FEELS LIKE HEAVEN

"You're perfect, Marjorie."

If her eyes had been open, she'd have blinked in surprise to hear such words coming from the lips of Jason Abernathy, the man whom Marjorie had come to consider the bane of her existence over the past few years. She almost came to the conclusion that she ought to act shocked, even if she didn't feel it, when his lips replaced his hand on her breast and the thrill was such that she forgot about acting any way at all.

Heaven. His touch, his lips, his hands, they were all heaven on her body. How fascinating.

"Everything will be all right, Marjorie. I promise you." Jason's voice was husky.

With a sigh, Marjorie sank back on the pillow, the fragrance of sandalwood wafting around her and her conscience at bay. Everything would be all right. She had Jason's promise on it. "Aye," she whispered.

BOOK YOUR PLACE ON OUR WEBSITE AND MAKE THE READING CONNECTION!

We've created a customized website just for our very special readers, where you can get the inside scoop on everything that's going on with Zebra, Pinnacle and Kensington books.

When you come online, you'll have the exciting opportunity to:

- View covers of upcoming books
- Read sample chapters
- Learn about our future publishing schedule (listed by publication month *and author*)
- Find out when your favorite authors will be visiting a city near you
- Search for and order backlist books from our online catalog
- Check out author bios and background information
- Send e-mail to your favorite authors
- Meet the Kensington staff online
- Join us in weekly chats with authors, readers and other guests
- Get writing guidelines
- AND MUCH MORE!

Visit our website at
http://www.kensingtonbooks.com

A PERFECT WEDDING

ANNE ROBINS

ZEBRA BOOKS
Kensington Publishing Corp.
www.kensingtonbooks.com

PROLOGUE

April 15, 1912

Marjorie MacTavish raced along the corridor of the first-class deck of the *Titanic*, her heart in her throat. Where was he? Dear Lord in heaven, where was he? She'd managed to get all the first-class passengers out of their cabins and upstairs, but where was Leonard?

Her heart leaped when she beheld him swinging 'round a corner at the end of the corridor and running toward her. "Marjorie! Why aren't you in a lifeboat?"

"Och, Leonard!" Under normal circumstances, Marjorie, who kept her emotions under strict control, would have been embarrassed at bursting into tears. These were extraordinary circumstances, however, and she didn't care. She threw herself into Leonard's arms when they met in the middle of the hallway.

"We've got to get on deck, Marjorie. The ship is foundering. It's going down fast."

"Lord have mercy," Marjorie whispered. She'd known, of course, that the ship was sinking, but hearing Leonard say it made it terrifyingly real.

"Come along with me, darling." Leonard took her

hand and pulled her to the stairway. He pushed her up the stairs ahead of him, never releasing her hand.

Marjorie heard the throng before she saw it, and she also heard the band playing. The music amid the noisy panic added to the surreal atmosphere of the moment. The night was black as tar, but the ship's lights still shone. The lights and music made the scene look as if it were taking place at a carnival instead of on the largest ocean liner the world had ever seen.

And it was supposed to have been unsinkable. *Tell that to the bluidy iceberg*, Marjorie thought bitterly.

"There!" Leonard shouted, pointing. "They're loading a lifeboat over there." He fairly dragged her toward the boat, shoving people aside.

"But, Leonard, I should wait until the rest of the passengers are loaded."

He stopped running, turned abruptly, and took Marjorie in his strong arms. As he held her in a desperate embrace, he whispered, "There aren't enough lifeboats, darling. There aren't enough lifeboats for half the number of people on the ship."

Marjorie let out a cry. "Nay! Nivver say so! Och, Leonard." When her emotions were stirred, Marjorie forgot the King's English and reverted to her Glasgow roots.

"It's so, Marjorie. Now be a good girl and come along. There are boats left, and I want to see you into one."

"Nay, Leonard!"

"It'll be all right, darling," he said tenderly.

For the very first time since they became engaged to be married, Leonard Fleming held Marjorie MacTavish in his arms and kissed her. It was a gentle kiss but thorough, and it was filled with the love of a wonderful man for the woman he'd chosen to be with forever. Marjorie didn't realize until much later that it had been a farewell kiss. They were both breathless when Leonard reluctantly pulled away from her.

"There," he said, smiling down at her. "That will have to hold us for a while."

She stared into his beautiful dark eyes. She loved him *so* much. He was not only a fine, upstanding man but a handsome and ambitious one as well. He was already the chief steward on board the *Titanic*. They would have a good life together. Marjorie knew it in her heart and soul.

Turning once more, Leonard kept her hand snugly in his and resumed his progress toward the lifeboat. "Out of the way. We have a lady here. Women and children first!"

The deckhand who was helping load the lifeboat recognized Marjorie and Leonard and gestured them forward. Pushing and shoving, Leonard managed to work his way to the boat. "Thank you, Jenkins. Take Miss MacTavish here, will you? That's a good fellow."

"Sure thing, Mr. Fleming. Miss MacTavish?" Mr. Jenkins took Marjorie's arm gently.

Marjorie, confused, resisted. Turning to Leonard, she cried out, "But, Leonard, ye mun get in t'boat, too!"

Leonard leaned toward her and gave her one last kiss on the lips. "I'll be along, Marjorie. Just get in the boat now."

"No!" Marjorie began to struggle.

A significant glance passed between Mr. Jenkins and Leonard. Marjorie saw it, and for the first time she knew what it all meant. "Nay!" she screamed again, trying to wrench herself away from Mr. Jenkins.

But Mr. Jenkins, with a smile and a nod from Leonard, picked her up and put her in the lifeboat.

"Leonard!" she shrieked. Firm hands prevented her from climbing out of the boat.

"I love you, Marjorie!" he called back. He waved. And she never saw him again.

ONE

September, 1915

The summer weather seemed to have gone into hiding, much as Marjorie MacTavish wished she could do. The air was chilly, and the fog had lingered into the afternoon. It swirled around her feet and crept up the walls of buildings like a cat burglar, slipping into rooms under doorways and through cracked windows and stealing the warmth therefrom. The atmosphere, damp and dreary, matched Marjorie's mood.

She'd had enough fog in her youth and during her years as a White Star stewardess. Now she detested it and wished it would go away. For that matter, she wished *she* could go away.

"Third floor, ladies." The elevator in which she had been riding clunked to a stop, and the operator pulled the lever drawing the double doors apart. Marjorie hesitated for a moment before stepping out into the hallway. She felt as if she were heading to her doom.

"I thought summers were supposed to be warm in California," she said in something of a grump.

"It'll warm up," her companion assured her. "Summers in San Francisco are always a little foggy. It has something to do with the atmospheric conditions here on the coast." There was no hesitation about her, and not a hint of gloom. She was bright as the morning sun—a good deal brighter than *this* morning's sun, actually—as she led the way down the hall.

As ever, Marjorie thought darkly. Marjorie herself hung back as well as she could, although she didn't dare be too stubborn. After all, Loretta Quarles, today's companion and also the woman who employed Marjorie as her secretary, was almost nine months pregnant. What's more, it was widely suspected that she was going to give birth to twins. Loretta was the healthiest specimen Marjorie had ever met in her life, but she didn't want to cause her any trouble.

That didn't negate the fact that she thought this was one of Loretta's most harebrained ideas ever. And Loretta was full to the brim with harebrained ideas.

Not only that, Marjorie thought acerbically, but why a nine-months-pregnant lady should be displaying herself in public was more than she could fathom. Any woman with an ounce of propriety would stay at home if she were in Loretta's condition.

But since she'd first encountered Loretta aboard the ill-fated *Titanic,* Marjorie had known her to be one of a kind. And that, if you asked her, was a very good thing. While Marjorie clung almost desperately to her conventional standards, Loretta flouted public opinion wherever and whenever she could. She also promoted every radical cause that came her way and had about as much truck with conventional behavior as she did with opera singing—and Loretta couldn't hold a tune in a teacup.

"I dinna want to see this doctor, Loretta Quarles, and ye're daft if ye think he'll do me good." As a rule, Marjorie did her very best to sound like a dignified, educated Englishwoman.

The sad fact of her life was that she'd been born in a slum in Glasgow almost thirty years earlier. But she'd overcome her beginnings. Every now and then, and especially when Loretta became particularly pushy or nonsensical, her origins came out in her speech.

"Fiddlesticks," said Loretta stoutly, waddling quickly at Marjorie's side. "You know as well as I do that you've been suffering terrible neuroses and phobias ever since the *Titanic* disaster."

"Stuff!" Marjorie's heart suffered a painful jolt, as it always did when she remembered that horrible night.

"It's not stuff. That experience has given you a phobia of the ocean, and Dr. Hagendorf is just the person to help you get over it."

Marjorie huffed, vexed. She didn't like even thinking about the ocean . . . or that night, when she'd lost all that she'd ever held dear. She sure as anything didn't want to chat about it with a stranger.

"Dr. Hagendorf and his wife Irene are my dear friends, Marjorie. William is a kind man, and a brilliant alienist. I'm sure he'll be able to help you overcome your illogical fear of the water."

"I deny that it's illogical."

"Pooh. It's illogical to have such a terror of the sea that you can't even go to the Cliff House to dine with me without suffering palpitations and spasms."

"I dinna want to go to the Cliff House."

"You're being stubborn, Marjorie MacTavish. You

know very well what I mean. You have a definite phobia of the ocean, and you need to overcome it."

"Why?"

"*Why*? Because it's holding you back is why!"

"From what?"

"From *life!* From *fulfillment!* From *joy!*"

"Codswallop."

"It's not codswallop. It's the truth."

"Well, and what if I dinna want to overcome this so-called phobia?" Marjorie said through clenched teeth. "What if I consider my life fulfilled already and as full of joy as it needs to be? What do I want the ocean for? I dinna care to travel. I've had my fill of it."

"But it's so *silly*, Marjorie. Wouldn't you like to be free from the debilitating anxiety that grips you every time you get near water?"

"Fah." The truth was that Marjorie never wanted to see an ocean again as long as she lived. Every time she even smelled the sea, she thought about her lost darling, Leonard Fleming. She no longer had to fight tears twenty-four hours every day, thank the good Lord. It had been more than three years since that black night, after all. However, she still hated the ocean. As far as Marjorie was concerned, the ocean had taken her very life from her.

Perhaps if Leonard's body had been recovered, she wouldn't feel this empty, gnawing grief in her heart, this sense of business unfinished and a life full of promise that remained unlived, but there it was. Poor Leonard had been one of the more than eight hundred people who had gone down with the ship, and who, for all anyone knew, were still there, locked in its barnacled bulk like ghostly prisoners. Sometimes Marjorie envisioned his bones lying in the remains of the grand ballroom, picked clean by fish and covered in cockles and sand, and the urge to cry assailed her anew. She fought it with all the strength she possessed. Marjorie wasn't one to broadcast her woes to the world.

Since she lived in San Francisco, which was on the very edge of the Pacific Ocean, most of her days were endured with the smell of the sea in her head and the accompanying ache in her heart. But she didn't have the energy to move farther inland.

Besides that—although Loretta occasionally drove Marjorie daft with her constant harping on rights for women, and votes for women, and this and that and the other thing for women—Marjorie knew she'd never get a job that paid as well, or with an employer as kind, as the one she had.

Because she'd learned the futility of arguing with Loretta early in their acquaintanceship, she only repeated, "Ye're daft," and stopped fighting.

So she had to spend an hour lying on a couch and babbling to a doctor. So what? The hour might be well spent, even if it only managed to silence Loretta on the issue of "Marjorie's awful neuroses." Loretta had promised not to fuss at her anymore about seeing the alienist if she agreed to keep one appointment. An hour wouldn't kill her.

The building in which Dr. Hagendorf practiced his trade was a fairly new one, having been built after the earthquake and fire that all but destroyed San Francisco in 1906. It rose tall and shiny in its clean white bricks on Market Street, close to where Loretta's father's bank sat.

Glancing at the pretty desert scenes decorating the walls of the hallway, Marjorie murmured, "Dr.

Hagendorf must have a flourishing practice if he can afford to have his office in this neighborhood."

"That's because he's the best," said Loretta, her confidence in her friend plain to hear in her voice.

Marjorie said, "Hmm," and left it at that.

"Here we are." Loretta sounded eager.

That made one of them. Because she didn't want Loretta to strain herself, Marjorie hurried ahead of her and opened the door, a sign upon which proclaimed merely "William D. Hagendorf, M.D., Ph.D." There was no mention of his speciality, Marjorie noted with interest. Evidently she wasn't the only person in San Francisco who felt funny about being seen visiting an alienist's office.

Dr. Hagendorf's nurse-receptionist, in a pristine white uniform that reminded Marjorie of the crisp uniforms she'd worn as a stewardess for the White Star Line, greeted the two women with a smile. She sat behind a businesslike desk that sported a candlestick telephone and several pieces of paper.

"Mrs. Quarles, how nice to see you again," she said. Glancing at Marjorie with an expression Marjorie could only deem as *kindly*, and which she resented, she went on, "And is this Miss MacTavish?"

With her usual cheerful ebullience, Loretta rushed to the desk, her bulk giving her a rocking gait not, Marjorie thought, unlike that of a corpulent bulldog. Or an ambulatory barrel. She would probably have grinned and relayed her notions to Loretta, who had a lively sense of humor, had she not been so peeved with her.

Loretta took the receptionist's hand and shook it heartily. "How are you today, Miss Grindthorpe? It's good to see you, too."

"I'm fine, thank you," gushed Miss Grindthorpe.

Marjorie had to fight a scowl. She considered Dr. Hagendorf and those of his ilk, not to mention the people who worked for them, no better than sly charlatans who preyed on gullible rich folks. If it weren't for Loretta and her cursed bluidy fortune, Marjorie wouldn't have to be going through this humiliating experience today.

As a rule, Marjorie loved Loretta like a sister. Sometimes, Loretta strained that rule beyond bearing, this being one of those times.

"Please take a seat, ladies," Miss Grindthorpe said, sounding to Marjorie's sensitive ears like the condescending mistress at a boarding school, not that she'd know anything about boarding schools. But she'd met plenty of nannies and governesses and rich people during her years as a stewardess, and she knew what *they* sounded like. "I'll see if Dr. Hagendorf is ready for Miss MacTavish."

Loretta immediately did as requested, subsiding into a chair with a grunt. She was *very* large. Marjorie sat, too, with less noise.

After Miss Grindthorpe had swished out of the office, Marjorie muttered, "'T'would be better to ask if I'm ready for him."

Loretta playfully patted her arm, one of her favorite forms of communication. "Don't be silly, Marjorie. This will be good for you."

"So you keep telling me."

Loretta only laughed.

A few minutes later, Miss Grindthorpe ushered Marjorie into Dr. Hagendorf's lair—uh, his office. Her heart quailed when she saw the couch upon which she presumed she would be lying. Loretta had told her that Dr. Hagendorf used a "modified Freudian" method, whatever that was, in his practice.

When Loretta had tried to explain it to her, Marjorie had become so embarrassed that she'd fled from the room. Therefore, she still had no idea what to expect.

If the wretched man lectured her about the sexual urge and how repressed hers was, Marjorie might have to flee from *this* room, too. As dear as Loretta was to her, and as much as she tried to please her, there were some things she wouldn't do.

Perhaps *couldn't* was a more honest word. When she wasn't fighting for her emotional life against Loretta's outrageous incursions, Marjorie acknowledged to herself that she did have a problem or two, the main one being that she'd lost the only man she'd ever loved in the most catastrophic ocean liner disaster the world had ever seen. And she was absolutely, deathly, stomach-churningly terrified of the ocean. Still and all, as little as she liked what Loretta called her "neurosis," and as much as she would like to overcome it, she figured she'd earned it.

As soon as the door opened, Dr. Hagendorf, who had been sitting at his desk and writing something— probably a report on some other poor soul whose life he'd invaded—rose and walked toward Marjorie and Miss Grindthorpe, his hand extended. He had a nice smile, and he seemed friendly.

Marjorie wasn't sure what she'd expected, but she hadn't anticipated being greeted by this beardless man who looked more like a studious schoolboy than a doctor, with his thick-lensed eyeglasses, his rumpled suit, and his big grin. He had freckles across his nose, too, for heaven's sake. Perhaps she'd thought he'd look more like Dr. Freud with his pointy beard and grim Germanic expression.

"Here's your next guest, Doctor," Miss Grind-thorpe said brightly.

Marjorie thought, *guest?* That was a wee bit precious, in her opinion, and her initial evaluation of Dr. Hagendorf dipped a trifle lower. Having been born into the lower echelons of a society that placed a good deal of emphasis on class distinctions, she'd become an expert at hiding her inner thoughts as a child, so she didn't indicate her opinion by so much as a blink of her eye.

"Miss MacTavish?"

"Aye," Marjorie said, allowing a note of suspicion to color the word. Since he was still holding his hand out to her, she shook it, and firmly, too, as she tried her best to act as if she was as good as anybody else in the world, even though she knew she wasn't. No matter what Loretta said, and no matter that she'd been living in the United States for three years, where everyone was supposed to be equal. Marjorie knew it wasn't so.

"I understand Mrs. Quarles bullied you into visiting me today, Miss MacTavish, but I'll try to make the experience worthwhile. Or at least," he added with a laugh, "not excruciating."

Surprised and faintly gratified, Marjorie returned his smile. She did so tentatively, still worried lest he get in under her guard and make her reveal more of herself than she wanted to.

The door closed softly behind them, and her fear returned in a rush. She was alone with the alienist! Then she scolded herself for being a gudgeon. This man wouldn't hurt her. He was a professional doctor, for sweet mercy's sake.

"Please, Miss MacTavish, take a seat."

To Marjorie's surprise, he gestured at a chair

facing his desk. She'd always assumed that the crazy person was supposed to lie on the couch while the doctor sat at its head in a chair set so the patient couldn't see him, smoked a pipe, and took notes. She sat, cautiously glancing around the office.

It was a cheery place, with windows that had their curtains pulled aside, inviting the sunshine—the nonexistent sunshine today—access to the room. This also surprised Marjorie, who had expected curtained windows, dark-paneled walls, tall bookcases laden with hundred-pound tomes, and framed certificates on the walls.

After seating himself on the business side of his desk, Dr. Hagendorf smiled at her. "I know Mrs. Quarles can be a handful. It was good of you to come in today, Miss MacTavish."

Marjorie considered this statement, examining it carefully for hidden meanings, detected none, and said warily, "She only means the best."

He laughed. "You needn't fear me, Miss MacTavish. I'm not going to trap you into unguarded speech. I couldn't do that if I wanted to, which I don't. Anyhow, anything you say here stays here. I won't tattle to Loretta if you want to unburden yourself. As wonderful a woman as she is, she often fails to take into consideration that other people don't care to be, or are unable to be, as open and freewheeling as she is."

Her defenses zoomed up, although he sounded as if he meant what he said. Still, Marjorie deemed it prudent merely to nod.

Dr. Hagendorf, clearly sensing her uneasiness, gentled his smile. "Would you prefer to remain in that chair during our session, Miss MacTavish? We have a couch, if you'd rather lie down. Sometimes it helps to relax people if they lie down."

It would take more than a couch to calm *her* down. She didn't know which option to choose.

Again understanding her trepidation, Dr. Hagendorf explained more fully. "If you want to, you can sit right there, and I'll sit right here, and we can chat. If you'd feel more comfortable with me out of the way, you can lie on the couch, and I'll take that chair." He pointed to a chair that would be out of Marjorie's sight if she lay on the couch.

She pondered her choices. She didn't want to talk about the ocean or that horrid night, or Leonard with this man watching her. On the other hand, she'd feel uncomfortable with him sitting there, just out of her sight. She'd keep wondering if he was going to pounce.

Idiot, she scolded herself. *The man's na a panther.* Besides which, if Loretta could be believed, he only wanted to help her. She sighed deeply, inducing Dr. Hagendorf to smile again, this time in understanding.

"Take your time, Miss MacTavish. In spite of what Mrs. Quarles might have told you, I don't bite."

Marjorie actually smiled at that. She made her decision. On the off chance that this appointment actually *might* be of benefit to her, she thought she'd be more comfortable if she couldn't see the doctor. "I'll take the couch."

"That's fine. Just make yourself comfortable."

As if she could ever do that. Nevertheless, Marjorie arranged herself modestly on the couch. In anticipation of something like this, she'd worn a shirtwaist and a comfortable, loose skirt that she arranged neatly around the ankles of her high-topped shoes. She had always been a modest woman.

"Why don't you tell me a little bit about your background, Miss MacTavish. Take your time."

Marjorie hesitated, then began slowly. Although she hadn't intended to spill her guts, once she got started, her narrative gained momentum. For the first time since she'd arrived in the United States, she told someone about her poverty-stricken beginnings, her family, and her early years. She'd never even told Loretta about her childhood in Glasgow.

"We were vurra poor," she said softly, recalling her work-worn parents, who'd been beaten down by life before she was even born. "And we ate mainly cabbages and tatties."

The sound of own voice lulled her strangely. She couldn't recall ever talking so much at one time. By the time she'd talked Dr. Hagendorf onboard the *Titanic*, she didn't think she could have stopped if she wanted to. But by that time, she didn't want to. It seemed to her as if, for years, her life had been bottled up behind her. She'd blocked so much for so long that, once she began telling it, everything just spewed out.

When she arrived at the night of April 14 and the morning of April 15, 1912, she started crying, thereby humiliating herself totally. Still, she couldn't stop talking. "Och, it was turrible. Turrible." And, for the first time since the tragedy, she told someone about Leonard.

All this time, Dr. Hagendorf hadn't said a word. He didn't even offer her a "Hmm" or an "Mmm." When Marjorie's tale trickled to an end, however, he produced a clean white handkerchief. "Here, Miss MacTavish. You probably need this."

"Th-thank you," she sniffled, embarrassed to death. "I dinna know what came over me."

"Please don't be embarrassed," Dr. Hagendorf said soothingly. "You've endured a good deal. It's time you let it out."

Mopping her tears and still feeling like an ass, Marjorie muttered, "Ye think so?"

Dr. Hagendorf chuckled. "It's been my experience that people who keep their woes stuffed tightly inside themselves suffer more than people who share them with others."

"Like Loretta."

He laughed again. "You don't have to go *that* far. It's perfectly fine for a person to share his or her sorrow. She or he doesn't necessarily have to make others suffer it as well."

Marjorie could scarcely believe her ears when a chuckle came out of her own mouth. "Ye ken her vurra weel, Doctor."

"All my life," he confirmed.

She blew her nose. "She's a wonderful woman."

"That she is."

"And a pain in the neck."

"That, too." The doctor laughed again. "You see, Miss MacTavish, the whole point of my practice is to give people a safe place to share their life. It often helps to talk about the things that worry us and that we don't feel comfortable telling our friends about."

That actually made sense to Marjorie. Pushing herself up, she swung her feet around and planted them on the plush carpet. Shyly, she glanced at the doctor, who still sat in the chair, smiling gently. "Well?" she said half defiantly. "What now?"

He got up from his chair and took her arm, helping her to rise and make her way to the chair. "That's up to you, Miss MacTavish." He gestured for her to resume her seat before his desk, and he sat on the other side once more.

She gave him a rueful smile, still dabbing at her leaky eyes. "Ye mean you're not going to tell me what to do with myself?"

"I'm afraid I'm not able to do that. Only you can decide how to live your life. I did notice while you were speaking about things that, along with great struggle, poverty, and sorrow, you often seem to have turned to song as a means of brightening your life and easing your suffering."

"I have?" Marjorie blinked at the man, startled. When she'd heard him say "turned to," she'd anticipated the word "church," or perhaps "religion," to pop out next. And, while Marjorie considered herself an upstanding Christian woman, she didn't really want to spend her days decorating the altar and pining for the minister like so many elderly spinsters she'd met over the years.

He shrugged. "You spoke of singing more than anything else, other than trying to better yourself—which, by the way, you seem to have done admirably."

Shy all at once, Marjorie murmured something inaudible.

The doctor went on. "You're not alone, you know. Often people who are forced to endure hard lives cling to some form of artistic expression to give them relief from the difficult world. You mentioned playing the piano and singing time and again. It seemed to me that you turn to music in your times of struggle. You're fortunate to have been born with a natural talent, and you were wise to develop it."

"Oh." Marjorie thought about it, and came to the conclusion that the doctor might actually have a point. "Ye mean, like I sing now in the choir at church?"

"Exactly. And you sang in the chapel chorus aboard various ships when you were a stewardess." He grinned. "I got the impression it's the music, and not the religious aspects, that mean the most to you."

She felt herself flush. "Aye. You may be right."

"It's nothing to be ashamed of. Religious feeling is fine, but I've come to the conclusion that not all of us respond as much to sermons as we do to hymns." He chuckled. "I believe John Wesley came to that decision, too, some years back."

In spite of this reference to the Methodist Church, which Marjorie didn't particularly care for, a sense of confirmation settled on her heart. He understood. This young, bespectacled fellow, whom she'd never met before, understood. How astonishing. She murmured, "Aye, that's so."

"You might find that, as you conquer your grief for Mr. Fleming—and don't worry about what Mrs. Quarles tells you, you have every right to grieve— you might consider music as a device to expand your world."

Marjorie had never told Loretta about Leonard. Leonard was too precious to share—or so she'd always thought. She wasn't sure any longer. She repeated in almost a whisper, "Expand my world."

"Exactly. I understand that Mrs. Quarles is a delightful person and a generous employer, but I also sense that you might like to create more of a life for yourself, away from the Quarleses."

Amazed by how precisely Dr. Hagendorf had hit the nail's head, Marjorie actually jumped slightly in her chair. "You're right!" she exclaimed, then pressed a hand over her mouth, embarrassed by having spoken so loudly. Then she admitted, "But I'm so afraid of new things, Doctor. So fleefu'. It really *is* a flaw, although I keep telling Loretta it isn't."

"You're not the only one who's afraid of trying new things, Miss MacTavish."

Although she knew that already, hearing the respected Dr. Hagendorf say so made Marjorie feel slightly better. "D'ye think so?"

"Absolutely. Often a patient will come to me complaining that, while he or she wants or needs to do something, he or she is afraid to do it. Do you know what I advise them to do in that case?"

She shook her head.

"I advise them to do whatever it is, even though they have to do it scared."

She blinked at him.

"There's no law on earth or in heaven that mandates a person feel comfortable when he or she tackles a new behavior for the first time, Miss MacTavish. You've heard the expression, 'practice makes perfect'?"

He lifted an eyebrow, and Marjorie nodded.

"Well, it's true of human behavior, too. Practice is usually what it takes to ease a person's nervousness if he or she is experimenting with something new. If you begin in a small way, you can work your way up to bigger things and, while you might feel uncomfortable for some time, you'll avoid absolute panic along the way."

"What a novel notion!"

"Not really. We don't expect babies to start out running, do we? They have to learn how to turn over, crawl, and toddle first. It's the same principle."

"My goodness." A crack in the wall keeping her from a whole new world suddenly appeared to Marjorie. It was a small crack in a formidable wall, to be sure, but Dr. Hagendorf seemed to have faith in her. That meant a lot to Marjorie.

The doctor grinned. "I think you'll be fine, Miss MacTavish. Don't let Mrs. Quarles worry you with her chatter about neuroses and phobias. You're firmly grounded and are a proven survivor. I trust that one day, you'll find the happiness you deserve."

Marjorie felt her cheeks heat up. "Thank you." She'd never been complimented so effectively before. She honestly *believed* Dr. Hagendorf. Astounding.

That night, unexpectedly buoyed by her visit with Dr. Hagendorf and eager to escape Loretta's constant "I told you so," Marjorie put on her hat and coat and prepared to walk the few blocks to the Columbus Avenue Presbyterian Church, where she'd been actively involved in the choir almost since she moved to San Francisco. Dr. Hagendorf's comments about herself and music had rung true in her mind and heart, and she'd decided to do something about it.

"No, you can't come with me, Loretta Quarles!" she said in response to Loretta's question. "Ye mun stay home and take care of the wee ones!" Marjorie didn't think she'd ever come to grips with the way

Loretta paraded her contempt for convention all the time.

"Good idea," grumbled Loretta's husband, the long-suffering and plainspoken Captain (now retired) Malachai Quarles. "Shut up and let the woman do something by herself for once, Loretta, will you?"

"Fiddlesticks," said Loretta grumpily. "You're both against me."

Malachai rolled his eyes.

Marjorie said, "Codswallop. Ye mun take care of yourself, and that's that."

"I wish I could sing," Loretta said plaintively. "I'd try out for the opera with you."

"I wish you could, too," Marjorie said truthfully. "But ye canna. Now go sit down, for pity's sake!" It worried her, the way Loretta tried to do everything she'd always done, as if she wasn't huge as a house and about ready to give birth.

"Do you want Peavey to walk you to the church?" Malachai asked.

Marjorie eyed Derrick Peavey, the man in question, with misgiving. Peavey had been a good sailor, according to Captain Quarles, and he now worked for the Quarleses as some sort of house servant or footman. He was a nice man, but he was about two quarts short of a gallon, and Marjorie couldn't see what earthly good he could be to her. For one thing, he was constantly blaming the world's ills on the Moors' invasion of Spain a thousand or so years ago.

Still, he was a kind and gentle fellow, and she didn't want to hurt his feelings. Therefore, she smiled at him when she spoke. "No, thank you. I shall be fine." She was pretty sure Peavey was relieved, although he'd never say anything to that end. He sighed as he sat on a chair in a corner of the library, and his countenance lost its worried look.

With a grin, Malachai said, "Right. Then have a good time."

"I wish I could see your audition. I'm sure you'll get the role of Mabel," said Loretta.

"Pish-tosh," muttered Marjorie.

With a laugh, Loretta said, "That's the wrong opera. Pish-Tosh is in *The Mikado*."

"You know what I mean." Marjorie grinned in her turn. But, honestly, Loretta *was* being silly. Mabel was the lead role in the opera, for heaven's sake, and Marjorie had no aspirations in that direction.

Relief swept over her when she left Loretta and Malachai's lovely mansion on Russian Hill. The night was fine, and Marjorie felt more light-hearted than she'd felt in, literally, years.

Funny how merely talking had eased her mental burdens. She hated to admit that Loretta had been right. But Marjorie was, above anything, a fair person, and she'd thanked Loretta for forcing her onto the alienist's couch. She'd been suffering the results of her thanks ever since, but she didn't mind Loretta's constant self-congratulations too much. Still, it was pleasant to be on her own this evening.

Marjorie loved her church. It was a pretty building, and it reminded her somewhat of the church she'd attended in Edinburgh, when she'd worked as a clerk in a department store and taken a typewriting class at the YWCA. The Columbus Avenue Presbyterian Church, like so many buildings in San Francisco, had been reconstructed after the catastrophic 1906 earthquake. She felt comfortable in her church, more comfortable than she felt anywhere else in San Francisco, except Loretta's house.

Truth to tell, Marjorie found the United States too large and confusing for her taste. The society in which she'd grown up had been in existence for centuries, and its rules had been set down in . . . well, who knew? Antiquity, certainly. And if her society's existence hadn't always been stable, Marjorie at least understood it. She felt wobbly in San Francisco, as if she couldn't gain a firm foothold anywhere.

Lately, though, she'd been itching internally. It was as if, frightened as she was of the strange new world she'd entered, she was yet stifled and confined in her very circumscribed life. Something in her was ready to emerge. Actually, it felt more as if it were about to erupt like a volcano.

Marjorie had realized recently that, in truth, she'd been living not merely with Loretta, but through her. Loretta wasn't shy and retiring like Marjorie. She met life head-on and battered it into submission, or tried to. It was a quality Marjorie both admired and decried. As Loretta's secretary, she was required to tag along when Loretta attended, for example, suffrage rallies and unionization meetings.

In other words, for years Marjorie had endured. Now she wanted to do something by herself, *for* herself.

It had dawned on her in Dr. Hagendorf's office that one needn't orate on street corners in order to find more fulfillment in life. One could expand gradually, easing one's way into the world, as it were. One could jolly well practice.

Dr. Hagendorf's idea had been a brilliant one, in her opinion. If she started expanding her horizons by participating in more musical events, she believed she'd be safe. "Safe" was an odd word, but it seemed to fit, and Marjorie didn't try to find a better one.

As luck would have it, at the very moment Marjorie needed it, the Columbus Avenue Presbyterian Church had decided to mount a production of Gilbert and Sullivan's *Pirates of Penzance*. Marjorie, whose salary as Loretta's secretary allowed her the luxury of purchasing the sheet music to many of Messrs. Gilbert and Sullivan's works, decided to try out for a part. Perhaps she could be one of the Major General's daughters. It would be fun—and she *did* have a fine soprano voice. Even Dr. Jason Abernathy, the bane of her existence, had said so more than once.

Too bad Dr. Abernathy and Dr. Hagendorf couldn't exchange personalities, Marjorie thought sourly as she walked at a brisk clip along the street. Dr. Abernathy, however, was a childhood chum of Loretta's, and he seemed to be forever hanging out at Loretta's house. He teased Marjorie unmercifully, and Marjorie saw him far too often for her peace of mind.

Jason Abernathy rang the Quarleses' doorbell with the energy typical of him. He was an enthusiastic fellow, and he lived his life with gusto.

Chuckling, he decided that was the reason he found his dealings with Marjorie MacTavish so refreshing. She was his antithesis in every respect. While he was outgoing and ebullient, Marjorie was quiet and withdrawn. While he had a raucous sense of humor and laughed as often as he could, poor Marjorie, if she even saw the point of a joke, which was seldom, invariably disapproved of it.

The door opened, and Jason tipped his hat. "Good evening, Mr. Peavey. Are Mr. and Mrs. Quarles in?"

"Aye, aye, sir," Derrick Peavey said in a sober voice, saluting. "They're in the back parlor."

"Ah, good. I'll just go in and bother them." Jason, who had known Loretta from childhood, was intimately familiar with the Quarleses' mansion. It had belonged to Loretta alone until her marriage, but Malachai had fitted into it as if it had been made for him.

Jason deposited his hat and overcoat on the hall rack and strode to the back parlor. When he glanced back over his shoulder, he realized Peavey was taking his hat and coat from the rack and replacing them. He shook his head. Once Malachai told Peavey to do something, Peavey did it, even if that meant redoing something someone else had already done. Odd duck, Peavey.

Loretta saw him first and cried, "Jason! I'm so glad you're here. I have great news!"

Pausing at the threshold, Jason's cheer diminished slightly when he realized Marjorie wasn't in the room, too. Disappointed, he realized that Loretta was trying to bound up from her chair as she'd always done, and was having a hard time of it, so he hurried over to her.

"Sit down, Loretta. You can't jump around like you used to do." She subsided with a huff, and he said, "Where's Malachai?" He really didn't care where Loretta's husband was, but he knew if he asked about Marjorie, Loretta would rib him.

"The sweet thing went upstairs to get me a lap robe. I don't know why he fusses so." Loretta laughed.

So did Jason, mainly because it was difficult to

imagine Malachai Quarles, who was built like a monument and looked like a pirate, as a "sweet thing," no matter how much he pampered his wife. "He fusses because he loves you and he's afraid you'll overdo. You're carrying a mighty big load there, you know." He patted Loretta's bulk.

Loretta did likewise. "Believe me, I know."

Jason wasn't really worried about Loretta. She was short, being only slightly over five feet tall, but she wasn't thin or narrow-hipped. He'd balked a trifle when she'd insisted she have her baby—or babies—at home, but he'd given in without too much arguing. For one thing, a man was better off tilting at windmills than arguing with Loretta Quarles, and for another, Jason didn't perceive any problems as long as the baby—or babies—came out the right way. He subsided into another chair, feeling vaguely dissatisfied.

"But I have to tell you about Marjorie, Jason!"

He perked up, understanding that his dissatisfaction owed itself to Marjorie's absence and his unwillingness to risk Loretta thinking that he cared about her. Odd that, since Marjorie had never offered him a single grain of encouragement. "Yes?" he said politely, trying not to sound eager.

"She went to see William Hagendorf today!" Loretta sat back with a "whuff" that owed more to pregnancy than satisfaction.

Jason lifted an eyebrow. "How'd you get her to do that? You really oughtn't browbeat her, you know."

"She browbeats everybody," came a rumbling voice from the doorway.

Jason rose from his chair and greeted Malachai with a grin and a handshake. "Even you?"

"How do you think she got me to marry her?"

All three of them laughed at that, since they all knew—as, probably, did everyone else in San Francisco due to some rather loud arguments—that Malachai had only gotten Loretta to agree to marry him because she was pregnant. Malachai spread the robe over his wife's lap, tucking it around the bulge tenderly. He eyed Jason slantways. "Are you sure she's not going to pop?"

"I'm sure. Women have been doing this for thousands of years." Jason cleared his throat. "But you were going to tell me about Miss MacTavish and Dr. Hagendorf." He didn't want to sound too keen, but he didn't want Loretta to become distracted either.

So Loretta told him all about Marjorie's visit with Dr. Hagendorf, ending with, "And she's gone to the church to try out for a part in *The Pirates of Penzance!* They're staging the opera as a fund-raiser for their African missionaries."

Flabbergasted by this intelligence, Jason said, "My goodness." He had a hard time picturing the reserved, quiet Marjorie MacTavish he knew singing on stage, although he knew, from musical evenings at the Quarleses's home, that she had a superb voice.

Loretta nodded. "She's got a beautiful voice, you know."

"Oh?" He cocked the other eyebrow.

"You know she does, Jason Abernathy! You've sung with her often enough."

"True," he admitted.

"Yeah, she's got a great voice," Malachai confirmed. "Loretta's been dragging me to church on Sundays. Claims it'll be good for the kid if his—"

"Or her," interrupted Loretta, an ardent feminist.

Malachai gave an exaggerated sigh. "Or *her* parents attend church."

"The church might be stuffy," Loretta said pompously, "but the values it teaches are important."

"Right." Jason didn't laugh and was proud of himself. It occurred to him that he liked to sing, too. And he'd been told more than once that he had a fine baritone voice. And *Pirates* was one of his favorite light operas. "Um . . . is the church seeking performers only from their own congregation?"

Loretta's eyes widened. "Jason! Are you thinking what I think you're thinking?"

Embarrassed, he shrugged. "Just thought it might be fun to be in an opera is all."

Malachai gave an inelegant snort of derision. He, too, had a nice voice, but it was more suited to barroom ditties than opera.

With a grin a mile wide on her face, Loretta said, "Actually, Marjorie said the auditions are open."

"Is that so?"

"You sly dog, you, Jason Abernathy." Loretta tried to wink at him, but she couldn't shut only one eye at a time.

Jason got the point, however, and tried to deny its implication. "It might be fun," he insisted.

"Of course," said Loretta.

Jason left the Quarleses' residence shortly after that. He fairly ran to the Columbus Avenue Presbyterian Church.

TWO

It always amazed Marjorie that she, who generally felt as if she fitted into the world rather like a lamb in a lion's den, should feel so comfortable singing before people. But she did. Therefore, she had no trouble "projecting to the last seats in the balcony," as requested by the choir director, Mr. Proctor, when she sang *Poor Wand'ring One*.

Her heart was lighter than usual. She hoped the condition would last past this evening. Although she'd always been a rather quiet person, she could remember—faintly—being cheerful once. It seemed like a very long time ago.

It didn't hurt, of course, that Marjorie had taken particular care with her grooming this evening. Because she wanted to look good and feel comfortable, she'd worn her favorite poplin suit. It was dark green, thereby bringing out the green in her eyes, and it had a single-breasted jacket with military braid and a pleated skirt that ended just at her ankles.

It also didn't hurt that she loved *Pirates* or that Mr. Proctor and his wife, Julia, had been visibly delighted to see her arrive for the auditions. Mr. Proctor had long begged Marjorie to take on more solos during church services. Marjorie, who had held subservient positions all her life, hated to put herself forward.

"You're not putting yourself forward," Mr. Proctor had told her once. "*I'm* putting you forward. And I'm the boss." He'd laughed, but she'd sensed the frustration behind his statement.

It was true, however. Even though she knew that to admit it was tantamount to the sin of vanity, she had a better voice than anyone else in the soprano section of the choir.

Therefore, much to Mr. Proctor's gratification, she'd agreed to perform two solos during the past three months, with Mrs. Proctor accompanying her on the piano: *In the Garden,* a sweet, lilting hymn, and *Crown Him with Many Crowns,* which was quite stirring and dramatic. After the latter, the congregation had actually applauded, thereby embarrassing Marjorie almost to tears and confirming her opinion that she'd never, ever, as long as she lived, get used to American manners.

People applauded her this evening, too, when she concluded *Poor Wand'ring One,* but Marjorie didn't mind, this being a play and all. She was faintly surprised, however. This was, after all, only an audition. And it was, moreover, taking place in a church.

"I do believe we've found our Mabel," Mrs. Proctor said, rising from the piano bench and clapping, her smile broad and bright.

Marjorie felt her face flame, something it did far too often for her comfort. She blamed it on her redhead's complexion. Mabel was the lead female part in the opera. "But . . . but I only meant to try out for one of Mabel's sisters."

"Nonsense," said Mr. Proctor firmly. "You'll be

the perfect Mabel, Miss MacTavish. Now we just need to find you a suitable Frederic." Frederic was the male lead and Mabel's love interest.

"I'll take a stab at it."

The familiar voice coming from the rear of the sanctuary made Marjorie's heart, which had been floating in happy, if somewhat startled, surprise, drop to earth with a painful thud. Dr. Abernathy! Sweet God in heaven, it couldn't be!

But it was. Striding forward as if he went to church every day in his life—and Marjorie doubted that he ever went to church at all—he came, comfortable as only a man sure of himself could be. Spitefully, she wished lightning would strike him for daring to sully God's house with his presence.

She was also outraged that he should invade the only safe harbor in her life and said a little too forcefully, "What are *you* doing here?"

As ever, and in spite of his handsome face, he looked like a devil out of hell as he sauntered down the center aisle. He *would* take the center aisle, Marjorie thought resentfully. Dr. Jason Abernathy, like Loretta, didn't take a back seat to anyone, even God.

Mr. Proctor, too, turned to see who had spoken. When he spotted Jason, he smiled. "Dr. Abernathy! How good to see you here!"

Marjorie watched this phenomenon in horror and exclaimed, "You mean you *know* him?"

Mrs. Proctor had left her piano and joined her husband. "Oh, my, yes, dear," said she. "We've known Jason Abernathy since he was a boy. He went to the same school our Georgie did, and they were friends from the cradle."

"Oh." George Proctor, the Proctors' only son, was

attending school back east at the moment, studying for the ministry. Thinking better of saying anything else for fear her feelings about Dr. Abernathy might leak out and shock the choir director's wife, Marjorie left it at that.

She watched, though, and not with joy, as Mr. Proctor greeted Jason with a handshake and a pat on his back. If Jason joined the production, her peace and comfort would be destroyed for the duration. And if he got the part of Frederic, her life would become a living hell.

Naturally, as soon as Jason left off shaking Mr. Proctor's hand, he turned upon Marjorie. She wasn't fooled by his big smile or his twinkling blue eyes. She knew he was a demon sent from below to torment her. Sometimes, in her more cynical moments, she wondered why God had believed her so important that He'd gifted her with a devil all her own.

Also naturally, he walked up to Marjorie as if they were dear friends and as easy with each other as mutton and tatties. Because she couldn't figure out how not to without seeming rude, she offered him her hand. He shook it cordially and with none of the teasing for which she had braced herself.

Something encouraging occurred to her. Before she could think better of it, she blurted out, "But you have quite a deep voice, Dr. Abernathy. Frederic must be a tenor."

He frowned and turned to Mr. Proctor. "Is that so?"

Mr. Proctor, whose puzzled gaze went from Marjorie to Jason and back again, shrugged. "Why don't you sing one of the pieces, and we'll see."

Codswallop. Marjorie knew from experience that Jason had an excellent voice. However, he *was* more comfortable in the bass-baritone range. And Frederic *did* have to be a tenor.

As little as she wanted Jason in the production, she supposed it wouldn't be too bad if he were one of the pirates. As long as she didn't have to sing with him or, heaven forbid, kiss him, peace might be maintained.

Mr. Proctor handed Jason some sheet music and gestured for him to climb onto the platform. As easy as you please, he did so, grinning all the while. "I'm familiar with the piece," he said, "but let me read it through once, will you?"

"Take your time," Mr. Proctor said with a conspiratory smile.

Marjorie told herself to calm down and reclaim her rationality. The music director's smile wasn't conspiratory. It was friendly. These people weren't in a secret plot to destroy her composure and her peace of mind; it only seemed like it now because she hadn't expected Jason to show up. In fact, in the years during which she'd clung to her church as a refuge from life's storms, which meant in the years she'd been living in San Francisco, the largest and most violent of those storms had ever been Jason Abernathy.

Mrs. Proctor returned to her piano, Mr. Proctor scanned his own music, and Marjorie took a seat in the front row of the sanctuary next to Virginia Collins. Miss Collins was a young woman who attended Marjorie's Sunday-school class and who called herself Ginger, an affectation Marjorie considered silly, although no sillier than anything else about her. However, although Ginger chatted a bit too much, in Marjorie's opinion, Marjorie needed the comfort of a friend right then.

With a smile of intense curiosity, Ginger leaned over and whispered in Marjorie's ear. "Do you know that young man, Marjorie dear?"

"Aye," said Marjorie grimly. "I know him."

"He's ever so handsome." Ginger tittered softly.

Marjorie turned to squint at Ginger. "D'ye think so?"

With another giggle, Ginger said, "Why, of *course* I do! He's terribly handsome. Surely you think so, too."

"Hmm," was all Marjorie could manage in response. She turned her squint upon Jason, though, and tried to fathom what the idiot seated next to her saw in him.

Perhaps Ginger wasn't an idiot, exactly. If one didn't know him to be a fiend incarnate, Jason Abernathy *could* be considered a fairly good-looking man. Tall and lean, he had thick, dark brown hair that was slightly too long and that had a natural curl to it. His eyes were as blue as sapphires and twinkled as brightly, generally in mockery, Marjorie thought sourly. His smile was nice when it wasn't curled into a cynical twist.

He appeared serious at the moment as he scanned the words and music to the song he was going to sing. In Marjorie's experience, seriousness was an unusual condition for him. The Jason Abernathy she knew didn't take a single thing in the entire world seriously.

When she reconsidered her last thought, Marjorie guessed it couldn't be entirely true. According to Loretta, Jason fought like a madman to help and protect the people who took advantage of his Chinatown clinic. And he also espoused many of Loretta's radical causes, from women's suffrage to the elimination of the Chinese Exclusion Act. She supposed he wasn't *entirely* frivolous, even if he did tease her constantly and laugh at things Marjorie considered important.

"What do you suppose he's going to sing?" Ginger whispered. "I can't wait to hear him."

"You won't have to wait long," Marjorie said, a trifle irked with the woman, who all but vibrated in her excitement at being in the room with Jason.

Truly, Ginger was more of a girl. About twenty-one or twenty-two, Marjorie surmised, Ginger behaved rather like a spoiled debutante. She was pretty in a crimped-and-curled sort of way. She wore paint on her face every day, which had shocked Marjorie before she realized that the world had changed during the time she'd been trying to hide away from it, and most women wore makeup these days. Only the very prudish or the very poor eschewed face paint in this new century.

Marjorie counted herself among the prudes, although she didn't especially want to. It wasn't so much that she deplored the use of makeup as that she didn't know how to use it. The few times she'd attempted to brighten her complexion with rouge on her cheeks, she'd felt like a circus clown.

"I'm ready when you are," Jason said to Mr. Proctor at last.

Marjorie's thoughts snapped to attention. She felt Ginger stiffen beside her with eagerness, not unlike a hound scenting a hare, and she wanted to poke the ridiculous girl with an elbow to the ribs.

Mrs. Proctor played the introductory chords to the Pirate King's song. Marjorie sucked in her breath. As much as she wanted nothing whatsoever to do with Jason Abernathy for as long as she lived, she had to admit that he would make a perfect Pirate King, a role that required an abundance of exuberance and swashbuckling *joie de vivre*.

Loretta's husband, Malachai Quarles, looked like a pirate to begin with. Jason, though, now that Marjorie could study him without him knowing it, could be made up to look like a pirate without any fuss at all. Aside from his physical qualities, he also possessed a cockiness that would enable him to swashbuckle with élan. She knew for a fact that he was an excellent dancer, so he'd probably be able to learn the physically challenging choreography necessary for the part without much trouble.

From the first word, his voice filled the sanctuary. "'Oh, better far to live and die under the brave black flag I fly, than play a sanctimonious part with a pirate head and a pirate heart.'"

Clasping her hands to her bosom, Ginger sighed, "Oh, my, isn't he *wonderful*?"

Marjorie realized she'd been holding her breath, and told herself to stop it. There was no reason for her heart to be pounding so bluidy hard either. She disapproved of both of these behaviors, which she believed more properly belonged in a girl of Ginger's age and relative vapidity than in a woman of Marjorie's years and dignity. "Aye," she muttered. "He has a good voice."

"Good?" Ginger managed to pry her gaze away from Jason for only long enough to give Marjorie an incredulous glance. "He's simply perfect. Why, with you as Mabel and him as the Pirate King, we should have a first-rate show."

"Hmm."

"'For I am a pirate king!'" Jason sang, adding a spirited gesture, as if he were wielding a sword, that made Ginger clap her hand to her cheek and giggle.

He would do something like that, Marjorie thought caustically. She eyed Ginger out of the corner of her eye and thought, *and so would she.* She wondered if Jason would enjoy having a sycophant. Probably. He was assuredly going to get the part. He'd be perfect in it, too, curse him. And with Ginger and the other women in the chorus swooning over him, his big head would grow even larger.

The notion of all the female cast members worshiping at Jason's feet gave Marjorie a peculiar feeling in her middle. She pressed a hand to her thorax and wondered if she'd eaten something that had disagreed with her. She surely couldn't be worried about Jason taking up an intimate association with Ginger, could she? Ridiculous! In fact, the sooner he found another victim and left off bothering Marjorie, the better she would like it.

Another twinge in her middle vexed her.

The song came to an end, and an enthusiastic round of applause filled the sanctuary. In the seat next to her, Ginger was clapping as if she'd just heard Enrico Caruso perform an aria intended just for her. Marjorie eyed her with disfavor. Ginger was *such* a giddy female. Jason would probably fall madly in love with her. According to Loretta, men preferred idiots to women with brains.

Not that Marjorie cared. If Jason was fool enough to marry Ginger Collins, the happier Marjorie would be. He deserved her. And she deserved him.

And why, she scolded herself, was she even *thinking* about things like that? All she wanted to do was expand her social life by performing in this light opera. That's all. If the whole world fell in love and married, leaving her the only single female in it, it was nothing to her.

She wasn't seeking love, for pity's sake. She'd *had* love. Once. But it had been a perfect love, and there would never be another like it, any more than there was anyone in the world who could ever take Leonard's place. Never. And especially not Jason Abernathy, who was a lout.

"That was spectacular," Mr. Proctor said, clapping with enthusiasm. He was clearly overjoyed that Jason had showed up. "I had no idea you could sing so well, Jason."

"No? Well, I don't get much practice anymore, but I enjoy music."

"He'll be perfect as the Pirate King," Mrs. Proctor gushed. "Don't you think so, Elbert?"

Her husband nodded. "Absolutely perfect." He sighed happily. "So we now have our Mabel and our Pirate King. All we need is a Frederic, and we'll be all set. We have plenty of people set to be daughters and pirates."

As she'd feared he might—Marjorie knew that he'd do anything he could to discompose her— Jason handed his music back to Mr. Proctor and strode over to her side of the sanctuary. Steeling herself, she smiled at him, hoping the smile appeared genuine, since she didn't want to stir Ginger's curiosity. In an effort to preempt his sarcastic thunder, she spoke first. "You sang beautifully, Dr. Abernathy."

"Thank you, thank you!" he said, flopping onto the pew next to her. "I was hoping for Frederic, but I'll take the Pirate King."

"You'll play the part very well, I think," Marjorie said politely. Being around Jason was nerve-wracking because he so often needled her about one thing or another, and she never knew when he'd strike. Even when he didn't tease her, she remained on the alert, expecting an attack any moment. He was an exhausting man, and Marjorie hoped rehearsals would keep him so busy that she wouldn't have to be forever wasting her energy on protecting herself from him.

"Thank you, Miss MacTavish." He gave her a grin that would have done the Cheshire Cat, in full toothy mode, proud. "It wasn't as much fun as when we're singing at the piano in the Quarleses' back parlor, but I'm looking forward to the production."

Ginger Collins made a squeaky noise, and Marjorie realized she was still there. Following up on the squeak, Ginger trilled, "You mean you two actually *sing* together?"

One of Jason's bushy eyebrows rose in an ironic gesture he usually reserved for Marjorie. Ginger's bright blush could be seen faintly through her rouge.

Only because she knew she should, Marjorie said, "Please allow me to introduce the two of you. Miss Virginia Collins, this is Dr. Jason Abernathy."

She considered telling Ginger a little about Jason, but decided not to. Ginger would learn soon enough that Jason was not merely a doctor, but a well-to-do one, and then she'd be all over him like heather on the brae. Marjorie hoped to spare herself that prospect for a while longer. Not, of course, that she gave a rap that Jason would undoubtedly favor the petite, blond Ginger. She only objected to witnessing scenes that ought to be confined to the privacy of . . . wherever Marjorie couldn't see them.

"Oh!" squealed Ginger, "you're a doctor!"

"Guilty," said Jason. "That's why they call me Dr. Abernathy. How do you do, Miss Collins?"

"Oh, please, Dr. Abernathy, call me Ginger!"

Eyeing her critically, Marjorie decided that Ginger was an unusually pert young thing whose parents should have taught her better manners. Imagine, asking a man to call her by her Christian name upon first being introduced!

Jason said, "Ginger," in a bored-sounding voice.

Marjorie was surprised that he didn't appear more delighted at being introduced to the pretty, vivacious, and remarkably young, if silly, Ginger Collins. It was just like him to act as if he didn't care, thereby whetting the girl's interest. He was no doubt attempting to lull her and would pounce later. Even if Ginger was a ninny.

Ignoring Ginger, Jason said, "I'm sorry I didn't get to hear your entire audition, Miss MacTavish. What little I heard of it was beautiful, as usual."

Giving him a squinty-eyed peek, Marjorie detected no ulterior meanings behind his polite words or his bland demeanor. Knowing it was best to be on her guard at all times with regard to Jason, she said, "Thank you."

"Oh," tittered Ginger. "Marjorie has *such* a beautiful voice. I'm only going to be one of the Major General's daughters in the chorus since I *couldn't* sing in front of an audience all by myself."

And a good thing, too, Marjorie thought spitefully. She said, "Nonsense. You have a lovely voice, Ginger." Even if it was kind of thin and reedy.

Jason, who still acted as though he were uninterested in Ginger and her voice—Marjorie knew a devious stratagem when she saw one—leaned back in the pew, stuck his long legs out in front of himself in a negligent posture, crossed his arms over his chest and took note of a young man chatting with Mr. Proctor. "Who's that priggish-looking fellow?"

"What priggish . . ." Marjorie narrowed her eyes. The sanctuary was dimly lighted, and she couldn't see too well. "Oh. That's Mr. St. Claire. Hamilton St. Claire." She turned to frown at Jason. "I don't believe him to be priggish at all, Dr. Abernathy."

"No," said Jason dryly. "You wouldn't."

"Do you even know the man?" Marjorie demanded.

"Nope." Jason waved a hand in Mr. St. Claire's direction. "I can tell."

Ginger giggled. Marjorie felt her temper rise and her blood race. Under normal circumstances—say, if they were sparring in the Quarleses' back parlor, as usual—she'd say something cutting. Since they were in a church and she didn't want Ginger to witness her further humiliation, she merely huffed softly and dropped the subject.

Mr. St. Claire possessed a good tenor voice. Marjorie listened with interest since, before Jason had barged in and spoiled the auditions for her, she'd assumed Mr. St. Claire would be her Frederic. It looked as if her assumption would be proved correct. She told herself she was relieved. Hamilton St. Claire, unlike Jason Abernathy, was a gentleman. Even if he was an awful prig. Grimly, she told herself she wouldn't let on for worlds that she considered him so—especially not to Jason Abernathy.

"He's got a pretty good voice," Jason muttered, eyeing Mr. St. Claire. "Doesn't look much like a pirate."

"It was only through a mistake by his governess

that Frederic was apprenticed to a pirate at all," Marjorie reminded him. "So I suppose that doesn't matter much."

He grinned at her. "You think that guy is going be your Frederic?"

That guy, indeed. Really, Dr. Abernathy was the least gentlemanly person Marjorie had ever met, and she included Loretta's husband in the mix. Captain Quarles might be fairly rugged, but he'd never speak of a fine young gentleman as *that guy.* "I should think so," she said, striving for a neutral tone. If she by so much as a nuance hinted that she disapproved of Jason's assessment of Mr. St. Claire, he'd tease her abominably.

"You deserve better."

She swivelled her head in Jason's direction, incredulous. "I beg your pardon?"

"No need to beg, Miss MacTavish. It's so unbecoming. I said you deserve better than to have that fellow as your love interest."

Again, Marjorie felt her temper spike. "He will not be *my* love interest. It's only a part in a play."

He grunted. Marjorie got the impression he wasn't convinced.

They listened to Mr. St. Claire sing some more. Marjorie envisioned St. Claire in his *Pirates* costume. He was somewhat spindly. And his limp blond hair and indoor pallor didn't exactly shout to the world that here was a robust seaman. But makeup could fix that part. And the spindliness *might* be overcome with padding. The thought of being held and kissed by Hamilton St. Claire made Marjorie's lips clamp together.

Better than Jason Abernathy, she told herself.

Somehow, the notion didn't lift her spirits as

much as she thought it should have. She didn't have time to ponder the perversity of her own nature, though, because the song came to an end, and she applauded politely. Jason, she noted with disapproval, did not. She gave him a stony glance. He only grinned back at her, and she gave up on attempting to teach him manners by example.

"Splendid, Mr. St. Claire," proclaimed Mr. Proctor. Marjorie sensed his praise wasn't quite as sincere as it had been for Jason. Of course, the choir director and Jason were old acquaintances. That probably accounted for it.

"I think Mr. St. Claire would make a fine Frederic, Elbert," said Mrs. Proctor. She, too, didn't sound quite as enthusiastic as she might have.

Marjorie told herself to stop being ridiculous.

"Who's my Mabel?" asked Mr. St. Claire, clearly happy to have been given the role of Frederic.

"Miss MacTavish will be our Mabel," said Mr. Proctor, beaming in Marjorie's direction. "There she is, next to our Pirate King, Dr. Jason Abernathy."

"Miss MacTavish," Mr. St. Claire said in delight. "I'm so pleased!" He rushed over to Marjorie.

Jason, sprawled at her side, rose only reluctantly to meet Mr. St. Claire.

Marjorie smiled up at her Frederic, trying to discern what Mabel would see in him. "We should have a fine time," she said to Mr. St. Claire, shaking his hand. She suspected that he had designs on her, although she couldn't imagine why. She was a perfect nobody with no particular beauty or grace, and he was an up-and-coming attorney in the city. Her only claim to excellence was her singing voice, and what did that matter? Besides, she was older than he by a good two or three years. Perhaps four or five. Not that it mattered.

Scowling at the two of them, Jason interrupted. "Mr. St. Claire?"

"Oh, I'm sorry," said Marjorie, instantly recognizing herself as being at fault. It was an old habit, and a difficult one to break, of feeling responsible for everything. "Mr. St. Claire, please meet our Pirate King, Dr. Jason Abernathy. Dr. Abernathy, Mr. St. Claire."

St. Claire smiled happily at Jason. "How do you do, Dr. Abernathy? Pleased to meet you." He held out his hand.

After hesitating ever so slightly—Marjorie wasn't sure Mr. St. Claire even noticed, although she did—Jason took the younger man's hand. "Likewise, I'm sure." He sounded not the least bit happy to be meeting the other fellow.

"Good evening, Miss Collins," Hamilton said, as if noticing Ginger for the first time.

He eyed the pew. Marjorie got the undoubtedly silly impression that he wished Ginger would move so he could sit next to Marjorie. She was only being fanciful.

"Good evening, Mr. St. Claire," Ginger said, her pretty blond curls bouncing. In her younger and more frivolous days, Marjorie would have killed for hair like that. And those guileless blue eyes of Ginger's were lovely, too.

Bah. What did it matter what an almost thirty-year-old spinster looked like? Marjorie told herself she was too old for such petty jealousy. Besides, *she* was Mabel.

"Would you like to sit here, Mr. St. Claire?" Ginger got to her feet, smiling prettily. "I'll just move

over to sit beside Dr. Abernathy. I'm sure you and
Marjorie will want to discuss your roles."

The little cat! Marjorie watched in incredulity as
Ginger flounced herself over to the other side of
Jason Abernathy and sat as if she weren't in reality
an unmitigated flirt but was only doing a friend a
favor. Then she batted her eyelashes at Jason, and
Marjorie couldn't watch anymore. She turned her
attention to Mr. St. Claire. *He* appreciated her, even
if nobody else did.

"Have any of the other roles been cast?" he asked,
leaning a trifle too close for Marjorie's comfort.

With one more glance at Jason and Ginger—she
was clutching his arm now, the hussy!—Marjorie
turned as pretty a smile as she had in her repertoire
upon Hamilton. He blinked, startled, and Marjorie
guessed it had been a trifle *too* pretty. Nevertheless,
she gushed a bit when she replied to his question.
"I'm not sure. I got here a little late. I believe Miss
Collins is one of the Major General's daughters."

"Do you know who the Major General is yet?" Mr.
St. Claire's voice seemed a trifle breathy.

"I believe Mr. Proctor is going to play that part.
He'll be perfect for it." Marjorie simpered, then
marveled at herself. She'd never simpered in her
life before this evening. It was all Jason and Ginger's fault.

"Ah . . . yes, he will be wonderful."

Marjorie noticed that Mr. St. Claire's eyes, which
were a fairly washed-out blue, were taking on a soul-
ful cast. She decided to back off on the simpering
and prettiness. "I'm so fond of this opera," she said,
aiming for a bright tone that couldn't be misinter-
preted as flirtatious.

"Yes," agreed Hamilton. "It's one of my favorite—"
His words broke off abruptly.

Suddenly, Jason stood before her. She jerked
slightly as she hadn't realized he'd left his seat. "Are
you ready to leave yet, Miss MacTavish?" he asked
sharply. "I'll walk you home."

Casting a startled glance at Ginger, who returned it with a baleful scowl of her own, Marjorie
said, "I . . . I—"

"I'll be happy to drive you home, Miss Mac-
Tavish," Mr. St. Claire said with a small frown for
Jason, "if you'd like to stay a little longer and see
the rest of the auditions."

"She has to get up early," Jason snarled at Hamilton. "She needs her beauty rest."

"I don't see that she needs anything of the kind,"
Mr. St. Claire snapped back. "She's beautiful already."

Sweet Lord in heaven. With haste and a good
deal of confusion, Marjorie rose to her feet. It almost sounded as if the two men were arguing with
each other over her. Preposterous. Nevertheless,
because she sensed hostility in the air—and not
only from the men; Ginger was glowering at her
for all she was worth—she said, "I'd really better
be getting along." Later she guessed the devil had
entered her heart, in spite of her being in church,
because she couldn't resist adding, "I'm so glad
you'll be Frederic, Mr. St. Claire."

"And I, too, Miss MacTavish." Mr. St. Claire rose,
took her hand, and actually deposited a chaste kiss
thereon. Marjorie wanted to snatch her hand back
and wipe it on her skirt, but she didn't. Anyhow, the
kiss provoked a snort from Jason, so she guessed it
wasn't so bad.

"Come along, Miss MacTavish." Jason grabbed her other hand.

Marjorie pulled it away. "One moment, if you please, Dr. Abernathy. I want to say good-bye to my friends."

As Jason fumed beside her, she took her leave of the Proctors and the other people who had come to the auditions. Most of them were members of the congregation, and Marjorie prolonged her leave-taking in order to fuss Jason even more.

Surely, the devil was alive and well in San Francisco that evening, because it seemed to be firmly clinging to Marjorie's heart and tongue. Marjorie knew she should be ashamed of herself.

She wasn't.

THREE

Fog trotted along at their feet as if it were a play-
ful puppy bent upon following them home. It
curled around lampposts and stop lights and made
little curlicues in the air. Jason might have been
amused by it if he weren't so annoyed with everything else in his life.

"That man is too much of a sissy for the part," he
said sourly, stomping along beside Marjorie. He had
the strangest urge to put an arm around her shoulder and draw her close to his side. He couldn't understand what the devil was wrong with him. "And
that woman is an idiot. I don't know how you can
stand being with people like that."

"Which woman is that?"

"You know very well who I'm talking about. That
ninny who told me to call her Ginger. Huh. As if we
were long-lost friends or something."

"You didn't care for her?"

Jason eyed Marjorie in the feeble light provided
by the street lamps. She was staring straight ahead,
but he detected an odd note in her voice. "I just
told you. She's an idiot. I don't care for idiots."

"I'm sure she's not truly addle-brained, Dr. Abernathy, or empty-headed. She's only . . . well . . .
young."

"Young women can be idiots, too," he snarled. In truth, he had no notion in the world why he was so crabby. His mood had been pretty good when he'd auditioned. He'd been pleased to have the role of Pirate King bestowed upon him. And afterwards, when he'd been sitting beside Marjorie, he'd enjoyed himself. It tickled him that she always went on the alert when he showed up. He probably ought not to tease her so much—but she was such a good subject for teasing. She took everything so damned seriously.

He realized Marjorie hadn't said anything in response to his last barbed comment. Irked, he said, "Well? Can't young women be idiots, too?"

"Are you calling me an idiot, Dr. Abernathy?"

He stopped walking. Since Marjorie's hand was in the crook of his arm, this required her to stop, too. She frowned up at him. "Well? What did you mean by that *too*?" she demanded.

"What too?"

"You said that young women can be idiots, *too*. Were you implying that you consider me old and an—"

"Good God, no!" His roar bounced off the tall buildings near them and echoed into the distance, the fog muffling it eerily. "What the devil made you think that?"

She sniffed. "I wouldn't put it past you, is all."

"Nuts." All right, he really had to stop needling the woman. He didn't understand his compulsion to do it, anyhow. There was just something about her. Something . . . something . . . aw, nuts. He didn't know what it was. Plowing through the fog as one might plow through snowdrifts, Jason contemplated Marjorie and the quality in her that seduced his wicked side out into the open.

It was as if all of her warmth and passion were backed up inside her. Jason sensed womanly passion there, lurking, peeking out from time to time from behind her reserve, although she did everything in her power to hide it. He wanted see it. To experience it for himself. So far, all he'd managed to do was make her mad at him.

He hadn't had these problems with his late wife, Mai. Of course, Mai had been so grateful to him that she'd adored him completely and unconditionally. She'd all but worshiped him. He'd been crushed when she'd died, although he wondered now if he mightn't have eventually felt smothered by her constant adoration. Even as he had the thought, guilt smote him.

Mai had been his one true love. His soul mate. He'd never find a woman to take her place.

That didn't negate the fact that he found Marjorie MacTavish fascinating, irritating, alluring, and absolutely baffling. He knew all about her, of course. She'd been born in Scotland, grew up in Glasgow, became a stewardess for the White Star Line, met Loretta aboard the doomed *Titanic*, and the experience of its sinking had left her with an exaggerated fear of the water. It was a reaction Jason considered perfectly understandable, but which Loretta deemed a "phobia."

Since Jason was a medical man, he didn't have any truck with phobias, *per se*. He doctored people's physical ailments and left their mental and emotional problems to others. Therefore, he didn't have an opinion on the phobia issue. He acknowledged that if he'd been forced to watch the destruction of his livelihood, not to mention watch hundreds of his friends perish, he might have a phobia or two himself.

"You're not an idiot," he growled.

"I should say not."

She sniffed, and Jason saw her pert little nose lift slightly. For so stuffy and upright a woman, she was remarkably . . . beguiling. And this was in spite of her best efforts to make herself unpleasant.

All this contemplation and introspection made him incautious. Before he could think better of it, he blurted out, "Why do you try to make yourself unpleasant?"

This time it was she who stopped walking. As the fog played games with her silly hat and deposited dewdrops on her gorgeous red hair, she gazed up at him in shock. "I beg your pardon?"

He shrugged, feeling a little silly. He hadn't actually meant to ask the question aloud. "Well . . . what I mean is . . . well . . ."

"I do not try to make myself unpleasant," Marjorie stated firmly. "I *do* try to avoid *you*. You've been awful to me since the day we met."

He had been. And he was ashamed of himself. "You're right," he said in a subdued voice.

Her eyes opened wide. "I beg your pardon?"

Irked, he said, "Stop begging my pardon, damn it. I know I've teased you a little—"

"A *little*? It didna seem like a *little* to *me*. And don't curse at me, if you please!"

He felt like a little boy being chastised for using bad language. "All right, it was more than a little," he admitted sheepishly. "But it was for your own good."

"My ain . . ." His explanation seemed to shock her. After the two words, her mouth merely hung open, as if she were unable to think of anything foul enough to say to him.

"You see," he said, feeling pressured to defend himself, although he realized what he'd done was probably indefensible, "I thought you needed to loosen up a little bit, that's all."

"To . . ." Again, she stopped speaking. This time she sucked in approximately four gallons of fog-laced air. "And what," she said in a voice he'd never heard her use before—it scared him— "would you know about my needs, Dr. Abernathy?"

This time it was his mouth that hung open for a second or two. He hadn't anticipated such a question. "Well . . . Loretta said that—"

"Loretta," Marjorie interrupted, which was a sign of just how agitated she was, "is a wonderful woman, but she has na wee *inkling* of my needs. Or, indeed, of my life before we met aboard that accursed ship."

"Really?" Jason found this quite interesting. "I thought you two had been exchanging girlish secrets since the day you met."

"Codswallop. We have'na. Nobody, not even Loretta, knows aught about me."

"Is that so?" He gazed down at her. She had delicate features and fine eyes that were green most of the time. He supposed that technically they were hazel, but she wore green a lot, which brought out the color. Her hair was a brilliant coppery red and, even though she tried to keep it confined, just as she did her personality, it wisped out of its bounds and feathered around her face, giving it a soft look even when she was at her most withdrawn or irate. He knew about the latter because she was definitely irate now.

"Aye."

"Why not?"

She blinked at him.

He expounded. "I mean, why doesn't anyone know anything about you? Your background? Your life before you moved to the United States? What are you trying to hide?" He grinned, knowing it would irk her. "Don't tell me you used to be a bank robber back home in bonny Scotland."

Her lips thinned, and he backed off slightly. "I didn't mean that, of course. Our Miss MacTavish would never do anything so outrageous as rob a bank."

"Nay, she wouldna." Marjorie turned and started off again toward Loretta's house. She didn't take his arm.

He rushed to catch up with her. "Say, Miss MacTavish, I didn't mean to rile you—"

"Ha."

"Honestly. I'm only curious. Why don't you want anyone to know about your life before the *Titanic?*"

"Because it's private."

"Well . . . but don't you like to share things with your friends?"

"My friends are all dead."

The declaration stunned Jason. "But . . . but . . ."

She stopped again and turned around. He almost ran over her. "Anyhow, why should I want anyone to know about my life before I came to America? D'ye think it'd pay me to spill my guts to *you*, who denigrates every single thing I say or do? You're daft, Dr. Jason Abernathy, if ye think that. And Loretta only wants to *fix* me, as if I were a watch that's been wound too tightly."

He knew she was hopping mad because she'd let

some Scottish expressions slip out. "I don't denigrate you either," he cried, hurt.

"Ye do." She turned as abruptly as before and took off at a sturdy clip. He had to trot to catch her up.

"Well . . . I'm sorry if you think that."

"I don't *think* it, it's the truth."

"I'm not *that* bad, surely."

"Ha."

"No, really, Miss MacTavish. I never meant to hurt your feelings."

"Fidditie-fa. Ye did, too. And it worked, ye'll be happy to ken."

He wasn't happy to ken it, whatever that meant. In fact, he was moderately chagrined that she thought so. "Well . . . maybe at first I did, but I haven't wanted to hurt your feelings for a long time."

"That makes me feel ever so much better."

He winced. Her tone had been *very* dry. "In fact, I'd like to get to know you better."

"Well, ye canna," she said flatly.

"Bet I can."

"Over my dead body."

"I won't go that far; I promise."

"Not funny," she snapped.

They walked in silence for about a block. The fog had thickened until it was like a mysterious, smothering gray mist out of a Gothic novel, and Jason began to feel depressed and misunderstood. He wished Marjorie wasn't such a tough nut to crack. He supposed her attitude was at least partially his fault, since he'd been kind of rough on her at first.

But anyone with half a sense of humor would have caught on to what he was doing and laughed. She was getting better at fighting back verbally, but he had thus far noticed not a whit of humor in her barbs. And all of his little barblets had been meant merely in fun, and besides all that . . .

Oh, very well, he'd been downright mean a couple of times. It pained him to admit it to himself.

But it hadn't really been his fault. When he'd first met Marjorie almost four years earlier, he'd still been reeling from Mai's death and in the throes of violent grief. He'd seen Marjorie sitting on Loretta's sofa, pale as a snowbank, all drawn into herself and nervous, with her lovely full mouth pinched up and with that red, red hair that fairly screamed of defiance in spite of her withdrawn demeanor, and something in him had reacted with rancor.

Although Jason didn't put as much stock in the new science of psychology as did Loretta, he now wondered if his instant antipathy toward Marjorie had owed something to his finding her attractive. At the time, such feelings about another woman had seemed a betrayal of Mai. They still did, but he was far enough removed from the worst of his grief now that he could understand that, logically, they weren't.

"I truly am sorry I gave you such a hard time, Miss MacTavish." *Miss MacTavish.* Jason gave an internal grimace. If she were any other female in the universe, they'd have been on a first-name basis for a couple of years by this time.

She squinted up at him, her face softened by the fog, as if she were assessing the truth of his apology. Because he didn't like having his sincerity questioned, he said, "I'm serious, Miss MacTavish. I'm sorry if I hurt your feelings. I promise never to do it again."

Her eyes widened. He raised his hand, palm out, in a gesture a Boy Scout would have been proud of. "I mean it."

"Vurra well," she said at last. "I accept your apology."

"Can we be friends?"

Another sharp glance at his face preceded her grudging, "I dinna know . . ."

"Can we at least not be enemies?"

"Well . . . aye, I expect we can. If ye keep your promise."

Phew! Jason was exhausted after conquering that one teensy little barrier. He wondered if he was up to pursuing friendship with the woman. Peering through the fog at her, he opted to shift to a neutral subject. "I'm looking forward to being a pirate king."

"I expect you are. The role suits you."

Jason wondered why she thought so, but decided only to say, "Thank you," and leave it at that.

"I've never been in a production like this one before."

"Nor have I. It should be fun."

"Aye. I didn't expect to be chosen as Mabel. I dinna know if I want that much responsibility."

"But you have a beautiful voice. I think you'll be great in the part." He mentally added, *if you'll loosen up and let yourself go.*

"Thank you."

He sensed that she was holding her breath, waiting for him to say something teasing, and another dart of guilt pricked his conscience. Because he was used to speaking his mind, and because he couldn't see how it could hurt her feelings, he said—and diplomatically, too— "And it might help you come out of your shell a little."

Instantly, he cursed himself as an addlepated fool. Before she could take him to task, he added, "I didn't mean that in a negative way." Oh, brother, what a stupid thing to say. When would he ever learn how to talk to this woman?

"No? Well, and what if I don't want to come out of what you and Loretta are pleased to call my *shell*, Dr. Abernathy? It might interest you to know that some of us don't *care* to have our business shouted to the world. We *like* having a little privacy. Unlike *some* people I could mention, many of us aren't comfortable fighting every rule known to mankind or marching for women's suffrage or agitating for unions or orating on street corners. And there's *nothing wrong with that.*"

She opened her mouth, as if to say something else, but she shut it again. Jason wondered what she was keeping inside herself this time. She already had so much stuff jammed up in her smallish body, he marveled that she didn't explode with it. "Absolutely," he said. "I didn't mean to offend you."

"So you say." She went on, much to his surprise. He wasn't accustomed to having Marjorie stick up for or explain herself. If she got really mad at someone, she'd erupt, and then go back into her . . . her shell, damn it. "It's a wonder to me that someone who claims not to want to injure a body's feelings can do such a good job of it without, if you're to be believed, half trying, Dr. Abernathy."

He flinched. "Ow. I didn't realize you were so sensitive, Miss MacTavish."

"Sensitive?" Her frown was as gloomy as the fog. "Sensitivity is a relative thing, Doctor. When one is accustomed to being flayed by a person, one automatically expects any comments from that source to be intentionally hurtful."

Another flinch. "I never intended to flay your feelings, Miss MacTavish."

She gave one of her ladylike snorts of disbelief.

He cleared his throat. "Um . . . I don't suppose you'd be willing to call me Jason, would you?"

After eyeing him mistrustfully for a moment, Marjorie said, "Well . . . I dinna know . . . I suppose it couldn't hurt. You may call me Marjorie."

Another hurdle o'erleapt! Jason was right proud of himself. "Thank you, Marjorie."

They walked along in silence. The fog muffled their footfalls and blotted out everything farther away than a couple of feet in front of them. A taxi-cab emerged like a phantom carriage from out of the mist, giving Jason quite a start. He wasn't normally a whimsical man, but San Francisco's fogs could make anyone feel as though he'd wandered into another, and very sinister, world.

Beside him, Marjorie shivered. Again, Jason had an impulse to draw her to his side. In spite of her having accepted his apology and agreeing to call him by his Christian name, Jason didn't think he'd better go that far. Not yet. "Are you cold, Marjorie?" Her name tasted sweet. How strange. That used to happen to him when he spoke Mai's name too.

"A little. But we're almost—"

A screech of tires and a grinding of gears interrupted Marjorie's sentence. Jason whirled around, stretching his arms out to protect her. Marjorie uttered a sharp, shocked cry, and the taxicab raced backwards out of the fog and shrieked to a stop right next to where Jason and Marjorie stood. The back door of the cab flew open, and a Chinese man hurtled out.

"Jason! You've got to come now! There's trouble and some bad injuries."

Jason, who had been primed to punch the daylights out of whatever thug had frightened Marjorie, stared in astonishment at the Chinese man. "Lo Sing!"

Lo Sing grabbed Jason's sleeve. "I'm really sorry, but there's trouble. I'm not even sure what it is, but a couple of the Chan tong got cut up pretty badly, and—" He seemed to notice Marjorie and broke off abruptly.

Jason whirled on Marjorie. "I'm sorry, Marjorie, but I have to go."

Looking dazed, Marjorie said, "Oh, that's all right. Um . . . can I help you?"

The notion of Marjorie actually being of help to him hadn't ever, not once in more than three years, occurred to Jason. He was all set to thank her and say no when Lo Sing preempted him.

"I beg your pardon, ma'am, but if you can bandage cuts, we can use you."

Jason's mouth shut with a snap of teeth. He almost barked at Lo Sing that Marjorie shouldn't be exposed to what he anticipated the evening had brought to his Sacramento Street office, when Marjorie said, "Certainly. I've had a small amount of simple nurse's training."

"You have?" Jason stared after her as she entered the cab, leaving him on the sidewalk gaping. He hurried over and climbed in beside her.

"Aye. We needed to have some basic nursing skills as stewardesses for White Star. They taught us how to apply ointment, bandage wounds, and stitch up minor cuts."

"Ah." That made sense.

Lo Sing took the front seat next to the cabbie. "Back to the clinic on Sacramento and Grant, Shen."

"Right."

Marjorie whispered in Jason's ear, "Is the driver Chinese?" She sounded surprised.

"Yeah, there are several Chinese taxi drivers in town. They mainly operate in Chinatown."

"Oh."

"Listen, Marjorie, this may be unpleasant and it'll almost certainly be bloody. I'd rather you not have to—"

"I want to," she interrupted. "This very day, I decided to expand my horizons."

"Yeah?" His gaze stuck when he turned and saw her face. She was by-God radiant. How . . . unusual.

"Yes. So I tried out for the play, and now I'll pretend to be your nurse for a wee bit."

"It's probably going to be ugly in there. I anticipate a mess. There's a full-fledged tong war going on in Chinatown, and the results are never pretty."

Her countenance sobered. "I shan't faint. You needn't fear about that. I've been through bad things before."

Recalling how she and Loretta had met each other and why she was now living in San Francisco, Jason nodded slowly, acknowledging the truth of her statement.

Marjorie hadn't lied to Jason. She had been through bad things before. None of them had been quite as gory as this particular thing, however.

The coppery reek of blood checked her in the doorway to Jason's office before she even entered the room. Jason himself, along with Lo Sing, to whom Jason had introduced her as his assistant, had rushed inside as if they smelled such nauseating odors every day. For all she knew, they might.

Marjorie hadn't kept up with the Chinese situation in San Francisco, particularly. Loretta had lectured at her once or twice—or thrice or more—about how the Chinese were discriminated against, and she'd read articles decrying the so-called "yellow peril." She'd heard about the Chinese slave trade in young women—she joined Loretta in deploring such a practice—but she hadn't heard about tong wars until recently.

Now it looked as if she was going to get a first-hand introduction to the results of a battle between members of different tongs. Five men sat in chairs or lay on the floor in Jason's office, all of them soaked in blood, a couple of them moaning softly. A woman sat on a sofa in the corner crying, her face a map of bruises. She, too, was covered in blood. Marjorie didn't know if any of the men were dead, but a couple of them lay mighty still.

"Here, Miss MacTavish, why don't you put on this coat? You don't want to get your clothes soiled."

She took the white coat from Lo Sing, thinking as she did so that the young man was incredibly polite, not to mention diplomatic. "Thank you."

"Marjorie, will you please go to the cupboard and bring me my black bag?" Jason asked the question as if he didn't intend to be denied and pointed. Marjorie complied.

Those were the last English words she heard for what seemed like a million years. Jason, making a quick assessment of his priorities, went first to examine the men lying down, questioning the more coherent of his patients about their various wounds. He shook his head and said something to Lo Sing.

Snatching his bag from Marjorie, Jason pulled out his stethoscope. He pressed it to the chest of one of the men on the floor, then snapped an order at Lo Sing. They communicated in Chinese, and Marjorie didn't understand a word. The two medical men gently transferred the man on the floor to the operating table in Jason's examination room. Then Lo Sing returned to the reception room and started inspecting another patient.

Feeling totally useless, Marjorie went back to the cupboard where she'd found Jason's bag and grabbed two rolls of gauze, one of adhesive tape, and some scissors, and returned to Lo Sing. He glanced up, smiled when he saw the supplies she'd brought, took a roll of the gauze, and gestured for her to put the other roll on a nearby bench and cut strips of tape for his use. Again, she complied.

Because she knew that wounds needed to be cleaned, she then went to the sink, filled a bowl with hot water, and brought Lo Sing the bowl and some carbolic soap and a washcloth. Again Lo Sing smiled at her. It was some comfort. She might not know what was going on, and she might not understand anything anyone was saying, but at least she felt as if she was doing something worthwhile.

While talking to one of the Chinese men, Lo Sing made a gesture, which Marjorie interpreted as one asking her to clean the first man's cut arm. It was a nasty cut. Marjorie recalled a Chinese ceremonial knife that Loretta owned and wondered if such a weapon had made this wound. She'd heard of hatchet men. Did these people really use hatchets on one another? She would have shuddered if she hadn't been otherwise occupied. Her patient hissed once or twice, but didn't complain. She tried her very best to be gentle.

She had no idea how long a time she and Lo Sing worked in that little room, surrounded by wounded people muttering comments in Chinese, a welter of blood, and the sickening stench of gore, but it was far longer than she wanted to be there. Following gestures by Lo Sing, she cleaned wounds, swabbed them with iodine, padded them with gauze, and secured the gauze pads with tape. Long before Jason returned to them, wiping his hands and looking grave, she wished she hadn't been so eager to volunteer to help him. Broadening her horizons, she told herself, didn't necessarily have to mean delving into the murky realm of Chinese tong wars.

At least she didn't get sick. The good Lord knew she felt like it often enough.

When Jason did emerge from his operating room, both she and Lo Sing glanced up. Lo Sing said something to him in Chinese. Jason shook his head and said something back that made Lo Sing shake *his* head. By that time, Marjorie wanted to stamp her foot and demand that somebody tell her what was going on.

Since she would never do anything so unconventional, she spoke up. "How is your patient, Dr. Abernathy?"

He shook his head again grimly. "Lost him."

Lost him? He'd *lost him?* Did he mean that the man had *died?* "You mean . . ." She couldn't say the words. They were too appalling.

Ignoring her unasked question, Jason turned to Lo Sing. "What's going on in here?"

"I think everyone will be all right if infection doesn't set in. Miss MacTavish has been very helpful."

He shot her a brief smile, and Marjorie didn't believe a word he said. She'd been virtually useless, except for cleaning and binding cuts, and she felt awful about it. Glancing at Jason, she shook her head but didn't explain herself, afraid she'd start crying if she tried.

"Did you find out what it's all about?"

"Yes. Evidently, the problem isn't solved yet." Lo Sing looked nervous when he peered from Marjorie to Jason. "Er, it's not a nice story. Perhaps . . ."

Impatiently, Jason said, "Just say it, Lo Sing. I'm sure Miss MacTavish won't faint from shock."

Marjorie wasn't sure about that, but she didn't let on.

"Well, then," Lo Sing continued, "it's a tong fight, as we already knew, but now I know the reason—or as much of a reason as there can be for so unreasonable a conflict."

Jason grunted in agreement.

"The Chan warlord bought Jia Lee over there"—he gestured at the girl in the corner—"from someone. Nobody seems to know from whom, although I gather it's a white man who imports women along with Chinese art and artifacts."

Marjorie stared at the girl. She had stopped weeping but looked as if she might start again any second.

"Unfortunately, the Gao warlord claims he bought her, too, from the same source."

They'd bought that girl? Marjorie's horrified gaze turned to the girl. She opened her mouth to ask the question, but a peek at Jason's face stopped her. It had taken on the aspect of a thundercloud about to burst and rain over everyone and everything in his

sight. Anyhow, she'd known the practice existed, in-
tellectually, at least. She hadn't expected ever to be
this close to it.

He snapped, "Miss MacTavish, come here, please."

Under normal circumstances, Marjorie would
have objected to his tone of command. This
evening, she rose from her knees—with some difficulty, as she'd been kneeling for what seemed like
weeks—and joined Jason, who had walked over to
the girl. He'd already started speaking softly to her
in Chinese. The girl's gentle voice replied. She
didn't once lift her head to look at Jason, but stared
at her hands, which were clasped tightly in her lap.
Marjorie would have paid money to know what they
were saying to each other.

She jumped slightly when he wheeled around to
face her. "This woman's name is Jia Lee. She's had
a nasty experience tonight and, as you can tell,
she's been badly treated. Will you please take her
into the—oh, damn." Without excusing himself for
using profanity, he called out to Lo Sing. "Help me
get the body—uh—the man out of my operating
room, Lo Sing. Miss MacTavish needs to take care
of Jia Lee."

Turning back to Marjorie as precipitously as he'd
turned away, he said, "Can you clean up the table in
there, Marjorie? It's a mess. But I don't want Jia Lee
to see it, and it would be better for her if a woman
checked her for bruises and cuts. I don't think she's
seriously injured."

Marjorie didn't want to see the mess, either, and
she didn't want to inspect this Chinese girl for
wounds, but she supposed she had to. She'd volunteered, after all.

She took another peek at Jia Lee and doubted

Jason's assessment of her injuries. She might not be badly hurt physically, barring those purpling bruises on her face and a few scrapes and scratches that had stopped bleeding long since, but she was scarred inside. Marjorie knew it, because she'd seen that same expression, a combination of agony and numbness, on her own face. Countless times.

Marjorie didn't want anything to do with Jia Lee or with the gruesome mess she knew she'd find in Jason's operating room. She had enough problems of her own.

So she said, "Of course I will."

And she went and did it.

FOUR

The clock at the Chinese Methodist Church on the other side of Grant Street had struck four, and Jason felt as if someone had thrown sand in his eyes when the last of the evening's patients was taken away by family or tong members. The dead man had been carted off by his own familial tong, and his body would be shipped to China for burial. It was a tradition. Along with killing each other.

No need for cynicism, Jason told himself. Every culture the world had ever seen, including his own, was irrationally brutal. Jason would like to acquit the American culture of brutality, but he couldn't. Men—and women—were merely products of their animal instincts, Loretta notwithstanding. He didn't understand it, but he knew by this time that he couldn't do much about it except to bandage the results of such insanity as best he could.

He rubbed his gritty eyes with a hand he'd just washed for the fiftieth time and sought out Marjorie. He'd lost track of her in the urgency of his medical dispensations. He appreciated her taking care of Jia Lee, and he dreaded the moment when he had to tell her that the Chinese girl had been restored to her singsong house—a pretty name for a disgusting place.

But the truth was that Jia Lee was a slave and was being used as a prostitute. Unlike most American prostitutes, she didn't even get to reap the rewards of her services. Her owner had that privilege, whoever he was. The whole thing made Jason sick.

But back to Marjorie . . .

"There you are," he said, surprised to find her sitting in a chair against the wall, and with almost the same expression on her face as he'd seen on Jia Lee's.

"Aye." She managed a little half smile, but he sensed her heart wasn't in it. His conscience smote him. It was beginning to do that a lot where Marjorie was concerned.

"You were a big help, Miss MacTavish," said Lo Sing. "Thank you."

Her head jerked a negative. Jason, who felt like a bloody mess himself after doctoring so many vicious stab and slash wounds, shook his own head. He wanted to hug her, but didn't dare do so—and not only because she'd probably scream and slap his face. He didn't want to rub his gore onto her. She already wore enough of her own.

That white coat Lo Sing had given her—and bless him for it, too, since Jason wouldn't have thought of doing that—was smeared red and pink, and it wasn't long enough to have protected her skirt. He noticed with dismay that smears and drops of blood had stained it. With a lopsided grin, he said, "You look like you've been through a battle."

Her huge green eyes pinned him and she didn't speak.

"We all do," said Lo Sing with a grim chuckle.

"I owe you a new skirt, Marjorie."

She didn't smile. "Nay. Ye donna."

Deciding to hell with it, Jason walked over and sat in the chair next to her. She watched him as a prisoner might watch a particularly untrustworthy guard. "We really do appreciate your help. I didn't anticipate the extent of the injuries we'd be handling, or I wouldn't have exposed you to the mess."

"Yes," agreed Lo Sing. "When I went to get the doctor, only Jia Lee and a couple of the men were here. I was shocked when we got back to find the room filled with the wounded."

"Please," she said in a voice like shattered silk, "dinna worry aboot me. If I did help, which I doubt, I'm glad to have done it."

"You did help," insisted Lo Sing.

"You did," Jason confirmed, taking her hand. It was limp and cold, and she didn't draw away from him, from which he deduced she was more upset than she cared to show. "Jia Lee was much more comfortable with you than she'd ever have been with Lo Sing or me. It was important that she have a woman to help her, and it was good of you to take care of her."

"She's just a girl," said Marjorie in a voice full of wonder.

Jason sighed. "Yes, she is." What else could he say?

"I wish I could have been of more help. I wish I spoke Chinese."

"I'll be happy to teach you." Jason cursed himself as an idiot. Oh, he wouldn't mind teaching Marjorie Chinese, but he sensed she wanted to learn in order to help Jia Lee and other Chinese women, and he didn't want her anywhere near Chinatown and its problems. He asked softly, "Are you all right, Marjorie?"

When she turned to face him, he saw tears standing in her eyes. He felt terrible for her.

"Why?" she asked, her voice trembling. "Why do they do that to each other? Isna life hard enough for them without fighting each other?"

Lo Sing muttered something under his breath.

Jason heaved a huge sigh. "You'd think so, wouldn't you?"

"It's not a simple problem," said Lo Sing.

A tear slid down Marjorie's cheek. Jason's heart squeezed painfully. "Here now, don't cry, please, Marjorie. You did splendidly. We couldn't have asked for a better assistant."

"But it's all so *senseless*." Marjorie's voice was thick.

Without thought, Jason stripped off his blood-stained coat and took her in his arms. He didn't care if he ruined his suit. "There now, Marjorie. It was a horrible experience for you, but you helped, and that's the important thing."

Her shoulders shook and she clutched him as if he were her lifeline. Jason's heart expanded a couple of cubic feet. He glanced at Lo Sing over Marjorie's head and found his assistant shaking his head.

As he patted her heaving shoulders, Jason spoke softly. "The tongs in and of themselves aren't the problem. They're only meant to be social clubs for a disenfranchised people. The problems come about when tong leaders become like the gangsters you read about in New York and Chicago. They each want the major portion of the illegal trades, and that fosters these so-called tong wars."

"Th-the trade in w-women?" Marjorie asked shakily. Her sobs were quieter now.

Both Lo Sing and Jason sighed in unison. "Women and drugs," said Jason. "If the United States Congress would repeal the Chinese Exclusion Act, the slave trade would probably die a natural—or perhaps an unnatural—death. I don't know what to say about the drug trade. People have been taking drugs to escape from reality for centuries. I don't suppose anything the government does or doesn't do will wipe out the drug trade."

"If you had to live like some of the Chinese people live, you might want to escape, too," Lo Sing said bitterly.

"Too true," Jason said with yet another sigh.

Marjorie lifted her head, and Jason sensed her desire to pull away from him. He didn't want to let her go. Because he knew her and knew that if he didn't release her, she'd pitch a fit, he gently drew back, still gripping her shoulders tenderly. "Will you be all right, Marjorie?"

She nodded and reached for her pocket. Encountering her bloodstained coat, she shuddered and snatched her hand back. Jason reached into his own pocket and withdrew a clean white lawn handkerchief. "Here. Use this." He almost added a *darling* to the last sentence, thereby shocking himself and making him release her shoulders with haste.

Standing and shoving his hands into his pockets, he continued to gaze down at her, wishing . . . wishing . . . well, he wasn't sure what he wished. "How about I pour each of us a little drink? I've got some rice wine in one of these cupboards somewhere."

"I'll get it," said Lo Sing, rising from his own chair.

Still mopping tears from her face, Marjorie looked up with a tremulous smile. "A payment from one of your patients?"

It embarrassed Jason that his friends all knew

about his habit of taking inconsequential tokens in payment for his services. He tried to laugh it off. "Mr. Hsiu. He's always paying me in rice wine. I think he makes it in his cellar." Marjorie blew her nose, then looked guiltily at Jason's handkerchief. "I'll wash it," she said.

"Don't bother. I have plenty of handkerchiefs." He made an awkward gesture meant to be comical. "Mrs. Fong makes 'em for me."

After sniffling a couple of times, Marjorie whispered, "Thank you."

"Don't mention it." He began to get nervous, standing there, peering down at her. His insides were fluttering as if a hive of bees had taken up residence in him, and he didn't understand why. He vaguely recalled having had this reaction to Mai once or twice. But Mai and Marjorie were polar opposites of one another. He shouldn't be feeling for Marjorie anything at all akin to the feelings he'd had for Mai.

Because this was so, and because he was having the feelings anyway, he forced himself to turn away from her and mosey over to his desk. He sat in his regular office chair. Marjorie and Lo Sing had worked in tandem and without speaking while Jason was stitching up his last patient. They'd mopped up the blood from the floor and washed down all the furniture. He felt guilty for having put Marjorie through this, even if she'd volunteered.

"I've never heard of wine made from rice," she said after a few moments of silence.

"Aha! There it is." Lo Sing withdrew a brown crockery bottle from a cupboard and turned to smile at Marjorie. "My people make just about everything from rice."

"Oh?"

"Everything from noodles to wine to floor mats."

"I had no idea," said Marjorie in a thread of her normal voice. "How enterprising of them."

"Oh, we're very enterprising." Lo Sing brought the bottle to Jason's desk, along with three tiny teacups. "Guess we'll have to use these."

Marjorie stood up, swayed slightly, and sat again with a thump. Jason jumped to his feet. "Marjorie!"

She flapped a hand at him. "I'll be fine. I'm just a wee bit shaky on my pins." She unbuttoned her bloodstained coat, slipped it from her shoulders, inspected it briefly, shuddered, and thrust it into the chair Jason had recently vacated. Bracing herself on the arms of her own chair, she pushed herself to her feet.

Fighting the impulse to dash over and pick her up, Jason remained standing until he was reasonably certain she wouldn't fall over. He'd been holding his breath, although he only realized it as he expelled it in a whoosh when Marjorie smiled and said, "I'm fine now." He sank back into his desk chair as she walked over to his desk with her old, sturdy gait. "I don't know what came over me."

Jason, thinking he knew what had come over her, splashed wine into a teacup and thrust it at her. "Here. Drink this. Maybe it'll settle you."

"Don't feel bad, Miss MacTavish. When I first started working for Dr. Abernathy, I was sick for days." Lo Sing chuckled softly.

"True, true," agreed Jason with a grin.

"Thank you for telling me that." Even Marjorie managed a small smile. "It makes me feel less of a nyaff."

Both men eyed her with blank expressions, and she sighed and said, "A fool."

Jason's eyebrows drew together. "Say, didn't you call me a nyaff once or twice?"

He knew she was recovering when her green eyes twinkled. "Probably. If I didn't, I'm sure I meant to."

The sky had just begun to display faint, blurry rays of pink and orange when Marjorie, after shaking hands with Lo Sing and telling him how glad she was to have met him—and almost meaning it—walked out the door of Jason's clinic and into the new day. Glancing down, she realized she couldn't see her feet. Bluidy fog. Or . . . the word *bloody* had taken on a new meaning in her life during the last several hours. How interesting. Or . . . perhaps she meant how appalling.

Nevertheless, she didn't appreciate the fog this morning. Shivering, she muttered, "I'm tired of the infernal fog."

"Me, too," said Jason. He hesitated. "Do you mind if I leave you here and go look for a cab?"

After thinking about it for a second or two, Marjorie said, "Aye, I do mind. I'll walk wi' ye."

"You sure? I know you're exhausted."

She offered him a grim smile. "As Loretta would say, so are you, and women are as capable of motion even when exhausted as men. I'm fit to walk, thank you."

"Let me take your arm then," Jason said with a grin.

So she did, and they started walking from Sacramento to Grant, where there was a greater chance they'd find a cab. After the night's adventures,

Marjorie wouldn't want to hazard a guess as to why a cab might be lingering in Chinatown at this hour of the day. Her happy ignorance had been shattered with a vengeance, and she didn't expect she'd be able to ignore at least one of Loretta's many causes any longer. She heaved a big sigh and wondered if her congressman would bother to read a letter from an immigrant Scotswoman.

"You all right?"

She nodded. "Aye, I will be."

"I really do appreciate your help, Marjorie."

With a shrug, she said, "I didna do much. I didna know how. Wish I did."

"No, you don't. It's very discouraging work."

Fog had beaded Jason's hat brim with little water pearls. Marjorie felt as if she were slogging through a mush of the stuff, although it really was weightless. Her heart was heavy, though, and the fog might as well have weighed a ton. Smudges of light streaked the air as it filtered through the mist from the street lamps.

Looking around her, she decided that this part of San Francisco might as well be Glasgow, although this fog wasn't as foul as the coal-smoke fogs that smothered her homeland. The things that went on under its muffling blanket were every bit as cruel, though, and Marjorie's head and heart both hurt.

Although she knew that to do so was tantamount to surrendering in a war, she said, "You're a good man, Jason Abernathy. I didn't realize it until tonight."

She sensed his shock a moment before he shrugged off her compliment. "I only do what I can do. It's pitifully little."

"You try, though, and that's what's important."

He didn't speak for a moment. Marjorie figured he was trying to think up a withering retort. Therefore, she was surprised when he only said, at last, "Thank you."

Their footsteps made muffled claps on the sidewalk. The streets in this part of the city had been paved years before, mainly because Chinatown attracted so many tourists. According to Jason and Loretta, if the city fathers had only the Chinese who lived in Chinatown to consider, the streets wouldn't have been paved at all ever. As much as Marjorie wanted not to believe them, she couldn't do it any longer. Lost innocence was a right burden, and she wished she hadn't so blithely rushed to accept it. How did that line of poetry start? "Fools rush in?" Well, she was a fool, and no mistake.

After a little while of walking and not speaking, Jason said, "I think I hear a horse. It must be a cab." He stepped away from her and was swallowed up by the fog.

For a few seconds, Marjorie felt as if she'd been abandoned in an evil land of frothing gray nothingness. Her joy when Jason emerged from the fog smiling was as overwhelming as it was strange. She'd never been glad to see him before. Because she was ashamed of herself for her reaction to the fog and to him, she forced herself to speak. "Was it a cab?"

"Yes." He took her arm again. "The only horse-drawn vehicles in the city these days are the cabs that work at night."

"Ah. They're too slow for daytime traffic, I expect."

"Right." He led her to the waiting horse and carriage. The vehicle was a shabby affair that had probably been dashing in about 1880. The horse didn't look much younger. "Here we go."

"You needn't see me home. You must be beat."

"Nuts. I'm going to see you to the door. You performed yeoman's service tonight, Marjorie, and I appreciate it."

"It was . . . interesting." She hoped he didn't see her shiver.

"Right." He gave the address to the cabbie and climbed inside the carriage with Marjorie. "Say, are you really interested in learning Chinese?"

She sighed. "I suppose so. Might as well. But, Jason, what's going on in Chinatown? Is there really a war between the tongs? And that poor girl. Where did she go? That man who picked her up, who was he? I canna stand the notion of her going back to . . . to . . ." She couldn't say it and chided herself for her cowardice.

"I'm afraid she did. Women aren't legally allowed to immigrate to the United States from China, you know."

"Aye. Loretta's told me as much." Many and many a time, as a matter of fact.

"Yes, I'm sure she has." He chuckled softly. "Anyhow, the result of the Exclusion Act is that a Chinese man either has to marry an American woman—and most of them don't want to—or they have to import women illegally."

She shuddered and again hoped he couldn't see her in the dark. The notion of human beings being bought and sold disturbed her and made something way down deep in her soul ache. "I thought America abolished slavery half a century ago."

"It did for plantation slaves in the South. The problem is that slavery of Chinese women is not supposed to exist. Rather like the Black Hand, I suppose."

"The Black Hand?"

"An Italian organization that terrorizes neighborhoods in New York City."

"And it's real?"

"Oh, yes, it's real, all right."

Marjorie thought about that for a few seconds. "Are governments always so blind?"

"Yes." His voice was firm. "When they're not lying to us, they're pretending such horrors don't exist."

"That's a vurra bleak assessment of things."

"I suppose it is, but I believe it's accurate."

She shook her head, thinking he was probably right, and wishing he was wrong.

"Conditions are so bad in parts of China these days that families sometimes sell their daughters into service of one sort or another. Daughters aren't regarded as being as valuable as sons, except insofar as they can marry well. If that's out of the question for one reason or another, there's always been a lively market for prostitutes. Now it's spread to the United States."

"The Chinese government sanctions such trade in human beings?"

"Oh yes. So does ours, by turning a blind eye to the problem." Marjorie heard the smile in his voice. "You should hear what Loretta says about the old-fashioned notion that women are only good for one thing."

Marjorie couldn't make herself smile. "That's terrible."

"Yes, it is. Any kind of slave trade is vile, and buying women to work in—" He broke off suddenly.

Marjorie thought she knew why. "You can say it, Jason. I think I can take it."

"It's such an ugly word."

"The words aren't as ugly as the deed."

"True, true."

"And that poor woman tonight—Jia Lee? Is that her name?"

"Yes."

"That man who came to get her was her owner?"

"I guess. There seems to be some dispute as to whom she really belongs."

"But she's so young."

"Probably fifteen or sixteen."

"Och, God." After thinking about the world, she added, "I dinna know why He allows such goings-on."

"I doubt God has much to do with it."

"Nay. He couldna. He gives us His gifts, expecting us to use them wisely, and we both just saw what some of us have done with them."

"Eloquently put."

Marjorie heard the dryness in his voice and didn't blame him. It was difficult to believe in a good God sometimes. Giving up the fight to remain strong and in control, Marjorie buried her face in her hands. She didn't cry. She just wanted to escape from the world and its horrors for a moment or two. When she felt Jason move to her side, she turned into his arms. "I canna stand life sometimes," she whispered.

"I know. A few hours ago we were singing delightful music in your church. Music has to be one of man's highest accomplishments. And then we were plunged into the depths of degradation that only man seems capable of."

"Aye." She didn't draw away. His arms felt warm

and comforting, a refuge from the damp, foggy, gray, miserable world that contained women like Jia Lee and men like those who claimed to own her.

"I think we're getting close to Loretta's house," Jason said after a long, silent respite.

Since he didn't seem to be in any hurry to let her go, Marjorie subsided against the shabby bolster, but allowed his arm to remain around her shoulder. It was warm and strong and gave her a measure of solace. "I'm tired."

"You and me both. I'm going to rest for a couple of hours and go back to the clinic, though. Maybe I can get to the bottom of the troubles."

"Do you need help?"

She felt his head turn and knew he was eyeing her sharply. With an odd-sounding laugh, he said, "Didn't you get enough ugliness tonight to keep you satisfied?"

"Aye. But it's work that needs doing."

"What about your duties to Loretta?"

"I don't *have* any duties to Loretta," she said on a grim note. "That's one of the problems. She's been all but keeping me for years now." She was disappointed when he drew his arm away and moved to the other side of the cab.

"I know that's not true, Marjorie. Loretta has told me many times that she relies on you for everything. She says you take care of her correspondence and accompany her to different meetings and keep track of her appointments and all sorts of other secretarial things."

"She's only being kind. She really doesna need me. Or," she amended, "if she *does* need a secretary, it's surely not a full-time job. I could help at your clinic." Feeling foolish all of a sudden, she added,

"If I can be useful. If ye canna use a person with little training and fewer skills, I'll understand."

"Nonsense." Jason stopped speaking as the cab pulled into Loretta's long drive.

The sky had lightened enough for Marjorie to be able to make out the tall iron fence she now knew so well. She loved Loretta's house, but even though she'd lived in it for more than three years, she considered herself an interloper there. Loretta had done, and continued to do, everything in her power to vanquish that feeling in Marjorie, but Marjorie still felt like a fish out of water. Perhaps getting involved in something worthwhile—or that *she* considered worthwhile—might lessen her sense of alienation.

It looked, however, as though Jason didn't need her. She wasn't surprised. She'd made a first-rate stewardess for White Star, but since the *Titanic* sank, she'd been rather like a feather floating on the breeze, with nothing to anchor her to any specific spot. Except her fear. Fear kept her at Loretta's house, and in a position that was, at best, a sinecure. Fear kept her from doing anything useful with her life. It was a melancholy thought.

The clip-clopping of the horse's hooves stopped and so did the cab. Jason said, "We're here."

"Aye."

He pushed the door open. "Let me get out first, and I'll help you to the door."

"You needn't."

"Yes, I do."

She didn't argue. Her spirits had plummeted during the last few minutes. She was *so* useless, and she felt her uselessness acutely right then. Jason flipped the stairs down and, accepting his hand, she stepped out of the cab. When her feet hit the gravel walk, she swayed slightly. Jason steadied her, and she felt foolish.

"Sorry. I'm a wee bit tuckered."

"More than a wee bit I think."

Jason's chuckle sent a shaft of heat through Marjorie. She chalked up this strange reaction to her state of exhaustion.

They both jumped slightly when the front door flew open and light spilled out, getting lost in the fog before it reached Marjorie and Jason. "Marjorie? Marjorie, is that you?" It was Loretta's voice, anxious and tense.

Jason led Marjorie up the porch steps. "It's both of us, Loretta. Sorry we've been so long. I should have telephoned."

"What in the world are you doing coming home at this hour?"

Marjorie might have been embarrassed had Loretta not been who she was. As it was, she knew that Loretta probably would have thrown a party had Marjorie ever done anything outré. "It's naught scandalous, you may be sure," she said, and she actually smiled for real.

"Of course it's not. I know you too well to think you actually did anything unusual, Marjorie Mac-Tavish." Loretta made a pretty picture, framed in the light from the entryway of her house. She was enormously pregnant, and her blue brocade dressing gown pooched in front of her as if she'd strapped pillows to her waist. Her masses of dark hair had been braided and fell over her shoulders, and her big brown eyes were wide with avid curiosity.

"Let Marjorie inside, Loretta, and I'll tell you all about it," Jason said.

Loretta's eyes grew even wider. "You mean you had an adventure, and you didn't take me along?"

Marjorie, recalling Jia Lee, the dead man, and the others whom Jason had bandaged, said tightly, "Aye, it was an adventure all right."

Taking a gander at Marjorie and Jason, Loretta gasped. "Marjorie! Is that blood on your skirt?"

Peering down at herself, Marjorie was surprised to discover that yes, there was blood on her skirt. "Aye, it's blood all right."

"Let Marjorie go to her room, clean up, and get some sleep, Loretta. I'll tell you about it."

"Oh my, you really *did* have an adventure!" Turning on Marjorie solicitously, Loretta took her arm. "Will you be all right, Marjorie? Do you need any help?

"Thank you, Loretta, but I'll be fine. I'm only tired."

"You poor thing. Did Jason rope you into helping at his clinic?"

"Nay. I volunteered." Marjorie didn't even resent the shocked glance Loretta shot at Jason or the wry grin he shot back. She'd proved herself to be magnificently conventional during the years they'd known each other. Tonight, from auditioning for a part in *Pirates* to helping Jason at his clinic, had been an aberration of enormous proportions.

"Was it bad?"

Thankful that Loretta had asked the question of Jason so she didn't have to answer it, Marjorie started up the stairs.

"Very bad," said Jason grimly.

In truth, Marjorie was relieved to hear his answer. If the poor man had to face casualties like that every day of the week, Marjorie might just have to forgive him for being a thorn in her side all these years.

"Are you sure you don't need any help, Marjorie?"

Marjorie was about halfway up the wide staircase. Turning, she looked down upon Loretta and Jason, both of whom were staring up at her, Loretta with a troubled expression on her face, and Jason with a puzzled one on his. Marjorie understood, and smiled. "Thank you, no, Loretta. I'm only tired."

"Are you sure?"

"Aye, I'm sure."

She felt their gazes upon her until she reached the top of the staircase and walked away from them toward her own room.

FIVE

Staggering out of bed a little past noon that same day, Marjorie was aghast that she'd allowed herself to sleep so long. She had duties to perform. She had a job to do. No matter that she hadn't fallen into bed until half past four that morning, she was shirking her responsibilities, and Marjorie Mac-Tavish didn't do things like that. She was ashamed of herself.

A clap of thunder had awakened her, and another had accompanied her out of bed. She shuffled to the window and wasn't surprised to see that the day was gray and overcast and that a fine drizzle was falling. Those thunderclaps presaged heavier rains to come. Well, good. Marjorie would have hated it if the day was brighter than she was—and she was definitely not bright.

After bathing—thank God for modern plumbing!— and dressing in record time, Marjorie twisted her unruly red hair into a knot at the back of her neck and clattered down the staircase and hurled herself into Loretta's sitting room. Loretta, seated at her desk and writing furiously, glanced up in alarm.

"Marjorie! Whatever is the matter?"

"I'm so sorry!" Marjorie gasped. "I dinna know what came over me that I forgot to set the alarm!"

A frown creased Loretta's brow. "I should certainly hope you *didn't* set the alarm, Marjorie MacTavish. After what you did last night, you deserve to sleep all day if you want to."

Frowning in her own right, Marjorie pressed a hand over her thumping heart. "But I have duties to you, Loretta. I am your secretary." She gestured at the pen and paper before Loretta. "For instance, I probably should be doing that."

"Piffle." Loretta waved Marjorie's duties away with a small hand. "Your work with Jason last night was ever so much more important than your work for me."

"But you're the one who pays my salary."

"That's right. Therefore, you should obey my orders, and I order you to rest today."

"But . . ." It was no use. Marjorie never won arguments with Loretta. She didn't know why she even tried to make her employer understand her point of view.

Loretta put her pen down and leaned as far forward over her desk as she could, considering the impediment in her way, and grinned at Marjorie, her bright eyes avid. "Jason told me all about it, Marjorie. How awful it must have been, and yet how thrilling!"

Because Marjorie knew it would be impossible to bring Loretta to a proper understanding of how she was failing in her duties as Loretta's secretary, she sank into the chair on the other side of Loretta's desk. It had frustrated her from the beginning of her association with Loretta that the woman seemed so little concerned with the way things were supposed to be. Marjorie, who clung to convention the way a drowning man might cling to a life raft, was uncomfortable when her employer waved rules away with such abandon. "I'm your secretary, Loretta. I'm supposed to be working for you, not for Dr. Abernathy."

"Fiddlesticks. Tell me, Marjorie!" Pressing a hand to her stomach and making a face, Loretta sat back in her chair. "I can't wait until this is over with. If I'd known how awful pregnancy would be, I never would have tried it."

"One presumes you didn't try it on purpose," Marjorie said dryly. She had been more shocked than usual when Loretta had begun an affair with Captain Quarles. She'd known that Loretta claimed to favor what she called "free love," but she hadn't expected her ever to practice it.

Free love. Marjorie almost snorted. There was no such thing in her experience. Love exacted a price, no matter what a woman's beliefs about it might be.

Loretta laughed in delight. "Oh, Marjorie! When we first met, I was sure you had no sense of humor at all, but you do. It's just wry, is all."

Mortified, Marjorie muttered, "I beg your pardon. It wasna my place to—"

"Oh, bother your place!" Loretta interrupted her. "If you haven't learned by this time that there are no set *places* for people in the United States, you're beyond redemption, Marjorie MacTavish! But I don't want to get sidetracked. Tell me all about what happened last night."

Marjorie opened her mouth to comply, when Loretta spoke again.

"Start with the auditions. Jason said he's going to be the Pirate King."

"Auditions?" Marjorie said blankly. It took her a few seconds to recollect. For pity's sake, she'd forgotten all about the auditions. How funny. Until she'd become involved in Jason's doctoring efforts, trying out for a part in *The Pirates of Penzance* had been the most outrageous thing she'd ever done. Now, even the auditions had been eclipsed. "Aye. The auditions."

"Jason wouldn't tell me which part you got. He said you should be the one to tell me. I hope you're Mabel. You'd make a perfectly gorgeous Mabel."

Marjorie's mouth clanked shut. "You think I'd be a gorgeous Mabel? Why ever d'ye think that?"

Loretta waved her hand in the air again. She was given to such broad gestures. They matched her personality. And her figure, at the moment. "Because you're so beautiful, and because you have a spectacular voice."

Beautiful? Her? Marjorie MacTavish? She could understand—and almost agree with—the voice issue. But as far as looks went, Marjorie had always deplored hers. Red hair was so . . . so . . . gaudy. It didn't suit Marjorie's personality, which was quiet and withdrawn. Confused, she sat there in frowning silence until her employer spoke again.

"Well," prodded Loretta. "What role did you get? If you were offered Mabel and opted for one of the Major General's daughters, I'll never speak to you again!"

"Nay. Ye needn't fear that we'll have to communicate by notes, Loretta. I accepted the role of Mabel."

"Hurrah!" Leaning back, Loretta clapped her hands. A boom of thunder shook the house, she sat forward again, said, "Ow!" and hugged her huge bulge with both arms.

Startled, Marjorie sprang to her feet and rushed

around the desk to the other side. "Loretta! Whatever is the matter? Are the bairns coming?"

Grimacing horribly, Loretta panted, "No, I don't think so. I don't know. I just had a sudden pain, was all."

"D'ye need to lie doon?"

Loretta shook her head. "No, I'm all right."

Another thunderclap sent Marjorie to the window to pull the curtains aside. "The rain's coming down in a torrent."

"Good. Knowing the weather's foul will make me feel less stifled when we stay home today."

"Aye. It might be pleasant to sit and read a book while it rains outside." Marjorie hadn't had many opportunities to waste time like that until she became Loretta's secretary. But Loretta handed out free time as if it were candy. Naturally, the thought made her feel guilty.

"Yes. I've got the latest Mary Roberts Rinehart book from the library. I've been looking forward to—Ow!"

Marjorie jumped, let go of the curtain and dashed back to Loretta's side. "Och, Loretta, what's the matter?"

Her employer shook her head. "I don't know what's going on, but it certainly hurts."

"Och, my God! Are these the first contractions, or have ye had others?"

"First contractions?" Loretta looked at her in astonishment. "Do you think I'm going into labor?"

Marjorie wished Loretta wouldn't speak so plainly, although she should be used to it by this time. "I dinna know. But we probably ought to start timing the pains."

"Timing the pains? Oh my goodness. Maybe I *am* going into labor. It hurts like mad."

"Aye. It'll hurt worse before you're through, too."

"Don't be so encouraging, Marjorie. I might forget myself and enjoy the experience."

Marjorie had never heard her employer speak so sarcastically. Loretta wasn't given to sarcasm. Unlike Marjorie herself, Loretta had no need for it, since she always spoke her mind. Loretta groaned again and would have doubled over had she been able.

"Ye needn't fret about enjoying it," Marjorie muttered. "Here. Sit on the sofa. I'm going to fetch Captain Quarles."

"Telephone Jason!" Loretta hollered after her.

"Aye, I will."

Fortunately for both of them, Marjorie nearly ran over Mrs. Brandeis, the Quarleses' housekeeper, as she dashed out the door. Grabbing the woman's arm, Marjorie cried, "Get the Captain, Mrs. Brandeis. The bairns are on their way!"

Mrs. Brandeis clapped her hands to her cheeks and uttered a shocked cry before tearing off in the opposite direction. Marjorie called after her, "And telephone Dr. Abernathy!"

"Yes, yes!" Mrs. Brandeis sang back. "I will!"

"Marjorie!" Loretta screeched from her sitting room. "Come back here for a minute!"

Her heart battering against her ribs like hailstones against a tin roof, Marjorie ran back to Loretta. "What? What's the matter?"

Rain pelted down outside the window, sounding like the drum of a military band. Marjorie wondered if the thunderstorm had brought on Loretta's labor. She'd heard that the weather played a role in these things, although she didn't know if such stories were old wives' tales or based on scientific fact.

"I'm having a baby is what's the matter," Loretta said, sounding grouchy.

"You're having twins," Marjorie corrected her, although she wasn't sure how she knew.

"It doesn't matter. But I want to go up to my bedroom before it's too late. You can telephone Jason after I'm settled there. I don't want to be stuck here for the duration."

"Aye. That's a good idea. Mrs. Brandeis is calling the doctor." Taking her tenderly by the arm, Marjorie helped Loretta struggle out of her chair.

Like a breeching whale, Loretta lumbered to her feet. Marjorie was frightened when she saw her eyes pop wide open, as if in shock. "What? Och, Loretta, what is it?"

But Loretta didn't look at Marjorie. She took a step sideways and peered down at the sitting-room carpet. A small puddle of water lay there. "I guess it's time, all right," Loretta said. "My water just broke."

Because of her service with White Star, Marjorie knew what that meant. She'd never been present at a birthing before, but she'd heard all about the couple of incidents that had taken place aboard ship. "Merciful heaven," she whispered. "Here, Loretta, can ye walk?"

"Of course, I can walk. I'm not dying. I'm only having a baby."

"Or two."

"Or two. It better not be more than that, or I'll never forgive Malachai."

Because she loved Loretta, and also because she valued her job, Marjorie didn't bother to point out that it took two to make babies. Anyway, trying to get Loretta to see reason wasn't worth the effort. In her more sardonic moments, Marjorie thought it must be nice to have so much money that you didn't have to care what others thought of you.

She wasn't sardonic now. She was frightened to death. Loretta was a very small woman. As she guided Loretta out of the room, Marjorie glanced back at the clock. Twelve forty-five. She knew somebody had to keep track of the contractions and how far apart they were, and she also knew that Loretta wasn't the one to do it.

The boom-boom of heavy footfalls smote their ears, and Marjorie breathed more easily. It was the captain. A body could hear him coming from miles away. The pitter-pat of his minion, Derrick Peavey, rat-tatted an accompanying counterpoint. As far as Marjorie was concerned, Mr. Peavey was pretty much useless as a house servant, but Captain Quarles valued his long-term service aboard the captain's ships, so he'd given Peavey a job when he and Loretta had married. She admired the captain for his loyalty and couldn't help but wish that Mr. Peavey were a more . . . sane was perhaps too strong a word for it . . . a more perspicacious individual.

"What's going on?"

Malachai's roar almost deafened her.

Mr. Peavey, close on his heels, muttered something about the Moors being at fault.

"Don't shout, Malachai," Loretta said querulously. It was an unusual tone of voice for her.

Malachai took her by the arms, ignoring Marjorie completely. His face couldn't go white because it was too deeply tanned, but the lines of fear and strain could be read by anyone who looked. Marjorie stepped aside, thinking how nice it would be if someone cared for her as much as the captain cared for Loretta. Then she remembered that someone had cared for her that much. Once. Her heart crunched painfully.

"Good God, Loretta, is it coming?"

Marjorie couldn't understand why everyone kept insisting on one baby when she knew there were two in there. Loretta wouldn't be so enormous if there was only one. Besides, Marjorie just *knew*. In her heart.

Loretta said, "Yes. What do you think all this fuss is about?"

Without bothering to answer his wife or take exception to her tone of voice, the captain swept her up in his arms and started for the stairs. He called back over his shoulder, "Telephone Dr. Abernathy!"

"I did, Captain," Mrs. Brandeis said. Marjorie hadn't seen her because the captain was so bulky, but she spotted her now, backed against a wall and wringing her hands. Derrick Peavey had folded himself up in a chair and looked as if he were trying to disappear.

"D'ye need me, Loretta?" Marjorie asked.

From her husband's arms, Loretta glanced back at her. "Not right now. Why don't you make some tea or something to keep Malachai occupied. He's going to be acting like a big baby until this is over."

Malachai growled, but Marjorie finally smiled. If Loretta's instinct for management had returned, she'd probably be all right. She turned to Mrs. Brandeis. "Shall we make sandwiches and tea, Mrs. B?"

Worriedly staring at the captain's retreating back and Loretta's dangling feet, Mrs. Brandeis said, "I suppose so. I wonder if the doctor will need help, though."

"He can tell us when he gets here," Marjorie said, taking the other woman by the arm and gently turning her around toward the kitchen. "He'll probably need sustenance, too, depending on how long this takes."

"I wish she was going to the hospital," muttered Mrs. Brandeis.

"So do I. But children have been born at home for centuries," Marjorie pointed out.

"Yes, I know that, and I also know that women have died in childbirth for centuries."

Marjorie had never known Mrs. Brandeis to be tart before. She didn't blame her in this case. Loretta was huge, she was having twins, and Marjorie, too, would have been more comfortable if she'd agreed to have them in a hospital, where emergencies could be dealt with more efficiently than from home. "Ah, well, you know Loretta."

"Yes. I do know Mrs. Quarles," Mrs. Brandeis said darkly. "Stubborn woman."

Marjorie couldn't argue with that.

Leaving Mrs. Brandeis and the two housemaids, Molly and Li, preparing food in the kitchen, Marjorie, nervous and worried, went to the front hall to await Jason's arrival. Mr. Peavey hadn't moved from his chair, but he had commenced biting his nails and muttering about the Moors.

Anxiety ate at Marjorie's innards, although she wasn't absolutely sure it all had to do with Loretta. In truth, she was jittery about seeing Jason again. They'd actually shared a confidence or two the night before, and Marjorie, who had locked everything inside herself for so long, felt strange about that.

His automobile pulled up in front of Loretta's porch a few minutes later, and Marjorie, who had been watching through the window in the door, had opened the massive thing before she realized she might appear eager to see him. How embarrassing.

On the other hand, Loretta *was* having twins. That being the case, Marjorie excused her eagerness and rushed out onto the porch. "Hurry, Jason! Loretta's having the babies."

He looked tired and drawn, but he produced a smile for her. "So I hear. How's she doing?"

Feeling a little silly—after all, nothing had gone wrong yet—Marjorie said, "All right, I think. But . . . well, she's so big and all . . ."

Rather than bounding up the porch stairs as was his wont, Jason trudged up them today. "I know. It's a little worrying, especially if she's carrying twins."

"Aye. D'ye think she is?"

He nodded. "Two heartbeats."

That made sense. "You look tired, Doctor."

He uttered a dry chuckle and lifted his head to smile at her. "I am. You look perky, though, Marjorie. And as lovely as ever. I'm glad you slept in."

Detesting her redheaded tendency to blush at the least little provocation, Marjorie turned around, pretending to lead the way, although that wasn't necessary. Jason knew Loretta's house better than she did. "Thank you. I did sleep in. Then I felt guilty about it." Her laugh was slightly strained.

"That's our Marjorie. But guilt becomes you, so I guess it's all right."

"Whatever d'ye mean by that?" demanded Marjorie, resenting his words, although she didn't know that he meant them to be unkind. She'd become accustomed to mistrusting every word that came out of his mouth.

Jason shrugged. "I don't even know." He hung his hat and coat on the hall rack and hefted his black bag. "Where is she?"

"Upstairs. In her bedroom. It's the first door—"

"I know where it is." He started wearily up the steps.

An angry, "Ow! *Damn* it!" floated down from upstairs, and Jason grinned.

"Ah, Loretta. This should be fun."

Marjorie almost said she was glad he thought so, but didn't. Her mind was still hovering around his comment about knowing where Loretta's bedroom was. Whatever did that mean? And how could he know where it was unless he'd been there? And what would have prompted him to go there?

But that was a silly question. Marjorie knew, because Loretta had told her, that she'd been a virgin until she met the captain. Anyhow, what did it matter to Marjorie if Loretta and Jason had been lovers? Not a thing, that's what.

That being the case, Marjorie couldn't account for the white-hot rage that engulfed her when her mind's eye pictured Jason and Loretta together in an intimate embrace. Or the burning jealousy the image brought.

Shaking her head and telling herself she was hopeless, Marjorie dragged back through the hallway toward the kitchen. Mrs. Brandeis and the maids didn't need her help any more than Jason did. She'd probably only be in the way. She was so useless.

As she walked past the staircase, she heard a noise

and glanced up. The captain, looking strained and rather like a whipped dog, was halfway down the stairs. He saw her, nodded, and muttered, "She kicked me out."

Marjorie felt her eyebrows lift, and she grinned in spite of herself. "Did she?"

He nodded again. "Said she hated me."

"Poor Captain Quarles. She didna mean it, ye ken."

"I guess." He made it to the bottom of the staircase, stuffed his hands in his pockets, and stared gloomily at the carpet at his feet. "I suppose I'll just have to wait here."

"Aye, I suppose so. D'ye want tea?"

"Tea?" The captain wrinkled his nose. "No thanks. I think I can do without tea."

"Coffee?"

"Maybe a cup of coffee."

"I'll fetch it for you, Captain. You just sit down here. I know you want to be as close to Loretta as ye can be."

"Damned Moors," Derrick Peavey mumbled from his chair against the wall.

A scream tore through the house, and Malachai's face scrunched up even as his shoulders lifted. He looked like an enormous schoolboy being punished for some heinous sin. Marjorie would have laughed had she not felt such sympathy for the poor man.

"I can't sit," he said.

"Well, you can pace then," advised Marjorie. "I think it's the time-honored way of fathers-to-be."

"God," he said. "This is awful."

"It was the Moors done it." Peavey sounded as if he might cry.

Chuckling under her breath, and silently thanking the captain for making her feel useful again, Marjorie trotted to the kitchen. She was ever so glad that the captain didn't drink as seafaring men often did. Drunkenness was the bane of many of the sailors she'd known in her own seafaring days.

When she returned to give the captain his cup of coffee and a sandwich to keep him busy, Marjorie saw that he was talking to Jason. Her heart sped up. She disapproved. Her heart had no business doing things like that.

In order to teach her heart a lesson, she spoke in a businesslike voice, "How's she doing?"

With a chuckle, Jason turned to grin at her, making her heart misbehave yet again. Stupid heart. "She's fine. She's short, but she has broad hips, and everything seems to be going quite well."

A shrieked "*Jason!* Where the devil are you?" sailed down the stairs to them. Marjorie winced, Jason chuckled, Peavey crossed himself, and the captain cringed.

"But I'm going to need help. I think Mrs. Brandeis has helped deliver babies before. Do you think you could ask her to assist me, Marjorie?"

"Of course." Without waiting for the captain to take the tray she'd prepared for him, Marjorie clunked it down on the hall table and raced back to the kitchen.

She exploded into the room, startling Li into dropping a piece of buttered bread and causing Mrs. Brandeis to turn pale and slap a palm to her bosom. "Oh!" cried she. "What is it? Something's going wrong, hasn't it? I *knew* she should have gone to the hospital!"

Guilt smacked Marjorie upside the head. "I'm

sorry. I didn't mean to frighten you. Nay, Loretta's fine. But the doctor needs help. There are two bairns, y'see, and he asked if you could help him."

Mrs. Brandeis straightened her shoulders. "I'll be happy to help. Let me wash my hands, and I'll be right there."

"Have you done this before, Mrs. B?" Marjorie was curious. She hadn't pegged the Quarleses' stately housekeeper as a midwife.

"Twice. I recollect telling Dr. Abernathy about it one time. I suppose he remembered."

There was a hint of pride in her voice. Marjorie didn't begrudge her the emotion. Mrs. Brandeis might shoulder a large responsibility as the Quarleses' housekeeper, but she was still a servant. From long and often bitter experience, Marjorie knew how difficult it was to find anything to feel good about when one worked as a servant. "Aye. It's good that you can help."

"Let me get a clean apron. Cleanliness is next to godliness, especially where babies are concerned."

Molly waited until Mrs. Brandeis had left the room before saying under her breath, "When you've got five brothers like I do, cleanliness is next to impossible."

Marjorie and Li both laughed.

Mrs. Brandeis pressed a cool, damp cloth to Loretta's brow. Jason told himself it was selfish to regret that he'd asked for Mrs. Brandeis rather than Marjorie. He appreciated the housekeeper more than he could say, really. She was efficient and self-contained, two qualities that came in extremely handy when dealing with childbirth.

Loretta was anything but those two things, as he'd expected. Neither meek nor mild, Loretta had no trouble expressing her opinions even during the most favorable of conditions, which childbirth wasn't. Although he'd never been in labor himself, Jason knew that it was one of the most painful experiences known to humanity. He'd often had occasion to thank his lucky stars he'd been born male.

"It *hurts!*" Loretta shrieked.

With a wink for Mrs. Brandeis, Jason said, "I know it does, Loretta. We're all going to be deaf by the time this is over."

"Curse you and your cursed deafness!" shouted Loretta. Another contraction racked her and she subsided into panting huffs. Jason was doubly glad he'd spared Marjorie this experience. For her. As for himself, he wished she was here. How strange.

The contractions were coming fast now, and Loretta was fully dilated. Jason could just see the top of a black head beginning to emerge. "It's looking good, Loretta. Next time a pain comes, push hard."

"Looking good my eye! Can Malachai hear me?"

"The whole of Russian Hill can hear you, sweetie," Jason told her. Mrs. Brandeis clucked her tongue.

"Good. *Damn you, Malachai Quarles!*"

"Poor Captain Quarles." Chuckling, Jason added, "Push hard now. I see a head. It's coming fast, Loretta. You're going to have a fine, healthy baby."

She pushed, her face turned red, and Mrs. Brandeis mopped sweat like mad.

"*Aaaagh!*"

"You're doing fine, Loretta."

"Am not!"

"Are too." Jason grinned, but there was a hurt deep in his heart. In spite of Loretta's current state of anger and anguish, this was going to be a joyous occasion for her and Malachai. He seldom got to participate in a happy infant delivery.

His practice in Chinatown was general, and even though it was illegal for Chinese women to immigrate to the United States, he'd delivered many a baby to a singsong girl who had been impregnated during her work as a prostitute. More often than not, the babies were half-breeds. The same white males who had legislated the Chinese Exclusion Act were not at all averse to taking advantage of the illegalities resulting from their work. The situation infuriated and saddened Jason, and there wasn't a damned thing he could do about it.

Delivering Loretta's baby was much more to his liking. Loretta and her husband loved each other dearly, and they had all the money they'd ever need to rear a tyke or two. Or three or four. Also, and not least among his reasons for gladness, was the fact that he'd known Loretta since she was born, and she was one of his best friends. She'd be a spectacular mother, and Malachai would be a wonderful father.

Still, a tiny ache accompanied the happiness in his heart when he remembered Mai. She'd wanted his children, and he had, too. But by the time they married, she was already dying from tuberculosis.

He wondered if Marjorie ever longed for a family. Jason did. Often. "Push again, Loretta. We're almost there."

"What do you mean, *we?* Oh! *Ow! Ack!*"

And Jason was holding a slippery little baby. Mrs. Brandeis whispered, "Oh, my, will you just look at that."

Loretta couldn't speak. She was too busy pushing. Her face ran with tears.

"Let me take care of this one, and we'll catch the next one," Jason said, his heart soaring. "You've got a beautiful little girl, Loretta."

"A *beautiful* little girl." Tears were leaking from Mrs. Brandeis's eyes now, as well as Loretta's. Jason judged the housekeeper's to be tears of joy.

Working quickly, he soon had the umbilical cord cut and tied. "I'll set this one right here on your tummy, Loretta. We've got another one coming."

"Ow! *Another* one?" Loretta panted like a racehorse for a couple of seconds before beginning to push again. "*I'll never speak to you again, Malachai Quarles!*"

She delivered her son less than five minutes later. Because he knew that Malachai was in a state of advanced anxiety downstairs, Jason worked with Mrs. Brandeis with speed and skill. As soon as he'd taken care of the umbilical cord on the boy and cleaned both babies, he said, "Wrap these two little bundles of joy in some swaddling clothes, will you, Mrs. Brandeis? I've got to fetch Malachai."

Loretta was at present resting with her eyes shut. He figured she'd last until her husband came up to sit with her. Then she could berate Malachai in fine style if she still wanted to. He suspected she'd be too overwhelmed and overjoyed to bother with recriminations.

"I'll be right back," he told her, and he leaned over to deposit a kiss on her forehead. "You did well, Loretta. The captain will be proud."

She said, "Huh." Her eyes opened. Jason's heart squeezed. He'd never imagined his feisty little Loretta looking so bedraggled. "Let me hold my babies." Her voice was a ragged thread. "I want to feed them."

"In a minute, sweetie. Mrs. Brandeis is swaddling them. I want to get Malachai up here."

"Huh." She settled back against her pillows. "I want to see Marjorie, too."

"I'll send her up." Jason wasn't sure if she was still mad at her husband or not, but he'd never yet met a mother, including all the mothers-by-rape he'd met in Chinatown, who didn't love their babies.

His heart hitched when he remembered Mai. It hitched again when he thought about Marjorie. Strange, his reaction to Marjorie. Jason didn't understand it.

SIX

"Damn you, Malachai Quarles!"

Marjorie winced in sympathy for the captain.

"It was the Moors done it," Derrick Peavey whispered, cowering in his chair. Every time Marjorie looked his way, he seemed to have shrunk more.

Malachai didn't respond. Marjorie expected he hadn't even heard, such pronouncements from Mr. Peavey being too common to require rebuttals.

She wished she could comfort Captain Quarles, but such a thing was beyond her capability. By this time, he'd nearly paced a hole in the carpet, and every time Loretta screeched, especially when she screeched at or about him, he cringed like a schoolboy having his knuckles smacked with a ruler. She hadn't realized the energetic, masterful captain could do such a thing. She smiled to herself when she recalled that it was the tiny Loretta who had brought him to his figurative knees.

Outside the weather was as stormy as was the atmosphere indoors. Thunder continued to rattle the windows, and rain came down in buckets. Marjorie heard it battering on the roof like tiny fists pounding to get in. Usually, she enjoyed a good brisk rain. It was life-giving stuff, rain was.

Today the storm seemed somehow suggestive of

malignant forces, and she wished it didn't. It was pure fancy, of course. Nothing could possibly happen to Loretta with Jason watching over her. She hoped.

Malachai, who was chewing a cigar—he didn't often smoke, but Marjorie figured he needed it right now—stopped suddenly. "I can't stand it any longer."

"I doubt that it will be much longer," murmured Marjorie.

"It's been quiet for too long. Something's gone wrong."

"Nothing's gone wrong." Marjorie spoke in her most soothing voice.

"She's not screaming, though." He gazed with tragic eyes up the long, beautifully carpeted staircase.

"There now, Captain Quarles, everything will be fine. You'll see." Marjorie wished she dared get up from her chair and go over to him. Pat him on the shoulder or something. But her inner reserve held her in her chair. Unlike herself, her inner reserve was also wringing its hands and moaning when it wasn't biting its nails. It wasn't at all as calm as she was trying to pretend to be.

She also wished Jason had called on her to help, although she didn't know why. Yesterday's bloodbath had been enough to put anyone off the medical profession for life. Nevertheless, she wished he'd trusted her to help him today. Moreover, it would have given her something to do besides watch the captain pace and listen to Mr. Peavey mutter about the Moors.

"I can't stand it," Malachai repeated. "I'm going to go up there and see what's wrong."

"Please don't, Captain Quarles. I'm sure Dr. Abernathy will be out in a minute."

A baby's thin wail filled the air and Malachai's own wrenching cry joined it almost immediately. "Loretta!"

Marjorie sucked in her breath. The bairn, at least, was alive. Smiling, she said, "Ye have a wee bairn, Captain."

Loretta screamed one last time, and Malachai, who didn't seem to have heard Marjorie's comforting words, said, "I'm going up there!"

With a massive internal push, Marjorie overcame her reserve and heaved herself out of her chair. Rushing over and grabbing one of Malachai's arms, which was rather like grabbing onto a tree trunk, she said, "No, Captain! Don't, please. Dr. Abernathy and Mrs. Brandeis must be vurra busy right now. Donna interrupt them."

He strained against her grip. Marjorie got the impression she might as well be trying to hold back a locomotive or a charging rhinoceros. She didn't mind. The poor man was almost out of his mind with worry for Loretta. How beautiful was their love, really, even though it had also caused Marjorie more than a few instances of pure shock.

"But . . ." He didn't go on, although he stopped struggling so hard against Marjorie's weakening grasp. "Damn." His shoulders slumped, he resumed pacing, and Marjorie went back to her chair. She felt much more at home there, against the wall, out of the way. The perfect wallflower. That's what she was.

Several more minutes passed in silence. Li and Molly stood against the wall on the other side of the room, their eyes wide, their faces worried. More wallflowers. Marjorie felt the tension radiating from

Malachai in waves. It filled the hallway, curled around the stair railings, and slithered up the stairs, much as the fog often did out of doors.

Finally, the captain's patience snapped. He threw his chewed-up cigar across the room. Molly and Li ducked, and the cigar hit the wall and fell to the floor in a soggy lump. "I'm going up there."

Recognizing the finality and the authority in his voice, Marjorie only sighed, knowing that nothing could stop him now. He had begun charging up the staircase, taking the steps three at a time, when suddenly Jason appeared like a vision at the top of the stairs. His broad smile brought Marjorie to her feet and the captain to a halt, leaving Malachai clinging to the banister and swaying slightly.

Marjorie clasped her hands to her bosom when she saw Jason reach out a hand to Malachai.

Raising her clasped hands and pressing them to her mouth, Marjorie felt tears sting her eyes. Jason caught her attention and winked. It was the first time in their acquaintance that she didn't resent one of his audacious winks.

Malachai's own eyes were huge. Squeezing his arm, Jason said, "You can go on up, Captain. You have a fine, healthy son."

"A son?" Malachai's voice came out in a shaky croak.

"And a daughter."

Marjorie heard the captain gulp from where she sat. "Twins?"

"Twins," Jason confirmed. "They're fine. You're the father of two beautiful, healthy infants."

"Two." Malachai sounded as if he were in a daze. "Two."

"Two. A boy and a girl."

"Two. My God."

And with that, Malachai thrust Jason aside and bounded the rest of the way up the stairs. Marjorie saw his coattails flap as he disappeared down the upstairs hallway. Jason laughed softly. "Do you want to see her, Marjorie?"

"Aye, but I want to see the bairns first."

Mrs. Brandeis appeared behind Jason, carrying two swaddled bundles. Marjorie gave a soft cry of wonder.

"They're as fine a pair as I've ever seen," declared Mrs. Brandeis. "They're fat and healthy and just beautiful."

Molly and Li surged forward as if someone had cut the strings binding them to the far wall. "May we see, too?" It was Molly, of course. Li, a young Chinese girl who had gotten into the country in a manner that hadn't been explained to Marjorie, was too self-effacing to utter a word except to Molly, and then only when they were working in the kitchen.

Since the question had been addressed to Marjorie, she said, "Of course. Let's all look at the wee bairns, and then I'm sure Mr. and Mrs. Quarles will want to cuddle wi' them."

Jason was looking upon her with approval, and his notice embarrassed Marjorie. She tried to shake it off and sound neutral and practical when she said, "Do you think Loretta and the captain want me in there?"

"Well . . . better give them a minute, but I know she wants to see you, because she asked for you."

"You look fagged, Doctor. Why don't you go on to the kitchen and get something to eat and drink?"

"What I really need is a bed and about twelve hours of sleep." But he was grinning as he spoke, and Marjorie could tell he was both relieved and happy that the birthing had gone so well.

"After last night and now this, I'm sure that's so."

"But I'll take you up on the food. I'm about to starve to death."

"Go to the kitchen, if you will. There are sandwiches laid out and coffee. I'll be there as soon as I can."

He took her hand as they passed on the staircase. "Don't stay too long with Loretta. She needs her rest."

"And she needs her husband," said Marjorie, squeezing his hand in spite of herself.

"And her husband," Jason agreed.

With a tired sigh, he released her hand. He seemed to do it reluctantly, although Marjorie figured she was probably imagining that part. Neither before nor since Leonard had a man been particularly anxious to be in her company. As she headed down the hallway, eager to see Loretta but reluctant to interfere in a loving domestic scene, she heard Derrick Peavey say, "It was the Moors done it," and she thought with a grin, *The captain won't stand for that.*

Humming to himself, Jason pondered his present mood. He felt as if a huge weight had been lifted from his shoulders, when in reality, the person who'd had weight lifted from her was Loretta. Still and all, she was one of his oldest and dearest friends, and he was extremely gratified that the births of her twins had been accomplished with so little trouble. In spite of what Loretta probably thought about the matter.

He sank into a kitchen chair, and could only be thankful that nobody else shared the room with him so he didn't have to be polite or make small talk. Lord, he was exhausted. Thank God for this day's blessed event, or he'd have been depressed for a week. Jason always took it personally when bad things happened in Chinatown. It was ridiculous of him. Just because he'd had a Chinese wife, the Chinese community would never be more than grateful to him. He wasn't a part of their culture except by grace, and he never would be.

Grace. Good word, that. Chinatown could use a good dose of grace. So could he. With a heart-weary sigh, he folded his arms on the kitchen table and rested his head on them. He was so tired.

He'd dozed off when, little by little, he became aware of a hand lightly resting on his shoulder. Blinking sleepily, he sensed that Marjorie stood beside him. Smiling in spite of his weariness, he sat up in his chair. She drew away as fast as she could, but not fast enough for Jason not to know it had been her hand that had so tenderly rested there. He felt oddly as though she'd blessed him.

"How's she doing?" His voice pronounced his grogginess, and he sounded like a frog. So he cleared his throat.

"She's vurra tired." Smiling, Marjorie sat in the chair farthest away from him at the table. "But she's happy."

Jason sighed at this typical, distancing behavior on Marjorie's part. "She's going to be tired for a long time. It's difficult enough giving birth to one infant. Two takes twice as much stamina."

"Loretta has lots of that."

"Yes, she does."

"Have you eaten, Jason?"

He liked the way his name sounded when she said it. "Not yet. I think I fell asleep."

Her smile made his toes curl and sweetness bubble in his heart. He *knew* he was exhausted when he had such a reaction to anything Marjorie, the Reserved and Occasionally Caustic, did.

"Aye, you did take a wee nap. You need rest."

She got up again and headed to the kitchen counter. Jason noticed a silver tray with a white kitchen towel draped over whatever it held. His fuzzy brain conjured an image of the head of John the Baptist, and he shook his head to rid himself of the grizzly vision. Last night must have rattled him more than he'd realized.

"True, true. But I'll be able to get some sleep now. There's nothing doing in Chinatown that needs my attention at the moment."

"Do you think that state of affairs will last?"

"Not long enough." He sighed again, in discouragement. "I'm worried about Jia Lee."

"The girl from last night?"

"Yes."

She shook her head. "Aye, what a terrible life that poor thing must live. It's a wonder to me the authorities allow such goings-on in this country."

"They tend to ignore what goes on in Chinatown."

Marjorie had lifted the towel. "Would you prefer a chicken or a ham sandwich? Mrs. Brandeis made some potato salad, too. I'll fetch you some from the icebox."

The thought of food made Jason's mouth water. "I'll take one of each. And the mere thought of

Mrs. Brandeis's potato salad is making me salivate. Thank you, Marjorie."

"You're welcome. Here, start in on these while I get your salad." She set a plate of sandwiches on the table in front of him.

Before she could turn away from him, he grabbed her hand and lifted it to his lips. He wasn't surprised when her face flamed. "Thank you, Marjorie. You're an angel."

"An angel?" As soon as he released her hand, she tucked it behind her back and turned to walk toward the ice box. "You've changed your opinion of me then."

"Not really." He must have stuffed half of the ham sandwich into his mouth on his first bite. He hadn't been lying when he'd told Marjorie he was hungry. Thinking back, he realized he hadn't had a bite to eat since dinner last night, and it was now . . . Jason looked up to check the kitchen clock. Good Lord, it was going on five o'clock in the afternoon. No wonder he was having visions and kissing Marjorie's hand. He really *was* starving!

Rehearsals for *The Pirates of Penzance* began two weeks after the captain and Loretta's babies were born. Marjorie found herself in the awkward position of not wanting to tear herself away from the twins to participate in the opera. She loved them as if they were her very own, and she told the new mother about her reluctance.

"Fiddlesticks," said Loretta, who was suffering from uncharacteristic crabbiness.

Marjorie chalked her mood up to weariness, lingering soreness in some delicate spots, and irritation at the nanny who'd been hired to care for the infants. Loretta had said in ringing tones that she didn't want or need a nanny to take care of her children. The captain had insisted, and the argument had grown quite fierce at times. The household staff had taken bets on who would win, with Loretta favored two to one. But the captain had prevailed, much to Marjorie's surprise.

"You need to get out of the house. Anyhow, you're Mabel. You *have* to go to rehearsals. The play can't go on without you."

"Aye, I know all that, but I hate to leave Oliver and Olivia. They're so wee and precious."

"They're little monsters is what you mean."

"Nay. I love them, Loretta."

"Well, so do I," Loretta said snappishly. "You'd have babies of your own to take care of if you'd stop being so standoffish with all the men who fancy you."

Accustomed as she was to Loretta's habit of speaking her mind, this sentiment so jolted Marjorie, it actually robbed her of breath. She stared at Loretta, her mouth hanging open with not a word to be found in it anywhere.

Loretta glared back. "It's the truth and you know it, Marjorie MacTavish. You're beautiful and smart, and there are tons of men who'd love to court you, but you treat them all like dirt." Since she was occupied in nursing both babies at the moment, she was unable to make one of her extravagant gestures. Her scowl was magnificent, though, and Marjorie got the point. "Why, only look at *Jason*, for heaven's sake."

Marjorie, who was trying to regain her breath, didn't know if she was more hurt than angry or the other way around. She was spared thinking up a response to this preposterous allegation. The door had opened without either woman being aware of it, and Jason poked his head around the jamb.

"Did I hear my name being taken in vain?"

To judge by the twinkle in his vivid blue eyes, he'd had plenty of sleep since the last time Marjorie had seen him, which had been the day of the babies' birth. She'd managed to avoid him since then during his frequent visits to check on Loretta and the bairns.

She frowned, thinking it was just like him to interrupt an argument. He did everything he could to discompose her. Not that she'd have hollered at Loretta, naturally, especially not with the babies in the room, but she'd have liked to have given her a piece of her mind. There were more important things to do at the moment, however.

"Och, wait a minute!" Flapping her hands at Jason, Marjorie glanced around wildly, searching for something to throw over Loretta so that Jason wouldn't see her breasts. Granted, they were mostly covered by babies, but still, it was shocking to nurse children in front of a man not one's husband. Even in front of one's husband, actually.

"For heaven's sake, Marjorie, never mind about covering me up," Loretta barked, having instantly discerned Marjorie's purpose. "Jason knows what women look like. Hell's bells, he saw the whole of me when the babies were born."

Rather than teasing Marjorie as he generally did, Jason looked upon her with a kindly expression. Marjorie wasn't sure she appreciated it. "There's no taming her, you know, Marjorie. But it's all right. She can't shock me."

"All I'm doing is feeding my children," growled

Loretta. "There's nothing wrong with that. It's a process decreed by God. It's stupid to be embarrassed by so natural a process. Anyhow, I'm not trying to shock anyone."

She'd managed to shock Marjorie, displaying herself before Jason Abernathy. Deducing it would be unwise to admit it, Marjorie only said, "I'll get my wrap."

Jason had telephoned earlier. Since he wanted to examine Loretta and the twins anyway, he'd offered to drive Marjorie to the first rehearsal. She'd agreed with a strange fluttering in her bosom.

Her bosom remained stony this evening when she marched out of Loretta's sitting room. She had to pass by the captain, who was standing behind Jason, and who gave her an understanding smile. Malachai had been Loretta's primary target of late. His sympathy didn't make her feel any better.

A half-hour later, she was bundled up and sitting in Jason's Hudson, glaring out through the front windscreen at a scene of early autumn chill. A brisk breeze whipped up Lombard Street, sending leaves eddying skyward from the pavement and striking against the automobile. The usual evening fog hadn't rolled in, and it might not, given the prevailing windiness. Jason had lighted the Hudson's front lamps, but Marjorie wasn't sure how long they'd stay lit, due to the breezes.

A full moon hung in the sky, looking like a silver dollar. Marjorie, who was accustomed to considering the moon a benevolent ruler of the night, felt a shiver run through her this evening. This particular moon seemed strangely sinister, pallid and cold as it was. She sensed no benevolence there, only unfeeling Nature.

Because indignation and hurt had been building in her breast for at least thirty minutes, the amount of time Jason had spent examining Loretta and the babies, Marjorie finally blurted out a statement she knew would earn her a jibe or two. She didn't care. She was furious. If Jason said anything mean to her, she'd just give him what-for and walk to the bluidy rehearsal. "The woman has no shame!"

To her surprise, he didn't attack. He only said, "She's rich. Rich people can get away with lots of things poor people can't."

Marjorie turned and narrowed her eyes at him. He didn't appear to be joking. Nor did he appear cynical. Sad, perhaps, but not cynical. How peculiar. Uncertain as to whether his rational mood was sincere or only hiding a teasing attack about to be let loose upon her, she said cautiously, "I'm surprised to hear you say so."

He shrugged. "You know it's the truth. Loretta can afford to bare her bosom to the whole wide world if she wants to, just as she can espouse her many causes, and she can do both with impunity. She can afford to ignore custom and tradition. No one is going to punish her, or take her job away, or sell her into slavery if she misbehaves." With a discouraged sigh, he added, "Hell, half the slaves I know didn't even misbehave. Their only sin was poverty."

"That's . . . that's tragic." It was the only word Marjorie could think of.

"Yeah, it is. Too bad Shakespeare's not alive today. He could write a play about it."

The Hudson chugged along. Marjorie hugged her shawl closer to her body, remembering the dreadful night she'd spent in Jason's office. "Have you seen that poor girl lately?"

"Jia Lee? No." He shook his head. "She's being kept carefully hidden away from prying eyes. I've learned a little more of her story, though."

"Oh?"

They'd reached the foot of Russian Hill, and Jason turned right onto Leavenworth. "She was brought to San Francisco by an importer of Chinese goods. A white man, naturally, since we don't care to deal with Bret Harte's heathen Chinee." His mouth twisted, and Marjorie saw his customary cynical expression emerge. "Most of this fellow's so-called Chinese goods are poor girls from the province of Canton whose parents or guardians have sold them into prostitution. It's not an unusual custom in China, girls being worth very little otherwise, although I'm sure most of them would prefer to stay in brothels in China, near their parents."

Knowing it was inadequate, but also knowing it expressed her feelings, Marjorie whispered, "That's horrible."

"It is horrible. And it's also illegal, but, as you've already learned, the authorities tend to turn a blind eye to the Chinese problem unless it gets in their way." He shot her a glance. "Did you know that the tongs post murder notices right there on the public streets? They're called red sheets, and they proffer rewards for the deaths of certain people."

Marjorie felt her brow furrow. "I . . . I don't understand. What people? I mean, rewards? For the deaths of certain people? What people?"

"If someone annoys a tong leader badly enough, the tong leader will decide to get rid of him. Then he'll either use one of his own hatchet men to accomplish the deed or, because most enemies of tongs try to hide if they know what's good for them, he'll post a notice stating that he'll pay so much money to whoever gets rid of so-and-so."

Still confused because what she thought he meant was so outrageous as to be unbelievable, Marjorie said, "Um . . . I don't . . ."

"Yes, you do," Jason interrupted, his voice hard. "You understand perfectly. You just don't want to. I meant exactly what you think I meant. A man's name will appear on a red sheet, and the amount of the reward for his murder will be posted. A red sheet is, literally, a piece of bright red paper so that it's clearly noticeable, and it's posted throughout Chinatown on buildings and fences and lampposts and anything else handy. Heaven forbid that the word not get out. You understand all right."

"But . . . but that's . . ."

"Incredible? Unconscionable? Yes. Both of those things. But the white authorities don't read Chinese, and the Chinese people don't trust the authorities, and they're also terrified of the tong bosses, so nobody tells anyone and the practice continues."

"But doesn't anyone *tell* the authorities?"

Again, Jason gave her a cynical glance. Marjorie felt it in her heart, which ached. "What for? Not only wouldn't the so-called authorities believe it, but if they did believe it, they wouldn't do anything about it because they wouldn't care. Besides, anyone who dares snitch gets killed. It's a fact of life. Hell, even *I* don't tell the authorities about such goings-on, because I figure I can do more good to the Chinese in Chinatown as a living medical man than as a dead one. God knows, there's no one else to see to their ills and injuries. Anyhow, the fewer Chinese in San Francisco, the better the authorities would like it."

"But . . . then why are the Chinese here?"

A sharp bark of laughter from her chauffeur didn't make Marjorie feel appreciably better. "They're here because we needed them once." A pregnant silence preceded Jason's next comment. "Have you ever heard the expression, 'a Chinaman's chance'?"

"I think so."

"Know how it came about?"

"No." Marjorie's whole being felt flat and sore, rather as if someone had jumped up and down on her heart and pounded on her soul with a mallet.

"They imported Chinese—Chinese men, that is—to work on the railroads and in the mines. They imported Irishmen, too, but, even though nobody much likes them, the Irish are white, and the powers that be allowed their wives in, too. Anyhow, whenever there was a particularly dangerous job to do, most often involving dynamite or poisonous gas, they'd send in a Chinaman to do it, sparing the white men. More often than not, the Chinaman didn't survive the experience. Ergo, when a job seems impossible to do and survive, anyone is taking a Chinaman's chance when he tries to do it."

Marjorie's mouth had dropped open as soon as the word *dynamite* left Jason's lips. It shut with a clack. "I don't believe it."

Again Jason shrugged. "Fine. Don't believe it. It doesn't matter to me. I know what goes on." A little more harshly, he added, "And after you saw what can happen when the tongs get mad at each other,

I should think you'd be a little more open-minded than the bulk of your white kin."

"I . . . I don't have any kin."

He shot her a scowl. "You know what I mean, damn it."

She swallowed the painful lump that had risen in her throat. "Aye, I know what you mean."

Neither of them spoke again until they'd reached the church. People were pouring into the sanctuary for this, the first *Pirates* rehearsal, and Marjorie was glad to divert her attention to something other than Jason's grim narration.

She was interested to see instruments arriving, as well as people. A bass drum, carried by a boy who couldn't be more than twelve years old, made her smile, which was a distinct improvement in her mood. The atmosphere had been chilly—and not merely out of doors—since Jason's unpleasant disclosures.

Yet she couldn't get Jason's words to leave her alone. Even after rehearsal began, she couldn't stop thinking about them.

It should be impossible that such things as Jason had related occurred. Marjorie didn't want to believe in them. But she had a sinking feeling she was looking at the world through rose-tinted glasses. The idea surprised her. After all, her own life had been far from easy.

When she compared a poor childhood with loving parents in Glasgow, a good career as a stewardess for White Star, and a pleasant job as a secretary to a wonderful woman, however, her own hard life paled in comparison to the life Jia Lee was forced to live. Marjorie wanted to hide away from the very notion of being sold into prostitution.

Years ago, Loretta had told her that Jason had been married to a Chinese woman who had died of consumption not long after their wedding. Had Jason's wife once been a prostitute? According to him and Loretta, the only women who came into this country were slave girls imported illegally to work as prostitutes, as if they were so many pieces of porcelain. Good Lord. Marjorie's mind boggled.

"Are you with us this evening, Miss MacTavish?"

Marjorie looked up, startled, and found the entire cast of *Pirates* staring at her—not to mention both Mr. and Mrs. Proctor. "I'm vurra sorry. My mind went wandering."

"Poor wand'ring one," Mrs. Proctor said with a titter. Everyone laughed. Marjorie herself managed what she suspected was a wan smile.

The rehearsal went well, however, and after a half-hour or so, Marjorie was able to concentrate on her role. This first rehearsal was a read-through and a sing-through. Mr. Proctor would break down future rehearsals into different scenes and groups after this initial one.

Marjorie stood beside Jason, who must have been used to sectioning off portions of his life, because he didn't seem at all concerned about the Chinese problem as he laughed, read, and sang. Marjorie admired the ability as she understood that it must have been a difficult one to achieve, and her heart, which had been hard-set against him for years until recently, softened a little more.

SEVEN

Jason, leaning comically toward the fellow who had been cast as Samuel, one of the Pirate King's underlings, was putting every melodramatic cell he possessed into singing, "'Although our dark career sometimes involves the crime of stealing, we rather think that we're not altogether void of feeling.'" Then he glanced up, and his heart dropped into his boots.

Lo Sing, looking abashed and out of place, crept along the west wall of the sanctuary as if he were a real pirate sneaking up on his prey, rather than a trained nurse and an assistant in a doctor's office and one of the best men Jason had ever met in his life. Jason held up a finger, thereby asking Lo Sing to wait until he was through with this number. Lo Sing nodded in understanding.

The song, which was about the Major General pretending to be an orphan and thereby tricking the softhearted Pirate King into allowing him to live, had seemed funny not three seconds earlier. Lo Sing had managed to vanquish any hint of humor in Jason's breast, and without even speaking a word. Astonishing.

Even more astonishing was the sight of Marjorie, who had silently slipped away from the rest of the *Pi-*

rates company, hurrying toward the young Chinese man with her hands held out in greeting. The expression on her face was one of understanding and worry, and Jason cursed inwardly even as he sang.

Damn it, he didn't want her involved in any more tong problems. Resisting the impulse to jerk away from the cast and rush after her, Jason nevertheless hurried the tempo of the song considerably. He felt a little guilty when the violinist, who was sawing away furiously at his instrument, shot him an accusing glance.

As soon as he hit the last note, he muttered, "Excuse me, please," and darted over to Lo Sing and Marjorie.

Turning toward him, Marjorie displayed a face as pale as the full moon outside. "Och, Jason, there's been another fight. There are more casualties."

"Good God, now what?" he snapped, irked with himself for having allowed Marjorie to witness the dark side of his life. She probably thought she belonged in it now, and she didn't. He didn't want her there. She was too . . . the word that popped into Jason's mind surprised him. It was *fragile*. Odd. He'd never thought of Marjorie as fragile before.

He didn't have time to think about it now, however. "Do you need me instantly?"

"Well . . ." Lo Sing turned a worried glance onto the cast of *Pirates*, all of whom had turned to see what had taken Jason and Marjorie away so precipitously.

"Just tell me," barked Jason. "Yes or no? If you need me, say so. This is only a rehearsal. People's health is more important than a rehearsal."

"Then . . . yes. I'm afraid we do need you. There are a couple of wounds that definitely need to be stitched up."

"I'll get my coat and hat."

Jason had already turned to fetch these articles of dress when Marjorie's hesitant voice brought him up short. "Do you need me to help?"

He whirled around and pinned her with a scowl. "Good God, no. Just because you butted into my business once doesn't give you the knowledge or ability to actually be of help in a doctor's office."

Marjorie gasped.

Lo Sing, obviously shocked, said, "That's not fair, Jason. Miss MacTavish was an enormous help to us."

"Never mind," said Marjorie, her cheeks red as fire. "You dinna need me, I ken. I'll return to rehearsal."

Jason was ashamed of himself, but he didn't back down. His feelings about Marjorie had plagued him for weeks now. Months, actually. Maybe even years. It angered him that he'd allowed her to witness anything so near and dear to his heart as his Chinatown clinic during a crisis. He wasn't sure exactly why, although he thought it was because he didn't trust her to understand his involvement. Why he even wanted her understanding was beyond him.

It had occurred to him more than once that perhaps he was clinging to his late wife's memory rather as a talisman, and that it wouldn't really hurt him to allow another woman access to his life and work. He'd cherished his poor, sick Mai. More, he'd pitied her. Perhaps it was time to allow a whole, healthy woman into his heart.

But . . . Marjorie MacTavish? Jason thought not. No matter how helpful she'd been that one time, and no matter how attractive he found her, he didn't believe she could stay the course with him. And, outrageous as it seemed, if he allowed her to get close and she failed him, he wasn't sure he could stand the pain.

Anyhow, she was no damned nurse. "I'll drop you off at Loretta's first, Marjorie."

"I can walk," she said stiffly.

"Nuts. I'm taking you home. You shouldn't be walking alone at night."

Several people had drawn near. Hamilton St. Claire, the fellow who'd been chosen to play Frederic opposite Marjorie's Mabel, stepped forward. "I'll be more than happy to see Miss MacTavish home if you have to leave us, Dr. Abernathy."

Shooting a black frown at Hamilton, Jason snapped, "Fine." He stomped over to fetch his hat and coat, thinking that Marjorie and St. Claire deserved each other. They were both unmitigated prigs.

He knew he was being irrational. After all, Marjorie had offered to help him in his clinic, and he'd chosen instead to all but throw her at St. Claire. But he didn't care; if he felt like being irrational, he'd damned well *be* irrational. It annoyed the hell out of him that Hamilton St. Claire, a handsome enough fellow, if a bit weak-chinned, seemed to find Marjorie attractive. Worse, Marjorie was nice to him.

Hell, he thought savagely. *They* do *deserve each other.*

He couldn't recall exactly when his reason had left him, but it definitely had left him, at least on the Marjorie issue. Thank God he had patients to attend to, or he might brood about it—and he was too damned old to brood.

The weather hadn't improved since the beginning of rehearsal. Neither had Marjorie's mood.

Her pride still stung from Jason's rebuff. And she didn't even want to consider the state of her heart, which had of late been behaving like a naughty child where the handsome, albeit irritating, doctor was concerned.

However, Hamilton St. Claire was kindness itself as he assisted her into her coat. And he was extremely solicitous when he took her arm and assisted her up the aisle toward his automobile, which was parked outside on the street in front of the church.

In short, unlike Jason, he treated her like a lady. He treated her as he might treat a delicate flower. Marjorie, who was unused to such gallantry, appreciated him. His behavior stood in stark contrast to Jason's peremptory dismissal of her, as a woman and an assistant.

"The wind is howling out there, Miss MacTavish," Mr. St. Claire murmured as soon as he'd opened the sanctuary door.

The statement was unnecessary, since Marjorie had seen for herself that the wind had caught the door, ripped it out of Mr. St. Claire's hand, and slammed it with a crash against the outer wall of the church. Nevertheless, she simpered a trifle when she said, "My, yes. It's just terrible." She reminded herself of Miss Virginia "Ginger" Collins and nearly giggled. Loretta would be furious if she ever found out about this.

But Loretta wasn't here, and Marjorie decided she *wanted* to be treated with deference for once. It would be a pleasant change from being treated with disrespect or savage mockery by Dr. Jason Abernathy. Ergo, if she had to simper to get the attention she craved—and deserved, confound it— she'd jolly well simper.

"Please, Miss MacTavish," said Mr. St. Claire in a voice that would have earned him ridicule from Jason, "allow me to fetch the Model T and drive it up in front of the door. I'd hate for you to have to brave that awful wind."

Marjorie's first instinct was to tell him not to be silly; that she'd braved worse weather than this without melting or coming down with the colic. However, because she appreciated his courtesy, she smiled sweetly and said, "How kind of you, Mr. St. Claire."

He bowed slightly, causing Marjorie to open her eyes quite wide—she wasn't accustomed to having American men bow at her—and, clutching his coat with one hand and his hat with the other, he forged out into the wind to fetch his automobile. Clasping the libretto to *Pirates* to her bosom, Marjorie sat on a convenient pew and waited.

She hadn't waited long before she was joined on her pew by Ginger Collins—not the person she would have chosen to spend time with. But she smiled at the girl.

"You were wonderful tonight, Marjorie," Ginger gushed. "You have *such* a beautiful voice."

"Thank you."

"But where did the doctor go? Didn't you arrive with him? He rushed off in a terrible hurry."

Was there the merest hint of malice in the young woman's voice? Probably. Marjorie said, "He was called away to his clinic on an emergency."

"Really? How annoying."

Ginger's eyes were too wide and innocent to be believed. "Yes. That was his assistant, Lo Sing, who came to fetch him away."

"He has a Chinaman as an assistant?" Ginger tittered. "How . . . unusual."

With more acidity than she'd heretofore used with Ginger—or anyone else, for that matter—Marjorie said, "His clinic is in Chinatown. Naturally, he employs a Chinese man to assist him. It only makes sense."

"Why in the world would anyone want to deal with *those* people?" Ginger smirked.

Suppressing the urge to smack the young woman smartly across her cheek to eliminate her smirk, Marjorie said calmly, "*Those* people are the ones who helped build the railroad across the United States. *Those* people have also been extremely useful in mining operations and dozens of other businesses and industries." She wished she'd paid closer attention to some of Loretta's impassioned lectures on the so-called "Chinese problem." If she couldn't slap Ginger, she'd love to be able to fling statistics in her face.

Ginger flapped an elegantly gloved hand in the air. "Oh, but they're so *dirty*. So *barbaric*."

Marjorie noticed that she was crinkling her libretto and unclenched her fingers. "The Chinese civilization was flourishing for thousands of years before that of Europe and the British Isles, Ginger. The Chinese were writing great epic poems while our ancestors still wore animal skins, lived in caves, and stabbed their food with sharpened sticks." Taking note of Ginger's incredulous expression, she added, "And they're no more dirty than we are."

"Well," said Ginger with a sniff, "all I know is that they smell funny."

"They cook different kinds of foods than we do. Personally, I enjoy a good Chinese meal." A slight—but only a slight—twinge of guilt bothered Marjorie. In truth, she generally tried to avoid Chinese food whenever she could, although she never had much luck in doing so since Loretta was always eager to try new things, including recipes and restaurants. She vowed to be more open-minded on the food issue in the future, if only to distance herself from the Gingers of this world.

"Well, I still think Dr. Abernathy ought to open a practice on Market Street. He'd make ever so much more money."

Marjorie eyed her with blatant disfavor. "Some things," she said sententiously, "are more important than money."

She had the satisfaction of seeing Ginger blush before the door crashed open again. Both she and Ginger jumped to their feet, startled. It was Mr. St. Claire. He faltered slightly when he beheld Ginger waiting with Marjorie, and he actually frowned for an instant before recovering his composure. Although she knew it to be a sin, Marjorie felt a surge of triumph. So Mr. St. Claire considered Ginger silly too, did he? How extremely gratifying.

"Er . . . do you need a ride home, Miss Collins?" Mr. St. Claire asked politely.

Ginger, who had evidently noticed his hesitation, said with a smile that belied the spark of anger in her eyes, "No, thank you, Mr. St. Claire. I'm waiting for my father's chauffeur."

"Ah." Mr. St. Claire brightened. "Well, then, good evening to you." He gave Ginger a perfect, and very brief, bow.

"Yes," Ginger ground out between her teeth. "Good evening, Mr. St. Claire. And to you, Marjorie."

Feeling more sure of herself than usual, Marjorie gave the younger woman a kindly smile and hoped she'd choke on it. "Good night, Ginger. I'm looking forward to our next rehearsal."

Ginger's own smile looked as if she'd found it in a vinegar cruet. "Indeed."

With great tenderness, Mr. St. Claire guided Marjorie to his Model T Ford, which was chugging away at the curb. The wind was howling so loudly, Marjorie scarcely heard his, "Take care, Miss MacTavish. There's a lot of rubbish being blown about."

She took care. Since the Model T had no door on the driver's side, she also appreciated his smile and his, "Please pardon me for being ungentlemanly," as he got in first and slid over to his side of the machine. As she got into the auto after him and took her place beside him, Marjorie noticed that it wasn't as fine a machine as Loretta's Runabout or Jason's Hudson. However, at least Mr. St. Claire was a gentleman, unlike some other men of her acquaintance. Anyhow, recalling the tiny lecture she'd recently delivered to Ginger, Marjorie reminded herself that there were some things more important than money. She wished she could think of a few more of them.

As Mr. St. Claire fiddled with the choke and pressed the low-speed pedal, he said, "You live on Lombard Street, don't you, Miss MacTavish?"

"Yes. I live in my employer's home."

"It's quite a home, if I recall correctly." Mr. St. Claire gave a jolly laugh. "My parents and I have attended parties there."

"Ah." Another grown-up rich kid, Marjorie thought crabbily, then she wondered why she should be crabby. It wasn't Mr. St. Claire's fault she'd been born into a poor family. Trying like mad to think of something to say that could get a conversation going, she said, "Whereabouts is your law practice, Mr. St. Claire?"

"Please, Miss MacTavish, call me Hamilton." He laughed. It wasn't a hearty laugh, Marjorie noticed. Not at all like one of Jason's laughs, but rather thin and reedy. Mentally, she gave herself a sharp shake. "I joined the family firm, St. Claire, St. Claire, and Thomas; we're on Market Street."

They would be. Another mental shake, and Marjorie reminded herself that sarcasm was no more sterling a character trait than ill humor. "How nice."

"Yes, it's a good practice. The pater doesn't believe in handouts, though, so I'm starting from the bottom."

Somehow, Marjorie fancied a St. Claire's bottom and another person's—hers, for instance—probably weren't equivalent. She didn't say so. "That's good," she said sweetly. "It's supposed to be bad for one's character to have too many things given one." Not that she'd know anything about that.

"That's what the pater says."

Why in the name of wonder is he calling his father "the pater"? Again, Marjorie kept her comment to herself. "He's a wise man, Mr. St. Claire."

"He's a great egg, my pater," said Hamilton cheerfully. "But won't you please call me Hamilton?"

Oh yes, she'd forgotten about that. Producing another sweet smile—although why she was bothering, she wasn't sure, since he couldn't see her—she said, "Of course. And please call me Marjorie."

"Marjorie and Hamilton. Why, they go together like ham and eggs, don't they?"

Did they? Marjorie thought not. But she laughed and told herself she was being far too critical where

Mr. St. Claire—she meant Hamilton—was concerned. He was a nice boy, and he liked her. He was ever so much nicer to her than Jason had ever been. She ought to be lapping up his attention as a kitten lapped cream.

Somehow, though, she couldn't overcome her gut feeling that Hamilton was something of a lightweight in the overall order of human events. Jason might be sarcastic, he might be occasionally unkind, and he might tease her unmercifully, but he was a good man who did good works, and his goodness pervaded his entire life. She sensed Hamilton was only interested in his own pleasure and in succeeding in his so-called *pater's* law firm.

Sweet Lord in heaven, was she serious? As Hamilton babbled beside her, Marjorie tried to decipher her feelings on the issue of Jason Abernathy. The task proved formidable, and she ultimately determined not to tackle it right then, with so much noise in the air to interfere with her thought processes.

"So, you see, Marjorie, I'll be well fixed in a couple of years."

"Er . . ." Marjorie hadn't been paying any mind to Hamilton's chatter. In an effort to disguise her inattention, she said brightly, "Yes, indeed, Mr.—I mean Hamilton. That's wonderful."

"It sure is. Why, I'll be able to take a wife, buy my own home, start a family, and carry on the St. Claire tradition in fine style."

In order to decipher his expression—she wasn't sure why he'd suddenly started blathering about wives and families—Marjorie squinted hard in his direction. The darkness prevented her from accomplishing her quest, so she decided on another noncommittal "Yes, indeed."

The sound of the motorcar's engine and the shrieking wind accompanied the two of them for a few minutes. The Model T didn't take kindly to San Francisco's many hills, Marjorie noticed. It was neither as zippy as Loretta's Runabout nor as powerful as Jason's Hudson. Not that it made a particle of difference to her.

"Say, Marjorie, have you been to the Pan-Pacific Exhibition yet?"

Momentarily befuddled by this abrupt change of topic, Marjorie made a frantic search in her brain's archives to figure out what the man was talking about. Then she remembered. San Francisco was playing host to a World's Fair this year, and the city had titled it the Panama-Pacific International Exhibition. "Why no, I haven't had the opportunity." She and Loretta had both wanted to go, but neither of them had made it yet. Marjorie couldn't remember why at the moment.

"Would you like to see it? It's quite something."

Was Hamilton going to ask her to attend the fair with him? What was it people called these types of rendezvous? Assignations? No, that was far too ominous. Trysts? No. Too romantic. Dates? Perhaps that was it.

"Er . . . yes, I've been meaning to go."

"Well then, how would you like to visit the Exhibition with me? I'd love to escort you. Would this coming Saturday be a good day for you?"

Fear instantly erupted in Marjorie's breast. Her heart gave a huge spasm, her mouth went dry, her nerves skipped, her libretto crinkled in her suddenly clenched fists, and she told them all to stop misbehaving. Dr. Hagendorf's advice and her own sincere, if timid, desire to expand her horizons ricocheted about in her brain.

She wanted to get out and about more, didn't she?

Yes, she did.

But did she want to do so with Hamilton?

Um . . .

Anyhow, she was frightened of the very thought of attending even so public an arena as a World's Fair, alone, with a man—and with Hamilton St. Claire of all people. She entertained the fleeting and ridiculous notion that if Jason had asked her, she'd have agreed on the instant.

So, what should she do? A quick glance in Hamilton's direction didn't help, since she couldn't see him. But she couldn't just sit here and not answer him. "Er . . ."

Hamilton didn't seem to notice her state of panic, thank God. "We can have supper at the Fairfield afterwards."

Good Lord. The Fairfield was a first-class hotel and the site of one of San Francisco's most expensive restaurants. Her good friend and fellow *Titanic* survivor, Isabel FitzRoy, used to dance there. Marjorie's heart started beating against her ribs like a frantic woodpecker.

With a quick, panicky nod at Dr. Hagendorf's sage advice to do things even when scared, Marjorie said, "Why, thank you, Hamilton. That would be very nice."

"Super! I'll pick you up at noon, if that's all right with you. There are all sorts of wonderful restaurants at the fair itself, many of them featuring foreign fare. Perhaps we can take luncheon at the Russian House."

Holy heaven. Marjorie guessed her horizons, especially in the realm of food, were going to begin expanding sooner than she'd anticipated. "My goodness. I don't believe I've ever eaten Russian food."

Hamilton chuckled. Unlike Jason's deep chuckles, which sent rivers of prickly sensation through Marjorie's veins, Hamilton's chuckle was thin and tinny, rather like his voice, and it left her unmoved. "It's super, really. I'm particularly fond of the piroshki. And they serve hot tea in glasses."

"Hot tea? In glasses? How . . . um . . . interesting." Wouldn't the hot tea make the glass break? She didn't feel up to asking.

"Yes, and they serve some kind of rice that's tasty, too."

Curious, Marjorie asked, "How often have you visited the fair, Hamilton?"

"Oh, five or six times. I enjoy seeing how the rest of the world lives. They don't have it as good as we do, let me tell you."

She did let him tell her the rest of the way home, and was grateful to the Pan-Pacific Exhibition for sparing her the trouble of unearthing topics of common interest between them. More and more, she thought there weren't any.

The day was fine, the weather crisp but not cold, the air beautiful and unmarred by fog or mist. A gentle breeze stirred the fall leaves on the sidewalks, making music with their rustling and crunching. In short, the sun shone down with benevolence upon the city of San Francisco . . . and Jason Abernathy was furious.

He paced before Loretta in her sitting room, his hands clasped behind his back, a scowl on his face, and his heart in a raging turmoil. Every now and then, his peripheral vision took in Loretta or Malachai, both of whom were staring at him, Malachai in befuddlement, Loretta with what Jason could only describe as unfounded and inappropriately wry humor.

"I can't believe she went to the Exhibition with that idiot St. Claire!"

Malachai said, "Uh . . ."

Loretta said, "And why shouldn't she? She and I were going to attend, but we never got around to it, and then I had the twins and that took care of that. Besides, Mr. St. Claire asked her, unlike some people." Her voice was as dry as the leaves smacking against the windows outside.

Still pacing, Jason muttered, "Well, but he's such a . . . a . . . prig!"

"And you," Loretta reminded him, "haven't bothered to speak to Marjorie since you were called away from rehearsal on Thursday night." She lifted a baby—the girl, Olivia—to her shoulder and gently patted her on the back. A hefty belch rewarded her effort and she smiled as if the child had performed a feat of wonderment and awe. "And, if I recall correctly, she said you were none too friendly when she asked if she could assist you."

Turning on his heel, Jason roared, "She's not a nurse!"

The boy baby, Oliver, who had been napping on his mother's lap, woke with a start and let out a bellow that was almost as loud as Jason's. Olivia made a face and spat up.

Jason grimaced. "Sorry."

"Honestly!" said Loretta. "Men are such nitwits."

Her husband gave her a frown, but didn't con-
tradict this broad statement. He probably didn't
dare, Jason thought unkindly.

"Marjorie may not be a nurse, but she's had some
training. Besides, she's got a good heart, the best of
intentions, she's smart as a whip, and as capable as
anyone you could ever find to help you. You could
train her as your nurse, Jason Abernathy. Did you
ever think of that, pray tell?"

No, he hadn't thought of that, as a matter of fact.
He'd slipped up and told her he could teach her to
speak and understand Chinese, but he hadn't
thought about training her as a nurse. The notion
made his stomach hurt. It wasn't that he didn't like
the idea of having Marjorie around more often, but
he didn't want her exposed to the violence and
pain Jason witnessed daily. "It's too difficult a job
for a woman." Instantly, he regretted his choice of
words.

Before Loretta could screech at him, he held up
a hand. "I didn't mean that, exactly. But . . . well,
curse it, I don't want Marjorie exposed to that sort
of thing. It's . . . it's . . ." He sighed. "It's really ugly,
Loretta."

Malachai glanced at the ceiling, his lips pressed
together tightly. With burgeoning indignation,
Jason realized he was trying not to laugh. This was
no laughing matter, damn it!

"I believe," said Loretta in a voice that would have
withered leaves if they hadn't already fallen from
the trees, "that Marjorie is intelligent enough, and
vigorous enough, not to mention sensible enough,
to decide for herself what's too difficult for her and
what isn't." She'd picked up Oliver and was cud-

dling him in an effort to soothe his shattered nerves. Therefore, this speech was interspersed with a number of coos and "there, there's" and one "Uncle Jason is just being an old meanie."

"Vigorous," repeated Jason. It seemed a strange word to describe Marjorie MacTavish, the least forthcoming person of his acquaintance. He had to admit, however, that when stirred, she could be quite outspoken. And she hadn't fainted or run away during that catastrophic night in his office.

He still didn't want her exposed to the mess that Chinatown could be. Knowing full well that to say so was to court rebuke, he didn't. He resumed pacing, however.

"Mai survived Chinatown," Loretta reminded him. "Or she would have, if she hadn't contracted tuberculosis."

His late wife's name on Loretta's lips brought Jason up short. Again, he whirled around. This time, he didn't yell; he only stared. Loretta and he had never discussed Mai. Most people, including Loretta, knew the subject was painful to him and tried to spare him. Of all the people he knew, Loretta was the only one who hadn't tried to dissuade him from marrying a Chinese woman. His breath lodged painfully in his throat.

"You know it's true, Jason." Her voice had gentled. "Poor Mai wasn't nearly as strong as Marjorie either, physically speaking. If anyone can survive the tong wars without fainting or flinching, it's Marjorie MacTavish."

After clearing his throat and swallowing his breath, Jason said, "Do you really believe that?"

"Well, of course I do." Emphatic. "Mind you, I don't have a notion about her life before the *Ti-*

tanic, because she's never told me anything, but I can tell you this much: She's not a quitter, and she's been through hell. She has no relatives that I know of. At least, she's never written a letter to Scotland since she moved into my house. That leads me to believe that her family is dead and that her friends probably all perished in the *Titanic* catastrophe. Her life as a stewardess involved service, and I know she feels stifled working as my secretary. I honestly believe she wants to continue to be of service to mankind."

Fascinating. And utterly unexpected. Jason tried not to gawk at Loretta, who'd finally calmed her son into a state of hiccuping stillness. Malachai had stuck his feet way out in front of him, folded his hands in his lap, and was watching his wife and his friend as if he were taking in a tennis match.

Because he didn't want to talk about it any longer, Jason said, "Where did you say they were going to take lunch?"

"You're not going to follow them there!" Loretta erupted into laughter, once more disturbing poor Oliver, who whimpered. She picked him up and kissed his pudgy cheeks until he quieted down again.

Frowning, Jason said, "I'm not following them. I just wondered, was all."

"Right." Still grinning like mad, Loretta added, "The Russian House is the place Mr. St. Claire mentioned."

"Piroshki and hot tea in tall glasses," Malachai supplied helpfully. "Marjorie doesn't understand how the glasses survive the hot tea." Leaning toward Loretta, he relieved her of Olivia. Jason thought the rugged sea captain made quite a charming spectacle with the infant cradled in his arms. Who'd ever have thought?

Heading toward the door—he couldn't get out of the Quarleses' presence fast enough; he had the uncomfortable feeling that both Loretta and Malachai were seeing through him—Jason said, "Thanks."

Loretta's voice trilled after him. "Tell Marjorie hello from Olivia and Oliver."

Malachai's deep chuckle followed Loretta's trill. Damn them both.

Anyhow, he wasn't following anyone. He'd been meaning to go to the World's Fair for months now.

EIGHT

"This is quite tasty."

Marjorie nibbled another bite of her piroshok. She'd been hesitant at first, but finally told herself that Russians ate these things every day and none of them had ever died from the experience. She couldn't help but wonder what was in it. Every time she did so, she hesitated as she plied her fork. In the back of her mind, Dr. Hagendorf's voice kept repeating, *Eat scared.*

So she took another bite, thinking she was behaving like an explorer venturing into new territory. Had Sir Richard Burton felt this way when he journeyed into Mecca, disguised as an Arab and certain to suffer death if his identity was discovered?

She told herself not to be silly. "They remind me of Cornish pasties." In a way.

"I love these things." Hamilton had no trouble eating his own luncheon. He took another big bite of pilaf.

Marjorie found herself admiring his ability to experience new things with gusto. It was an attribute she wanted to cultivate in herself, if she could find its seed. Until her visit with Dr. Hagendorf, she'd believed herself unable to embrace novelties with anything other than fear and loathing.

Eat scared, Marjorie reminded herself. Thank God loathing had nothing to do with this particular experience. "The rice is good, too."

"Delish."

Delish? Marjorie wished she knew how old her luncheon companion was. He behaved rather like an adolescent, but he had to be in his twenties. "I'm enjoying the tea, too. I didn't realize the glasses would be placed in wicker holders. They're quite charming."

"They'd be too hot to hold otherwise."

"Yes." She spooned up a driblet of borscht. It was quite savory, actually. It was fortunate for her that she'd never encountered a beet she didn't like. "The soup is wonderful. I wonder if Mrs. Quarles has a Russian cookery book in her library. Perhaps Mrs. Brandeis might make it one day. I'm sure it would be quite nourishing for a new mother." Especially one who was determined to nurse her own children. Naturally, she didn't mention Loretta's odd behavior to Hamilton. One didn't discuss breasts with men.

Hamilton didn't respond. Since he was a chatty fellow, Marjorie glanced up from her soup dish to see if he'd discovered something unpleasant in his piroshok. If he had, she might have to reconsider . . .

But no. Evidently his silence had nothing to do with the food. She discovered him staring fixedly into the throng of fair-visiting diners. His expression wasn't one of warmth and joy. Curious, she turned her head.

Her mouth fell open. Lucky for her, and for anyone who might be watching, there was no food in it.

"Say, isn't that your doctor friend?" Hamilton's

tone of voice was no more warm or joyful than his expression.

Stifling a spurt of elation that was liberally laced with fury, Marjorie said calmly, "I do believe it is. I had no idea he had planned on coming to the fair today."

As she spoke, she searched the sea of faces for Jason's possible companion. If he'd brought a woman with him . . . well, Marjorie would endure. She was a past master at that. And, since she really didn't want to see the other woman—why, it might even be Ginger Collins, perish the thought—she returned to her borscht.

Hamilton said, "Hmm," in a somewhat menacing tone.

Peering at him closely, Marjorie detected signs of annoyance on the young face. How strange.

"He's spotted us."

Marjorie resisted the urge to turn around and stare. After all, Jason had every right to attend a World's Fair on a Saturday afternoon if he wanted to, and even bring a female companion with him, confound the man. One thing of which Marjorie was certain was that he hadn't followed *her* here. He couldn't have. He hadn't known she'd be here.

But here he was. Right next to her chair.

After first giving Hamilton, who had stood politely, a curt nod, Jason spoke to Marjorie. "Loretta said you'd be here." Only then did he remove his hat.

Her mouth fell open. Nothing came out of it but an inquisitive syllable that wasn't quite a word, undoubtedly because her brain had suddenly stopped working.

"Miss MacTavish was kind enough to accompany

me to the fair today, Dr. Abernathy." Hamilton placed slight emphasis on the word *me*.

Jason whipped his head around and pinned Hamilton with a vicious scowl. Hamilton flinched. "Yeah? Well, she shouldn't have. We had a prior engagement."

Her teeth came together with a distinct click, all befuddlement fled in a flash of ire, and Marjorie surged to her feet. Fury supplanted the green-eyed monster of jealousy that had so recently infested her heart. "We did not! We had no engagement, prior or otherwise, ye haggis-headed nyaff!"

"Now see here, Dr. Abernathy . . ."

Ignoring Hamilton as if he were of no greater import than a pesky fly, Jason interrupted his sputters in favor of berating Marjorie some more. "You were supposed to come to my clinic to learn how to nurse people. Or to learn Chinese." He flipped his hand in the air as if the distinction between the two activities was minute.

"I wasna!"

"Yes, you were."

"Ye nivver asked me to!"

"Well, I meant to!"

In an uncharacteristic gesture, Marjorie slammed her napkin onto the table. "Well, ye didna! And I'm'na a mind-reader!" She went so far as to poke him in the chest, something she'd never done to anyone before in her life. "What's more, when I asked to help, ye told me I'm'na a nurse! And then ye told me ye didna want my help!"

"Well . . ."

"And furthermore," Marjorie said, getting her English pronunciation back under control, "If you *do* want my help or if you *do* want to teach me Chinese, you can jolly well ask me politely and set up an appointment!"

Jason sucked in approximately eight cubic acres of piroshki-scented air. Before he could use it to say anything, Marjorie had at him again.

"Anyhow, do you mean to tell me that you paid good money to come to the fair only to scold me? For not doing something ye nivver told me about in the first place?" Offhand, Marjorie couldn't recall ever being this angry at anyone about anything.

Grabbing a handkerchief from his pocket, Jason mopped his gleaming face and turned to Hamilton. "Listen, St. Claire, I'm sorry about this. I'm totally at fault here."

"Aye, ye are," growled Marjorie, forgetting proper English once more. "Gudgeon. Baffin." She was confused, however, because Jason wasn't known for apologizing for his bad behavior.

Hamilton said stiffly, "It's Miss MacTavish to whom you should apologize, Abernathy."

"Damn it . . ." But Jason turned back to Marjorie. "I'm sorry, Marjorie. I've . . . ah . . . been under a good deal of strain lately, and I must have forgotten to ask you to come to the office today."

"Well, she can go to your office another time," said Hamilton, seeming to gather his own courage together as Jason lost his. "Today, she's seeing the Pan-Pacific Exhibition with me."

"I don't think so, Mr. St. Claire," Jason pushed out through his clenched teeth.

"But I do," countered Hamilton.

Enraged at both of these men who seemed so eager to disregard her free will and desires—and in the United States, too!—Marjorie raised her voice and spoke in a piercing tone. "*I* shall decide what I shall do in this instance, thank you, gentlemen."

Both men paused with their mouths open. They reminded Marjorie of a couple of trout. Jason spoke first. He would.

"Certainly, Marjorie."

"Of course, *Marjorie.*"

When Jason heard her Christian name come out of Hamilton's mouth, his face, which was already high in color, turned puce. Marjorie had no idea why, and she wasn't going to ask. She'd have liked to march out of the restaurant, leaving both men to their own devices, but she'd miss seeing the fair if she did that.

Besides, Jason was undeniably the guilty party, and she aimed to let him know it. She hoped he'd suffer, too, although she didn't expect much along those lines. She'd often reflected that his conscience must be a bluidy impervious object.

In her coldest voice, she said to him, "Since you didna bother to invite me to learn nursing skills today—indeed, you rebuffed me in no uncertain terms when I offered my services—and you didna ask me to have a Chinese lesson either, I shall remain in Mr. St. Claire's company this afternoon, Dr. Abernathy. Perhaps we can discuss nursing and Chinese at another, more appropriate time."

"But, Marjorie, listen . . ."

"No, thank you, Dr. Abernathy, I needn't listen any longer. I plan to enjoy the fair."

Jason slammed his hat to the floor. Marjorie hastily glanced around, hoping they wouldn't be asked to leave. "Now see here, Marjorie MacTavish—"

"Hush up, will you?" she hissed. "Ye're making a spectacle of yersel'!"

"Damn it!"

"And don't curse, if you please!"

"People are beginning to stare," Hamilton pointed out in a strained voice. "Really, Dr. Abernathy, I don't understand—"

"No. You wouldn't!"

And with that, Jason stooped, swept his hat off the floor, slammed it onto his head, and marched out of the restaurant. Everyone in the room watched him, goggle-eyed and gape-mouthed, including Marjorie and Hamilton.

Resuming her seat, Marjorie was overwhelmed with embarrassment and guilt—which was not at all as it should be. After all, she'd done nothing wrong. Yet she felt her face flame, and she wished she could dive under the table and cower there until everyone went away or the world stopped turning, whichever came first.

Not daring to scan the rest of the room for fear she'd see everyone staring at her, she gazed somberly at Hamilton. "I'm so sorry, Hamilton. I have no idea what prompted Dr. Abernathy's strange behavior."

"I have an idea," Hamilton said darkly.

"You do?"

"You mean to say that you *don't*?"

He sounded sarcastic, and Marjorie couldn't account for it. "Well . . . no, I don't. I know good and well that Dr. Abernathy and I had no appointment today."

"Marjorie, do you honestly not understand what just happened here?"

She pondered the question for a moment. "I'm not sure what you mean." Her appetite had fled. She considered this phenomenon a great pity, since it was the first time in a long, long time she'd actually been almost eager to experience a new-to-her cuisine.

"Your friend the doctor just had a fit of jealousy, my dear. *That's* what just happened."

Marjorie had picked up her fork, determined to taste at least one more bite of her piroshok, but Hamilton's statement shocked her so much, she dropped it again. It clanked against her plate most embarrassingly. "You're daft."

"I don't think so."

Daft or not, after about fifteen minutes of discomfort, Marjorie was pleased to note that Hamilton regained his composure. She couldn't be said to have done the same, but she pretended very hard. One thing that helped was that Hamilton didn't seem to hold Jason's outrageous behavior against her. She almost had a good time visiting the rest of the fair and dining out afterwards.

If she'd had more experience in doing things for pure enjoyment, she was sure she'd have enjoyed it a lot. This all added up to one more proof, if one were needed, that Dr. Hagendorf had been correct about the benefit of practice.

When Hamilton escorted Marjorie to her door that evening, rather like a knight escorting a lady to the castle keep, Marjorie thought whimsically, she could hardly wait to tell Loretta all about her day. She found her in the first place she looked: the babies' nursery, where she was changing Oliver's diapers. Marjorie instantly picked up Olivia.

"Where's Miss Forrest?"

"I sent her to the kitchen to find something useful to do." Loretta made a face. "I keep telling Malachai I want to take care of my own babies."

"I should think you'd be grateful for the help of a trained nanny like Miss Forrest."

With a grin, Loretta said, "Well, I am, really. Because I'm *so* exhausted. But still, I want to do as much as I can for them." She blew a raspberry on little Oliver's tummy. The infant was too young to appreciate such motherly behavior, and only kicked Loretta in the nose.

Rubbing said nose, she said, "Tell me all about it, Marjorie. Don't leave anything out."

So Marjorie spent thirty minutes or so relating to Loretta everything that had happened at the fair. After those thirty minutes, she hadn't yet left the Russian restaurant, but Loretta was so weak from laughing, she fell into a chair. "I can't believe Jason actually chased you down at the fair!" Then she contradicted herself by saying, "I just *knew* he was going to do it! He came here and was furious when he learned you'd gone to the fair with Mr. St. Claire."

"Well, he did." Marjorie resumed crooning to Olivia, who seemed to have a touch of colic. "Idiot."

"He's in love with you, of course. That's what the matter is."

Marjorie gave such a violent start, Olivia opened her eyes and frowned at her. "Sorry, darling," she whispered. To Loretta, she said, "You're daft." In actual fact, she was beginning to wonder if the whole world—or at least the American part of it—was daft.

"Am not."

"Well, he's not in love with me, I can tell you that much. The man humiliated me today. It's a wonder Hamilton still spoke to me after he finally left the restaurant."

"You call him Hamilton?"

Loretta's tone of voice made Marjorie glance sharply at her. "It's his name."

"Ah."

Marjorie decided to drop the first-name issue. She'd never win. "At any rood, the fair was most interesting once Dr. Abernathy left us in peace."

"It's a good thing Mr. St. Claire remained kind to you, because Jason's behavior wasn't your fault."

"Mmm. True, but you know men."

"I certainly do."

Loretta's tone matched Marjorie's for the darkness of its quality. She went on, "Did you see Jason lurking in the background and around corners during the rest of your visit?"

"Nay." Giving Olivia a smooch on her chubby cheek, Marjorie said, "I don't want to talk about that madman. I mun tell ye about the fair, Loretta. I hope you and the captain can see it before it closes in December. It's very interesting."

With a sigh, Loretta threw Oliver's dirty diaper in a bucket intended for the purpose. "I'd love to see it. I was a fool not to take you before I got so huge. And now with the babies and all . . ."

"You have a nanny to care for the bairns," Marjorie reminded her.

"I hate that stupid nanny."

"She's a fine woman," Marjorie objected, shocked by Loretta's unjust condemnation of Miss Forrest, who was a qualified nurse and had been highly recommended by Jason.

"Oh, there's nothing wrong with *her*," Loretta said, backtracking. "I just don't need her, is all, except when I'm especially tired."

Shaking her head, Marjorie muttered, "I never

heard of a new mother who didn't need help, and you can afford it. Yet you don't want it. I recollect when . . ." She broke off, realizing with a start that she was about to relate something from her youth. She'd never done that before.

"You recollect what?"

Perhaps this was another new thing she should try, Marjorie thought. She hadn't intended to; it had just sort of popped up. Perhaps now that she'd initiated a leak in the floodgates, they'd rupture entirely and she'd begin to spill her guts all over the place. What an appalling thought. However, the story she'd begun to relate wasn't one that would hurt in the telling, so she finished telling it.

"When I was about fifteen or so, a friend of mine, Susan McNally, married a nice young man. They had a baby not a year later, and the poor girl was overwhelmed. Her mother was gone, you see, and she had no help to speak of. She could have used a Miss Forrest."

Loretta clucked her tongue. "Poor thing. I wish I'd known about it. I'd have helped."

With a smile of genuine love, Marjorie said, "Aye, I know you would have. You've a heart bigger than yoursel', Loretta Quarles."

"Pooh."

Loretta went to her bedroom shortly after that, allowing Miss Forrest to perform her duty as a nanny now that the children were settled in for the first part of the night—they wouldn't stay asleep, of course—and Marjorie changed into her nightgown, robe, and slippers, and moseyed down to the kitchen to make herself some hot cocoa.

Could Loretta possibly be right? Could Jason

Abernathy, of all unlikely men, be in *love* with her? In love with *her*?

No matter where Marjorie placed the emphasis, the sentence still sounded ridiculous.

Nevertheless, since she was alone in the kitchen and felt pleasantly tired from a full and interesting— and sometimes frustrating—day, she sat at the nice clean kitchen table, propped her elbows on it and her chin in her hands, and let her mind wander. Naturally, it wandered over to Jason Abernathy.

Could Marjorie ever be a real nurse? Could she learn Chinese? Could she, if she accomplished the first two formidable tasks, actually become a helpmeet for . . . well . . . someone like Jason?

Balderdash, Marjorie MacTavish. Allow yoursel' to think what you mean. So she did. Could she—did she—love Jason? At once her conscience smote her.

"What about Leonard?" she whispered into the silence.

Well, for one thing, Leonard was dead. Marjorie would gladly have died with him, but she hadn't, and she was still alive. Therefore, was it really necessary that she remain in silent mourning for the late, lamented Leonard Fleming for the rest of her life?

A little frantic after having entertained so revolutionary a notion, Marjorie whispered again. "I love you, Leonard."

Usually when she whispered such endearments, she heard Leonard's precious voice return the compliment in the back of her mind. This evening, Leonard's voice sounded a trifle tart when she heard it say, "So what?"

Startled, Marjorie sat up in her chair. So what? So *what!* Well . . . well . . . Well, actually, she didn't know so what, although the two words sounded frivolous and mocking in the face of so noble and true a love as the one she and Leonard had shared.

Annoyed, Marjorie heard Jason Abernathy's voice then. It said, "He's been dead for more than three years, for Pete's sake."

Well, but so had Jason's wife, confound it, and according to Loretta, Jason was still mourning her loss. So why should Marjorie be less faithful to her own beloved one?

An entirely new voice, one Marjorie couldn't place, said, "All that proves is that you're both nitwits."

She was about to take exception to the phrasing used by this mystery voice, when she was nearly frightened out of her skin by a vicious pounding at the kitchen door. Leaping to her feet so abruptly that she knocked her chair over backward, Marjorie grabbed the first item to hand, a cast-iron skillet standing on the stove. It was so heavy it nearly broke her wrist when she dragged it off the stove. After it had clunked onto the kitchen linoleum and Marjorie had wrapped her other hand around it, she staggered to the door and realized she couldn't see who was without because the curtain covered the window. And she couldn't draw back the curtain without relinquishing her weapon. Not that she'd be able to use it effectively if she couldn't lift it, but—

Her reflections stopped abruptly when Jason Abernathy's angry voice hissed, "Open the damned door, whoever you are! This is an emergency."

Marjorie abandoned her skillet and pulled the door open. Her shock when she beheld Jason, holding in his arms the battered body of a Chinese girl, held her speechless.

Jason rushed into the kitchen, stumbled over the skillet and barreled into the kitchen table. He sat with a crack of pottery, still clinging desperately to the Chinese girl.

"Who the devil put a damned skillet in the middle of the kitchen floor?" he demanded, his bushy eyebrows drawn into a furious v over his nose, his face red with fury, his blue eyes flashing sparks.

Stooping to rescue the skillet and hefting it with difficulty, Marjorie frowned at him. "There's no need for profanity. And it was the only weapon I could find."

"What the hell do you need a weapon for?" He stood and glared at the table, where Marjorie's squashed teacup and saucer and a good deal of hot cocoa were spread out. The rest of the cocoa and some splinters clung to the seat of Jason's trousers. "Damn it, now I've got chocolate all over my butt."

With a mighty heave, Marjorie replaced the skillet, which landed on the top of the stove with a hideous crash. The girl in Jason's arms moaned.

"Damn it, will you be quiet?"

"Stop swearing at me and tell me what you're doing here in the middle of the night with a girl in your arms!" Marjorie was proud of the steadiness of her voice. She was also pleased with its volume. In truth, when she'd beheld Jason holding a woman in his arms, her heart, which had been lodged in her throat after his attack on the door, had dropped straight to the floor at her feet. She didn't want to see another woman in Jason's arms, confound it. "Who is that?" she demanded crossly.

With a weary sigh, Jason turned around. "Brush off my trousers, will you? And it's Jia Lee. Either the Chan tong or the Gao tong—unless it was the importer of Chinese goods, who's in deep trouble with both sides—tried to kill her tonight."

"Merciful heavens!" Jason's explanation so startled Marjorie that she almost wasn't embarrassed when she took a kitchen towel off the rack and wiped Jason's rear end of extraneous china bits. There wasn't much she could do about the chocolate stains except to fold the towel and place it on the seat of the chair before he sat in it, which he did with a grunt. She fetched a washrag and began wiping the table.

"I brought her to Loretta's because I can't imagine anyone finding her here," Jason went on. He gazed critically at Jia Lee.

So did Marjorie. She was distressed to see awful swelling and bruising on her face. She expected that the rest of the girl's body was similarly disfigured. "Does she have any broken bones?"

"I haven't had a chance to examine her yet," Jason said with rancor. "For pity's sake, I just got here."

Vexed that he should be snapping at her, who had done absolutely nothing wrong, Marjorie snapped back. "Well, how should I know how long you've had her?"

"Just find a place to put her and stop crabbing at me, will you?"

"Well, for heaven's—"

Neither of them could continue their argument because the kitchen's door from the pantry swung inward, and Loretta, clasping her pretty brocade dressing gown to her throat, marched into the room. "What in the name of glory is going on in here? First I heard a crash, and then—" She broke off when she saw Jason and Jia Lee. "Jason! What's wrong? Who's that?"

Marjorie could but admire Loretta's instincts. She seemed instantly to realize that Jia Lee was in trouble. "The poor girl has been beaten up, Loretta. Jason brought her here to hide her."

"And nurse her." He scowled at Marjorie. "You wanted nursing practice? Well, you can have it."

"But . . ."

Loretta interrupted what was going to be a sensible caution on Marjorie's part. "Of course. You must keep her here. She can't be moved, poor thing. There are two rooms off the kitchen. She can stay in one of them. We'll have to make up the bed, but you can lay her down on the coverlet in one room while we prepare the other one in the meantime."

"But . . ."

This time it was Jason who interrupted her. "Thanks, Loretta. That would be great. She's in pretty bad shape. I'm not sure if anything's broken because I haven't had the opportunity to examine her."

"But . . ."

Loretta had hurried across the room. "Here. Bring her in here. It's small, but it'll be handy to water and so forth. There's a bathroom between the two rooms."

Jason rose with Jia Lee still firmly clasped to his bosom.

"But . . ."

"Thanks, Loretta. You're a real pal."

"But . . ."

Loretta laughed. "Of course I am. If the authorities would only see fit to repeal the Chinese Exclusion Act, this sort of thing wouldn't happen."

"But . . ."

"Amen. But just try to make a politician see reason. I'm beginning to think it can't be done."

"*Wait!*" Marjorie stamped her foot. The gesture

wasn't as effective as it might have been if she'd been wearing something more formidable than her bedroom slippers. Still, it got Loretta and Jason's attention. Both turned and looked at her, Loretta with astonishment, Jason with irritation.

"What is it now?" he asked sourly.

"It's dangerous, is what it is now," said Marjorie. "It's as dangerous now as it was then." She wasn't sure that made sense, but she meant it.

"Dangerous?" Loretta blinked at her.

"Oh, brother," muttered Jason.

Irate with him, Marjorie all but shouted, "Oh, brother, my foot! You yoursel' said that three individual parties were out to kill the lass, if you'll recall, Jason Abernathy!"

"So what?"

"So *what*? I'll tell you so what, you damned, bluidy man! There are wee bairns in this house nowadays, lest you forget! What if the tongs and that other devil *do* trace the poor girl here. What will happen then?"

"Three individual parties?" Loretta looked confused.

"Let me put the girl down, and I'll tell you about it," Jason said wearily. "Marjorie's right." So saying, he shot Marjorie a hideous scowl, leading her to deduce that, while she might be right, he didn't appreciate her for it.

"I'll get clean bedding," Marjorie muttered. "And clean clothes. The poor thing can't wear that scandalous dress any longer. It's ripped to shreds." She disapproved in general of the shimmering brocade gown barely concealing Jia Lee's slim figure, but even if it were a more demure and proper dress, it was ruined now.

Loretta, in command as ever, said, "Good idea. You get the bedding, and I'll get one of my old maternity gowns. They're big as houses, but they're clean."

So the two women left Jason in the room off the kitchen while they went about their business.

NINE

Impotent fury raged in Jason's breast as he examined Jia Lee. The injustice of her situation was so overwhelmingly obvious to any right-thinking individual that he couldn't understand why everyone in the entire city of San Francisco wasn't agitating for relief for people like her and incarceration or death—Jason was very upset—for the villains who profited by her condition.

And Marjorie MacTavish, whom Jason had almost begun to believe was actually human, was worried about the damned babies!

His conscience tapped him on the shoulder and reminded him that Marjorie had been correct about the fact that there were three individual—and remarkably vicious and violent—parties after Jia Lee and that Loretta was a new mother with two new children to protect. Not to mention the household staff, her husband, and herself. Jason also wasn't entirely sure about Malachai's interest in having his home used as a refuge for battered Chinese women with bloodthirsty villains on their trails.

"Bah," he grumbled. Damn it, it wasn't his fault the world stank and bad things continued to happen in it with a relentlessness that sometimes left him reeling with outrage and frustration. He was only trying to clean up what few messes he could and make things better in his own small way.

And the Quarleses, not to mention Marjorie, might still be in danger from the tongs and whoever had bungled the importation and sale of Jia Lee.

"Sale," he growled. "A human being. There ought to be a law."

"I think there already is." The deep, grumbling voice coming from behind him startled Jason.

He glanced over his shoulder and almost managed to smile. "Sorry about the interruption of your beauty sleep, Malachai."

Slipping around her husband, Loretta hurried to Jason's side. "How is she?"

"I don't think anything's broken. I'm not sure about internal injuries. I wish that fellow who invented the X-ray machine would hurry up and create a way to carry them around in a doctor's bag." Another glance at the parties in the small room made him frown. "Where's Marjorie?"

"She's making tea." Loretta grinned in spite of the nature of the gathering.

"Huh. She ought to be here if she wants to learn how to nurse people."

"I thought you didn't want her nursing your patients," Loretta said sweetly.

As Jason was already in a bad mood, Loretta's teasing didn't improve his temper any. He snapped, "I don't. But Jia Lee needs her."

"Why don't I let Miss Forrest nurse the poor girl. Give her something to do besides interfering with my babies and me."

"No!"

Jason's vehemence caught Loretta by surprise. She gave him a questioning look.

"Nobody should know she's here except the few who have to, and that means you, Malachai, and Marjorie. Is it possible to keep this from your domestic staff?"

Loretta and Malachai exchanged a glance, and Jason felt another stab of guilt. Brushing his fingers through his hair, he said, "I'm sorry, you two. I'm assuming too much." Damn Marjorie for being right. "Do you mind hiding her here? It might be dangerous if anyone finds out. As Marjorie mentioned, both the Chan and the Gao tongs are after Jia Lee, and whoever bought her in China seems to want her back, too. If I knew who it was, I might be in a better position to see that his career as a slaver is brought to a conclusion, but I don't know who he is. He'll probably be looking for her, too. I probably shouldn't have brought her here, but I didn't know what else to do."

"Your pursuits aren't exactly benign, are they, Doctor?" Malachai asked acidly. "I don't know that I want to put my family in jeopardy for the sake of this stranger, however much in need she is."

"Malachai," Loretta said, reproach in her voice. "You know we talked about it."

The big man nodded, frowning. "I know we did, but this is a real mess, Loretta. And we have the children to think about now, remember. This isn't just another one of your street-corner rants."

"They aren't rants!"

Malachai rolled his eyes, and Jason felt a quarrel coming on. He loved these two like kin, but he didn't have time for a domestic spat right now. "May I keep her here until her condition is stabilized? I don't know where else to hide her, but . . ." He frowned, puzzling the matter over in his head. The only other people he dared ask would be Isabel and Somerset FitzRoy, and they, too, had a child to protect. And Eunice, the child in question, was extraordinarily bright and inquisitive. They also didn't have a Marjorie handy.

Damn it, he didn't mean that. He didn't want Marjorie involved in this problem in any way. Except as a nurse, of course.

After another exchange of glances, Malachai and Loretta both turned to him. It was Malachai who spoke. "You can leave her here. We'll watch out for her. I wouldn't hesitate for a minute, except that we have Oliver and Olivia to think about now."

Contrite, Jason nodded. "I know. And I'm sorry. I just couldn't think of anywhere else to bring her."

Patting him on the back, Loretta said, "It's all right, Jason. Finish up your examination, and then come back to the kitchen and give us instructions."

"Thanks, you two." The kindness of his friends humbled Jason. In many respects, he knew he was a very lucky man.

It didn't take him very long to determine that Jia Lee was suffering from a concussion and that her ankle was badly sprained. He bound it with strips of linen and decided to splint it to keep it from moving. To do so, he had to call upon Marjorie's services, which she performed admirably. And in total silence. Fury radiated from her in waves, and he expected he'd be in for it once the operation was concluded.

With one last strip of tape, he finished fastening the makeshift splint into place and stood back with a sigh. "There. I think she'll do."

Marjorie said, "Hmm."

He gave her a sidelong glance and decided it would be better if he didn't look her full in the face yet. Best not to antagonize an angry bull by waving a red flag in front of it, after all.

"I'm primarily concerned about her head injury. I think the instrument of damage was a man's fist, although I don't know that for a fact. I didn't see any blunt instruments, but it was dark, and everyone scattered as soon as I showed up."

Marjorie huffed.

"Even so, there may be swelling in the brain. She's a small woman, and her head might have been knocked against a building. They were having at her in an alleyway."

Another huff.

"If I hadn't come along, she'd be dead now."

"Aye. Undoubtedly."

Shooting her another slanty-eyed glance, Jason kept talking. "I recognized the Chan and Gao enforcers. I'm assuming the other man was a bully boy hired by the white importer. At least that's the gist of what little conversation I heard. They weren't interested in chat at the time. They were more interested in poor Jia Lee."

"Hmm."

"The bully boy was trying to grab her away from the other two. I don't know what he aimed to do with her once he got her, assuming he ever did, but it probably wouldn't have been anything good."

"Undoubtedly."

Her voice was dry enough to turn a grape into a raisin. With a sigh, Jason guessed he couldn't put it off much longer. "I hate to move her . . ."

"Then don't." Crisp. Remarkably crisp.

Jason decided to brave her fury. Turning and looking her in the eye, he said, "So, may I leave her on the coverlet? You can put sheets on the bed once we're sure she's going to survive. I don't want to move her around anymore."

Marjorie's face was as stony as could be.

Jason dared to say more anyway. "Because of the concussion. Anyone with a concussion shouldn't be moved, and I've already had to haul her all over the city."

She said, "Fine," turned on her heel, and left the room.

For a moment, Jason just stared after her. Then, with another sigh, he shoved his hands into his pockets and went out into the kitchen to face the Quarleses and Marjorie. Of the three, he dreaded Marjorie the most.

The Quarleses' large kitchen was toasty warm and everyone in it looked quite bright-eyed and alert, considering it was the middle of the night. If one didn't know that catastrophe lurked in the very next room, anyone would consider the room cozy and inviting, and the people gathered there merely friends chatting after a nice day. Marjorie knew, and she was furious.

"You canna leave the woman here!" she hissed. "Ye'll call down the wrath of the whole of Chinatown on the heads of Loretta and Malachai and the children!"

"Now, now, Marjorie, I'm sure it's not that bad." Loretta patted her hand.

Marjorie suppressed the urge to grab and shake

the woman who was a brand-new mother with two wee bairns to consider.

Jason passed a hand over his eyes. He looked as if he were feeling guilty about having brought Jia Lee into the Quarleses' home. As well he should, although his guilt was rather late in arriving, if you asked Marjorie.

"She's right," he said wearily. "I probably should have taken her somewhere else. But I couldn't think of anywhere else to take her."

"Hmph." Marjorie folded her arms across her chest and glared at him.

This time it was Jason's hand that Loretta patted. "Nonsense. You were perfectly correct in bringing her here, Jason. No one in the entire city of San Francisco would ever think to look here for her."

"Codswallop. You're known as one of his best friends, and also as a supporter of the repeal of the Chinese Exclusion Act and any number of other radical causes. Yours is the first place anyone would think of to look. After all, I'm sure they know it was Jason who took her."

"Well, but will anyone bother to search for her?" They all turned to gape at Malachai. "Look at it this way," he continued. "You had two tongs trying to beat her up and perhaps kill her. You had someone else trying to wrench her away from the tongs. Maybe they all just want her out of the way." He shrugged. "She's out of the way."

Loretta liked this idea a lot. Marjorie could see it in her face, which brightened right up. Marjorie herself didn't believe it for a second. In her experience, life was never that easy.

"I don't know," said Jason doubtfully. "I think that, somehow or other, Jia Lee's become some kind of playing piece in a game of power going on in Chinatown. I doubt that anyone's going to stop searching for her." He dragged his fingers through his curly dark hair. "Damn, I wish I knew what the problem was."

"I thought you knew," said Marjorie accusingly. "What you told me was that the same girl was sold to two different tongs and that they're fighting over her now."

"Yes, but why? I don't know why. As a rule, women aren't considered all that important."

Loretta began to puff up, and Jason held out his hand. "I didn't say *I* felt that way, Loretta. But I can't change several thousand years of Chinese culture overnight all by myself."

"Humph." Malachai squeezed his wife's shoulder and grinned.

Marjorie always felt vaguely jealous of Loretta when her husband demonstrated his affection so openly. Not that she wanted Malachai, but it must be wonderful to have a man love you that much. In fact, she knew it was, because she'd been loved that much by Leonard. He'd died for her. It seemed like a million years ago now. She sighed heavily.

When Jason's hand covered hers where it rested beside her teacup, Marjorie started violently.

"I'm sorry, Marjorie. You're right, of course. I've put everyone in this house at risk, and it was thoughtless and stupid of me."

Marjorie's mouth dropped open.

It was Loretta who spoke. Naturally. "Don't be silly, Jason. Marjorie knows you only did what you had to do."

"I should have thought harder before putting you in danger."

Marjorie's hand felt as if it were on fire, and prickles of heat radiated from the point of contact to the entire rest of her body. She knew she was blushing, because she always blushed, confound it. And she was gratified that Jason had finally admitted her correctness in the Jia Lee affair. Yet she felt guilty for having been such a wet blanket about it. After all, the poor woman wasn't at fault for any of the things that were happening to and around her. "Well . . . I suppose it isna your fault, Jason. Not entirely."

When she saw his right eyebrow lift in an ironical twist over his bright blue eye, she regretted her compassion instantly. "And you still put the whole family in danger," she stated firmly. "Including the wee bairns."

He squeezed her hand. "That's my Marjorie."

Scowling at him, Marjorie thought, *I only wish.* Then she couldn't believe she'd had so alarming a thought. Backpedaling furiously in an effort to banish it, she asked a question she'd wanted to ask Loretta before everyone had so brusquely confiscated the kitchen bedroom. "I thought Li and Molly had the bedrooms off the kitchen."

Loretta looked puzzled for a minute, then her expression cleared. "They moved upstairs last year. I asked them if they'd rather have rooms on the third floor where they'd have more privacy, and they said they would."

"Oh." However had she missed that? The fact that she had missed it proved with finality that Marjorie's job with Loretta was nothing but a sinecure provided by a bighearted woman to another woman who ought to be more independent. Marjorie was ashamed of herself. As usual.

"That's probably for the best," said Jason. "No-body need know that Jia Lee is here at all." He turned to Marjorie, and his eyes were pleading. Marjorie wished they weren't, because they made it difficult for her to resist the man. "I know it's ask-ing a lot, Marjorie—"

Marjorie huffed.

"—but do you think you could take up residence in the room next to Jia Lee's for a couple of days? Just until she's out of the woods?"

"And how, pray, will I know if the woman's out of the woods?" Marjorie regretted her harsh tone as soon as she saw Jason's expression stiffen. She wasn't really a hardhearted woman. Truly, she wasn't. But she became so flustered when any-thing out of the ordinary happened that . . .

No. There was no excuse for her attitude. Again, shame washed over her. Her gaze dropped to the table where she tried to ignore the fact that Jason's hand still held hers.

"You can report to me, for one thing." Jason's own tone was as hard as steel.

Her gaze passing between the two, Loretta said, "Would you mind sleeping down here for a few days, Marjorie? It probably shouldn't take longer than that for us to be sure the poor thing is out of danger. I'd do it myself—"

"The hell you would," growled her loving husband.

Loretta smiled at him. "Well, I can't, because of the babies."

"And me," grumbled Malachai.

"And you," agreed Loretta.

"I dinna mind at all," said Marjorie, wishing she could erase her prior question. "And I'll stay for as long as need be. After all, if anyone does come looking for her, someone ought to be with the poor thing."

Jason's hand tightened painfully around hers. "No."

Confused, Marjorie frowned at him. "No? But you just said . . ."

"I know what I just said, damn it, but I don't want to put you in danger."

You should have thought about danger long before this. Marjorie bit her tongue and didn't say it.

"Fudge," said Loretta. "Nobody's going to sneak into my house and kidnap the girl." She laughed merrily. "That's absurd, Jason. There's not a chance in the world that anyone will suspect us of harboring the girl here. And even if they do, how can they gain entry? They'd have to scale that huge wrought-iron fence and then break into the house. I do keep it locked up at night, you know."

Jason's smile was faint and rather sickly.

Marjorie wished she believed it.

Rehearsals for *The Pirates of Penzance* were going very well. Mr. Proctor, who made a delightfully stuffy and very funny Major General, called various segments of the cast together on Monday and Thursday evenings and Saturday afternoons.

More often than not, Marjorie and Jason were called to rehearse at the same time, thereby enabling Marjorie to give Jason regular reports on Jia Lee's recovery. Jason didn't want to be seen visiting Loretta's house more than he normally did, since he was known to have rescued Jia Lee from the rival factions, and he didn't want anyone to suspect he'd taken her to Loretta's.

During the scene they were rehearsing this evening, the last one, the Pirate King has just confessed to theft. Pursing his lips comically, Mr. Proctor looked suitably prim and fussy when he condemned Jason and his pirate cohorts to prison. Mrs. Proctor, as Ruth, charged into the fray.

In her role as Mabel, Marjorie stood with her hands clasped to her bosom, her eyes wide, her posture fairly shrieking maidenly innocence as she watched the scene unfold.

"'For they are all gentlemen's sons who have gone wrong!'" Mrs. Proctor sang, flinging out her hand toward the pirate mob.

At once, Jason, without his prop top hat but faking for all he was worth, adopted a pose. Marjorie was hard put not to giggle, he played the role so well as he strutted out toward the stage's apron, singing a refrain of Mrs. Proctor's announcement. When he got there, he sidled slightly toward Marjorie and mouthed, "How's the lotus?"

Lotus had become a code word for Jia Lee. Sometimes Marjorie felt as if she'd become involved in a plot from a Fu Manchu novel. "Better. Her ankle is still awfully black and blue, but the swelling is going down."

With his nose in the air in stereotypically snobbish fashion, Jason said, "Good," an instant before he broke out singing again. This time, because it was written thus, Marjorie and the rest of the cast joined him.

Hamilton St. Claire, in his role as Frederic, clasped Marjorie to his side and whispered, "What are you two so cozy about?"

Shocked, Marjorie would have turned to stare at him, except that she was supposed to be Mabel.

"'Poor wand'ring one,'" sang she, hissing as she drew breath to continue her song, "We're not!"

"Huh." Hamilton swirled her off into a waltz that had been choreographed by Mr. Potter. "Listen, Marjorie, I don't think that fellow is on the up and up."

"You *what*?" Marjorie could scarcely believe her ears. In all the years she'd been acquainted with Jason, she'd known him for a tease, an irreverent jokesmith, and a frustrating fellow who laughed at the most important things, but she'd never once considered him in any way disreputable. "Don't be silly."

"No, no," Hamilton insisted. "There's something shady about him."

"That's ridiculous." They stopped center stage, Hamilton released her, and Marjorie began her final aria, gasping slightly because of the dance and her conversation.

Behind her, Jason whispered, "I'll come over late tonight to examine her."

She gave the slightest of nods, wishing all the men in her life would leave her alone so she could concentrate on her solo. Then she almost spoiled the song entirely by laughing at the thought of herself with "men in her life."

Again, the cast broke into a waltz, and Marjorie found herself in Hamilton's arms. "Say, Marjorie, are you sweet on that fellow? Because if you are—"

"*What?*"

She'd shrieked the word, and several people hesitated in the dance, causing a brief pile-up on the stage. Most of the cast turned their heads to stare at her, including Jason and his dancing partner, who happened to be Ginger Collins, much to Marjorie's disgust.

Lowering her voice to a furious whisper, she said,

"Are you daft, Hamilton St. Claire? What kind of question is that to ask a lady?"

Sounding sulky, Hamilton said, "I only wondered. After all, you must know by this time that I'm . . . interested in you myself."

"You are?" Astounded by this news, Marjorie forgot her own footing and nearly caused them both to fall over.

"Well, of course I am!" Now Hamilton sounded more angry than sulky. "Why else would I be paying you so much attention?"

Had he been paying her particular attention? Marjorie tried to think back upon their interactions during the last couple of weeks, but she was out of breath and surprised, and her mind couldn't wrap itself around the problem.

Fortunately, the grand finale was upon them, and with a flood of music, the entire cast hit their marks for the last pose. Hamilton clutched Marjorie in a comical embrace. Jason, doing likewise with Ginger, dipped her so low that she giggled. Marjorie was not amused. Jason had no business flirting with Ginger Collins when so many awful things were happening. Anyhow, as far as Marjorie knew, he didn't even like the woman.

She wasn't able to think about it after the music ended, because Mr. Proctor clapped his hands to get the cast's attention. "That was better," he panted. "But we need to be much smoother in the dance." He turned to Marjorie. "Was there some problem, Miss MacTavish?"

"Problem? Er . . . Why, no." *Yes, there had been a problem,* Marjorie thought angrily. Two infernal men kept talking to her when she was trying to concentrate on her role. Naturally, she didn't say that.

"Well," Mr. Proctor said, his voice kind, "Do try to keep yourself focused, will you, Miss MacTavish? You're very important to the production, you know." He gave her a knowing smile.

Ginger tee-heed.

Marjorie wanted to belt Ginger first, then Hamilton, and then Jason. Ultimately, however, the entire bobble could most properly be laid at Jason's feet. Perhaps she should belt him first.

Jason couldn't understand why Marjorie had acted so peeved with him after rehearsal. He hadn't done a thing to rile her, had he? He hadn't teased her for going on weeks now.

Oh, very well, perhaps it had been days. He was appreciative of her efforts at nursing Jia Lee and of her singing in the role of Mabel. She was the best Mabel he'd ever heard, actually, and she was displaying a streak for comedy that he'd never have guessed existed. He was doing an exceptionally splendid job in his role as Pirate King, too, dash it. So what the devil was the matter with Marjorie?

Mai never used to be unreasonable like this.

Mai worshiped you as her savior, a little voice in his head whispered. The voice annoyed him. It had been interrupting his peace quite often of late.

It was also wrong. Or . . . well, perhaps Mai had been grateful to him, but that was only normal. He and she had adored each other. Theirs had been a love unequaled in the annals of humankind.

You loved her, the pesky voice said. *She would have loved anyone who rescued her.*

Now, Jason *knew* that wasn't true.

At least, he thought it wasn't true.

Anyhow, so what?

So, wouldn't it be nice if a woman in full possession of her freedom and free will chose to love you? the voice asked. Jason detected the faintest hint of a taunt in it. *Marjorie MacTavish, for example?*

Good God, he must be losing his mind.

When he saw Hamilton St. Claire escorting Marjorie out of the church, gripping her arm as if he had a right to her body, his infernal internal voice, Mai, and the rest of the world evaporated from his consciousness as if it had never been. "Hey!" he hollered, running up the middle aisle, uncaring that he was in a church or that people might be staring. "Wait a minute!"

What the devil was that silly boy doing escorting his Marjorie? That's what he wanted to know. Even in his exasperated state, he understood that he needed to rephrase the question before he allowed it out into the open air.

He resented the look both Marjorie and Hamilton gave him when they turned to see who was causing the commotion. Not that it *was* a commotion. Not exactly. He only wanted to catch the two before they left the church. Together. And why were they thus? He wanted to know that.

"Dr. Abernathy," Hamilton said coldly.

"Yes?" Marjorie's voice was similarly icy, although her cheeks were flushed, Jason presumed, from ire. If there was another cause for those rosy cheeks— say, because she enjoyed Hamilton St. Claire's escort—he didn't want to know about it.

Panting a little, Jason said, "I thought I was taking you home."

Marjorie lifted an eyebrow. Jason hadn't seen her do that before. It was rather intimidating.

"Oh?" More ice, damn it.

Hamilton's eyebrows lowered over his pallid blue eyes. He, too, said, "Oh?" as if he thought it was Jason's place to explain himself.

Then the two of them simply stood there and looked at him. How . . . uncomfortable. "Um, didn't we agree that I was going to see you home, Marjorie?" he asked at last.

She said, "No."

He said, "Oh."

Then he watched the two of them turn back toward the door, open it, and walk out, leaving him in the aisle feeling like an idiot. When he turned around and slumped back to the front of the church to fetch his hat and coat and saw several of the cast members watching with avid interest, he felt even more idiotic. He gave everyone a glare, then wished he'd smiled with insouciance instead. It would have been more in character for him to be flippant. Or at least uninterested. He sighed. Too late now.

There was no doubt about it: Marjorie MacTavish was bad for Jason Abernathy's peace of mind.

"Ye should be knackered, Marjorie MacTavish. So why canna ye sleep?"

A very grumpy Marjorie sat at the kitchen table, staring balefully at her cup of hot cocoa and wishing Jason would show up and get his examination of Jia Lee over with. It was just like him to pretend they'd had an arrangement whereby he would see her to her home, and then not show up to examine Jia Lee when he'd said he would.

As for Jia Lee herself, the girl was sleeping peacefully. Marjorie almost envied her. Well, except for the illegality of her presence in the United States, her status as forced prostitute, the way she had been abused since she got here, and her current state of injury.

At least Jason had kept his promise to teach Marjorie some rudimentary phrases in Chinese. She could now ask Jia Lee where she hurt, if she wanted tea, and if she was hungry. If Jia Lee did more than point or said more than "yes" or "no" to any of these inquiries, Marjorie was lost.

Still, it was better than no communication at all. If Li, Loretta's housemaid, were allowed to tend the girl, they might be able to get more information from her, but neither Loretta nor Jason—nor Marjorie, if she were to be honest—wanted anyone else to know the girl was being hidden in the Quarleses' mansion. The more people who knew, the more apt someone was to leak the news, and that might be catastrophic.

They kept Jia Lee's bedroom door locked during the day. Not that any of the Quarleses' household staff was wont to snoop, but it was safer that way. After all, Mrs. Brandeis, Molly, and Li were the ones most likely to be in the kitchen during the daylight hours. Or they had been until recently, now that Marjorie was also sleeping downstairs.

In order to perpetuate that particular ruse, Loretta had arranged to have Marjorie's upstairs bedroom painted and redecorated. Marjorie had protested the expense, but Loretta had pooh-poohed her reservations.

"It's for a good cause. Anyhow, I'm in a decorating mood," Loretta had declared airily and with one of her characteristic broad gestures. "I guess it started with the nursery."

Marjorie had accepted this, as she accepted all the rest of Loretta's largesse, with a feeling of failure in her bosom, even though she understood that the lie was primarily meant to be of benefit to Jia Lee. She knew she ought not remain as Loretta's secretary, because she certainly didn't earn her keep. As small as Loretta was, though, she was a powerful force and one that wasn't easily defied.

The remainder of Loretta's household staff had readily believed the lie, Loretta being as well known for her impulsive behavior as for her large heart. Hadn't she redecorated the maids' quarters on the third floor a year or so earlier? Yes, she had. Therefore, no one thought twice about her redecorating Marjorie's quarters. And the fact that Marjorie seemed to be using both of the downstairs bedrooms didn't cause anyone else in the household to bat an eye.

A sound at the kitchen door made her jerk her head up. Glancing at the kitchen clock, she saw that it was well past midnight, confound Jason Abernathy.

Gathering her robe to her bosom, she marched to the kitchen door and yanked it open. "It's about—"

But she didn't get to finish her complaint. In fact, Marjorie was so startled when two large, hooded men swarmed into the kitchen, forcing her to stumble backwards, that she didn't even scream.

TEN

"All right, lady, where's the Chinese gal?"

Marjorie's first, insane thought was that these two blackguards weren't Chinese. Her second thought was that she'd be damned for all eternity before she told the brutes anything at all, much less what they wanted to know.

Anyhow, since the villain's hand covered her mouth, she was unable to speak. Therefore, she stood in his grip, silent, defiant, and as thoroughly angry as she'd ever been in her life. If she'd been able to move her mouth even a fraction of an inch, she'd have chomped down on his fleshy palm, even though to do so would probably have given her ptomaine poisoning. It was clear to her that these particular criminals didn't bother to bathe regularly.

"I don't think she can talk, Bart," the man's companion said.

Whoever Bart was, he growled, "Don't use names, damn it, Frank."

"Well, I still don't think she can talk with your hand over her mouth," Frank said in an aggrieved tone.

Bart, who appeared to be a slow thinker, took some time to contemplate this sensible remark.

Marjorie sucked in air, preparatory to screaming bloody murder should the hand fall from its place. Her plan suffered a check when Bart showed her what looked like the largest and sharpest knife in the universe.

"All right, lady, I'm going to move my hand, but if you try to yell or anything, you'll get it across the throat. Do you understand me?"

She managed a nod with difficulty. Codswallop. Now what? She assuredly wouldn't reveal Jia Lee's presence in the house, but she also couldn't scream. Damn Jason Abernathy to perdition! He should have been here hours ago.

Cautiously, Bart slid his hand away from Marjorie's mouth. As it was a particularly dirty hand, she spat as soon as she was able. This annoyed Bart enough that he said, "Hey!" and administered a blow to her cheek that made her ears ring and her eyes water. It might also have made her fall had Bart not maintained a bruising grip on her arm. She blinked furiously, unwilling to cry in front of these two beasts.

"The boss didn't say nothin' about hurtin' her, Bart. Better not hit her too hard." Frank sounded worried.

The man named Bart glared at Frank and growled, "She spat on my damned hand!"

Frank shrugged, unable to deny the fact.

"And I'll do it again if you put your filthy hand over my mouth," declared Marjorie, regaining her spirit in spite of her stinging cheek and watering eyes. Feeling the inside of said cheek with her tongue, she tasted blood and hoped Bart hadn't loosened any of her teeth. She also wished Jason would get here before very much longer, confound the man. In fact, while she was at it, confound all men.

"Where's the Chinese gal?" Bart repeated.

"I don't know what you're talking about. What Chinese girl?"

Drawing his hand back to strike again, Bart checked the action when a sound came from the kitchen door. Unwilling to hope for fear she'd be disappointed, Marjorie still couldn't help but pray it was Jason this time and not more crooks.

Above all the other emotions roiling within her at that moment in time, she felt absolute rage. That being the case, and because she hoped to disconcert her foes, she said in a fair semblance of her normal tone, "It's the police. They patrol this house regularly, you know, because—" Fudge. She'd thought quickly, but not quite quickly enough to think of a good reason for the fictitious patrol. "Because Captain Quarles pays for it. Because of all the valuable antiques." There. These two couldn't possibly know that she'd just lied.

"She's lying," said Frank matter-of-factly.

"Sure she is. Stupid lie, too."

Fie on them! "I am not! It's the truth! The Quarleses are enormously wealthy!"

"Marjorie?"

So relieved was Marjorie to hear Jason's voice, she nearly fainted. Catching herself in time, her heart pounding like a bass drum, she shrieked, "Jason! Help!"

With a mighty shove, Bart grunted, "Let's get out of here," as he rushed toward the door.

"The boss ain't going to like this," muttered Frank, following his cohort at a dead run.

As for Marjorie, she staggered across the room with arms flailing in an attempt to keep her balance, bounced off the far wall, ricocheted back again, and ended up pitching onto the kitchen table, upending her hot cocoa and sending another of Loretta's beautiful china teacups crashing to the floor. Cocoa, she thought inanely, seemed to be a dangerous beverage in this household.

Terrified that the two villains would harm Jason, and still so angry she could have spat tacks, she shoved herself upright and raced to the door, punching the light switch on the way. The kitchen garden lit up just in time for her to see the back end of one of the culprits slither over the wall. She heard a thump and a muffled curse, and then the sound of retreating footsteps racing down the alleyway. She cried, "Jason!"

A form picked itself up from the graveled walkway running between the rows of vegetables Mrs. Brandeis and the gardener tended. "Yeah, it's me."

Marjorie raced outside to help him. "Confound you! Why didn't you come earlier?"

He frowned at her. "I'm quite all right, thank you. No bones broken. A few scratches here and there."

"Confound you!" Her heart was hammering so hard it hurt by the time she reached his side and grabbed his arm. He seemed basically unharmed. Thank God, thank God. "If you'd been here on time, none of this would have happened!" She eyed him critically as he dusted himself off. "What *did* happen?"

"A couple of ruffians ran into me." Jason scowled. "Ran over me is more like it."

Relief washed through Marjorie like flood water. "Why the devil weren't you here earlier?" The mere thought of that huge knife plunged into Jason's heart made her want to weep. She'd be cursed forevermore before she'd do that.

"What the devil are you going on about the time for?" Jason demanded.

"You said you'd be here earlier, confound you! Those men wouldn't have . . . have . . ." Pooh. She didn't know what they wouldn't have done actually. They might have come anyway and killed them all.

"Who were those fellows anyhow?"

"I don't know!" A tear slipped out in spite of Marjorie's rigid control, and she wiped it away angrily. "But they asked where the Chinese girl—or, rather, gal—was."

"Damn."

"And well you might swear," Marjorie said, furious that she had actually shed a tear over fear for his welfare. "Why weren't you here earlier?"

"I knew I was being followed," he said in a voice conveying hurt that Marjorie should be blaming him. "I thought I'd shaken them off my tail."

"Well, it looks as if you didn't." Repressing the urge to feel Jason to make sure none of his limbs were damaged, Marjorie clasped her hands together instead. She was so angry with him, both for being late and for worrying her, that she also had to resist the urge to kick him.

"Damn it, I'd been hoping no one knew about Jia Lee being at Loretta's place."

"It's a forlorn hope now," Marjorie said sourly.

"Evidently." Jason took a step; said, "Ow;" frowned; and continued, "There's a rock in my shoe."

Once more Marjorie's heart began to pitch and roll. "Are you sure it's only a rock?" Oh, Lord, what if the knife had fallen and stabbed his foot?

"Yeah, it's only a piece of this cursed gravel Loretta has spread all over the place. I'm all right. Why'd they spread gravel? Wood chips would be better."

"How should I know?" Feeling very cross, Marjorie stamped to the kitchen door.

He squinted at her in the light provided by the one lamp over the door. "What the devil's the matter with you?"

Indignant, Marjorie snapped, "I've just been accosted by two black villains, for heaven's sake!"

"Right." His continued scrutiny made her nervous. "Damn, I wish I could have caught one of them."

"I know their names," Marjorie said, taking his arm and turning him toward the kitchen door. "Bart and Frank."

"Big help."

Annoyed, Marjorie said, "It's more than you know!"

"Right. Sorry. I'm only upset that this happened."

"So am I."

Upon entering the kitchen, they saw Jia Lee, obviously terrified, standing at her bedroom door, her hands pressed to her heart. She looked delicate and fragile, which she was, and her perfect, beautiful, oval face conveyed terror. Marjorie thought she'd never seen anyone look more beautiful and pathetic at the same time, and a surge of jealousy, as unexpected as it was unworthy, shot through her.

Jason hurried over to Jia Lee, saying something in Chinese that, naturally, Marjorie couldn't understand. She frowned at the two as they talked with each other.

A notion had just struck her, and she didn't like it one little bit. Was Jason interested in Jia Lee like he'd been interested in his late wife? Was his concern for the poor girl more than purely medical or kindly intentioned? Her heart, which had been performing erratically all night long, plummeted sick-eningly.

As she continued to watch Jason and Jia Lee, she absently fingered her bruised cheek, recalling as she did so that Loretta had been similarly injured several months earlier. Marjorie prayed that her own cheek wouldn't swell as Loretta's had. Loretta had been a mess for a couple of weeks, and she'd been unable to speak clearly for several days.

With that in mind, Marjorie hurried to the icebox, grabbed the ice pick, and chipped off a good mound of ice. With soft Chinese murmurs floating in the background, she wrapped the ice in a clean kitchen towel and pressed it to her cheek. Then, since Jason obviously didn't need or want her help, she went back to the table and retrieved the broken pieces of the teacup and mopped up the spilled cocoa. She thought about making more, but decided to wait until Jason was through with Jia Lee. Maybe he'd want some, too. Or maybe he'd want his latest Chinese love to have a cup.

Marjorie told herself to stop it. Even if Jason did fall madly in love with Jia Lee, it was nothing to her. Absolutely nothing. Less than nothing.

Another tear slid down her cheek, and she cursed herself as a blathering, haggis-headed gudgeon.

Jason settled Jia Lee down in her bed, pleased with her relative progress since she'd been staying at Loretta's house. He was very concerned, however, that her enemies had discovered her whereabouts. He couldn't understand how they had done so. He thought he'd been so careful.

"Get some sleep now," he advised the girl.

She thanked him, and Jason was surprised and a little worried to see the same expression on her face that he'd so often seen on Mai's. The little voice in his head couldn't be right about his first wife's devotion, could it?

Oh hell, what difference did it make now? He was very, very weary as he went back into the kitchen, shutting the door softly behind him. He was rather surprised to see that Marjorie had waited for him as she'd seemed unaccountably irritated with him before he'd examined Jia Lee. Narrowing his eyes, he peered at her, wondering why she was holding a kitchen towel to her cheek.

"What the devil are you holding a kitchen towel to your cheek for?"

Narrowing her own eyes, Marjorie looked up at him, a scowl on her lovely face. She lowered the towel, revealing the angry red imprint of a hand on her cheek.

Gasping, Jason darted over and knelt next to her. She drew back, as he should have expected her to do but hadn't, thereby irritating him. "What happened?" he demanded.

"One of those beasts—Bart, it was—hit me."

In less than a heartbeat, rage consumed him. He grabbed her by the shoulders and lifted her clear out of her chair. "I'll kill the bastard!"

And then, before he even knew what he was going to do, he'd clutched her to his bosom and was kissing her on the lips. Before his own eyes closed, he saw hers open wide in shock, register an instant's anger, and then close in rapture. He assumed it was rapture, because that was his condition.

He hadn't expected to experience such sweetness from the prickly Marjorie MacTavish, but awe, joy, and lust all built in him until he ran out of breath and resumed thinking. When his initial surprise lessened, he gentled both the kiss and his grip on her. One of his hands went to her hair—the fiery hair he loved so much—and stroked it softly.

Sanity returned to him slowly. When it did, he braced himself for an explosion—but he didn't let her go. She felt too good in his arms. Remembering her poor cheek and worried lest the pressure on her lips hurt it, Jason reluctantly withdrew his own, but pressed her head to his bosom. "Your skin is like silk, Marjorie."

She said, "Mmmm."

Not only was her skin like silk, but her breasts were also pressing against his chest, and he could feel her puckered nipples through the silk of her robe. Lord, he couldn't recall ever thinking of Marjorie MacTavish in terms of breasts before, but he sure did now. His arousal was rock-solid and ready for action, and he was afraid to so much as move for fear something embarrassing might happen.

He didn't know how long they stood in the kitchen holding each other, before Marjorie's whisper drifted over his senses, rather like falling feathers. "You . . . you kissed me."

Jason discovered that he had to clear his throat. "Yes, I did." What's more, he wanted to do it again. And again and again and again.

She didn't try to pull away from him, which surprised him moderately. "I dinna think you liked me, Jason."

"Oh, I like you all right, Marjorie." What worried him was that he had a sinking sensation that he more than merely liked her. In fact, when he briefly considered the idea that Marjorie might marry that dimwit St. Claire, his insides crunched up into a tiny, seething ball and began to throb. "But I didn't mean to shock you."

"You dinna shock me, Jason."

Thank God, thank God. He licked his lips. "In that case . . ." And he kissed her again, thereby shocking himself.

When, after several blissful seconds, his hand moseyed over to one of Marjorie's enticing breasts—the breasts he hadn't noticed until this very night, the more fool he—and she gasped, Jason brought himself up short.

What the devil was he thinking?

He wasn't thinking at all, was what the matter was.

What was he doing?

He was fondling one of Marjorie MacTavish's breasts.

At once he removed his hand. Sucking in a huge breath, he then uttered a bald-faced lie. "I'm sorry, Marjorie." He wasn't sorry. What he was, was intensely frustrated. What he wanted to do was rip that damned robe off her body and ravish her. Right here. Right now. On the damned kitchen floor if he had to.

"Dinna be sorry," she whispered, thereby robbing him of breath. "It's all right."

Damned if it was. This was especially true since Jason had just recollected that he wouldn't have to use the floor because Marjorie now slept in a room only a few feet away from them. He almost wished he hadn't remembered.

"No." His voice was ragged. "It's not all right." With almost savage force, he tore himself away from her. It hurt. "I'm acting like a damned wretch."

Was that disappointment he saw in her eyes?

Good God, he was losing his mind. Scrubbing a hand over his face, Jason turned away, fearing that if he kept looking at her his resolve to remain a gentleman would crumble.

Silence issued from Marjorie. It worried him. Greatly daring, he turned halfway around and peeked at her. There she stood, looking totally bewildered, and so lovely he could hardly stand it. He steeled himself against his intense attraction to her. "Um . . ." But he didn't know what to say. They probably ought to discuss the Jia Lee situation, but at the moment, Jason wished Jia Lee to the devil.

Marjorie shook her head once sharply, as if to rid it of detritus, and spoke. Her voice was stronger than it had been. "Would you care for some hot cocoa?"

The question was so utterly prosaic and so far removed from everything Jason had been thinking and feeling that it jarred him into a semblance of sanity. "Cocoa?" He shook his own head, although it still felt moderately fuzzy. "What the devil would I want cocoa for?"

That did the trick. In an instant, Marjorie transformed from an angelic creature out of his most soul-satisfying dreams and back into a prim Scottish former stewardess. "I have'na notion. But I thought it wuid be polite to ask, you bluidy contentious nyaff."

And with that, she turned on her heel, went into her bedroom, and pulled the door after her with such force that Jason braced himself for a slam. She caught it just before it could waken the whole household and shut it quietly.

When he heard the key turning in the lock, Jason felt as if he'd just lost his one true friend.

"Ah hell." With that, he sank onto a kitchen chair, folded his arms on the table, placed his head on his arms . . . and wished he had a nice, hot cup of cocoa to drink.

An abbreviated but hideously loud screech awakened Marjorie from a troubled slumber the next morning. Fearing another attack on Jia Lee, she stumbled out of bed, grabbed her robe, and dashed for the door while still trying to put it on. Then she grasped the doorknob, gave the door a mighty push, and ended up mashing her nose against it. She'd forgotten all about having locked it the night before.

"Confound it," she mumbled, turning the key and rubbing her nose, praying it wasn't broken or bleeding or anything else of a like nature. Her cheek took that opportunity to twinge, reminding her that she was already injured. Stupid day. Stupid door. Stupid Jason Abernathy.

And, more than anything else, stupid Marjorie.

She finally emerged from her room—rumpled, grumpy, and sore—to find Mrs. Brandeis lavishing adoration upon Jason. Apparently, she'd been the one who'd screeched when she'd discovered Jason in the kitchen.

Marjorie frowned at the scene. "What the deuce is going on?" Her tone was sharp enough to pierce Jason Abernathy's black heart.

He glanced over at her and grinned. "You look like the wrath of God, Marjorie. You should have let me tend to that cheek last night. And what happened to your nose?"

To the devil with sharp voices—Marjorie was going to use a butcher knife. She stamped over to the stove where she'd set a kettle the night before in preparation for the morning's tea. "You don't look so chipper yourself, Dr. Abernathy." Her growl seemed to startle Mrs. Brandeis, who glanced at her quickly, then glanced away again.

"Probably not." Jason rose and stretched. "I slept at the kitchen table."

After lighting the burner under the kettle, Marjorie turned, crossed her arms over her bosom—that same bosom Jason had lavished so much gentle and tender attention upon only a few hours earlier—and glowered at him. "Why'd you do that?"

"Oh, Miss MacTavish," Mrs. Brandeis interrupted, which was most unlike her. Marjorie supposed she'd done it to avert an all-out battle in her kitchen. "Dr. Abernathy said that some awful ruffians came to the house last night and broke in."

"Aye, I know it. It was those men who hit me and injured my cheek." She rubbed her cheek. It was very sore. So was the inside of her mouth. So was her nose. Stupid door.

"My goodness gracious sakes alive!" Mrs. Brandeis dropped the pot she'd been holding. It crashed onto the stove with a frightful noise.

Marjorie winced and repressed the urge to punch Mrs. Brandeis on the jaw. It was rare for her to harbor violent impulses, but so far this morning, she'd fancied murdering Jason and knocking out Mrs. Brandeis. What's more, she'd enjoyed doing both. She wondered who would be next.

As if in answer to her unspoken question, Loretta appeared at the kitchen door, a baby in each arm and a huge grin on her face. "Good morning, all!" she cried in an ungodly cheerful voice. "My goodness, what a crowd!"

Marjorie scowled at her.

Jason got up and went over to take a baby from her arms. "Hello there, Oliver, old man. How are you today?"

The baby burped in his face.

"That's Olivia," said Loretta.

"Olivia, I mean." He turned to Loretta. "You'll be able to tell 'em apart pretty soon."

"*I* already can," Loretta informed him pertly.

Marjorie wished they'd all go away and be happy somewhere else. All this jolliness was making her queasy. Unless that was pain from her nose and cheek. And heart.

Mrs. Brandeis said, "Oh, Mrs. Quarles, you'll never believe what happened here last night!"

Spotting Marjorie still standing like a statue of injured dignity before the stove, Loretta gasped. "Marjorie! What happened to your poor face?" She rushed over to her.

And, to her absolute humiliation, Marjorie burst into tears. Loretta was so kind to her. And Marjorie was such a miserable, wretched, unworthy specimen of womankind. The previous night had been so horrible and frightening and had ended with such a stupendous kiss that Marjorie knew she'd taken much too seriously because nothing Jason Abernathy ever did was serious, and she was so very unhappy about it all that she couldn't hold her misery and indignation and confusion inside of herself another single second.

Darting past Loretta, she raced to her room. She didn't get the door closed in time, and Loretta followed her. She must have foisted Oliver off on someone in the kitchen because both of her arms were free when she threw them around Marjorie.

"Oh, Marjorie, whatever is the matter?"

"I'm an addlepated gudgeon is what's the matter," Marjorie said, her voice thick with tears. "And a nyaff and an ass!"

"Good heavens."

Wrenching away from Loretta, Marjorie flung herself onto her bed sobbing. "I'm such a fool!"

She didn't see what Loretta did, because her face was buried in her pillow, but she heard the door close softly. "What happened, Marjorie?"

The bed dipped as Loretta sat beside her. Marjorie rolled over and tried to wipe her eyes, but tears kept leaking out. And now she was going to have swollen red eyes to go with her fat cheek and broken nose. Life was perfectly hateful, and she wished she were dead. She said as much to Loretta.

"Oh, you poor dear." Loretta hugged Marjorie in an effort to comfort her. "You're such a wonderful person, and you have so much to offer the world. I'm so sorry you were attacked last night. It's probably all my fault for allowing that poor girl to stay here."

"Nay, it isna," snuffled Marjorie. "It's just . . . everything." She couldn't admit to having been seduced into an indiscreet kiss by Jason Abernathy. Or that she'd enjoyed it and wished it had gone on and on. That would be too pathetic an admission.

She heard the door open quietly and her heart fell. Oh good. Just what she needed were more witnesses to her pitiful condition. She wiped her cheeks and eyed the door malevolently. She wasn't surprised by what she saw. It was as if God had decided to heap coals of fire upon her head this morning for some reason beyond her ken, unless God just hated her for no particular reason.

Jason Abernathy stood there, in her bedroom, an expression of concern upon his face. She didn't believe that concerned expression for a second and fell back onto her pillows with a groan.

Turning to see who had entered, Loretta said, "Oh, hello there, Jason. I think Marjorie needs to be examined. Her cheek is horribly bruised, and her nose is swollen."

As were her eyes, although her self-respect had shrunk to about nothing. "Nay," she muttered. "He needn't bother. I'll be fine."

"Pooh," said Loretta briskly. She would. A wail from the kitchen made her pop up from the bed. "I think the babies want to be fed. I'll just leave the two of you here for a few minutes. Check her nose, Jason. I hope it's not broken." With a pat to Marjorie's shoulder, Loretta trotted out of the room.

Abandoned again, Marjorie thought bitterly. She frowned at Jason. "Ye needna bother examining me. I iced my cheek last night and can do as much for my own nose, thank you."

"Nonsense. Let me have a look."

As if she had a choice with the entire household parked right outside her bedroom door waiting to pounce if she should scream or shout at Jason or slap his arrogant face. With an aggrieved sigh, she sat up. "Do your worst."

He sat next to her on the bed—a shocking thing to do, even for a doctor, in Marjorie's considered opinion, not that Jason or Loretta would think so—and took her hands. "Please, Marjorie, what's the matter? I hope you're not holding last night against me."

Through her swollen eyelids, she glared at him, thinking *as you held* me *against* you? But of course, he wasn't thinking about the kiss. The kiss that had meant nothing to him and everything to her. He

was talking about the attack upon her person by the
two brutes, Bart and Frank. "Nay. I'm'na."

"I'm relieved to hear it. Now, let me take a look
at that cheek."

So, her humiliation complete, Marjorie submitted to forces more powerful than she, and allowed
the man she'd come to love—

Good Lord, she didn't mean that!

With a sinking feeling in her heart, she feared
she did.

Well, whatever her state of emotion regarding
Jason, she allowed him to probe the bruise on her
cheek, then stick his finger and a tongue depressor
into her mouth and observe the cut on the inside of
said cheek. How utterly and completely embarrassing.

"Hmm," Jason noised. "I'd better dab some iodine on that cut."

Marjorie said, "Uhk." It was all she could say
under the circumstances. Then she submitted
docilely while Jason dabbed iodine on the inside of
her cheek. It stung like fire, but she bore it without
a whimper.

"Nasty cut," Jason murmured, frowning. "I hope
it heals quickly. It should."

"Mmm."

"Now let me take a look at your nose. How'd you
do this?"

"Ran into the door." Because she'd locked it
against him the night before and had forgotten
about it when Mrs. Brandeis screeched and woke
her up this morning. Because of him. She didn't
add that part.

"How strange," he muttered, reaching for said
protuberance. When he wiggled her nose gently, it
didn't hurt much. "Do you often run into doors?"

"No." She didn't like having him this close to her. As he probed her nose, she had to stare straight into his sparkling, sapphire-blue eyes, and that made the impulse to throw her arms around him rise up in her like a persistent ache.

"Wonder why you did this morning." His voice had gone softer. "Does this hurt?" He tweaked a little harder.

"No."

"Good." His hand moved sideways from her nose and caressed her cheek.

Marjorie repressed an urge to purr. She couldn't account for why his amazing blue eyes seemed to be getting larger. Blinking because the sensation was so odd, she opened her mouth to say something—she didn't know what—when suddenly she understood everything, because he kissed her. Sweetly and deeply and thoroughly. With a sigh, she sank back onto her pillows again, this time taking Jason Abernathy with her.

She'd completely lost track of time—and space and everything else—and could never afterward say what might have happened if a knock hadn't peremptorily sounded at her bedroom door. Jason leaped to his feet as if he'd been shot from a cannon. Marjorie, dazed but noticing that her bosom was peeking out from her nightgown for all the world to see, snatched a pillow and covered herself with it.

"Aha," said Loretta, grinning from ear to ear. "I see the examination is over."

Marjorie was perhaps more shocked than she'd ever been in her life when Loretta deliberately glanced at Jason's crotch. When she looked herself, she saw an enormous bulge, and felt herself go hot with embarrassment.

ELEVEN

"Marjorie's going to take a bath now," Loretta announced, coming back into the kitchen whence Jason had fled as soon as he could. He heard the bath water running even as she spoke in the bathroom between Jia Lee and Marjorie's bedrooms. She added, "You sly dog, you."

Acutely uncomfortable, he resented Loretta's knowing grin. "It was a momentary aberration," he muttered under his breath. "I need to examine Jia Lee now."

"Momentary aberration, my hind leg." Loretta added a snort to her caustic comment. "You're in love with the woman, Jason Abernathy. Why don't you just admit it and marry her?"

"Nonsense. Who said anything about marriage?" He groped around in his black bag irritably. *Who'd said anything about love, for that matter?* Love. Huh. "Where's my stethoscope?" If he'd left it in Marjorie's room, he might just have to buy another one. He'd be damned if he'd risk going back in there again. Not that Marjorie would let him.

Damn, he was a fool! How could he have been such an ass? And the worst part was that if Loretta hadn't interrupted them, Marjorie would no longer be a virgin at this moment—and Jason would be staring matrimony square in the face with no way out.

Ah, there it was. "I have to examine Jia Lee." Stethoscope dangling, he frowned at Loretta. "Shall I just knock on the door?"

Mrs. Brandeis and the maids had left the kitchen, and Loretta was at present occupied in feeding the twins. Although Jason had never once, in all the years he'd known her, thought about Loretta as a particularly maternal woman, she certainly seemed to have taken to motherhood with élan. He was happy for her. Even though he was also angry with her at the moment for having seen him in a compromising situation with Marjorie. *Damn* it! How could he have done such a damned fool thing?

"Go ahead. Just be sure to shut the door after you. I'll keep anyone busy who comes to the kitchen until you're through."

Marjorie had fled the house by the time he was finished examining Jia Lee. So had Loretta. It was Mrs. Brandeis who told him so when he found her in the front parlor arranging a bouquet of fall flowers from Loretta's garden.

"They trotted out together as happy as you please, to *take a walk* as if the missus hadn't just born twins not a month ago." The older woman shook her gray head in disapproval. "It's scandalous."

Although he didn't feel the least bit jolly, Jason managed a laugh. "You ought to be used to Loretta by this time, Mrs. B. Anyhow, the twins are almost four weeks old. I don't suppose a walk will hurt her. The exercise will do her good."

The housekeeper sniffed.

Another thing about brisk walking was that it helped a person release pent-up frustrations. Jason feared it would take more than a walk or two to release his own frustrations, but he didn't have the option anyway. He'd driven his Hudson to Loretta's last night, and he supposed he had better drive it home again.

So, his breast seething with confusion, anger, and perturbation and trying to decide what the devil Marjorie meant to him, he cranked his Hudson, stomped on the low-speed pedal, flooded his engine, and swore. That didn't help either.

Nevertheless, and because the Chinatown situation was almost as much of a worry to him as the Marjorie situation, he decided to stop by his office before going upstairs to his living quarters above the clinic to change into clean, unwrinkled-by-sleeping-at-a-kitchen-table clothes.

As the Hudson approached the Chinatown district, Jason began to feel better. As little as he had been or ever would be accepted into the Chinese community in San Francisco as a member, he still understood it better than he did his feelings regarding Marjorie.

And, also unlike with Marjorie, he could admit freely and openly that he loved it. He loved the food, the music, the colors, and the art. He loved the faint scent of incense that always and forever permeated the air in the neighborhood of his clinic. He loved the click of Mah-Jongg tiles and the chatter of the men gambling in upstairs rooms that floated down into the streets.

He had loved Mai with his whole being. No matter what that damned little voice in his head kept implying, he had adored her with all the ardor within him. He'd redirected that ardor to his medical practice with some success. Marjorie had no place in his real life. Not in Chinatown. Not in his clinic. Not in his work. She'd be completely out of place there.

She did pretty well that night when the tongs battled, his pesky little voice reminded him. He told it to shut up. Everyone was allowed a deviation or two in his or her lifetime. That evening at his clinic had been Marjorie's one and only deviation from a life of absolute conformity.

His heart sank when he started down Grant and he saw what was going on. Clustered here and there were groups of people. To a man—since there were no women on overt display—they were talking and pointing at something stuck on a lamppost or a wall or the side of a building. Without even being able to discern the object of interest, a telltale flash of red every once in a while told him what it was: a red sheet.

"Damn." He supposed it would be too much of a coincidence for this particular red sheet, or murder-for-hire notice, to be unrelated to the Jia Lee incident of the prior night. What in the name of God was this going to mean for Marjorie? For Loretta's entire household for that matter?

He told himself that no one as yet knew for certain that Jia Lee was *in* Loretta's house. If Marjorie was to be believed, and Jason told himself she was, she hadn't let on by so much as a blink of her eye that she knew what the men were talking about when they asked for the "Chinese gal."

Why in the world were they looking at Loretta's house anyway? It didn't make any sense. Loretta had for years agitated for her causes, but the Chinese problem hadn't figured large among those causes. Sure, she wrote letters to the *Chronicle* and the *Call* decrying the Chinese Exclusion Act and demanding that it be repealed, but she was more apt to be vocal about women's suffrage and unionization than that.

So what spark of inspiration had led someone to direct his hatchet men to Loretta's house?

The question was a vexing one, and Jason hadn't solved it by the time he pulled the Hudson to a stop in front of his clinic where another small crowd of Chinese men had gathered. As soon as they saw him, they hurried to surround his automobile, all asking him questions and waving red sheets at him.

With a sigh, he climbed out of the Hudson and greeted the men, all of whom were either patients or neighbors of his clinic. One of the men handed him a red sheet that had been torn off a wall. Jason read it with interest, his brows beetling.

"Who is this?" he asked, pointing to the Chinese characters that meant "Great Boss." He'd never heard of this person before, and he'd believed himself to be familiar with all the tong leaders and their associates. Anyhow, no self-respecting Chinese would call himself Great Boss, for God's sake. He'd use his family name. That was the purpose of the tongs in the first place: to provide social clubs for the various extended families.

"Nobody knows," said Lo Sing, who had come outdoors to greet Jason. "I've never even heard of anyone called Great Boss. It's absurd."

A chorus of babble rose up around the two men. Jason held up a hand to stop the confusion. "Hold on. I can't hear any of you if you all talk at once. Does anyone know who this is?" He pointed at the name on the red sheet.

Mr. Hsiu, a bent old man who had to use a cane, nodded, and Jason, deferring to him because of his age, nodded back. "Mr. Hsiu?"

A spate of creaky Chinese informed Jason that nobody knew who the Great Boss was. They only knew for certain that the man was white, that he dealt in importing girls from China, and that people in Chinatown were afraid of him.

Jason heaved a huge sigh. "I've heard that, too. But nobody has any clue as to who he might be?"

Apparently they did not, or they weren't saying. In so many damned ways, Chinatown was a society closed to him, a white man, even though he'd lived there for years. Feeling stymied and hating it, he asked the man who'd handed him the red sheet, "May I keep this?"

The man nodded, and the crowd began to disperse, mumbling and still chattering among themselves. Jason and Lo Sing went into the clinic. Jason sat behind his desk, sagging and discouraged. "What the devil's going on, Lo Sing?"

With a shrug, Lo Sing said, "You have as much information as I have."

Jason shook the red sheet. "Is this the same guy who brought Jia Lee to the States?"

"I guess so. It makes sense that it's the same person. Of course, he's not the only white man importing singsong girls, so maybe it's not. Your guess is as good as mine."

Jason didn't begrudge Lo Sing the taint of acrimony in his voice. Jason was pretty bitter about the situation himself. "This is only going to make things worse," he muttered.

"For a while anyway."

This time both men sighed in chorus.

To Marjorie, it didn't seem right that the world should go on as if nothing had happened in it, when her own personal life had just been tipped on its ear. From her obtaining the part of Mabel in *Pirates,* to Jason hiding a Chinese girl in the room next door to hers, to a couple of brutal thugs breaking in to snatch the girl away again, to Jason's impassioned kiss, Marjorie was fairly certain her own personal world would never be the same again.

Yet Mrs. Brandeis still cooked meals, Li and Molly cleaned the house, Loretta and the babies thrived, Captain Quarles managed his extensive business affairs and got richer, Mr. Peavey still muttered about the Moors, and Marjorie still sang in the church choir.

That being the case and it was Sunday morning, she set out to walk to church feeling even more out of place in the universe than usual. She had taken special pains with her toilette that morning, hoping to make herself feel a little more human. It hadn't worked emotionally, although she did look quite fine, thanks to Loretta. Loretta paid her much more than her duties were worth, and she was forever buying her clothes.

Today's ensemble consisted of a pretty cotton crepe dress with woven stripes. The overall impression was of brown stripes on a cream background, and the dress had piping on the collar and turned-back cuffs made of mercerized crepe.

Her shoes and handbag matched the brown stripe in the dress, and her hat, also brown, was made in a design Loretta had designated as a "Matador's hat." It sported a brown pheasant feather in its brim. Marjorie wore it at a jaunty angle, although it didn't make her feel particularly jaunty, more's the pity. Loretta had allowed the pheasant feather because, she said, she found pheasant feathers in the park all the time. Marjorie didn't exactly connect her feather with those feathers, but she didn't argue. She never argued with Loretta. Almost never.

As luck would have it, her costume earned her admiring glances as she walked briskly up the walkway toward the church's front steps. In fact, Hamilton St. Claire, who stood at the top of the stairs chatting to Ginger Collins, excused himself to Ginger and trotted down the steps to join Marjorie when he spotted her. Marjorie got the impression he'd been waiting for her, although she told herself that was only her vanity speaking.

"Marjorie!" Hamilton took her hand and squeezed it tenderly. "You're looking lovely today."

"Thank you, Hamilton." She bowed her head, faintly embarrassed by Hamilton's public display of approbation—and Ginger's equally public display of fury as she glowered at the couple, turned on her heel, and flounced into the sanctuary. Oh, dear.

Hamilton tucked her hand into the crook of his arm and guided her toward the stairs. "It's a lovely Sunday morning, isn't it?"

"Aye, it's a fine day." A little chilly, but that was to be expected in the autumn. Also, the day was gray and glum, overcast and threatening rain. She supposed many people favored rainy days. Perhaps Hamilton was one of them.

"And the choir's anthem today is one of my favorites."

"Aye, it's a pretty one."

In truth, Marjorie didn't much care for *Nearer My God to Thee*, because every time she heard it, she remembered the night she'd lost her one true love. The *Titanic*'s orchestra had played to the bitter end, and all the musicians had died for their ef-

forts. It was one of the tunes she'd heard as she and
Leonard had parted for the last time. She found it
difficult to keep from crying when she sang it, and
she wasn't looking forward to the experience today.

"I do love autumn," Hamilton said brightly,
thumping his thin chest. "Makes me feel alive."

"Ah." And what, Marjorie asked herself, was a
body supposed to say to that? She hadn't a notion.

Fortunately, she was spared the need to answer
because they entered the church and there were
other people to smile at, greet, and shake hands
with. Hamilton seemed reluctant to release her
arm, but he did, thank God. After saying hello to
several acquaintances, Marjorie hurried to the
choir room to don her robe, Hamilton hard on her
heels.

As luck would have it, the first person she met in
the choir room was Ginger Collins. Because she
could perceive no polite alternative—anyhow, it
was Ginger who had the problem, not Marjorie—
she smiled graciously. "Good morning, Ginger."

"Good morning, Marjorie."

One could have iced a drink with Ginger's tone
of voice. Marjorie hated it when people had a grievance against her. Most of her life had been spent in
an effort to avoid such conditions. The fact that
Ginger's grievance wasn't her fault bucked her up
only slightly.

When Ginger, robed and with her choir book
clutched to her bosom, pushed past her to go to
the stairs to the choir loft, Marjorie sighed.

"What's the matter with her?" Hamilton stared
after Ginger in plain bafflement.

You, thought Marjorie. She said, "I don't know."

The choir proceeded to their assigned chairs

while singing the introit as soon as Reverend Sargent greeted the congregation. It was a tradition.

Tradition. Sometimes it seemed to Marjorie as if tradition was the only thing that held the battered bits of her internal self together. She valued it this morning as she'd seldom had reason to in recent days. She prayed hard during the opening prayer, too, asking the Lord for strength to survive this present chaos in her life. Not to mention the strength to resist Jason's embraces and her own unladylike impulses.

Not for Marjorie MacTavish was Loretta's devotion to free love. Whatever that was.

And then she opened her eyes and beheld Jason himself sitting halfway down the right-hand row of pews, his neck twisted, and his bright blue eyes sparkling directly at her. At once, she squeezed her own eyes shut and sent another desperate prayer to the heavens. Her fervent prayer didn't keep her from hearing a feminine snort from the row behind her. Ginger. Second soprano. Who had also spotted Jason in the congregation. Wonderful. Simply bluidy wonderful.

She managed to get through the church service somehow. So alarmed was she by Jason's unexpected appearance in church, of all unlikely places, that she didn't even think about Leonard as she sang the soprano part to *Nearer My God to Thee*. Small mercy. Now she had to face Jason a mere day after she'd made a total fool of herself with him. On her own bed. In Loretta's house. How would she ever live it down?

Having no clue how to answer that question, Marjorie endured. Every now and then, she entertained the caustic notion that that's what she'd done all her life: endure. A little enjoyment now and then wouldn't be unwelcome.

Except that she wasn't sure she knew how to enjoy things anymore. How pathetic.

Reverend Sargent, an ardent speaker whose sermon this morning Marjorie hadn't heard a word of, said the last prayer and intoned the last "Amen," and Marjorie and the choir stood for the choral benediction.

And then it was over, and she had to face her doom. That is to say, she had to face Jason. For only a moment, Marjorie wondered if anyone would notice if she remained in the choir loft for the rest of the day. A glance at the congregation, surging toward the sanctuary door, and of Jason, who had stood and was now posed rather like a statue staring at her from his pew, disabused her of that notion in a hurry.

"Marjorie, you sounded simply wonderful today. You're in superior voice, my dear." Hamilton took her arm.

He would. "Thank you." Wanting to shake off the fellow's hand, but knowing she was being unreasonable, Marjorie again endured. Fortunately, the choir had their own hallway leading to the choir room, so she could take her time as she hung up her choir robe and readied herself for public inspection once more. With the no doubt ridiculous hope that Jason would get bored and go away before she showed herself in street clothes, Marjorie dawdled. To her dismay, Hamilton dawdled with her.

Then again, perhaps it wasn't a bad thing that Marjorie should face Jason with Hamilton at her side. His presence would at least prevent Jason from making snide references to her moral lapse of

the preceding day. Or perhaps it wouldn't. Jason
didn't possess the respect for social structure and
manners that most people exhibited.

"Are you ready, my dear?"

Why did he persist in calling her his dear? Bother.
"Aye. I'm ready." She took Hamilton's arm, thinking
that not even Jason would allude to a passionate in-
terlude in front of another man. Would he?

She sucked in air when she realized she was
going to discover the answer to that question in
only a few seconds.

"I say, Marjorie, isn't that your friend Dr. Abernathy?"

Marjorie glanced at Hamilton sharply. He didn't
sound as disappointed as Marjorie might have anticipated he would. Another puzzle, and one she didn't
feel like thinking about at the moment. Turning
back to the people gathered in Fellowship Hall for
refreshments after the service, she spotted Jason.
"Aye." She sighed. "It's he." *Confound the man.*

"Fellow seems to be hanging around you a lot
lately, Marjorie. Is there something you're not telling
me?"

Another sharp glance at Hamilton informed
Marjorie that he was enjoying the situation. His
pale blue eyes were bright, although his smile
looked fairly tense. Perhaps he was only young and
unsure of what to do in the face of a rival. If Jason
was a rival. If *Hamilton* was a rival. Marjorie didn't
bolt in the opposite direction as she was tempted to
do and was proud of herself.

One thing was for certain: there was no escape.
Jason had spotted them, frowned, and was now
marching straight at them, reminding Marjorie
of a cavalry charge she'd see in a motion picture

recently. Before he was close enough to do so properly, he spoke. "Marjorie!"

Everyone in the hall turned to see who had spoken so loudly. Marjorie winced before she could stop herself; faked a smile; hurried to meet Jason, dragging Hamilton with her; and hissed at him, "Don't yell at me, confound you!"

"Sorry." Appearing neither sorry nor happy, Jason glared at Hamilton. "St. Claire."

Returning Jason's glare with a silly grin, Hamilton said, "Dr. Abernathy." He didn't let go of Marjorie's arm.

Since Hamilton didn't appear willing to release Marjorie's arm into Jason's custody in spite of his threatening scowl, Jason said, "Listen, Marjorie, I need to talk to you. Right away. It's important."

She just bet it was. "Now?" She put as much incredulity and scorn into the one word as she was able.

"Yes, now." It didn't seem fair to Marjorie that Jason should be able to out-scorn her without even trying.

Marjorie wavered for only a few seconds. Although she didn't want to be alone with Jason ever again for as long as she lived, she knew they had to discuss the Jia Lee situation.

Perhaps he'd found another place to hide the poor girl. A happy notion. And possible.

Perhaps he wanted to discuss strategies for keeping Jia Lee and the Quarleses safe. Less likely but also possible.

Perhaps he wanted to apologize for putting her in a compromising position. Not bluidy likely.

Nevertheless, she recognized her duty when she saw it, even if it did entail speaking with Jason privately. "Vurra weel," she muttered, her Scots coming out in force as it did when she was perturbed.

"If you don't care to speak with this fellow, Marjorie . . ." Hamilton let the sentence hang.

Irrational annoyance with Hamilton warred with gratitude that he would be willing to take up the cudgels of righteousness on her behalf. She opted to demonstrate gratitude. "No, no. I really mun— must—speak with Dr. Abernathy for a moment." Judging from Hamilton's lifted eyebrows that he couldn't understand why she should be interested in a private conversation with a doctor, she added lamely, "It's about the bairns, ye see."

"Yes," Jason said with much emphasis, ignoring Hamilton's unbelieving eyebrows and taking Marjorie's other arm. He yanked on it. "We need to discuss the babies. Loretta needs help."

And with that esoteric comment, Jason managed to tug Marjorie away from Hamilton but not without a small stumble on Marjorie's part. "Stap hailing on me, ye pernicious gudgeon!"

Stopping short so abruptly that she bumped into him, Jason muttered, "Sorry." He turned to glower at her. "What the devil are you doing with that ridiculous jackass?"

With a step back and a tug at her vest-like waist, Marjorie matched him glower for glower. "We sing in the choir together, ye daft nyaff. And he's'na ridiculous jackass!" Casting a glance around, she hoped no one else had overheard her indelicate speech. Drat Jason Abernathy forevermore!

"Bah. Come here." Taking her hand, Jason pulled her toward the back of the room. "Damn it, now everybody's staring at us."

"I wonder why." Marjorie might have toasted the

words before handing them to Jason, they were so dry. "I'm sure we're all accustomed to seeing men yank women all over church halls."

Jason stopped, turned, and released Marjorie's hand. He threw a guilty glance around Fellowship Hall. Sure enough, at least half the congregation was staring, shocked, in his direction. Hamilton St. Claire scowled at him from across the room. "Sorry, Marjorie. Guess I got carried away for a minute."

"I'm the one who got carried away," Marjorie pointed out. "And if you want to speak to me privately, I might suggest you be more subtle next time."

With a roll of his eyes, Jason said, "Yeah, yeah. I said I was sorry. But listen, Marjorie, we really do need to talk."

Marjorie's chest lurched suddenly and painfully. If he was going to chat about that kiss, she might just have to hit him with her handbag, ruining her forever in the eyes of her church. If he wanted to discuss the problem of Jia Lee, she could survive without doing violence to his person. "About what?"

"About *what?*" Jason goggled at her, something Marjorie resented greatly.

"Yes, ye haggis-headed gudgeon, about what? That poor—" She broke off speaking when she saw Jason's hideous grimace. He was right, drat him. She shouldn't speak of Jia Lee in public, even at a whisper, which she hadn't actually been doing. Trying to make up for it, she hissed, "I meant, do you want to talk about the lotus?"

"Let's get out of here." Again, Jason grabbed her hand.

She managed to shake him off with some difficulty. "Let me say good-bye to my friends first. If you don't want to stir up interest, you're going about this rather the wrong way, don't you think?"

"Oh, for . . . you're right, damn it."

"And don't swear in church."

"We're not in church anymore. We're in . . ." Jason looked around and waved his hand. "Whatever this place is."

"It's the fellowship hall, ye daffle-brained gudgeon." And with that, and assuming an air of confidence she was far from feeling, Marjorie smiled graciously, as if she were taking leave of a friend for a moment, and headed back into the fray. It was a very embarrassing thing to do, thanks to Jason's having called unwanted attention to the two of them, but she braved it out.

Naturally, Hamilton and Ginger wanted to know what the fuss was about. "And why did he grab you like that?" Ginger giggled slyly. "Don't tell me you're secret lovers, Marjorie."

Marjorie refrained from kicking the infuriating, nitwitted, birdbrained twit with her pointy-toed shoe. "Don't be daft, Ginger." Her tone was more curt than usual. "I've been helping Dr. Abernathy at his clinic, and he needs my assistance today." It wasn't too much of a lie. She had helped him there once. And he did need her assistance.

"I thought you were talking about the Quarleses' children," Hamilton said, confirming Marjorie in her opinion that he was rather a pest occasionally.

"That, too," she said through her teeth.

Ginger's pretty little nose wrinkled up. "I don't know how you can bear to do work like that, Marjorie. And on Chinamen, too."

"No," said Marjorie coldly. "I'm sure you don't."

"I think Miss MacTavish is a noble soul," Hamilton said. Although she appreciated the sentiment, his tone of voice was somewhat too syrupy for Marjorie's taste, and she glanced at him sharply. He appeared to be sincere. "But what's this I've heard lately about trouble in the Chinese district, Marjorie? Are you quite sure you'll be safe there?"

Since she discerned nothing but honest concern in the question, Marjorie smiled when she replied. "Indeed, I'll be quite safe there. Dr. Abernathy and his assistant will be at the clinic, you see, and the Chinese in the neighborhood appreciate their work very much." She didn't add that, at the moment, she considered Chinatown a good deal safer than her home with the Quarleses in the upper-crust Russian Hill district.

"Dr. Abernathy's assistant is another Chinaman." Ginger sniffed. "What good will *he* be?"

Marjorie didn't react to Ginger's statement. Rather, she turned to Hamilton. "What have you heard about the troubles in Chinatown, Mr. St. Claire? I'm surprised you've heard anything at all."

Hamilton waved a well-manicured hand in the air. "Oh, you know, I'm a lawyer. We hear all sorts of things. And the situation has been written about in the local newspapers recently, too."

"Really? I don't recall seeing anything about them." Marjorie tried to recall articles concerning the tong troubles, but couldn't.

With a chuckle, Hamilton said, "Oh, my office subscribes to many papers and journals I'm sure you ladies have never heard of."

A spark of resentment rose in Marjorie's breast, no doubt as a result of her association with Loretta. She didn't offer Hamilton a sarcastic rebuttal of his implied slur against women's abilities to comprehend social problems as Loretta would have done. She merely smiled and said, "I'm sure."

As soon as possible after that, she made her escape. Jason had been leaning against the back wall of Fellowship Hall, his arms crossed over his chest, his expression black, and his foot tapping impatiently. He did speak civilly to the Proctors, but he didn't extend himself any farther than that. Marjorie joined him with a frown as dark as his.

"If you want to keep your dealings wi' me a secret, Jason Abernathy, you're going around it in a very queer way."

"I don't want to keep my dealings with you a secret, for God's sake!"

"Shhhh."

Lowering his voice, Jason said, "I only want to keep one aspect of them a secret."

"Hmm."

"Anyhow, why should we try to hide our relationship? We're in the play together, aren't we?"

Their relationship? Marjorie squinted at Jason. Did they have a relationship? What kind of relationship? Although she was dying to know what he meant by the comment, she didn't dare ask. "Where are we going?" she asked instead.

"I'm taking you to lunch. We can be private in a booth at a restaurant I know nearby."

She didn't object. In fact, the notion of being private with Jason held a strange—and dangerous—appeal. She didn't even object when he led her down the street and toward a restaurant that obviously served Chinese fare. After all, she'd eaten Chinese before and lived through the ordeal.

Besides, she'd survived piroshki, hadn't she? Could chow mein be any worse?

TWELVE

The aroma of Chinese food should have made Jason's mouth water. It usually did. Today, however, he couldn't stir up much appetite for anything but the woman seated opposite him in a tucked-away booth of Quan Den's Chop Suey House.

Gilded Chinese paintings hung on the wall, and a scratchy gramophone played recorded Chinese music. Jason wondered where the owners had found such things. Hong Kong or Shanghai probably, imported via ship, as were most Chinese goods. Including girls. Most recorded-music shops didn't carry much in the way of Chinese music even here in San Francisco.

"So what do you propose?" Marjorie sat, stiff and prim, in the seat opposite his. Her lips scarcely moved when she asked the question, and she hadn't made a move to pick up her spoon. This boded ill.

Jason also wished she hadn't used that word. It was too close for comfort to what he'd been wanting to do. Not, naturally, that he'd ever ask Marjorie, of all people, to marry him. No matter how much he lusted after her.

"I don't know." He scowled into his bowl of egg-drop soup. Better than scowling at Marjorie. Each of the booths in this small restaurant were made private by a screen of hanging beaded strings. A few tables were set in the middle of the restaurant for those who didn't need or want to be private. The dim electrical lights on the ceiling made colors dance across Marjorie's face, giving her a mysterious air. Not that she wasn't mysterious anyway, given her aloofness and defensiveness, but she looked even more so today.

"I hate to move her," he went on. "She's beginning to trust us. If I take her somewhere else, she'll have to adjust to a whole new set of circumstances and people, and she'll only become frightened again. Besides, the more we move her around, the more chances there are for someone to spot her."

"But if they keep trying to find her in Loretta's house, they'll probably succeed one of these days, because she's there. Besides, if you keep her there, more people than she will be in danger."

"I know." He heaved a gigantic sigh and sipped his soup.

Finally, Marjorie condescended to pick up her spoon. She took a very small sip of her own soup, then eyed her spoon with misgiving. "I've never seen a spoon like this before."

"Chinese," muttered Jason. "They carve them out of bone." Her nose crinkled, and he added, "Don't worry, they wash the bone first." With a stab at sarcasm, he said, "Be brave for once, can't you? It's only soup, and it hasn't killed anyone yet."

She gave him a very good frown and dipped her spoon again. "I'm not refusing to eat the stuff. Besides, I've eaten Chinese food before." She sniffed meaningfully.

The stuff. Huh. "It's tasty. You have to admit that it's tasty."

"Aye," she said grudgingly. "It is tolerably tasty."

He put his spoon down. "Do you think they know she's there? Really *know*?"

At last she made eye contact. She'd avoided doing so until this moment. "I don't know. Those two hoodlums asked for the Chinese girl, and I said I didn't know what they were talking about."

"Hmm. I wonder why they chose Loretta's house to look for her."

Shaking her head, which was at present crowned with a flat hat tilted at an angle that looked remarkably fetching on her, she said, "I have no idea." With unbecoming sarcasm, she added, "Perhaps because you and Loretta are known to be best friends, and you both support all sorts of unorthodox causes."

"They aren't unorthodox," Jason grumbled.

"Hmm."

The beads at their sides rattled, and a smiling Chinese waiter in a crisp white robe appeared. "Main course," he said in heavily accented English.

"Thank you." Jason sat back as the plates were placed on the table before them. He didn't watch the food; he watched Marjorie. In spite of his mood and the seriousness of what they needed to discuss, he felt a tingle of amusement as she eyed each dish as the waiter set it down in front of her. He could tell what she was thinking. She recognized the rice for what it was. She had grave suspicions about the chicken with cashew nuts. And she was clearly afraid of the shrimp with vegetables and garlic.

"It's all very good, Marjorie. Don't look so frightened."

She lifted her head with a jerk. "I am'na frightened!"

"Right." He lifted his chopsticks. Marjorie had been provided with a knife and fork. "I'll just put a little bit of this on your plate. You'll see. It's delicious."

He did as he said he would, piling approximately a tablespoonful of rice onto her plate, and a teaspoonful each of the other delicacies. On his own plate, he mounded as much as would fit, then dug in with relish.

Marjorie didn't exactly dig in at all. She forked up a tiny bit of chicken with some rice and tasted it, a thoughtful expression on her face. Her eyebrows lifted in surprise.

"Good, isn't it?"

"I must admit that it is." She took a deep breath and forked up some of the vegetables and shrimp, leaving the rice aside as if she were finally willing to chance something new without something familiar along with it to give her comfort. Again her eyebrows lifted.

"See?" said Jason, swallowing. "It's good." He reached over and dished up more of all three selections onto her plate.

"Thank you. Aye, it's vurra good."

To his surprise, she looked him square in the eye and smiled. "And it's the second time I've experimented with food recently, too, so your nasty comment about my not being brave was off the mark." She sounded proud of herself.

"The second time?"

"Aye. I had Russian food at the Panama-Pacific Exhibition."

"Oh. Right." He frowned, having forgotten about that humiliating day. Damn Hamilton St. Claire as a benighted prig and a bounder.

"Aye."

They ate in silence for a few minutes. Jason discovered that his appetite had come back to him the instant Marjorie gave her approval of the fare. Strange, that. After demolishing most of the food on his plate, he sat back, sighed, and returned to the pressing issue of Jia Lee. "I'm worried that even if we move her, people will still try to invade Loretta's house."

"Why should they if she's not there?"

"Because if they don't know she *is* there, they won't know when she's *not* there," he pointed out. Picking up his tiny teacup, he sipped some fragrant tea. He really did feel a special kinship to Chinese history and culture, which was one of the reasons he found his attraction to Marjorie so remarkable. She was as remote from anything Chinese as a body could get.

"Ah. Aye, that's so."

Her frown made him itchy. "I know, I know. I should never have brought her to Loretta's house. It put all of you in jeopardy. But I didn't know what else to do at the time, and it was critical that I take her somewhere before the louts who'd been after her traced us. She was badly injured, don't forget, and I couldn't very well just let her go. She had no place *to* go."

Setting her fork down, Marjorie sighed. "Aye, I know. You made a quick decision. I'd probably have made the same one."

His own eyebrows shot up. "Is that a conciliatory statement from our own Marjorie MacTavish? How unusual."

"Blast you, Jason Abernathy!"

He winced. "Sorry. I didn't mean that the way it sounded."

"I'm sure." With sharp, angry gestures, Marjorie

folded her napkin, set it beside her plate, and scooped up her small handbag from the seat beside her. "I willna stay here and be insulted by you! I've taken enough of that sort of thing from you. And I willna do it anymore."

Reaching across the table, Jason grabbed her wrist. "No, Marjorie, don't run off in a huff. I'm sorry. I didn't mean it."

The beads at their side rattled again, and a most unwelcome and entirely too hearty voice said, "I thought I heard your lovely voice, Marjorie!" Hamilton St. Claire nodded at Jason. "Dr. Abernathy. Sorry for intruding like this, but I wanted to see if I was correct." He giggled, thoroughly irritating Jason, who didn't approve of men giggling. "I do love this restaurant, don't you?"

"Hamilton!" Marjorie, clearly as startled as Jason by this sudden intrusion, dropped her handbag on the table. "I didna know you were here."

"Miss Collins and I were taking a bite of lunch. I see the two of you had the same idea."

"Yes, we did." Jason eyed him suspiciously. "I don't suppose your table is anywhere near ours, is it?"

Marjorie gave him a searching glance.

"No indeed. We're across the room." Holding the beaded curtain back, Hamilton pointed, and Ginger gave them a finger wave. She wore a silly smile on her face, as if she felt she had somehow scored a point against Marjorie.

Jason, who couldn't account for his sudden jolt of suspicion, nodded. He didn't chalk this meeting up to coincidence of course, although he guessed he could acquit St. Claire of having designs on Jia Lee. He definitely had designs on Marjorie, damn the fellow.

"We were just finishing up here," he said gruffly. "Then I'll see Miss MacTavish to her home."

"Of course, of course. Just wanted to say hello. Ta-ta, Marjorie."

"Good afternoon, Hamilton," Marjorie said formally.

Jason silently blessed her for sounding as annoyed as he felt. Maybe she wouldn't fall for the sissified Hamilton St. Claire and his money and his breeding. Not that Jason himself didn't have money and breeding but, according to his parents and their socially snobbish friends, he'd been flying in the face of both of those privileges his entire adult life. He'd expected his father to disown him when he married Mai, but since she'd died shortly thereafter, the old man had forgiven him. Not, Jason thought bitterly, that he had any reason to be forgiven, not having done anything the least bit shameful except love a good woman.

Damn it, he didn't want to think about that right now. The beads dropped back into place, and he scowled at Marjorie. "Do you think they heard what we were talking about?"

"Of course not!" She looked at him as if she considered him not merely an idiot but a particularly pernicious one. "And what if they did? Would it matter? Surely you don't suspect Hamilton St. Claire or Ginger Collins of attempting to abduct the lotus."

It did sound silly when she said it aloud. "Of course I don't," he retorted irritably. "I just don't like coincidences."

"Balderdash. This restaurant is close to the church. I'm sure there are others from the congregation here. You're not the only one who likes to dine out on a fine Sunday afternoon, you know."

"Of course, of course." Jason plucked some bills from his wallet and threw them onto the table. Marjorie's eyes opened wide, and he glanced at the money. Sheepishly, he scooped up a couple of the bills, understanding that ten dollars for a one-dollar meal was fairly excessive. Marjorie rattled his senses, damn it. It wasn't like him to throw money around.

"Come on. We can talk in the clinic." He took her arm; nodded at Hamilton and Ginger, who were smirking from their table; offered the Chinese owner a friendly good-bye; and left the restaurant. "It's not far. We can walk, if you don't mind."

"I don't mind. I can use some exercise after that meal."

"It was good, wasn't it?"

"Aye. Very."

Jason felt an unaccountable surge of pride at having succeeded in pleasing Marjorie for once.

The crisp autumn air was bracing after the warm, foody atmosphere of the restaurant, and Jason discovered his mood was bright and his step was jaunty. He allowed himself only a second or two to consider that this phenomenon might owe something to the company he was in. Down that path lay too many perils, and he didn't need any more things to worry about than he already had at the moment. Before he could even begin to think about what Marjorie was coming to mean to him, he had to solve the problem of Jia Lee.

"Weather's nice," he said, attempting in that way to reinforce his hope that it was the weather and not Marjorie that was affecting his mood.

"Aye," said she. "Brisk."

And that was that. Neither one of them spoke as they traversed the sidewalks of San Francisco. As they neared Chinatown, the atmosphere changed as it always did, and Jason's perky mood got even perkier. He couldn't really account for why he loved this part of his city. God knew, his appreciation had nothing to do with his upbringing.

Gradually, the conversations they overheard as they walked past other people changed from mostly English to mostly Chinese. The air they breathed, always tangy with salt and creosote, became mingled with the aromas Jason would forever associate with Chinatown: fragrant teas; salt vegetables; and always, always, a faint, elusive hint of sandalwood incense.

He'd just taken a deep breath, preparatory to breaking the silence prevailing between himself and Marjorie, when suddenly the air was knocked out of him by a vicious blow to his back. Marjorie screamed. Jason, scrambling to keep his feet under him, whirled around to see what had happened, and was horrified to find Marjorie crumpling to the sidewalk. Two brutish men, hooded and enormous and carrying cudgels, charged at him, their purpose clear, even if their faces weren't.

But Jason hadn't merely devoured Chinese food and culture during his years in Chinatown. He'd also become fairly well acquainted with the old Chinese martial art of Taijiquan.

Even though he was no expert, he still managed to kick out smartly and fell one villain with a blow to his midsection. In a flash, he'd snatched the fallen brute's cudgel and warded off a blow from his companion with it. Still in a crouched position, he knocked the second hoodlum in the knee with a sharp kick. The man bellowed, dropped his own cudgel, and as quickly as they'd attacked, the two men ran away. Both of them limped, making Jason's heart soar a second before it plummeted as he beheld Marjorie's still form huddled at his feet.

"Marjorie!" He knelt beside her, wanting to take her into his arms and knowing that might be the worst thing he could do for her.

She stirred.

"Don't move," he said, palpating her head like mad. It looked to him as though her pretty hat, now squashed and not so pretty, might have cushioned the cudgel's blow. He ripped it off her glorious, shiny hair, prompting a squeal of pain from her. "Sorry. Don't move. I want to see if you have a concussion."

A crowd had gathered. As a rule, the Chinese avoided the problems of whites who invaded their neighborhood, but everyone in the neighborhood knew and respected Jason, so the crowd consisted of a variety of facial characteristics and colors. Glancing around, Jason rapped out an order in Chinese. "Go to my clinic and fetch Lo Sing and a litter." Several people darted off.

"What happened?" Marjorie lifted a hand to her head and grimaced. "It hurts."

"I'm sure it does. We were attacked."

"Attacked?"

Her beautiful green eyes blinked at him. He longed to hold her in his arms, to cradle her and tell her that he wouldn't allow anyone to hurt her again ever. Because doing so would not only be dangerous if she had sustained a concussion but also incredibly stupid, he only answered her question. "Yes. And damned if I know why."

She lifted her eyebrows, and he understood the

question. "I can't imagine why they'd do this for that reason."

"Let me sit up, please," she said. "I dinna like it here on the ground."

"Not until I know you won't hurt yourself more."

"Jason!"

Looking up, Jason beheld Lo Sing and several other Chinese men racing toward him. "Thank God."

"What?" Marjorie blinked blearily.

"Here's Lo Sing with a litter. We'll take you to the clinic where I can examine you more carefully."

"This is vurra embarrassing," muttered Marjorie.

Her complaint was so utterly typical of her that Jason actually laughed. "It'll be all right in a few minutes," he promised, hoping he was right. "Don't talk."

A glance at the people surrounding her made Marjorie shut both her mouth and her eyes. Jason got the impression she was either wishing she could disappear or praying for deliverance.

For a moment or two after she awoke, Marjorie didn't know where she was, why she was there, or why her head hurt. When she reached up to feel the sore spot, she encountered a bandage covering a lump the size of an egg, and it all came back to her.

"Och, God," she moaned, unsure of whether she found the wound or the place she lay more of a problem for her. Because she was currently occupying Dr. Jason Abernathy's personal, private bed in his personal, private bedchamber located above his clinic on the corner of Grant and Sacramento Streets in Chinatown.

How shocking. Not to mention degrading. And then there was the fact that it was relatively frightening to know that she and he had been attacked on a public street by two armed—with cudgels as weapons but they still had been armed—hooligans on what should have been a peaceful Sunday afternoon.

Loretta would have been delighted if such a thing had happened to her.

Marjorie snorted. In some respects, Loretta was a fool. Not that Marjorie didn't love her like a sister.

With a groan, she swung her legs over the side of the bed. At least Jason hadn't undressed her but had allowed her to do the deed herself. Glancing down at the white Chinese robe now adorning her person, she couldn't understand the small stab of disappointment that speared her at the knowledge that she and not he had wrapped the silken garment around her. She frowned, knowing that the stab had been not merely outrageous and foolish but probably irreligious and immoral as well.

She glanced around the room curiously. So this was where Dr. Jason Abernathy lived. Interesting. His fascination with all things Chinese was evident here. The room was filled with Chinese art, both silk hangings and painted landscapes. They were beautiful, although they made Marjorie feel somehow alone and isolated, as if she and not they were the alien entity in this room of the man she . . . er . . . was beginning to trust as a friend. She scowled, knowing that wasn't the right description, but she didn't care to examine it further at the moment. She had plenty of problems to occupy her without having to worry about her feelings for Jason.

Jade and ivory ornaments sat here and there, artistically arranged on tables and bookcases. Marjorie wondered if Jason had accepted the gewgaws in payment for his medical services. It was a good thing the man came from money, because he assuredly didn't make much in his practice, which was all but a charity clinic.

With a deep inhalation of breath, Marjorie decided she liked the fragrance permeating the room. It was a flowery, somewhat spicy scent that she knew she'd forever associate with Chinatown and the jasmine and sandalwood incense so prevalent there. Pushing herself up from the bed, she stood still for a moment, testing her ability to maneuver without falling over or bumping into things.

After a few seconds, she decided that, except for the lump on her head, she felt fine, and the pain from that was isolated at the site of the lump. She didn't know if that was a good thing or not, but she suspected it was. Jason needn't worry about concussion if she was any judge. Of course, she wasn't, but that didn't deter her from her mission of exploration. After all, she'd never again have this opportunity.

The notion made her feel quite gloomy. She shoved the emotion away resolutely.

Discovering the bathroom without any trouble, Marjorie was pleased to note that he had full indoor plumbing. She took advantage of it, slightly embarrassed to be doing so in a bachelor's quarters, but more interested than abashed.

Delightful ginger-, sandalwood-, rose- and jasmine-scented soaps were heaped in a Chinese bowl on the wash stand. Marjorie recognized them from some he'd given to her and Loretta a while back. Naturally one of his patients had made them. She actually

smiled when she shook her head, thinking what a
wonderful man he was, really, in spite of his tendency
toward jocularity in the face of what Marjorie considered serious concerns.

The shake had been a mistake. She pressed her
hand over her lump to prevent her head from falling
off.

Nevertheless, and for the first time, she considered the possibility that Jason might use humor
rather as she used strict manners: as a way of protecting himself from emotional pain by keeping
people at a distance. It was an interesting notion,
and she contemplated it as she explored.

His bedroom was quite lovely, considering its windows opened out onto one of the busier streets in
the Chinese district. A good deal of noise entered
through those windows. But they were accoutered
with pull-down window shades and covered with
filmy curtains that Marjorie suspected had been
handmade for him by another of his patients, probably one of those poor slave girls like Jia Lee. How
sad their situation was. One could only thank Prov-
idence for one's own life, she supposed, even when
one's own life didn't seem exactly perfect.

The thing Marjorie appreciated most of all about
Jason's quarters was the lovely fragrance that permeated everything. Closing her eyes, she sniffed
deeply. Then she opened her eyes fast when she felt
dizzy. Stupid lump.

Some silk flowers stood in a gorgeous Chinese
vase on his bureau, and when Marjorie leaned
closer to inspect them, she realized that they were
fragrant, too. How unusual. The bureau itself was
covered with a perfectly splendid runner of em-
broidered Chinese silk with silken fringes. She

sighed, thinking how nice it would be to have such things in her own room.

Actually, there was no reason she shouldn't have such trappings; they were available right here in Chinatown. Marjorie wondered why she'd never thought about buying Chinese silks before, but not for long. She knew why. Buying Chinese silk would have been a departure from her rigidly structured life and, therefore, frightening.

What a bore she was!

Wandering back to the bed, she fingered the coverlet, which was also Chinese silk, this time in a brocade that was a feast for Marjorie's eyes. Dreamily thinking about Jason alone amid all this beauty, she sat on the bed and then jumped when Jason himself suddenly appeared before her. The jerk made her lump ache, and she pressed it, frowning.

"Marjorie! You're awake. How are you feeling?" Without a thought to propriety—not that it wasn't already too late for that—Jason plopped himself down on the bed beside her.

"My lump hurts," she said, trying to draw away from him.

He threw his arms around her, so she couldn't. "Oh God, Marjorie, I'm so sorry about all of this."

She felt a little fuzzy, perhaps because she'd taken a teeny drop of laudanum before lying down to rest at Jason's command, since he had said he wanted to keep an eye on her for a few hours. "Is it your fault this happened?"

He buried his face against her hair, and Marjorie opened her eyes *very* wide. This wasn't right. This was wrong. This man, who was not her husband or even her fiancé, was out of bounds, holding her in this shocking manner and burying his face in her hair. The embrace felt so good, she had a hard time making herself care.

"It must be my fault." His words were muffled, due to the aforementioned hair.

Marjorie said, "Oh."

"I'm so, so sorry. Lo Sing and I don't know who those fellows were or who sent them."

That was moderately unsettling, Marjorie supposed, although, again, she couldn't quite work up much indignation at the moment. In fact, undoubtedly because of her fuddled condition, she found herself struggling not to turn into Jason's embrace and let herself go entirely. When she felt his lips on her neck, she almost swooned.

Head injuries, she told herself. *They cause these problems*.

That being the case, and because her loose behavior wasn't her fault, she *did* turn into his embrace.

"Oh, Lord, Marjorie, I was so afraid for you."

How nice. She said, "Mmm."

"I'll never forgive myself for what happened today."

Dramatic, but also nice. She repeated herself. "Mmm."

"Look at me."

She did.

"God, your poor head."

And with that, he bent his own head and captured her lips with his. Marjorie melted into the kiss as if she were accustomed to such embraces. His lips were gentle but insistent, and she found herself eager to allow them to do their best.

She meant their worst.

No, she didn't.

She wanted this. She *needed* this. And whatever it led up to.

Did that make her an abandoned woman? She supposed it did. For once in her life, Marjorie discovered she didn't give a hang. Convention could go chase itself. She, for once, was going to enjoy a new experience that was more interesting than food.

"You drive me crazy," Jason mumbled into her hair. "I don't understand it."

Neither did Marjorie, but she was willing to accept whatever it was that seemed to draw the two of them toward each other. It made no more sense to her than it did to Jason. On the surface, they were as unlike as broccoli and newspapers. But oh, how good she felt at the moment. Her head didn't even ache.

She didn't realize her robe had come open until she felt Jason's hand on her breast. How shocking. How terrible.

How absolutely, perfectly wonderful. She knew her nipples had pebbled under his tender assault. She guessed she should be embarrassed, but she wasn't.

"You're perfect, Marjorie."

If her eyes had been open, she'd have blinked in surprise to hear such words coming from the lips of Jason Abernathy, the man whom Marjorie had come to consider the bane of her existence over the past few years. She almost came to the conclusion that she ought to act shocked, even if she didn't feel shocked, when his lips replaced his hand on her breast, and the thrill was such that she forgot about acting any way at all.

Heaven. His touch, his lips, his hands, they were all heaven on her body. How fascinating.

"Everything will be all right, Marjorie. I promise you." Jason's voice was husky.

With a sigh, Marjorie sank back on the pillow, the fragrance of sandalwood wafting around her and her conscience at bay. Everything would be all right. She had Jason's promise on it. "Aye," she whispered.

Her robe was completely open now. Marjorie lay in a soft bed of silk, and she felt rather like a pagan princess—if pagans had princesses—as Jason continued to caress her in places that Marjorie had never in her wildest imaginings dreamed could be caressed. She hadn't once thought about how blissful making love to the right man would be either.

That thought made her remember Leonard. Guilt assailed her so suddenly and sharply that she cried out.

Jason pulled away from her, alarmed. "Marjorie! What is it? Did I hurt you?"

"Aye." She gulped. "Nay. Och, Jason, I dinna know!" And she broke out sobbing.

As gently as if he were dealing with a newborn bairn, Jason took her into his arms and cradled her as she cried. "Marjorie, what's wrong? Did I upset you? I'm so sorry."

Her voice thick and shaky, she whispered, "It's'na you, Jason."

"Can you tell me about it? Did I frighten you? I didn't mean to."

"Nay." He was being so kind to her that Marjorie's guilt expanded to include him as well as Leonard. "I'm sorry," she sobbed. "It's auw my ain fault."

"Nuts. Nothing's your fault, darling."

Darling? Had he really called her darling?

But Marjorie wouldn't allow herself to become distracted. Jason deserved an explanation for her strange behavior. He handed her a clean handkerchief that he'd grabbed from somewhere and that smelled sweet, and she mopped her eyes as he continued to cuddle her to his large, warm chest. His arms were strong, and Marjorie felt safe. She hadn't felt safe for such a long time.

"I guess I got carried away, Marjorie. I'm terribly sorry. It was such a shock to see you injured that—"

She pressed two fingers to his lips. "It's'na you, Jason. It's . . ." A huge well of hurt rose in her chest, but she fought it down. "It's that I just remembered."

"Remembered? Remembered what?"

"It's'na what. It's whom." She took a deep breath. She'd never talked about Leonard with anyone except Dr. Hagendorf since the horrible, horrible night he died. She couldn't account for the urge to tell Jason about him, but she decided to give into it.

"A man?" he asked softly.

She nodded. "Aye. Leonard. Leonard Fleming. We were engaged to be married."

Silence greeted this revelation. Marjorie dared to open her eyes and look at Jason. She was surprised to find that he appeared almost stricken. "Jason? What's the matter?"

"I . . . I didn't know you'd been engaged, Marjorie. Who was the fellow?"

"I just told you. Leonard Fleming."

"But . . . who was he?"

"He was the chief steward on the *Titanic*."

Jason sucked in a breath.

"He died that night. He—" A sob interrupted her.

Jason's arms tightened around her. "I'm so sorry, Marjorie. I'm so, so sorry. I didn't know."

"Nobody knew."

"I'm so sorry."

His voice conveyed such honest sympathy that

Marjorie was strangely comforted. "You've lost a loved one, too, Jason."

"Yes," he said. "I have." After a moment, he said, "But I knew it was coming because Mai was sick. You had no warning."

They stayed that way for a few minutes, wrapped in each other's arms and neither speaking. Marjorie's tears gradually dried up. It was she who spoke first. "I've nivver spoken of Leonard to anyone before, except to that alienist friend of Loretta's."

After a second or two, Jason said, "Will you tell me about him now?"

He sounded as if he truly wanted to hear her story. Marjorie hadn't anticipated this, but she appreciated it. Bracing herself because she wasn't accustomed to confiding in anyone, she began. "We met during our employment, of course. I was a stewardess, ye ken, and he was a steward."

A soothing noise issued from deep within Jason's chest. Marjorie took it as a sound of encouragement. "I loved him." She choked slightly. "I loved him dearly."

"I know you did, sweetheart."

Sweetheart? First darling and now sweetheart. The endearments played upon Marjorie's senses like a healing balm. How odd.

"And that night . . ." Another wave of pain stopped her voice for a moment. Jason only held her, allowing her all the time she needed, God bless him. "I was working on the first-class deck." She almost chuckled but couldn't quite do it. "That's where I met Loretta."

"Good old Loretta."

"Good old Loretta." She paused to swallow the pain in her throat and take a strengthening breath.

"And then, after I'd cleared the first-class deck and everyone was aboon—above, I mean—I went looking for Leonard."

Jason shook his head, anticipating what was coming.

"We found each other, and he led me upstairs to the lifeboats."

"I understand there weren't enough of them."

"Nay. There werena. But he found one and put me into it. I thought he would get in after me, but he didna."

"Women and children first," muttered Jason.

"Aye." She heard the bitterness in her voice. "And he paid for my life with his ain." Her breath caught in her chest with another stab of pain. "Och God, that awful night."

"I know he felt the price was low, Marjorie. He loved you and wanted you to live."

She let that settle for a moment, pondering it and wondering if Jason was right. Unconvinced, she said, "I wanted him to live, too, though. I didna want to be alive in the world wi'out him."

A deep, shuddering sigh escaped from Jason. "I understand, Marjorie. I understand completely."

She looked up at him. "You felt the same, didna you, when your wife died?"

He nodded and looked very, very sad.

They lay on his bed wrapped up in each other's arms for a long time. Marjorie didn't know when she drifted off to sleep.

THIRTEEN

From the other end of the telephone wire, Loretta's voice conveyed deep shock. And extreme titillation. Jason, who was worried sick about Marjorie, was not amused. "I'm keeping her here for observation," he said sternly. "She took a terrible blow to her head."

"Good for you, Jason."

"I mean it, Loretta. This isn't funny. Somebody hired two thugs to intercept us on the street. Marjorie might have been killed. And I don't even know who the villain is."

His words seemed to sober her. "I'm sorry, Jason. You're right. Do you want me to move Jia Lee?"

"No. Just keep her locked in." Thoroughly puzzled and irate that he hadn't been able to spare Marjorie, he said, "I'm calling a private police firm to patrol your house."

"You'd better hire them to patrol your clinic, too."

Frowning furiously, he admitted, "You're probably right."

They hung up after a few more desultory words. After arranging with a private detective agency to patrol the Quarleses' home and his clinic, Jason went back to his office. The sun had set hours before, but Lo Sing had remained, waiting for Jason, because they both knew they needed to discuss the matter of the attack. As far as Jason knew, there were three possible sources of the bullies who'd attacked them on the street: The Chan tong or the Gao tong, either one of which might be worried about losing face in the community, or the white man who had imported Jia Lee. He suspected the last, but didn't have an idea in the world who the man could be. Lord, what a mess.

They didn't solve the problem that night, either, although they discussed it for a couple of hours, picking the pieces of the puzzle apart until there didn't seem to be anything left. And still they had no answer.

"It's unlike a tong to hire thugs to club people. They'd be more apt to send a hatchet man to do me in some night in a dark alley, although I don't know why they'd bother. I'm no threat to anyone." Except to whoever was so eager to get Jia Lee back. Why did they even want her back? He frowned, his confusion as complete and infuriating as ever.

Lo Sing finally said, "I don't think any of the Chinese tongs would go after you, Jason. You're too important to the community."

Too tired to be flattered, Jason muttered, "Maybe. It's probably the merchant. But who the devil is he, Sing? I don't have a clue. Have you heard anything from anyone?"

Lo Sing, who looked approximately as exhausted as Jason felt, shook his head. "Don't know. Could be any one of a number of importers, I suppose."

"Damn." They sat there for a few minutes without speaking. Then Jason swallowed the dregs of his tea, rose, and stretched. "I'm going upstairs. Are you staying here tonight?"

"Yes. I think I'd better."

"I've hired a guard for the building."

"I know, but I'd feel better knowing somebody's here in the office."

With a nod, Jason said, "Thanks. I know none of this is your problem."

Lo Sing gave him a wry smile. "Everything that goes on in Chinatown is my problem, Jason. You know that."

Jason clapped him on the back. "I know. You're a good friend, Lo."

"Likewise."

The two men parted, and Jason dragged himself up the stairs. In a way, he was glad he was so tired, because he wouldn't be so tempted by Marjorie's presence in his bed in his current state of exhaustion.

Or so he thought. As soon as he entered his room, tiptoed over to see how she was doing, and saw her lovely red hair spread out on his pillow, lust surged through him. Ruthlessly driving it back, he smoothed the hair back from her white brow, winced when he saw the bruising that had spread out around the bandage, and told himself he would just have to sleep frustrated that night.

Taking a blanket and pillow from the linen closet, he shucked off his coat and shoes and tried to make himself comfortable on the sofa. Fortunately, he was so tired that he fell asleep even though his efforts failed.

He didn't know how long he'd been sleeping when someone's voice awakened him. Sitting bolt upright, he blinked into the darkness, unable to see a thing and wondering why his back ached and he was hearing voices. Then he remembered, and he listened harder.

"Och nay," Marjorie muttered. Jason heard the bedclothes rustle as if she were thrashing about. "Nay, please."

Befuddled both by Marjorie's words and with sleep, he turned a lamp on low, got up from the sofa, and tiptoed to the bed. The dim light made her appear almost magical. With her fair skin and beautiful red hair, she reminded Jason of a fairy princess from out of the books he'd read as a youngster. She seemed to be asleep and dreaming. To judge by the worried expression on her lovely face, her restlessness, and her mumbled words, the dream was not a pleasant one.

"Nay, Leonard, come wi' me!"

With a jolt of painful clarity, Jason realized she was dreaming about her lost fiancé. He knew he shouldn't be jealous of the late Leonard Fleming, but he was. Hell, he hadn't even known Marjorie existed back then, any more than she'd been aware of his existence. Nothing that went on in her life before he met her should matter to him. But it did, damn it all. Everything about her mattered to him.

"Come wi' me! Leonard, don't leave me!"

Worried about her state of agitation, and feeling such a mixture of emotions in his chest that he couldn't even name them all—although jealousy and pity were uppermost—Jason sat on the bed next to her. Knowing better than to jolt her out of her dream, he laid a hand gently on her shoulder. "It's all right, Marjorie. Everything will be all right."

"Leonard! Is't thee?"

Pain ripped through Jason's chest. "It's Jason, Marjorie. It's Jason Abernathy."

With a gasp and a low cry, Marjorie opened her eyes. She stared up at Jason for a moment, confused. "I . . . I guess I was dreaming."

He nodded and tried to smile. "Looked to me like it was a pretty bad dream."

Lifting a trembling hand, she covered her eyes. "Aye, it was a vurra bad dream."

"I'm sorry, Marjorie."

"Nay. I'm sorry, Jason."

And then, to Jason's utter shock, Marjorie sat up and threw her arms around him. Burying his head in her silky hair, he held on to her with gratitude, not unmixed with desire.

"You're a good man, Jason Abernathy. I didna believe it for a long, long time, but you are."

"Thank you." He felt strangely humbled by her words.

"And I want to make love wi' you."

Startled, he said, "You do?"

"Aye. I do. I want to know what it's like. I do."

He accepted the invitation with joy—and a large dose of concern. "Are you sure about this, Marjorie?"

She nodded. "Aye, I'm sure. I've not been sure of vurra many things in recent years, but I'm sure of this."

"God, I want you. I've wanted you from the moment I saw you."

She laughed softly. "You didna act like it."

"I know it. It's because I felt so guilty about my feelings. I'm sorry."

As gently as he was able, he kissed her. She responded hungrily, and he deepened the kiss, tracing her luscious lips with his tongue and gently prodding her mouth open. She moaned softly, encouraging him to be bold, and he lowered her onto the bed.

Tenderly untying the belt of her robe, he caressed her stomach and feasted his eyes upon her. "You have a beautiful body, Marjorie. And your skin is like silk."

"I want to see what you look like, too, Jason."

His lips quirked into a slight grin. "I never thought I'd hear those words from your lovely lips, darling."

She responded to his humor with a smile of her own. "Nay, nor did I. But it's true."

Her breasts were a delicious handful—not large, but beautifully rounded—and her nipples were hard and delectable. He took one of them in his mouth, and her soft gasp was music to his ears.

"Och, Jason!"

"Does that feel good, Marjorie?"

"Are ye daft? Of course it feels good. Oh my . . ."

That being the case, he proceeded to lavish more attention upon her. She was such a surprise to him. She responded with what seemed like glee, although glee and Marjorie MacTavish didn't fit comfortably together in his brain, at least not in the same sentence. Nevertheless, when he realized she'd unbuttoned his shirt and had begun a tactile examination of his chest, he was more than a little pleased.

Her responses to his ministrations were so gratifying, in fact, that he began to wonder if he'd be able to perform as well as she deserved. It had been more than three years since he'd been with a woman, after all. And poor Mai had been so fragile. It was probably a good thing that he'd had practice being gentle right now, since this was Marjorie's first time—at least, he supposed it was.

"Did you and Leonard ever make love, Marjorie?" He made sure his voice conveyed only interest and not criticism. There was plenty of misery and violence in the world, both of which deserved condemnation. Jason wasn't about to judge people who were guilty only of loving each other.

The question must have shocked Marjorie, though, because her eyes flew open and she said again, only this time with a trace of rancor, "Are ye daft? What kind of woman d'ye think I am? I'm not like Loretta, ye ken."

He chuckled. "I ken. I didn't mean anything. I only wanted to know if this was going to hurt you."

"Hurt me?" She blinked those gorgeous green eyes at him and stopped what she'd been doing with her hands, damn it.

"Well, it sometimes doesn't hurt," he said, wondering where his brain had gone begging that he'd even brought the subject up. "I only wondered."

"Oh. Well, I've nivver done this before."

Now that he'd cleared up the question of her virginity, Jason decided he'd be better off if he just shut up and continued. Her body was a wonder to him. He'd been right about her, too: she hid her passion under a cold exterior, but it was there. And he was stirring it.

His own hunger almost frightened him. His hands shook when he unbuttoned his trousers. "Don't be afraid, Marjorie. I'll never hurt you."

"I know it, Jason."

He believed her, and again felt humbled. The feeling fled as soon as she touched his shaft. "Marjorie!"

"I've never seen one of these before. How strange it looks."

If she backed out now, he was pretty sure he'd die. "It looks worse than it is," he assured her.

She laughed softly. "It doesn't look bad."

Thank God!

"I just didn't expect it, is all."

"I'll make sure you enjoy this, Marjorie. Don't worry."

"Stop telling me not to worry, you gudgeon. I'm'na worried."

Thank God again! He nibbled on her breast, and she sighed with pleasure.

"I'm almost thirty, ye ken, Jason. I want to know what this is like. I'm no Loretta, but I'm a human woman."

His hand tracing her body from her rib cage to her gently swelling hips, he murmured, "You certainly are."

"And I have human feelings." Her hips arched as if seeking something.

He knew what it was, and he whispered, "We're all human, darling, and we all have feelings." He moved his hand slowly and caressingly to the soft red thatch of hair between her thighs, his heart thundering, uncertain how she'd react to this intimacy. "Don't be frightened."

A sharp slap on his shoulder worried him for a second before she said, "I'm not frightened, ye nyaff! Keep doing that. It feels like heaven."

So he did, and again he silently thanked his Maker. He'd have hollered his gratitude to the celestial regions themselves, but he feared Marjorie might consider it a blasphemy. Jason knew it wasn't. This was the physical expression of human love, and he honored it . . . as he honored this woman, whom he had come to love. He didn't want to think about that now, however. He only wanted to feel, for the first time in years, the most intimate and magnificent of human interactions.

Marjorie was moaning softly now, and her hips were arching in the sweet rhythm of love. Jason kissed her lightly, watching her, coveting her reactions to his stroking fingers. He could tell she was coming close to a climax. He was, too, for that matter, and he contemplated entering her.

But no. He wanted to make sure she achieved completion this, her first time with a man. He could wait another minute or two. At least, he hoped he could.

"Och, Jason." Her voice was ragged and a little uncertain.

"It's all right, darling. There's nothing to fear. Just let yourself feel it."

"Oh, *Jason!*"

And her hips bucked, and her arms went around him, and he felt the most amazing series of spasms wrack her body. It was time for him now, dash it, and he took full advantage of the situation. Throwing a leg over her hips and poising for only a moment over her glistening body, he plunged inside her.

Marjorie gasped, shocked. From the most spectacular sensation she'd ever experienced, suddenly she felt as if she were being torn asunder. Good heavens, was *this* what it was all about? She heard Jason's ragged, "I'm sorry, Marjorie. I never meant to hurt you," and her heart melted.

"You didna hurt me, ye daft thing," she whispered, holding him tightly and wondering how she could ever have fallen in love with him. But she had, God save her.

The sensation was interesting after she overcame her initial jolt of alarm about being so intimately invaded. In fact . . .

"God, you feel good."

Marjorie thought about that. Jason was at present plunging into and drawing out of her body in a most extraordinary manner. He was enjoying it, too, if she was any judge—and in this case, she believed she was.

Suddenly, he shuddered and stiffened, and Marjorie felt a man's seed pour into her body for the first time. How absolutely extraordinary! No wonder Loretta advocated free love. If a woman had no legitimate way to experience this, it probably *would* be worth sacrificing one's moral code to do it.

With that thought, Marjorie succeeded in totally scandalizing herself, so she decided it would probably be best if she ceased thinking altogether. It was easy to do, what with Jason's limp body on top of hers, their perspiration mingling in a way that was . . . well . . . rather thrilling, actually.

"Are you all right?"

She could scarcely hear Jason's voice. He sounded as if he'd just run a long, long race and had collapsed in exhaustion at its completion. She understood. "I'm vurra weel, thank you."

That was awfully formal. But Marjorie wasn't sure how to react after the last few astonishing minutes. She was rather embarrassed actually. How did married women face their husbands in the morning after doing this?

Jason's breathing slowed, and he pushed himself away from her, settling at her side, thus allowing her to breath more easily. His arm flopped onto her stomach and he cupped her body with his. The position was remarkably comfortable, especially when he sighed deeply and drew her close. How sweet. How . . . well . . . loving.

Marjorie, settling in, decided to let him speak first, if he wanted to, since he'd had more experience of this act than she did. A lot more. She took a deep breath, and waited. Perhaps he would declare his love for her. Was it possible that he actually *did* love her?

Probably not. While Marjorie didn't believe all the things Loretta said about men, because some of them were so outrageous as to be incredible, she still understood that men and women had different attitudes about love. And lust. If it weren't so, there would be no market for those poor, impoverished Chinese girls who were sold into prostitution and slavery right here in San Francisco.

She'd been thinking and waiting for Jason to speak for quite a while before she realized he'd gone to sleep. His deep, even breathing was her first clue. Surprised that so phenomenal an experience for her should have put her partner to sleep, she dared whisper, "Jason?"

He answered not.

A little louder, she whispered, "Jason?"

No answer.

"Bother." A tiny thread of resentment niggled in Marjorie's heart.

Now why, she wanted to know, should she harbor this gigantic feeling of awe and adoration in her bosom when Jason obviously considered this, her first experience with physical love, nothing more than a . . . a . . . a bluidy sleeping draft?

She told herself that she was being unreasonable. Naturally, the experience didn't mean as much to Jason as it did to her. She was being too sensitive. Jason was exhausted. He'd been through a lot recently.

After stewing over that one for a few minutes, her resentment grew an inch or two. *He'd* been through a lot? Well, so had she! What's more, *she* was the one who'd been hit with the bluidy cudgel. And that was after she'd been hit with a bluidy fist. Well, perhaps it hadn't been a fist, but . . .

Anyhow, why was it that she was being battered and bruised? Was it because she'd done something wrong? Was it because she'd been foolish? No. It was because Jason Abernathy had decided to play the hero and rescue Jia Lee from the clutches of bad men.

Not that Marjorie believed that Jia Lee deserved to be a slave or anything, but if Jason hadn't brought her to Loretta's house, Marjorie wouldn't have been hurt. So far, it seemed to her that the score lay heavily in Jia Lee's favor, as a matter of fact. As of this day—night, she meant—Jia Lee was recovering comfortably in Loretta's house, and Marjorie had been brutalized twice.

Perhaps she was being a teensy bit unfair. After all, Jia Lee had suffered a brutal beating first.

And that wasn't Marjorie's fault, either. With a huff, Marjorie discovered within herself a strong disinclination to be fair.

The attitude surprised her. Always before in her life, she'd bent over backwards to take the blame for whatever went wrong. This was thanks, in part, to her service as a White Star stewardess, and in even larger part to her upbringing, which had taught her that poor people were always to blame, even if nothing was their fault.

She'd even been blaming herself for Leonard's death since the ship sank. Yet the truth was that Leonard had, in effect, committed suicide when he'd refused to climb aboard the lifeboat with her.

Damn him! Why, if Leonard Fleming hadn't decided to play hero that night, Marjorie and he might be married and rearing a fine family this very minute! Instead, Leonard was dead—and a whole bluidy lot of good a dead man did anyone—and Marjorie had been living in a hell on earth for more than three bluidy years!

Men and their heroic deeds. Loretta was right. Heroic deeds ranked right up there with the oppression of women as insane and irresponsible masculine behaviors.

That being the case, and because she felt like a blooming idiot for having actually begged Jason Abernathy to deflower her, Marjorie eased herself out from under his arm. She felt a stab of soul-deep hurt as she did it, but she told herself that by taking this step, she was sparing herself not merely the embarrassment of seeing him in the morning, but also the humiliation of discovering that he didn't give a fig about her. As Loretta might have said—indeed, she probably had said it a time or two—he'd only wanted *sex.*

Well, he'd had it. And so had she. A shiver accompanied her into Jason's well-equipped bathroom. In spite of her present state of resentment, she had to admit that making love with Jason had been quite a spectacular experience. And she appreciated Jason for having enlightened her. If she could only bear the pleasure of the event in mind, perhaps she could keep at bay the sense of loss and emptiness lurking just outside her consciousness . . . at least until she got home and could cry in peace.

Suddenly, she wanted to see Loretta. To talk to her. To tell her everything there was to know about herself. All at once, Marjorie felt stupid for having kept her past to herself for so long. She couldn't remember why she'd decided to do so, either, although it had seemed like a good idea at the time. The plain truth was that all she'd accomplished was to shut herself away from the support of her friends and deprive herself of the love and understanding of another woman. Moreover, Loretta was a woman who only had Marjorie's best interest at heart, even though her means of accomplishing the same often left Marjorie breathless with shock and consternation.

A tear or two leaked from her eyes as she cleaned herself up. Dr. Hagendorf's words came back to her, giving her a measure of comfort: *You're a survivor.*

Aye, she was that, all right, and she'd survive this, too. She would *not* allow Jason Abernathy to get her down. She wouldn't.

After she washed up and donned her clothes, Marjorie, carrying her shoes, tiptoed down the stairs and into Jason's office. She almost suffered a heart attack when she turned on the light and saw a body on the sofa against the far wall. When the body blinked and sat up, she realized it was Lo Sing.

Somewhat blearily, he said, "Miss MacTavish!"

Marjorie pressed a finger to her lips. "Shhh. I need to get home, but I didn't want to awaken Ja— Dr. Abernathy."

"Uh . . . but don't you want to wait until morning?" He'd been sleeping in his shirtsleeves, and he grabbed his coat from the chair where he'd hung it. Looking embarrassed, he fumbled around, attempting to put on the coat.

"No. I really must be getting along now." Marjorie was approximately seventy times as embarrassed as poor Lo Sing, but she tried not to show it.

"But . . . you can't walk, surely. It's not safe."

There was that problem. The relative lack of safety surrounding Dr. Jason Abernathy and his bluidy damned clinic was the reason she, a former virgin, was here now in this predicament. Marjorie frowned, trying to think of a way to get home that wouldn't entail grave injury or death to herself. Not that she cared particularly, deeming life a waste of time, but Loretta would be crushed.

"Let me call you a cab at least."

Marjorie never would have thought about calling a cab as her life to date had required her to be of service, not to be served, but the suggestion relieved her a good deal. As graciously as she was able, she said, "Thank you! That would be so kind of you."

So Lo Sing called a cab for her, and Marjorie waited nervously, fearing Jason would awaken and come downstairs in search of her. Evidently, his sexual exertions had knocked him out, because the cab showed up before he did. Damn the man.

Marjorie was embarrassed when Lo Sing walked her out to the taxi and paid the fare for her. She shook his hand and thanked him, and her relief was almost as potent as her unhappiness when the cab—a motorized one this time—took off toward Russian Hill.

Feeling a good deal lower than dirt, Marjorie stared dejectedly out the window of the cab as it rattled its way toward Lombard Street. She'd gone and done it now, she guessed . . . and she didn't even find amusement in the fact that Loretta would be proud of her. Loretta was, at times, a remarkably fuddle-headed woman. She was also rich, which colored her outlook on life a great deal.

And then there was Jason, who was an advantage-taker if ever there was one. And she'd been so trusting and innocent, with her knock on the head and her . . .

"Fah," she muttered, knowing that she was blaming Jason for her own lack of moral fiber.

Still, it was galling to know that an event that was monumental in her life had sent him to sleep. Bah. Life was so unfair.

And speaking of unfairness, here she was, whining to herself about her love life, or lack thereof, when Jia Lee had been deprived forever of any sort of life at all, and only because she, like Marjorie, had been born poor. Marjorie should be counting her blessings instead of sitting in this cab trying not to weep with misery and unhappiness. It seemed terribly unjust that one's feelings about, and the truth of, any particular situation couldn't be made to coordinate more closely.

Why, if she had only . . .

Squinting out the window, Marjorie allowed the thought to trail off. Rubbing her fist on the isinglass, she tried to clear a spot on the foggy pane.

What in the world was going on? There seemed to be some sort of commotion transpiring in Loretta's neighborhood.

Marjorie's mouth dropped open when she espied the Quarleses' estate ablaze with lights. The gate gaped wide, too, and an automobile chugged at the curb in front of the open gate. Leaning forward, Marjorie rapped on the partition separating her from the driver. He pulled over and turned to face her. "Ma'am?"

"Stop here, if you will, please. Something seems to be going on ahead."

"Looks strange for sure," the cabbie agreed.

Since she didn't have to bother about paying the man—she assumed that Lo Sing had given him a decent tip since Lo Sing was a most responsible individual—Marjorie departed the cab several houses down from that of the Quarleses without further interaction with the cabbie. She had a sinking feeling that this unusual confusion in a top-flight neighborhood had something to do with the Jia Lee affair.

She wished she hadn't thought of the problem in terms of *affairs*.

But that was neither here nor there. Because she didn't want to be seen, Marjorie stuck as close to the shrubbery as she could as she approached the house. If there had been another attempt to abduct Jia Lee, perhaps she could discern the individuals involved from this vantage point. Maybe she would at least be able to offer reliable descriptions of the participants if the fiends weren't wearing hoods.

Then, to her utter dismay, she saw what she'd half expected and wholly dreaded to see: Two men, large, brutish, and hooded, running down the long drive to the gate. The man in front carried a huddled form over his shoulder. Marjorie knew the form was that of Jia Lee.

To her further horror, Marjorie then espied Loretta Quarles, in full fighting mode, racing after the two men and looking particularly tiny compared to them. She seemed to be wielding something in her hand, although Marjorie couldn't make it out. A rolling pin perhaps?

Oh dear. Loretta couldn't possibly foil those hardened villains with a rolling pin. And all Marjorie had with her was a small handbag that dangled from her wrist and contained nothing more formidable than a handkerchief.

The man carrying Jia Lee scrambled into the automobile. The other man leaped in after him, and with a terrific squeal of tires, the machine lurched away from the gate. It rumbled right past Marjorie before it had picked up much speed.

Then, performing perhaps the first truly spontaneous act in her entire lifetime, Marjorie decided it was her turn to play the hero. With a wild leap, she grabbed onto the vehicle's bumper and threw her arms around its protruding wheel case.

Then, with the sound of Loretta's horrified "Marjorie!" faintly pursuing her, Marjorie MacTavish took the ride of her life.

FOURTEEN

Jason rolled over and blinked his eyes, wondering why he felt so good. Life had been awful lately. There was no reason he should feel so . . . so . . . content. Happy. At peace with the world.

And then it all came back to him.

Marjorie. She had given herself to him last night in an act so beautiful, so fulfilling, so splendid, that he could almost weep with the wonder of it all. Marjorie.

He threw an arm about her. Odd. She seemed rather squashier this morning than she had the night before when her body had felt as firm and pliant as a wood nymph's. Not that Jason minded. She could get to be as fat as a whale, and he'd still desire and love her. And she was his now. She was his, body and soul. She was—

Damnation! She was gone!

Sitting up and hugging the pillow he'd mistaken for Marjorie, he blinked into the feeble light leaking through his bedroom curtains. He croaked, "Marjorie?" After clearing his throat, he tried again. "Marjorie?"

No answer drifted back to him from the bathroom or the room he used as a front parlor. Familiar sounds wafted up from the street below, sounds of business beginning to transpire in the Chinatown district, sounds he usually found comforting. This morning, they comforted him not a whit.

Where the devil was she? Swinging his legs over the side of the bed, he wondered if he'd dreamed it all. When he lifted the covers and checked, however, he discovered definite evidence that it hadn't been a dream. Marjorie and he had consummated their love last night.

So where in the name of mercy was she this morning? Had she awakened, felt embarrassed, and fled? Silly woman. He'd rectify *that* situation in a hurry.

With eyes gritty from lack of sleep, but still feeling pretty darned good in spite of that, Jason hurried through his morning ablutions, threw on some clothes, and clattered down the stairs to his office. Lo Sing and the fragrance of freshly brewed coffee greeted him, and both were welcome.

"Thanks," he said, taking the coffee cup from Lo Sing's hand. "Say, where's Miss MacTavish? I woke up and she was gone." Naturally, he felt no need to reveal the most intimate secrets of the previous night to his assistant.

"She left here some time after three. Said she had to get home."

Jason's soaring heart wobbled in its upward flight, turned a sickening somersault, and crashed to earth. "She *what?*"

"She left." Lo Sing's eyebrows dipped in a puzzled fashion. "What's the matter, Jason?"

"And you let her go?"

"I called a cab." Discerning symptoms of consternation in Jason's demeanor, Lo Sing added, "I paid the fare. Didn't want her to have to worry about anything. She'd been through enough."

"I'll say." Jason stamped to the window and glared

out onto the street. It was still early in the morning; Jason's bedside clock had told him it was only five-thirty. Pretty soon Chinese vendors would be plying their carts on the streets and sidewalks; old men would be padding here and there; and younger men would be scurrying thither and yon, taking care of business. There wouldn't be a woman anywhere, barring the occasional tourist or San Franciscan out for a jaunt in the "foreign" sector of her city. Naturally, the tourists and San Franciscans would only venture to Chinatown in clumps. For protection. Damn them all.

Well hell, what now? He'd have to go to Loretta's house, he guessed.

The silly woman would turn tail on him, wouldn't she? He ought to have anticipated something like this from Marjorie, who was the last person in the universe from whom he'd expect unusual behavior. Last night's surrender to his embraces had been an anomaly, and she was probably suffering pangs of embarrassment and regret this morning.

Why hadn't he awakened when she'd left, damn it?

But he knew why. He'd been so absolutely exhausted, and so utterly fulfilled, he'd just drifted off to sleep in an ecstasy of delight. Trust Marjorie to throw a damper on any situation that might foreshadow happiness, he thought crankily.

The telephone shrilled, and he jerked, slopping hot coffee onto his hand. "Damn."

Lo Sing answered the phone. After a brief conversation, he held the receiver out for Jason. "It's Mrs. Quarles."

Oh, great. Now Loretta was going to tease him about what he and Marjorie had done. Or maybe she was going to scold him. You never knew which side of any particular issue Loretta would be on, since she seemed to alter her standards to fit her mood of the moment.

He knew he was being irrational, but didn't care. "Good morning, Loretta."

"Good morning, my foot! Get over here, Jason Abernathy, and get over here now!"

Peeved, Jason said, "And why should I do that?"

"Why? Why?" Loretta had screeched the two words. Jason heard her suck in her breath in an effort to calm herself. "Listen, Jason, I don't want to talk about it over the phone. Get over here now."

"Damn it, Loretta, I won't go over there unless you tell me why." He was being stubborn for no particular reason, and he knew it, but he didn't like being dictated to. Besides, he didn't understand why she sounded so upset. "Anyhow, I thought you were a firm advocate of free love."

A pause followed this sentence. Then Loretta said, "I beg your pardon?"

Irked, Jason snapped, "You're always saying you support free love. Why are you so upset this morning?"

"Jason Abernathy, did you do something to Marjorie?"

"Did I *do* something to her?" Jason was no longer irked. He was furious. "Damn it, it was mutual, Loretta Linden! I mean, Loretta Quarles! What kind of man do you think I am, anyway?"

Another pause. "Jason, I don't know what you're talking about, but you need to get over here now. Jia Lee was kidnapped, and the last I saw of Marjorie she was clinging like a limpet to the back of the kidnappers' car! The police are here, and you've got to get over here to help. Now quit arguing with me, and come!"

Jason had gone numb when Loretta rapped out the news about Jia Lee. When she told him about Marjorie, he actually staggered slightly. Lo Sing shoved a chair behind him, and he collapsed into it. "Marjorie was what?" he asked weakly.

"You heard me." And she slammed the receiver into the cradle.

"Good God." Passing a hand over his face, Jason stared up at Lo Sing.

"What is it? You've gone white as a ghost."

"They've got Marjorie."

Lo Sing squinted at him. "Who's got Marjorie? Miss MacTavish, I mean."

But Jason didn't answer. Shoving poor Lo Sing out of his way, he raced to the door of his office without even pausing to grab his hat. He cranked the Hudson up faster than he'd done thus far in its existence, and with a screech of wheels that scattered pedestrians like chaff in the wind, he took off for Russian Hill.

Marjorie knew she'd made a massive blunder, but she didn't know what to do about it at this point. She couldn't just let go and leap away from the automobile. It had to be going at least fifteen or twenty miles per hour, and she'd kill herself if she tried so stupid a stunt. Yet if she stayed where she was, she'd probably die anyway.

Nyaff, she told herself. *Gudgeon. Haggis-headed ninnyhammer.*

Calling herself names didn't help her come to

any firm conclusions about what to do next, but it relieved her stress slightly. And perhaps all wasn't lost yet. She still had her handbag, for all the good it did her. But it did contain a few coins that she might be able to use to bribe someone so she could use a telephone once the automobile came to a stop and she figured out where she was, which would be where the kidnappers had taken Jia Lee.

The wind whipped her hair around her face and blew her skirt up to her knees, and she could only thank God that the hour was early and not too many people were on the streets of San Francisco yet. This was embarrassing enough without the whole world watching her make a fool of herself.

That thought consoled her until she realized the machine had turned onto the Embarcadero. Oh, no. They were on the wharf.

In less than a split second, a sickening, soul-destroying, mind-numbing panic engulfed Marjorie.

The ocean. The dark, cruel, life-taking ocean. It was right there, only yards away from her. She smelled it now: her bitterest enemy, her blackest foe. The ocean. The same ocean that had taken Leonard from her and destroyed her life.

Except that she still lived, so she guessed her life hadn't been completely destroyed. Yet. Marjorie entertained the cynical thought that there was yet time for the damned ocean to finish what it had started. Her heart was already hammering as if a crazed pile driver were operating it. She was liable to suffer an apoplexy and die from fright if the bluidy automobile got any closer to the water.

But the machine seemed to be slowing down. Marjorie prayed that she could get out of this pickle before either of the men inside it spotted her.

Knowing it was risky, but fearful lest she wait too long, when the automobile slowed down to turn onto a pier, she jumped down. With a good deal of skipping and flapping of arms, she remained upright, but she was distressed to see the car still moving forward onto a pier where boats were moored. And the sea, rolling and heaving and lurking in wait for her, slapped against the wharf. Seals barked. Gulls soared. Pelicans squawked. And Marjorie was sick.

She couldn't follow the automobile. She'd die if she had to walk out onto a pier.

As clearly as if he'd taken up residence in her head, Dr. Hagendorf's voice came to her. *You won't die, Marjorie. You'll be frightened. There's a huge difference.*

Bluidy hell, she hated when people got reasonable on her. She could still see the automobile. What she should probably do was turn around and see if she could find a telephone somewhere. She could call Loretta and tell her where the men had taken Jia Lee.

But she didn't know where they were taking Jia Lee. There were dozens of boats anchored off that stupid pier. Could the police search every one of them before the kidnappers sailed her away?

A couple of Jason and Loretta's more bitter denunciations came back to her, and she then paused to wonder if the police would bother to come at all. Her heart suffered another gigantic spasm. Pressing her hand against it, she hoped she'd survive this day's adventure without it giving out entirely.

"Och, God, please help me," she muttered, knowing that she had to go forward. Even if it killed her.

You're a survivor, Dr. Hagendorf's voice told her.

"I dinna *want* to be a survivor, curse it! I want a happy life!" Ah well, too late for that now.

Practice makes perfect, Dr. Hagendorf's voice chided her.

"Bluidy hell, how's a body supposed to practice for something like *this*?"

No answer occurred to her, and Dr. Hagendorf offered no opinion. The automobile was out of her sight now. Marjorie shut her eyes, hugged herself against her fear and the cold morning air, prayed hard for a few seconds, and spat out, "*Damn* it!"

And then, making sure she hid herself as well as she could, and with her heart racing and her ears ringing, she walked out onto the pier.

"Where did it go?" Jason's nerves jumped and his heart thudded, and he wanted to throttle somebody. "Didn't you have someone follow it?"

"How could we follow it? I was the only one in the house who was awake!"

Loretta's scowl bounced off Jason as if he were made of rubber. He glared at her. "You could have awakened someone!"

"Oh, for God's . . ." Loretta took his arm. "Listen, Jason, I know you're worried about Jia Lee—"

"To hell with Jia Lee! I'm worried about Marjorie!" As soon as the words left his lips, he could scarcely believe he'd said them.

Loretta's lifted eyebrows told him she felt the same way. To hell with it. He passed his hand through his hair in agitation.

"I know you're worried, but I called the police instantly. Even before I called you."

"The police don't give a—"

"They do, too. There's a white woman involved now, you know."

That was right. Marjorie. The police would surely care about Marjorie.

"And I'm involved, too. Don't forget the power of money, Jason. The police are always interested in whatever the famous Captain Malachai Quarles wants them to do. Or his wife, by extension."

"Right, right. But you don't know where the car went?" It seemed mighty irresponsible of Loretta not to have followed the automobile far enough to see which way it turned off of Lombard Street.

"Oh, of course," she said sarcastically. "I should have raced right down the street after the machine, brandishing my rolling pin instead of calling the police. That would have been a *much* more sensible course of action."

He hung his head. "Sorry. It's only that I'm so worried."

She patted his shoulder. "I know, Jason. Come inside and let Mrs. Brandeis feed you something."

"I'm not hungry."

"You've got to keep up your strength. Besides, I want to know what Marjorie and free love have in common."

Jason frowned at her. "You would."

Marjorie couldn't seem to take in a decent lungful of air. Her respiration was coming in short gasps, and she had to stop every couple of steps, press a hand over her heart, and try to suck in her breath. She couldn't.

This was simply marvelous. She was going to hyperventilate and pass out and get herself kidnapped if this kept up. So far, she'd been able to avoid looking at the ocean, which was probably the only reason she was still conscious at all.

Also, thank the good Lord, the fog was thickening. This not only helped conceal her from the kidnappers, but it also helped conceal the water from her. There were holes in the pier's flooring, and the black, deadly swirling water was right down there, not twenty feet beneath her. She could hear it sloshing against the pier's supporting posts, and the sound made her sick to her stomach. She was pretty sure that if she actually got a good look at the ocean, she'd faint dead away, Dr. Hagendorf or no Dr. Hagendorf.

Her heart still pounded in her chest like a thunderstorm; she was perspiring like a sailor in the sun; her tongue was so dry it stuck to the roof of her mouth; and she was so light-headed she had to keep one hand on whatever solid object was nearest to her to keep from collapsing. Her knees shook, too, but that was a minor problem.

She heard the sounds before she saw anything. Crouching behind a tall pile of cable, she poked her head up and saw that the automobile had come to a stop. The doors opened, and the two thugs got out. She noticed that they'd taken off their hoods—not that it mattered, since there was no one at hand to whom she could give a description.

One of the brutes reached into the tonneau and grabbed something. As soon as the something fell out of the automobile, Marjorie saw that it was Jia Lee. Poor thing. Marjorie hoped she was still alive and not too badly damaged from all the rough handling she'd undergone. Life was *so* confounded unfair to women! For the first time, Marjorie spared a

thought for Loretta's agitating for women's suffrage.
If she survived this ordeal, she might just have to join
in the next march.

"Careful, Bart. The boss don't want her hurt."

"Dammit, Frank, I know what I'm doing."

Aha. The dimwitted duo of Bart and Frank again.
They were as ugly as Marjorie had supposed they'd
be. Marjorie wished she had a gun. She might be
able to fire it into the air and get the villains to release Jia Lee. Of course, then she'd have to figure
out the to do with the girl. And herself. Bother.

Where was Jason Abernathy when she needed
him? He'd been ever so happy to deposit Jia Lee at
the Quarleses' house for other people to take care
of, but every time something happened to the girl
after that, he was sleeping. Bluidy damned man.

"The boss wants her on the boat," said Bart. "I'll
carry her."

The boat? Och God! Marjorie folded her arms
on the coil of rope and dropped her head onto
them. She prayed as hard as she'd ever prayed in
her life for approximately fifteen seconds. Then
she lifted her head and saw that Bart was carrying
out the fell scheme and that Frank was following
him onto the craft, a shiny mahogany pleasure
yacht with brass fittings of about forty-two or forty-
six feet in length. Anyone else in the world would
have considered the craft positively gorgeous. Marjorie hated it on sight.

But she knew she had to follow the men. She
couldn't *not* follow them without being plagued by
her conscience for the rest of her life. Damned inconvenient things, consciences. So . . . she'd have
to follow them.

Easy to say. She couldn't follow them either. She'd

die if she got onto a boat again. She knew it. No matter what Dr. Hagendorf said.

Anyhow, her legs wouldn't move and her feet didn't work, so it was impossible to board the boat. She was also having to gasp for breath at present, and was on the verge of fainting dead away.

Excuses, excuses.

Och good Lord, now it was Loretta's voice that had invaded her head. It had been bad enough when Dr. Hagendorf intruded, but Loretta?

Loretta wouldn't had daunted by a mere fear. And Loretta certainly wouldn't allow a fainting fit to stop her from perpetrating a rescue. Of course, Loretta didn't have an ounce of common sense, and didn't suffer from Marjorie's bluidy *phobias*, either.

"Take hold of yoursel', Marjorie MacTavish," she commanded herself in a murmur. "If ye canna do this, ye're a feeble excuse for a human being."

Big words. But they gave her a measure of courage. Since Bart and Frank and Jia Lee were long gone, Marjorie attempted to take a deep breath, failed, and decided the ability to breathe was overrated and that she had a duty to perform. Duty had been her salvation thus far in her life; it would see her through this ordeal—uh, this challenge.

So, with her heart in her throat further impeding her ability to take in more than tiny amounts of air, with her knees knocking together like castanets, with sweat pouring from her although her skin felt like ice, with a mouth so dry that she couldn't swallow, and with a feeling of doom pervading every cell in her body, Marjorie crept out from behind her protective coil of cable. Bracing herself for dear life on whatever solid object was closest at hand, she inched toward the boat. Before she'd taken her second step, she'd begun to cry. She hated herself for doing so, but she couldn't help it.

Why hadn't she gone with Loretta to the seashore for that picnic back in May? *Why* hadn't she gone to the Cliff House when Jason had invited her? *Why* hadn't she gone on that boat ride when Mr. St. Claire had taken her to the Pan0Pacific Exhibition? Those incidents could have served as practice for this crisis. But she'd been frightened of the water, so she hadn't done any of them. And now she had to pay the price for her cowardice and stupidity by doing this without any kind of practice at all.

Weaving her way to the boat—her steps were unsteady, and she was still gasping for air—Marjorie arrived at the gangplank. She was going to be sick. Her stomach heaved and pitched, and she bent over, clutching at it and squeezing her eyes shut. Her stomach settled gradually, but she realized she was just standing there, on the pier, holding on to the rope rail to the gangplank, and that somebody might see her any second.

Frightened by that possibility, Marjorie was spurred to scuttle across the gangplank, which swayed slightly, sending her stomach into turmoil once more. As soon as she was on deck, she jumped behind a barrel—and collapsed into a shuddering heap.

She didn't know how long she remained in that pitiful condition, but eventually she realized she wasn't dead. *Unfortunately*, an increasingly angry voice in her head said acrimoniously. This wasn't right. It wasn't fair. It was absolutely and completely rotten. Why should *she* who had a—justifiable, by

God—fear of the ocean, have to rescue this confounded woman? Jia Lee wasn't her problem, confound it!

In that moment, she hated Jason Abernathy, Jia Lee, Loretta Quarles, and God, not necessarily in that order but profoundly. And, recalling why this crisis was taking place in the first place, she added Jia Lee's parents, her purchaser, Chinese tongs, and Bart and Frank to her hate list.

It was, in fact, her hate that got her up and moving again. She decided she wasn't going to let them win. She was going to survive this ordeal, rescue Jia Lee, and, by God, tell them all what she thought of them.

First, of course, she had to find Jia Lee. Since she was already on the deck of the boat—she hadn't picked herself up yet—she peered out from behind the barrel. No sailors' legs and feet met her gaze. Lifting herself into a kneeling position and hoping she wouldn't throw up, she peeked again. No one. Not a soul. Where the devil were they?

Perhaps whoever had masterminded this event preferred to keep his fell business to himself and therefore had not employed a huge staff. That made as much sense as anything else about the business did, she supposed. If it were true, it might make this job of hers easier . . . if anything about it could possibly be easy.

After she had made it to her feet and stopped swaying, Marjorie dared take a step away from her barrel. At once, she retreated behind it again. She needed a plan before she tackled anything as panic-inducing as actually walking on the deck of a water-going vessel again, even so small a one as this.

First of all, she needed to find Jia Lee. Then she

could formulate further plans, even if that only meant returning to shore and reporting to the police.

Damn and blast, she'd forgotten that the police didn't care about people like Jia Lee. Well, she'd report it all to Jason. And Loretta.

So she sucked in a breath—and thank God, she could take one again—and once more sallied forth in pursuit of Jia Lee. Because her shoes sounded like cannon blasts when she stepped on the wooden deck, she again retreated behind her barrel, telling herself as she did so that she was merely being prudent and not giving in to her panic.

"Gudgeon," she muttered, knowing that prudence was only a tiny part of the reason she didn't want to leave the safety of her barrel. Not that it was much safety.

She hated having to leave her shoes behind, but in the interest of safety, she did so. Then, making herself as small as possible against the cabin of the yacht, she sidled along, listening for all she was worth. She hadn't gone far before she heard voices coming from inside the cabin.

"Good. Just leave her on the chair, fellows. I'll take care of everything now."

"What are the tongs gonna do to you?" either Frank or Bart wanted to know.

"That's not your problem."

That voice, which sounded awfully familiar to Marjorie, as well as quite supercilious, must belong to the leader of the gang. Marjorie was dying to know who he was.

She wished she hadn't thought the word *dying*. Ah well . . .

Inching toward the porthole and keeping a wary

eye out for signs that someone else might be on the boat, Marjorie crept forward. When she reached the porthole, she very gingerly crouched beneath it, trying to judge by the voices where everyone in the cabin was located. She couldn't, confound it.

Well, it couldn't be helped. Praying that no one was looking her way, she quickly took a peek inside the cabin—and nearly suffered a spasm. As quickly as she'd looked, she crouched again, her heart battering against her rib cage like gunfire.

Good God! Was that who she thought it was? Marjorie didn't believe it. It couldn't be. Her state of panic must have interfered with her vision. She must be seeing things. Or . . . God forbid, maybe Loretta was right, and she was a raving lunatic. She couldn't have seen whom she thought she'd seen. She must be . . .

Very, very slowly, she inched up toward the porthole once more. Praying that the attention of everyone in the cabin was still focused away from her, she allowed herself a slightly longer peek.

It was he.

Good Lord in heaven, it was Hamilton St. Claire! Was *Hamilton* the evil importer of Chinese prostitutes? How could he be? He was a lawyer! He was rich! He was a *baby*, for sweet Jesus' sake!

Baby or not, he seemed to be in charge of this situation. As she listened for all she was worth, Marjorie's opinion of Mr. Hamilton St. Claire underwent a revision. From thinking of him as a slightly silly young lad, she suddenly realized he was an intensely evil man.

Merciful heavens, wouldn't his *pater* have a fit when he heard about this, though?

She heard Hamilton tell Bart and Frank to leave

the cabin, and she searched around wildly for somewhere to hide. A lifeboat was suspended on a divot several feet away. Marjorie was about to make a dash for it when, before her eyes, flashed a scene from the last time she'd been aboard a lifeboat. She froze in place, a virtual pillar of salt like Lot's wife.

Stop it! She rubbed her eyes hard to eliminate the vision. Then, with a monumental effort of will, she forced herself to head for the lifeboat. *Do it scared,* her inner voice commanded. So she did.

Right before she left the porthole, however, she heard Hamilton say, "I'll just take the yacht out and eliminate this problem forever, boys. You won't be needed again. And if you ever come back and ask me for more money, you'll regret it. Believe me."

Marjorie believed him. She'd never heard such menace in a human voice. And she had no doubt he'd carry out his threat.

Evidently, neither did Frank nor Bart. One of them said, "Sure, boss. We won't do nothing stupid."

But whatever did he mean, he was going to take the boat out and eliminate the problem? Marjorie gulped painfully. She had a feeling she knew what he meant. Good God, what an evil person he was! She never would have guessed. He'd seemed so . . . so . . . insipid was the word that sprang to mind. Some judge of character *she* was!

And what would this do to the cast of *Pirates*?

Marjorie told herself not to be an idiot. She had enough to concentrate on right now without adding irrelevancies to the mix.

It occurred to her then that she'd become so engrossed in the conversation inside the cabin and her terrifying memories concerning the lifeboat that she'd forgotten to be afraid of the ocean.

Naturally, as soon as she thought about it, panic overwhelmed her. Since she was lying in a lifeboat, she could faint in peace, but she didn't. Again, fury and hate propelled her to shove her fears aside. Until this hair-raising experience, she'd never realized how convenient those two emotions could be.

When Bart and Frank lumbered past her lifeboat, Marjorie held her breath. If either one of them bothered to glance into the boat, she was sunk. Perhaps literally. *God, God, God, please help me!*

God was evidently hearing at least some of her desperate prayers, because the two men's footsteps veered onto the gangplank and disappeared. Marjorie heard the automobile rumble to life, and its noise, too, faded into the distance.

So. Now all she had to do was foil Hamilton's vicious scheme, rescue Jia Lee, and get the both of them back to the pier. Resisting the urge to pound her head against the bottom of the boat, Marjorie peeked over its side. No one seemed to be anywhere on the boat. Was Hamilton all alone except for Jia Lee? It was possible, she supposed. He probably didn't want too many people to know of his business dealings outside of his father's law firm.

Perceiving no choice, Marjorie slung a leg over the side of the lifeboat and hoisted herself down onto the deck. Again, she sneaked up to the port-hole and looked inside the cabin. Hamilton's expression was as black as any Marjorie had ever seen on a human face as he glared at Jia Lee. Poor Jia Lee was tied to a chair. Marjorie added one more thing to her to-do list. Secure some way of severing her bonds.

Oh, Lord, she wasn't cut out for this sort of thing!

Why hadn't it fallen to Loretta to rescue the bluidy woman?

Realizing that this sort of thinking signified a weak character—at the very least—Marjorie guided her mind onto a more productive path. Where the devil could she find a knife or a large pair of scissors?

Hamilton's voice scared her nearly out of her skin. She gasped loudly, and prayed he hadn't heard her.

"I'm going to start the motor now, my little dove. And then we're going to take a trip out into the bay."

Jia Lee probably hadn't understood a word he'd said, but she sobbed, thereby proving to Marjorie that she understood his intent, if not his words.

Marjorie didn't understand his words, either, if it came to that. Start the motor? Marjorie guessed she had heard about outboard motors propelling boats, but they were uncommon, and she'd never seen one—naturally. She wouldn't be seeing this one if necessity hadn't forced her to.

"Don't cry." Hamilton's voice was snide and vicious. "I know you believe yourself to have been hard used, but it's your parents' fault. Whoever heard of selling a daughter into prostitution? Christ, your people are barbarians."

And just what did he think *he* was, Marjorie wanted to know. The notion of buying a woman was absolutely appalling to her. She supposed some kind of cultural imperative might possibly allow for the sale of daughters in some places, but in the United States, where slavery had been abolished more than fifty years before, there was no excuse for Hamilton's behavior.

Och, God! He was leaving the cabin! As quickly

and quietly as she could, Marjorie scuttled back to the lifeboat and crawled inside. Her skirt caught on a divot and tore, leaving a scrap of fabric dangling in the open air, but she didn't have time to snatch it back before the cabin door opened. Squeezing her eyes shut, praying for all she was worth, and trying to scrunch into the smallest bundle possible, she waited for Hamilton to notice the tatter of her skirt flapping in the wind, find her, and murder her along with Jia Lee.

His footsteps approached. She swallowed and held her breath. Her heart hammered so hard, she felt certain he must be able to hear it. Her ears rang. Her nerves jangled like sleigh bells. A sob caught in her throat.

And the footsteps passed the lifeboat without a pause. Marjorie's relief was so great, she nearly cried. Firmly she told herself that she could cry later. As soon as Hamilton was wherever the engine was, she had to rescue Jia Lee, with or without a knife. For the first time in her life, she wished she went about armed. This would be so much easier if she could simply shoot Hamilton.

She told herself she was going crazy. It was impossible to account for her bloodthirstiness in any other way. Perhaps she'd get over it if she survived this adventure.

Listening hard, she heard a noise some distance away. She scolded herself for not ascertaining exactly where everything was on the yacht before she began spying, although it did no good to second-guess herself. When she'd first boarded the cursed thing, she'd been so terrified, it was all she could do to remain conscious. She ought to be proud of herself, confound it, not scolding herself!

That being the case, and as soon as she heard a
motor rumble, Marjorie again scrambled out of the
lifeboat. She hurried to the cabin, praying the door
wasn't locked. Thank God, it wasn't. With a finger
pressed to her lips to keep Jia Lee from crying out,
she pushed the door open.

Jia Lee had been drooping in her chair, hanging
her head, and looking as if she were already dead.
At Marjorie's abrupt entrance, she jerked violently,
and Marjorie barely had time to dash over and
catch the chair before it could topple over. There
was no gag covering Jia Lee's mouth, so Marjorie
clapped her hand over it just in case the woman's
astonishment led her to cry out.

"Shhh," Marjorie said. "I'm here to help you."
She wished she'd learned more Chinese words
and phrases. It would do no good to ask Jia Lee
where she hurt or if she'd like a nice cup of tea.
What she needed to know was where a knife could
be procured.

Despite the language barrier, Jia Lee understood.
She nodded vigorously, so Marjorie felt safe in removing her hand. She made sawing motions with
her hands over the bound woman's ropes and lifted
her eyebrows. Jia Lee appeared puzzled for a moment before she nodded her comprehension and
tilted her head to the left.

There, to Marjorie's utter astonishment, a knife lay
on the chair where Hamilton had sat. Something
had gone right for a change! Heartened by this, the
first indication that all wasn't lost quite yet, Marjorie
picked up the knife and set to work on Jia Lee's
ropes. It wasn't an easy task, since she was trying not
to cut the girl as she worked, but she finally succeeded.

"Can you walk?" Marjorie demonstrated her question by taking a couple of exaggerated steps toward the door.

Nodding, Jia Lee started to rise from her chair. Hurrying to help her, Marjorie said, "Careful. Your circulation might be impaired."

Again, Jia Lee nodded, although Marjorie was sure she didn't understand her admonition. However, she must have comprehended her intention because she hesitated before taking one tiny step and halting, Marjorie holding fast to her the while. She didn't topple over after that one step, so she took another one. Again, Jia Lee nodded.

Nodding back, Marjorie whispered, "Stay here and practice walking." She demonstrated with her fingers. "I'll peek outside and see if we can get to the gangplank." Borrowing from Loretta, Marjorie gestured broadly to indicate her purpose. Another nod made her hope she'd made herself clear.

So, while Jia Lee walked circles in the cabin, Marjorie sneaked out the cabin door, praying they'd be able to make their way to the gangplank unobserved.

The gangplank wasn't there.

What Marjorie saw when she went outside was so horrifying that she sank to her knees. The boat had left the pier. Nothing connected them to the shore but the black, freezing, bitter, murderous depths of the Pacific Ocean.

Och God, nay. For pity's sake, dinna do this to me.

But He had.

FIFTEEN

The police officer frowned at his notebook. "You don't have any idea which way the automobile went?"

"No. I've already told you that a million times."

"Yes, ma'am. Just trying to make everything clear in my mind."

Loretta rolled her eyes. Jason couldn't blame her, as the policeman did seem rather a dim bulb, but he didn't want to rile the man. He needed the police department's help now as he'd never needed it before.

"And you, sir," said the officer, turning to Jason, "you say you don't know where they might be taking the girl?"

Jason shook his head. "They might be taking her to Chinatown, but I don't know. They might just as well be taking her to Timbuktu. I suspect the men who carried her off were hired by the importer, who's a white man. And I don't know who he is. Or where he is. Or what he's going to do with Jia Lee. *Damn* it!"

He whirled around to pace away in the opposite direction, running a hand through his already wildly disarranged hair and cursing himself for not having found out the villain's identity before this. It was his fault. It *must* be his fault! And Marjorie was in their clutches now as certainly as was Jia Lee. And it was all his fault. What an ass he was!

As he passed the chair in which Loretta sat, she reached out to take his arm. "Try not to worry, Jason. Marjorie is a resourceful woman. I'm sure she'll be all right."

"Resourceful?" He stared at Loretta. "How can resourcefulness help her against armed thugs?"

With a sniff, Loretta said, "You don't give her enough credit. You never have."

The policeman cleared his throat. "And you say this Chinese woman was named . . ." He squinted doubtfully at his pad.

"Jia Lee," Jason said harshly. He was accustomed to the San Francisco Police Department's unfamiliarity with the city's Chinese citizens. The police and the politicians liked to pretend the Chinese didn't exist—unless they wanted some illicit fun. They made him sick. He spelled the name carefully, not that it would matter. "J-i-a L-e-e, I guess is the best way to spell it."

"I see. And the other woman is MacTavish?"

"Yes. M-a-c-T-a-v-i-s-h. Red hair. She was wearing a brown-and-white striped dress."

"Brown and cream," Loretta muttered.

Jason waved an arm in the air. "What difference does it make? She could be anywhere!"

"Try not to panic, Jason. Panicking won't help anything."

Jason glared at Loretta. They were in Loretta's front parlor, and the nanny had just taken the babies upstairs for their nap. Malachai was out with Derrick Peavey in a no doubt futile effort to garner information about the vanished automobile. He'd mentioned that someone might have noticed a speeding vehicle with a woman clinging to the back.

And that was another thing: What if she'd fallen off? What if right this very minute, she was lying somewhere, bleeding and unconscious after having lost her grip? Why the devil had she done so damn-fool a thing?

For that matter, why had she left him without a word? Had she awakened and been embarrassed? Had he done something she'd taken exception to? From his perspective, their lovemaking had been nothing short of magnificent, and he knew she'd enjoyed it. He'd felt it. He *knew.*

Damn her anyway! At least Mai had been pre-dictable. Marjorie was such a complicated person, he never knew what she was going to do next. And half the time, she did exactly the opposite of what he would have predicted, had he been in the habit of predicting.

Mai was a slave. Marjorie is a free and independent woman, the voice in his head told him. He was be-ginning to hate that damned voice. Besides, she wasn't that all-fired independent. She was a slave to convention, dash it. His voice said, *Pooh. You're as-signing traits to her based on your own life. What do you know of what's gone in to making her the woman you love?*

The woman he loved? Oh God he *did* love her. He ran his fingers through his hair for approxi-mately the hundredth time that day.

"If you don't stop that, Jason Abernathy, you're going to pull all your hair out." Loretta's voice was sharp. "It's not doing any good, and you're making me nervous."

He turned on her, glad to have a target for his

anxiety. "Making you nervous! If you aren't nervous already, you're a damned piece of stone, Loretta Linden!"

"Quarles," she said dryly. "And don't be an idiot, Jason. Of course I'm worried. But pacing back and forth and pulling your hair out isn't going to accomplish anything but exhausting you and making you bald."

"*Damn* it!"

When the telephone rang a second later, it so startled Jason that he let out a yell, then felt stupid. Loretta, preempting her housekeeper, hurried to the telephone room to answer it with Jason and the policeman hard on her heels.

Jason almost succumbed to the urge to yank the receiver out of Loretta's hand. Only the knowledge that Loretta would probably bash him with it, and that to do so would serve to prove her right on the idiot issue, prevented him. He fulminated, however, feeling rather like a volcano about to erupt as he listened.

"You're where?" Loretta sounded incredulous. "The pier? Good Lord, Marjorie, what are you doing there?"

As soon as he heard the word *Marjorie,* Jason's knees gave out on him, and he had to clutch the door jamb to remain upright.

Jason watched Loretta's eyes grow wider and rounder as she listened. His skin itched and he had to stuff his hands in his pockets to prevent them from getting away from him. He hissed, "What? What's she saying? Where is she?"

Flapping a hand at him in order to silence him, Loretta continued to listen, emitting the occasional gasp. Once she said, "You *what?* Oh, Marjorie!"

Jason damn near suffered a spasm.

After what seemed like an hour, at least, Loretta replaced the receiver in the cradle and turned around. She smiled.

"*What?*" Jason shrieked. "Damn it, Loretta, what did she say?"

Bullying Loretta Quarles was never the right thing to do, and Jason wouldn't have done such a stupid thing had he been thinking clearly. But his thought processes had been scrambled like breakfast eggs several hours earlier. He took Loretta by the shoulders and shook her.

"Here now, there's no need for that," the policeman said reprovingly.

Realizing what he had done, Jason released Loretta as he might drop a hot rock. Passing a hand across his eyes, he muttered, "Sorry. I'm going crazy."

Loretta patted him on the shoulder. "There, there, Jason, I know you're worried. Come into the parlor and I'll tell you all about it."

He sucked in a gallon or two of air, intending to use it to shriek again, but Loretta saved him the effort by saying, "She's fine, Jason. And so is Jia Lee."

The breath went out of him in a whoosh, and he followed her meekly back into the parlor. This time, he sat. In fact, he more or less collapsed onto a nearby sofa. All of his pent-up energy had deserted him as soon as he heard Loretta say the magic words affirming Marjorie's welfare, and he now felt as limp as a wet washrag.

"You look terrible, Jason," Loretta said.

To Jason's ears, there was a considerable lack of concern in the words. He didn't snap at her. "I feel terrible. So tell us. What's going on?"

Glancing up at the policeman, Loretta said politely, "Why don't you take a seat, Sergeant Harkwright? I'm sure you'll be more comfortable sitting."

Jason gritted his teeth. Was the damned woman deliberately prolonging his pain? He'd always believed them to be friends, but a friend wouldn't stretch out his agony in this inconsiderate way.

"Thank you, ma'am, but I'm used to standing."

Unable to stand it any longer himself, Jason barked out, "Get on with it, will you?"

"For heaven's sake, Jason, control yourself!"

Jason said, "Hrrrrr."

"All right. First of all, both Marjorie and Jia Lee are all right. At present, they're at the Police Station on Front and the Embarcadero. Evidently, Marjorie had to rescue Jia Lee from the kidnappers."

"She did that alone?" roared Jason. "*Damn* the woman!"

Frowning, Loretta said icily, "I gather there wasn't time for her to fetch help. Not," she added, this time showering her frown upon the policeman, who didn't seem to notice, "that the police would have done anything to rescue Jia Lee, I'm sure."

Sergeant Harkwright said nothing.

Through his teeth, Jason ground out, "Go on."

"That's all." Loretta shrugged.

"That's *all*?" Jason jumped to his feet. "What do you mean, *'that's all'*?" Rushing to the door of the parlor, he said, "I've got to get down there now."

"Jason! Stop it!"

Loretta's peremptory command actually did stop Jason. He spun around and pinned her with a gaze of frantic intensity. "But I have to get Marjorie."

Rising majestically—quite a feat for so small a

woman—Loretta said, "We'll *all* go. I have to take Marjorie some clothes. And Jia Lee, too, I'm sure."

"Clothes?" Unaccustomed to feeling frantic, Jason didn't appreciate it when panic nudged the earlier emotion aside and started jumping up and down on his nerve endings. "*Clothes?*" Good God, what had happened? His jaw bulging, Jason rasped out, "If those maniacs so much as touched Marjorie, by God, I'll kill them all."

"I told you they're both fine," Loretta snapped. "Now come with me and do something useful, will you? I'm tired of all this drama, Jason Abernathy."

"Drama?" Jason resented that.

She grabbed him by the hand and tugged. "Yes. Stop it this instant, and help me." Over her shoulder, she said, "We'll be right back, Sergeant Harkwright, and then we can all go to the police station."

"I don't understand," mumbled Jason. But he obediently followed Loretta down the hall and through the kitchen to Marjorie's improvised bedroom.

There he assisted Loretta in gathering up two complete sets of clothing, from underwear to sweaters. Loretta stacked everything into a neat bundle, tied it with string, and turned to Jason, thrusting the bundle into his arms.

"I have to tell Mrs. Brandeis where we're going and fetch my hat and coat. I can trust Mrs. Brandeis to tell Malachai where we are. Wait in the parlor with the policeman, will you? And don't do anything stupid."

Numbly, Jason nodded. Then, like a trained puppy, he dragged himself and the bundle of clothes back to the parlor, where he sat on the sofa and waited for Loretta.

* * *

Huddled in a hard, wooden, straight-backed chair, shivering and hugging a scratchy woolen blanket around her shoulders, Marjorie wondered if Loretta would *ever* get there. Jia Lee, in a similar condition, sagged in the chair next to her. Every now and then, when she remembered to do so, Marjorie patted the other woman on the arm, attempting in that way to give her courage. Too bad nobody was giving *her* any.

A foghorn sounded mournfully in the distance, and Marjorie wondered if Hamilton St. Claire had discovered he was missing a captive yet. And would the fog interfere with navigating his yacht? She sincerely hoped so.

Envisioning Hamilton finding that Jia Lee had fled, Marjorie allowed herself to feel satisfaction. Her mind formed a mental picture of him: first incredulous, then horrified, and then so angry that she allowed him to jump up and down in the cabin of his yacht, making it rock so hard it sank.

But no. She wouldn't mind if Hamilton St. Claire died. God knew, he didn't deserve to live, but Marjorie didn't want him sharing the same ocean as her late, beloved Leonard.

It's'na the same ocean, Marjorie MacTavish. This is the Pacific. That was the Atlantic.

Well perhaps. She still didn't like the notion of Hamilton and Leonard having anything at all in common with each other, even their deaths. Anyhow, it might be preferable if Hamilton had to face the consequences of his bad acts and endure a trial, although Marjorie wasn't sure the authorities would care much about a Chinese woman or a Scottish immigrant.

Codswallop. Where was Loretta?

"Would you care for more tea, Miss MacTavish?"

Marjorie looked up at the young police officer and smiled. "No, thank you." She didn't know how he could call this slop *tea*, but she was grateful that he was kind, even if he couldn't tell tea from dishwater.

"And you, ma'am?" The young man lifted an eyebrow at Jia Lee, who stared at him dumbly.

Thinking that at least she could help in this instance, Marjorie asked Jia Lee in her limited Chinese if she'd like another cup of tea. Jia Lee shook her head. The poor thing looked even more miserable than Marjorie felt, although that seemed unlikely since Marjorie felt ghastly.

But she'd survived. By God, she'd more than survived. She'd defied her fears, boarded a boat, rescued Jia Lee from a hideous death by drowning, swum in the sea, and they'd *both* survived. She felt rather heroic in fact. If she didn't also feel bedraggled, wet, cold, salty, sore, embarrassed—she'd actually appeared in front of perfect strangers practically naked—and itchy, she'd probably be enjoying her victory. As it was, well . . .

Where the devil was Loretta?

Marjorie didn't know how long she'd sat in that hard chair, freezing cold and uncomfortable and wishing herself elsewhere, but she'd almost succumbed to her exhaustion and nodded off when a loud cry startled her into sitting bolt upright and scanning the room for villains.

"My God, Marjorie, you look like the wrath of God!"

Jason! It *would* be Jason. Confound him!

"Oh, Marjorie, you poor thing!"

And that was Loretta. Thank the good Lord for

friends. By the time Marjorie had struggled to stand up, Loretta had hurled herself at her and flung her arms around her, and Marjorie decided she could shoot Jason later. Right now, she needed the comfort of a friend's caring.

Since Loretta was so much shorter than she and she had a perfect view of the room—and Jason— Marjorie gaped in astonishment when Jia Lee, too, leaped up from her chair. Then, dropping both her blanket and her stoicism, Jia Lee broke out into tears and ran straight into Jason's arms.

Well!

"I keep telling you it wasn't my fault." Feeling abused and misunderstood, Jason once again paced in Loretta and Malachai's front parlor. Marjorie and Jia Lee were both in their rooms off the kitchen washing up. Marjorie would come to the parlor shortly to explain what had happened.

"It's *all* your fault, actually," said Loretta without heat. "But I'm not blaming you for bringing the poor girl here. What will become of her now?"

With a shrug, Jason said, "I don't know. I'll have to find work for her, I guess. She'll have to stay here, since there's nothing for her in China any longer."

"Will there be trouble with the tongs?" Malachai had come home shortly before Loretta and Jason had brought Marjorie and Jia Lee back to the Quarleses' Russian Hill home.

Jason shook his head. Then he nodded. Then he sighed heavily and said, "Damned if I know. Maybe not with St. Claire out of the way. The tongs will probably be happy if I give each of them a cash payment to make up for their losses."

"Their losses?" Malachai's left eyebrow quirked.

"Both the Chan tong and the Gao tong paid for her. If I repay each of them, they won't have anything left to gripe about, I hope."

"It's still hard for me to imagine Hamilton St. Claire as a died-in-the-wool villain," said Loretta, shaking her head. "Just imagine. He seems like such a . . . conventional prig."

"He's a swine," said Jason, who'd had good reason to dislike St. Claire even before he learned of his criminal career as an importer of Chinese sing-song girls.

"His family is wealthy. I don't understand why he felt the need to do something so vile." Loretta shook her head. She held Olivia, and Oliver resided in Malachai's arms, propped against his shoulder, sound asleep.

It amused Jason to see the rugged sea captain so encumbered. "Your guess is as good as mine. Maybe Marjorie will be able to shed some light on the situation."

Loretta glanced at the ornate clock on the mantelpiece, but shook her head. "Olivia's had her fingers all over my eyeglasses, and I can't see the time."

Jason, who had been paying close attention to that clock, said, "It's a quarter past four. How long does it take a woman to get dressed, anyhow?"

"A long time, I suspect, if she's nearly been drowned in the ocean," said Loretta tartly. "She'll have to wash her hair, and you know our Marjorie. She probably won't want to come in while her hair is still damp. She's such a proper young woman, you know."

With a shudder, Jason wished Loretta hadn't

mentioned the ocean part of this debacle. Poor Marjorie. How had she ever overcome her terror of the sea to effect the rescue of Jia Lee? And her hair. He closed his eyes, remembering the feel of her glorious hair as they'd made love. God, he wanted her. He loved her. He was, by God, going to get her to marry him.

Anyhow, he wasn't worried about that. Loretta was right about Marjorie; she was an exceptionally proper young woman. Now that she'd given herself to him, she'd naturally expect him to marry her.

Jason could hardly wait.

Bother. Her hair was so thick, it would probably never dry. Marjorie kept brushing it while standing in front of the fireplace in her downstairs room, but it was still damp.

Her mind's eye kept remembering Jia Lee in Jason's arms, and every time it did so, her heart squeezed painfully. Bluidy damned heart. Bluidy damned mind's eye. Bluidy damned man. Loretta was right. Men were all fiends.

She never wanted to see Jason Abernathy again.

She wanted to see him right this minute and give him a piece of her mind.

She wanted to throw herself into his arms and beg him to marry her.

She wanted to shoot herself.

"Codswallop. It's no good. I'll just put the cursed mess up into a bun."

In spite of her mixed emotions regarding Jason, she didn't want him to get away before she could see him again. Just see him. That's all. Just once more. And she wanted to look her best at the time.

The urge to cry assailed her and she ruthlessly suppressed it. How could he have embraced that woman in front of her though? How could he, after taking Marjorie's virginity the previous night, fall into the arms of another woman? Marjorie didn't understand. She wasn't sure she wanted to understand, actually. If that's the way Jason Abernathy was, then she wanted nothing to do with him!

"And just who are ye trying to fool, ye blathering loony?" She wanted him to love her as she loved him; that was what she wanted, confound it. "Ye're a pathetic jackanapes, Marjorie MacTavish," she told herself as she stabbed hairpins into her bun. "He doesna care, and you'd be best off if you just accept it."

Not the least bit comforted by this piece of practical advice, Marjorie inspected the result of her efforts in the mirror. At least she no longer looked like a drowned rat. Actually, she looked rather good in her green poplin house dress. If life were fair, Jason would take one look at her and rue his callous behavior toward her.

Marjorie of all people knew better than to expect fairness from life.

Nevertheless, taking her courage in both hands, she sucked in a deep breath and prepared to meet her fate. Or, at least, to meet Jason, Loretta, and Captain Quarles, all of whom were awaiting her in the parlor.

Because she felt obliged to do so, she knocked on Jia Lee's door. It was answered at once, and Marjorie, by gestures and the few Chinese words she knew, asked the girl if she would like to join her in the parlor.

She was surprised when the girl shook her head and gestured at her bed. "Sleep," she said. "Please."

Although jealousy raged in her heart, Marjorie understood that nothing that had happened in the past few weeks was Jia Lee's fault. Therefore, she smiled; said, "Of course;" and was grateful for small favors. The upcoming encounter was going to be nerve-wracking enough without Jia Lee present and cuddling up to Jason.

Damn them both.

She didn't mean that.

Or maybe she did. At the moment, she was confused.

The telephone shrilled as she passed the telephone room off the hall. Glad for the reprieve of even a few seconds, Marjorie detoured into the room to answer the ring.

"Quarles residence."

"Mrs. Quarles?"

"Nay. She's in the parlor. May I tell her who's calling?"

"This is the police station at the pier. Is this Miss MacTavish?"

Marjorie's heart flipped over. "Aye, this is Miss MacTavish."

"Sergeant Harkwright here, ma'am. I was at the Quarleses' place earlier in the day. We met at the station. Don't know if you recall."

"Aye, I recall. Do you wish to speak to Mrs. Quarles, or will I do?"

"You'll do fine, ma'am." Marjorie heard the smile in his voice. "Will you take a message, please, and let them know that I'll be at their house in about twenty minutes?"

"Certainly. May I relay any more pertinent information, Sergeant? Have you found the boat? Mr. St. Claire?"

He hesitated for a minute, then said, "We've found the boat."

"And Mr. St. Claire?"

"I'd best tell you in person, ma'am."

Confound his confounded delicacy! Marjorie almost told him as much, but caught herself in time. Passing a hand over her brow, she reminded herself that she was still understandably upset. It wasn't in her nature to snap at strangers who were only trying to help her.

"Very well." She replaced the receiver in the cradle with care, took another deep breath, and resumed her aborted journey to the parlor.

The desultory conversation being carried out there stopped abruptly when she entered the room. Pausing in the doorway, Marjorie surveyed the scene. Loretta rose from her chair, a baby in her arms. The captain didn't rise, probably because he feared waking up another baby. Jason had been pacing, but he stopped as soon as he saw her and looked rather as if someone had glued the soles of his shoes to the carpet. Marjorie pointedly ignored him and went to Loretta.

"Och, let me take the wee bairn. I didna think I'd ever see them again in this lifetime."

She heard a squeak come from the direction of the Jason Abernathy statue in the corner, but didn't turn to acknowledge it.

"Oh, Marjorie, dear, I'm *so* glad you're safe!"

Loretta handed over the infant who was, Marjorie noted, Olivia. She'd asked to hold her primarily so she'd have something to do with her hands and eyes, but now that Olivia was in her arms, she felt a passionate desire to hug her close, press her cheek to Olivia's fine baby skin, and break down crying.

She fought the desire, although she did cling hard to the baby.

"Take a seat, dear, and tell us all about it. Was it you who answered the telephone when it rang just now?"

"Aye. It was Sergeant Harkwright. They found the yacht, and the sergeant will be here in twenty minutes or so to tell us all about it."

"The yacht?" Jason.

Marjorie said, "Aye." She didn't look at him.

"What about St. Claire?"

"He said he wants to tell us in person."

"What the devil does that mean?"

Since he'd managed to irk her, she dared look at him and frown. "I presume he'll tell us when he gets here."

Jason muttered something Marjorie didn't understand and sat in a chair across the room from her. Fine. If that's the way he wanted it, Marjorie couldn't care less.

Liar.

"So," said Loretta, "tell us all about it."

Marjorie did. She had gotten to the part where she and Jia Lee had stripped to their underwear in order to slip over the side of the yacht and into the water when they were interrupted by the doorbell. Marjorie took in a deep breath and held it, praying this interruption would prove to be Sergeant Harkwright, and that he'd be able to tell them more about the yacht and Hamilton St. Claire.

Sergeant Harkwright walked into the room carrying his hat, and he executed a pretty good bow to the ladies and shook hands with the men. Marjorie's heart sped up.

"So," said Malachai in a voice that rumbled even

though he'd tried to make it soft, "please tell us what you've found, Sergeant Harkwright."

"Yes, sir." He saluted. Marjorie would have rolled her eyes had the circumstances been different. For some reason, Captain Quarles inspired all sorts of people to salute him. "Mr. St. Claire's boat was found adrift in the bay about two hours ago. There was no one on board."

"Mercy," Marjorie whispered.

Again the telephone trilled in the background. The noise startled Marjorie, who jerked and woke little Olivia up. She soothed the baby as one of the housemaids answered the ring. Shortly afterward, Molly appeared at the parlor door.

"Yes, Molly?" Loretta smiled at the girl.

"If you please, ma'am, a person wants to talk to the sergeant."

"Ah," said Harkwright. "Perhaps they have more news for us."

He followed Molly to the telephone room, and the parlor's occupants all exchanged nervous glances. No one spoke. As the minutes dragged on, Marjorie inspected the sleeping infant in her arms. She wished Olivia was hers, but she doubted that she'd ever have children now. For a few hours earlier this day, she'd actually allowed herself to to think about having children with Jason, idiot that she was. Och weel. Too bad about that. She swallowed the lump in her throat.

Sergeant Harkwright, appearing once again at the door to the parlor, cleared his throat.

Loretta said, "Yes?"

Entering the room, still with hat in hand, he stopped and stood at attention several feet away from Captain Quarles. "They found Mr. St. Claire."

"Oh?" Malachai's left eyebrow lifted.

"Oh?" Jason's right eyebrow lifted.

Marjorie held her breath.

Loretta said, "Well?"

"I'm afraid Mr. St. Claire's body has just been recovered by one of the harbor tugboats. We're not sure how he drowned, but he *did* drown. I'm sorry."

Silence filled the room. After what seemed like hours, Jason said, "I'm not. It's best this way."

"Why do you say that?" Marjorie asked sharply. Not that she didn't agree with him, although she would have liked to see the pernicious monster stand trial for his crimes.

"Because he'd never have had to face charges."

Indignantly, Loretta cried, "But why not? He did a horrible thing!"

"Yes, he did. But how could he be arrested for a crime that is presumed not to exist? His father's rich, remember?" Jason's voice was dryer than Marjorie had ever heard it.

"That's baneful," she whispered.

"Yes," said Loretta, "it is."

"I'm glad the bastard's dead," said Malachai.

Marjorie had almost become accustomed to his swearing, although she doubted that she'd ever get used to Loretta's. "Aye," she said slowly. "Perhaps it is for the best."

And, although she knew it was foolish, she couldn't help but be happy that his body had been recovered. Now there was no possible way Hamilton's bones could ever intermingle with those of Leonard.

SIXTEEN

Rain battered the church roof, sounding like a hail of pebbles against tin. Jason had arrived at rehearsal early. He was determined to talk to Marjorie, no matter how stubborn she tried to be. The woman had been avoiding him for days now, ever since her heroic rescue of Jia Lee. He couldn't understand what she was up to.

Jia Lee had been taken in by one of Loretta's radical friends who intended to train her to do something useful. Jason didn't have any idea what that might be. Jia Lee was a very young girl—perhaps fifteen or sixteen—and she only knew how to do one thing so far. Knowing that Loretta's friends were every bit as moralistic as she was, he didn't doubt that Jia Lee would receive a proper education and learn to make an honest living. Perhaps one day, she'd overcome her dreadful experiences, both as a singsong girl and as a pawn in a battle not of her making.

He presumed that Marjorie had moved back upstairs to her own bedroom, although he didn't know it for a fact. Every time he showed his face at the Quarleses' house, she headed out another door. Even though Loretta was one of his oldest and dearest friends, he didn't expect she'd countenance his chasing Marjorie through her house. She was an ardent feminist, after all. He knew good and well she'd take Marjorie's side, whatever it was.

Damn it, though, what *was* it? If she'd only talk to him, he might have a clue.

"Oh, thank God you're here!" Mr. Proctor, his thick white hair standing on end, probably as a result of having thrust his fingers through it seventy-five or eighty times, rushed up to Jason. "We've got to rehearse the opening scene with our new Frederic tonight."

Since he already knew that or he wouldn't have bothered coming to the church on a Monday evening, Jason nevertheless only smiled and said, "Right."

"We have to rehearse every night this week and next. Do you realize our opening night is the Friday after this coming Friday?"

As the elderly man rushed away from him, Jason gave him another soothing, "Right."

Poor Mr. Proctor had been in a dither ever since the news of Hamilton St. Claire's death had reached him. Jason acquitted him of caring only about his opera. He was certain that the dear man truly regretted the loss of a man he'd considered a fine, upstanding pillar of the community.

If he only knew.

The newspapers and most of the people who had known Hamilton St. Claire were calling his death a tragedy. A travesty would have been more appropriate, but the only people who knew or cared about that were Jason, Marjorie, and the Quarleses. And Jia Lee, of course, but nobody but them cared about her, either. The hypocrisy of it all chafed on

Jason's feelings, although there wasn't much he could do about it, barring agitating on street corners and writing letters to elected officials as Loretta did all the time. The feeling of helplessness didn't sit well with him.

Hamilton's funeral was being held the next day, in this very church, and Jason planned to attend. He wanted to see for himself that the evil man was put away underground forever and covered with the dirt so appropriate to him even if he couldn't tell the world about St. Claire's viciousness. Well, he *could*, but nobody would believe him. It was frustrating, damn it.

But, by God, he could figure out what was going on with Marjorie, and he intended to do so. The damned woman drove him crazy. The sanctuary door crashed open, undoubtedly blown by the wind, and Jason saw Marjorie enter the room with Ginger Collins. Damn it, she was always *with* somebody. Jason needed to get her by herself.

Intending to do just that if he had to cut her out of the herd like a cow pony cutting dogies, he marched up the center aisle toward her. Producing a smile that was probably vulpine, he said, "Good evening, ladies!"

"Oh my, it's Dr. Abernathy!" Ginger trilled in that annoying little-girl voice of hers that made Jason's teeth itch.

Marjorie took one look at him and said, "Oh dear, Ginger, I forgot something. Do see what Dr. Abernathy wants, won't you?" And she made an abrupt left turn and rushed off in another direction. Finding himself caught between two rows of pews and Ginger Collins, Jason silently steamed.

Foiled again. But he'd get her to himself soon. What was the *matter* with the woman?

"Oh, good!" came Mr. Proctor's relieved voice from behind him. "Here's our Mabel. Mr. Kettering, will you and Dr. Abernathy please take your places? We'll begin at the opening scene."

Damn. Well, there was no talking to Marjorie now. Jason turned and, his shoulders sagging along with his mood, went back to the stage and took his place. The new Frederic, Theodore Kettering, had a pretty good voice. And he was a fairly nice fellow. But he was a trifle older than Hamilton St. Claire and, as far as Jason was concerned, had a much sounder character. It would be just like Marjorie to fall in love with the man.

Damn her. Damn Kettering. Damn them all!

Watching from the sidelines, Marjorie tried to view the opening scene of *Pirates* without allowing her emotions to interfere with the view. It wasn't an easy thing to do. And then there was Ginger, who wouldn't stop yakking in her ear.

"What do you think about your new Frederic, Marjorie?" Ginger tittered. Ginger always tittered.

"I believe he'll do very well." Marjorie strove to achieve a neutral tone of voice.

"It was such a *tragedy* about Mr. St. Claire. I just can't imagine such a thing."

Although she didn't look, Marjorie imagined Ginger with a crafty expression on her face, avidly inspecting Marjorie for any signs that she had cared for Hamilton and was now bereft over his death. She said, "Mmm."

"He was quite taken with you, my dear," Ginger went on.

Suppressing the urge to shudder, Marjorie again said, "Mmm."

"Why do you suppose he took his boat out on such a foggy day?"

"I've no idea."

"It almost seems as if he were trying to kill himself, although I know that's a shocking thing to say."

Good Lord! Marjorie said, "Mmm."

"I don't suppose he proposed to you, and you turned him down, and he then decided he could no longer live?"

"Nay. He didna."

"Are you sure he wasn't pining for you? And that you hadn't told him your heart belonged to another?"

That was enough for Marjorie. Turning on the sly cat in a fury, she said, "Ye daft gudgeon, if you begin spreading that story around town, I'll tell the whole world you're a scheming, lying vixen!"

Ginger's mouth fell open.

"And furthermore, if you ever so much as *hint* of such a thing in my presence again, I'll deny it and call you what you are—a mean-spirited, lying cat!"

Ginger's mouth stayed open.

"I didn't care much for Mr. St. Claire, even before—" She stopped herself before she could blurt out the truth. Frustration made her temper rise higher. "I'm sorry he's dead," she lied, "but I had nothing to do with his emotional or mental state of health. If he was stupid enough to go out on a day like that, perhaps he got what he deserved."

A gasp was all Ginger could manage.

"And furthermore," said Marjorie, hissing the words out through her teeth so that she wouldn't interrupt the rehearsal, "If you think I'm going to stand for your sly whispers and innuendoes, either, you're wrong. Just because neither Hamilton St. Claire nor Jason Abernathy wanted anything to do with you, that doesn't give you the right to tear another person's reputation apart."

Ginger gasped again.

"Anyhow," Marjorie concluded, "you don't know what you're talking about, and you'll only make yourself out to be the idiot you are if you start any such rumors." She might not dare enlighten her, but maybe she could get her to shut up.

The singing onstage had stopped, Marjorie realized. Turning, she saw the entire cast of pirates staring at her and Ginger. And then, to her utter astonishment, all the Major General's daughters who were clustered there began applauding enthusiastically. *Her*.

Ginger burst into tears and ran away, and ten women gathered around Marjorie to congratulate her for finally doing what they'd wanted to do for ages.

"It was terribly embarrassing," she told Loretta later that night. She'd managed to avoid Jason, though, which was the most important aspect of her evening.

They were in the nursery. Loretta was feeding Oliver, and Marjorie held Olivia, who had recently been bathed. She smelled as sweet as a spring morning, and her skin was like velvet. She never wanted to leave these children—at least, not unless it was for children of her own.

And there was a snowball's chance in hell of *that* ever happening.

"You did a noble thing, dear," said Loretta laughing. "And it's something the other women had been wanting to do for a long time evidently."

"Evidently," Marjorie agreed, still surprised about that.

It was an odd thing, too. She tried so very, very hard not to lose her temper, because she'd always held subordinate positions, and people didn't appreciate their servants displaying fits of temper. But when she occasionally did allow herself to blow up, nothing bad ever seemed to happen to her. Perhaps there was a lesson to be learned there somewhere. For a second or two, she even wished she could discuss the matter with Dr. Hagendorf.

Good Lord, she was truly mad.

"What about Jason?"

Marjorie's head snapped up. "Jason? What *about* him?"

"You can't keep avoiding him forever, Marjorie. What happened between the two of you, anyway?"

Because she'd prefer to be roasted over hot coals than admit to her foolish lapse with Jason Abernathy, Marjorie said, "Nothing."

"Fiddlesticks."

"Aye. It is." And she still couldn't bear to face him. Perhaps in ten or twelve years, she'd be able to hold a civil conversation with him—without breaking down and sobbing her heart out for her lost dreams and hopes.

Perhaps not.

The weather on the opening night of *The Pirates of Penzance* was as crisp and clear as San Francisco ever got, which was seldom. From the butterflies in Marjorie's stomach, she'd have thought it was spring had she not looked out upon fall leaves blowing around. Her butterflies fluttered not unlike those fallen leaves as she and Loretta and Captain Quarles climbed into the cab that would take them to the Columbus Avenue Presbyterian Church.

Loretta patted Marjorie's hand. "Are you nervous, Marjorie?"

"Aye." Marjorie sighed. She wasn't looking forward to this. Mr. Kettering had proved to be a competent and energetic Frederic, and he'd learned his lines and the lyrics very quickly, but she still faced the prospect of avoiding Jason all night—and for several more performances to come. She'd been doing so six evenings a week for two solid weeks now, and it was becoming quite tiresome.

He *wouldn't* leave her alone. Every time there had been a lull in rehearsal, he'd sidle up to her and try to talk. Marjorie was sick to death of sidling in the other direction. He'd humiliated her, hurt her feelings, and . . . and . . . not loved her as she loved him. It was a most lowering experience, perhaps the worst in a life that hadn't exactly been brim-full of delightful happenings.

She sighed heavily, and Loretta patted her hand again. "You'll do a wonderful job, Marjorie. You have the most beautiful voice I've ever heard, and you look simply smashing in your Mabel costumes."

"Do I?" Marjorie eyed her employer with scant interest. She couldn't seem to drum up much interest in anything these days. Except in avoiding Jason. She still had energy enough for that.

"Yes," said Loretta firmly.

Captain Quarles nodded. "They're fetching outfits," he rumbled, evoking mild surprise in Marjorie.

The captain wasn't one to notice much, especially as regarded feminine trappings.

"Thank you."

Her heart felt heavier and heavier the nearer they got to the church. She imagined Jason would escalate his attempts to approach her, since they were only giving six performances of *Pirates*, and he didn't have much time left. After the production concluded, she'd never have to see him again. She supposed it would be something of a miracle if she didn't have to speak to him again during those six performances but, in her considered opinion, she was overdue for a miracle or two.

A crowd had already gathered around the church. Happy playgoers chatted with one another outside the building, and more were gathered on the church porch and steps. Loretta, being Loretta, stuck her head out the window to see if she could spot anyone she knew. Since she commenced waving madly, Marjorie presumed she had done so.

As for Marjorie, she didn't care. She didn't care about anything. She didn't mind singing Mabel. She could do that in her sleep. In fact, she'd prefer doing it in her sleep. This being awake nonsense was for the birds.

Loretta called Marjorie's current condition "depression."

"I thought it was called melancholia." Not that she cared about that, either.

"That's the old word for it. The new word is depression."

"Oh." Marjorie couldn't perceive much difference, although she didn't bother to ask why the change had taken place.

"Anyhow, it's all because you overcame your

phobia and performed an heroic deed, Marjorie. And now, since you've achieved the utmost, your inner psyche is telling you that there's nothing left to conquer."

Nothing left to conquer? What was the woman talking about? Marjorie didn't care enough to ask.

"Also," Loretta went on—Marjorie rolled her eyes—"since you stepped so far outside the bounds of your usual behavior patterns, you frightened yourself and are now suffering the consequences."

It didn't take an alienist to tell Marjorie *that*. She didn't care enough to say that, either. All she knew was that she had no interest in anything any longer, and the sooner this stupid opera was over for good and all, the sooner she could get back to living her life the way she wanted to.

Loretta called the way Marjorie wanted to live her life "hiding away from the world." Marjorie thought she might have a point, but she didn't care.

Loretta wanted Marjorie to see Dr. Hagendorf again.

Marjorie didn't have the energy for that.

"Oh look!" Loretta cried, startling Marjorie, who had been slumped in her seat. "It's Dr. Hagendorf!"

Oh joy. Oh rapture. "Did you telephone him?" Not that she cared much. Anyhow, she didn't have anything against Dr. Hagendorf. He'd given her sound advice. It wasn't his fault that Marjorie had allowed herself to commit a moral lapse that had affected her more than she'd ever have dreamed it would.

"No. But I told him you were Mabel when we met at the charity benefit last Thursday."

"Oh."

"Why don't you make an appointment with him,

Marjorie? I'm sure he can do you some good. He did the last time, remember."

"Why don't you let Marjorie take care of her own life, Loretta?" grumbled the captain, stepping out of the automobile and assisting his wife to do likewise.

Marjorie smiled at him as he then helped her out. She didn't quite have the vigor to thank him. In fact, she was sleepy. It was a good thing the music always perked her up, or she'd be stumbling through her part in a haze.

"I'm not interfering!" Loretta said indignantly.

The captain rolled his eyes.

Marjorie said, "Aye, you are."

Loretta frowned, but didn't pursue the matter. Then she brightened. "Oh! And look, there's Jason."

Wonderful. Exactly what she needed. Jason. Finding herself the recipient of a sudden spurt of energy—fleeing for her life from a ravening lion would have produced much the same effect, she supposed—Marjorie spun around and started walking in the opposite direction toward the corner. There was another church entrance in the back. She'd just use that instead of— "Ow!"

Frowning, she turned and saw that it had been Jason who'd grabbed her arm. She stared pointedly at his offending hand.

"Damn it, Marjorie, we need to talk!" he hissed under his breath. He didn't release her arm.

Looking over his shoulder, Marjorie saw that he'd raced right past Loretta and Malachai, both of whom had turned to gape in their direction. Bah. Stupid man. "You're making a spectacle of the both of us," she said crossly. "Let me go."

"We have to talk," he insisted.

"No, we don't." She shook off his hand and marched on in the direction she'd started.

"Damn it, don't walk away from me!" He hurried after her.

Confound it! Well, she supposed it would be undignified to have a knock-down, drag-out fight on a public street—especially in front of her very own church—so she didn't run away or shout at him. Rather, she stiffened her spine and kept walking. If he wanted to talk to her, fine. Let him talk. She didn't have to talk back at him. Maybe he'd get bored with himself and shut up.

"Well?" he demanded.

She remained mute.

"*Damn* it, Marjorie, talk to me!"

She wouldn't.

They arrived at the back door, and Jason yanked it open. Mrs. Proctor, in her Ruth costume, jumped a foot and slammed a hand over her heart. "Oh my! You frightened me, Jason! I was just getting a broom out of the closet here." She gestured at an opened door. "I thought Ruth might like to carry a broom or a mop during the first scene."

Marjorie heard Jason's harsh intake of breath and deduced he was attempting to suppress further swear words. "Sorry, Mrs. Proctor. Door got away from me."

Liar. She didn't say the word aloud because she didn't want to start a conversation.

"That's quite all right, Jason, dear. You make such a splendid Pirate King. I just know we're going to do a wonderful job this evening."

"Thanks."

After smiling at the woman and hoping Mrs. Proctor wouldn't wonder why she didn't speak to her, Marjorie resumed her march to the sanctuary. Naturally, Jason continued to pester her.

"I won't leave off until you agree to speak to me, Marjorie. I don't understand why you're being so standoffish. For God's sake, I thought we'd overcome our problems! We've been intima—"

Marjorie slapped her hand over his mouth, so he didn't get to finish his sentence. Then she broke her silence long enough to whisper, "Haven't you done me enough harm, ye deevilish, gawkit gullion? Keep your mouth shut about my mistake, if you will!"

"Mistake?" Jason stopped dead still and looked stunned. "Mistake?"

Deciding that to say more would be imprudent, Marjorie huffed once and continued her trek to the sanctuary.

"You're calling it a *mistake?*" Again, Jason rushed to catch up with her. "How can you call that heavenly night a mistake?"

"Shut up!" They were nearing the sanctuary, and there were quite a few people milling about.

"I won't shut up! You have to explain yourself to me, Marjorie MacTavish! If you don't want the whole of San Francisco to know about us, you'd better talk to me, and do it now!"

Confound the man! Furious, Marjorie turned on him. "Will ye shat your trap, ye ghastly man? I'll talk to you if that's the only way to keep you from ruining my reputation! I won't do it now, though. I have to change, and so do you. The play will begin in less than an hour!"

His chest heaving, Jason glared at her. If he'd been an honorable man, he'd have looked guilty for threatening to expose her, but he didn't, the rat. Marjorie's hand itched, it wanted so badly to slap his insolent face. "Well?" she demanded. "Is that good enough for you, you underhanded, sneaking, slithering snake, you?"

He had the impudence to appear offended. "I am not any of those things. I'm only a man who's being driven to distraction by an irrational woman."

"Right." Turning on her heel, Marjorie stamped away from him. Let him shout her iniquities to the rooftops. She couldn't stop him, and she'd be confounded if she'd stay in the same room with him any longer than she had to. It was too difficult to remain angry when she wanted so badly to throw herself into his arms and beg him to love her.

How utterly degrading.

Jason's hand trembled as he strapped his sword belt on. He felt a little guilty for having threatened Marjorie as he'd done, but she'd driven him to it, damn it.

"Here's your sword, Dr. Abernathy."

"Thanks." Taking the rubber prop sword from Theodore Kettering, Jason reminded himself that he wasn't the only man in the world with a lot on his mind. Forcing a smile, he said, "You'll do very well this evening, Kettering. You're much better in the role than St. Claire."

The young man's face, which had been creased into intense lines, relaxed. "Do you really think so? I've never had a role this big before."

Jason clapped him on the back. "You'll do swell. I really think you're better than St. Claire." In more ways than Jason would say.

"Thanks. I appreciate your support."

Nodding, Jason tested his sword. It had a tendency to get caught as he was removing it from the scabbard, so he'd put a dab of petroleum jelly on it. It seemed to work better now. Good. That was one thing in his life that worked. Too bad nothing else did.

"Are we ready?" Mr. Proctor asked, rubbing his hands together. "The orchestra is about to take to the pit."

There was no pit per se, but Jason didn't mind the man taking liberties. Mr. Proctor's talents were vast; if he wanted to pretend that this was an honest-to-God theater instead of a church sanctuary pretending to be a theater, Jason didn't begrudge him the affectation.

"I've asked Reverend Sargent to say a brief prayer for our success this evening and in our succeeding performances," Mr. Proctor went on.

Some wag in the chorus muttered, "We can use all the help we can get," and a few titters erupted from the rest of the cast.

Everyone obediently bowed their heads as Reverend Sargent stepped up to stand in front of the assembled cast and members of the orchestra. Everyone except Jason, who searched the crowd for Marjorie. Ah, there she was. Although her head was bowed, he'd recognize her anywhere. All that amazing red hair. He loved her hair. He loved her.

For the first time, he wondered if perhaps he should tell *her* that. Hmm. It was an idea. A definite idea.

Could that be the reason she was avoiding him? Because she thought he'd only used her?

Indignation swelled in him. Did she honestly believe he was *that* sort of man? Did she truly think he was so lost to goodness that he'd take advantage of an innocent for his own pleasure?

And why shouldn't she? his inconvenient little voice asked him. *You've done naught but make her life miserable for more than three years.*

Have not!

Have, too.

Bother. All right, so he'd teased her a little.

More than a little, chappie.

Why the devil was his little voice speaking to him with an English accent? As Reverend Sargent intoned a sonorous "Amen," Jason wondered briefly if the spirit of the late, lamented Leonard Fleming had taken possession of his brain.

But the cast began hurrying to their places, the orchestra lugged their instruments to the front of the church, the audience erupted into applause, and Jason had to leave off contemplating his most recent bout with insanity in order to play the role he'd been assigned in *The Pirates of Penzance.*

Marjorie listened and watched moodily. The audience was eating up their production of *Pirates.* Even Marjorie had to admit that, if she weren't in the throes of depression or melancholia or whatever the current terminology was, she'd be enjoying it, too. Jason was excellent. And in spite of his hurried introduction to the part, Mr. Kettering was proving to be a splendidly comic Frederic.

"'What a terrible thing it would be if I were to marry this innocent person, and then find out that she is, on the whole, plain!'" said Mr. Kettering musingly as he eyed Mrs. Proctor as Ruth, who was preening coquettishly. The audience laughed.

"'Oh, Ruth is very well. Very well indeed,'" said Jason, with a look of absolute innocence on his face. The audience roared. Clearly, they were more intelligent than Marjorie, who hadn't understood the falsity behind that look until far too late.

The fellow playing Samuel, one of the pirates, said, "'Yes, there are the remains of a fine woman about Ruth.'" Yet more laughter.

Sighing, Marjorie thought that probably described her as well as poor Ruth. The remains of a fine woman. Aye, that's all there was left of her. And, worse, she'd never even blossomed. Not once. She'd believed her life would be complete with Leonard, but the confounded iceberg had taken that sweet hope from her. And then, idiot that she was, she'd fallen for the blandishments of Jason Abernathy. And his blandishments weren't even kindly! He was a benighted habbler, and she was a bluidy gameral. A gudgeon. A baffin.

"It's going very well," someone whispered in her ear.

Turning, Marjorie saw that it was Mr. Proctor, dressed in his Major-General suit, readying his play daughters for their grand entrance, even though it was quite a ways away. Jason was going to sing his Pirate King song first. And then every bluidy female in the whole bluidy audience would fall madly in love with him. A sob caught in her throat. Swallowing it unmercifully, she smiled at the elderly Mr. Proctor. "Aye. The audience loves it."

It was the right thing to say, and Marjorie congratulated herself. She seldom managed to say the right thing. In fact, it had begun to seem as if everything she attempted turned to garbage.

Dinna fash yoursel', she commanded. She had to pay attention to the play. As soon as Jason finished his song, Ruth and Frederic would have their confrontation, and then her play sisters would take to the stage. Her cue would come soon, and she had to be alert, even if she'd rather be asleep.

Picking up his sword, Jason slashed energetically at a stage prop. "'No, Frederic,'" he recited in response to Frederic's invitation to return with him to civilization. "'I shall live and die a Pirate King!'"

And the orchestra struck the thrilling opening to the Pirate King's special number, and Jason burst into song. Eyeing her supposed sisters, Marjorie noticed them all watching, enthralled.

Well, they would be. Even Ginger, subdued ever since the incident of Marjorie's temper tantrum, watched with fascination unmixed with sly glances at Marjorie. An improvement that, even if it had come about as the result of a rather massive and unfortunate explosion on Marjorie's part. Marjorie wasn't accustomed to having temper fits, and that one still embarrassed her whenever she thought about it.

"Oh my, isn't he in fine voice this evening?" said Kathleen O'Riley, the girl who'd been chosen to play Kate, slightly breathlessly.

"Aye," said Marjorie. "He's good."

"Goodness, yes. He's so good in the role," whispered Kathleen. "I've always thought the Pirate King should have been the romantic lead."

"Yes," sighed another smitten damsel.

If she could have, Marjorie would have walked away. Gone home. Reprieved herself from this cult of Jason-adoration. It was too painful. Too awful. Too—

Everyone backstage broke into applause along with the audience as Jason belted out the last note of the Pirate King's song. Startled, Marjorie, after a significant pause, joined in. It wouldn't do to let her emotions show, after all. Just because she was heartbroken and suffering from blighted hopes, she didn't want the rest of the world to know it.

She considered it a blessing that the pirates and Jason exited on the opposite side of the stage. With luck, he wouldn't come to this side and pester her. Too bad her luck had been so putrid of late.

A frantic rustling of skirts to her rear reminded her that as soon as Frederic and Ruth finished quarreling onstage, Mabel's sisters would appear. And they'd be singing before that. With a sigh, Marjorie stepped aside.

And, as soon as Mabel's sister Edith, played by Ginger Collins, sang, "'Let us gaily tread the measure,'" she knew her luck was holding.

"Marjorie, we have *got* to talk!" And there he was: the plague of her life.

SEVENTEEN

"Honestly, Jason, you do pick the least convenient times to conduct intimate conversations."

Her voice was as cold as the damned iceberg that had sunk the *Titanic*. Jason was so frustrated with her avoidance by this time that he could have cheerfully slung her over his shoulder and made off with her. Unfortunately for him, he valued the Proctors and this production of *Pirates* too much to remove two of the starring players before the final curtain.

"Oh, Dr. Abernathy," crooned Mrs. Proctor, attacking him from the rear. "You're simply smashing as the Pirate King!"

Damnation! Turning, Jason said, "Thank you, ma'am," and tipped his piratical hat at her. Naturally, during this brief exchange, Marjorie escaped.

Stomping softly due to his aforementioned respect for the Proctors and *Pirates*, Jason set off in search of her. She couldn't be too difficult to spot, this being a made-up stage and all. How big was a stage? How many places were there to hide?

Stage or not, Jason didn't find her.

"'Alas! There's not one maiden here whose homely face and bad complexion have caused all hope to disappear of ever winning man's affection!'" sang the chorus of Mabel's sisters.

Jason had searched everywhere. No Marjorie. But this was where she was supposed to be in order to make her entrance. He'd just wait here. She couldn't elude him. She'd have to show up a few minutes before she took to the stage, damn it.

Frederic, in despair, sang, "'Not one?'"

And the sisters chorused, "'No, no. Not one!'"

Again, Frederic crooned sadly, "'Not one?'"

The girls sang, "No, no—"

And Marjorie, emerging from behind a curtain on the opposite side of the stage from which she was supposed to appear, strode onto the stage, threw out her arm in a dramatic gesture, and sang with amazing bravado, considering her mood, "'Yes, one!'"

As the entire cast of *Pirates* turned, surprised at her unconventional entrance, Jason muttered, "Damn!"

A shocked gasp from Mrs. Proctor at his side prompted him to mumble, "Sorry."

But Marjorie was out there, and he was back here, and he'd lost another opportunity to talk to her. What was the matter with the woman?

"I wonder why she entered on that side," Mrs. Proctor mused.

Although he could have, Jason didn't enlighten her.

Her husband, who was soon to make his own entry into the onstage fray, rubbed his hands together and grinned hard. "I don't know, but it was very effective. Did you see how surprised they all were? It was perfect. Perfect!"

Perfect, my ass, thought Jason bitterly. He wouldn't allow her to avoid him any longer, damn it. If she wouldn't talk to him offstage, she'd damned well have to do it when they were both onstage.

Marjorie was quite proud of herself for managing to elude Jason so effectively. It was astonishing how much a heavy curtain could hide when used properly, even if it was a trifle musty-smelling and dusty. Must or no must, she was now onstage where Jason couldn't get at her.

Happy about this quick thinking on her part and free from Jason's intrusive presence for the nonce, Marjorie forgot her recent blue devils and put everything she had into her role as Mabel.

The audience was *very* receptive. When she sang the final notes of *Poor Wand'ring One,* the applause was deafening. And, as Frederic led her to the mouth of a cave where the two of them were supposed to pretend to chat as Mabel's sisters pondered what to do now that Mabel had butted in, Mr. Kettering whispered, "That was the best you've ever sung it, Miss MacTavish. Your voice belongs in grand opera."

"Och pooh," said she. But she was pleased. Terribly pleased.

Until Jason from inside the cave whence he had crawled, she supposed, from the wings hissed, "Psst, Marjorie! We have to talk."

"Och, ye bluidy blackguard! I'll na talk to thee again in this lifetime!"

Mr. Kettering, forgetting for the moment that he was the beauty-blinded Frederic, gasped. "Dr. Abernathy!"

"Don't pay any attention to me," whispered Jason. "I have to talk to Marjorie."

"Well, ye canna," said Marjorie, her Mabel smile firmly in place. "That's our cue to join the others."

It wasn't *quite* their cue, but it was close enough. To Jason's frustrated muttering, she took Mr. Kettering's arm and led him back to the group of girls who didn't seem surprised to have them appear a trifle early. It was a stretch, but Marjorie managed to look like a dreamy maiden in love when she began her next number.

"'Did ever maiden wake from dream of homely duty, to find her daylight break with such exceeding beauty?'" She batted her eyelashes at Frederic to the audience's overt relish. She wasn't sure, but she thought she heard the gnashing of teeth coming from the cave. Good. She hoped the vile deceiver was suffering. Not, naturally, that he was.

Offhand, she couldn't understand why he persisted in pursuing her with the intention of talking to her. It had become painfully obvious to Marjorie that it was Jia Lee whom he wanted and loved. She herself had been merely a . . . what? A convenience, she guessed. How demeaning.

And how comforting to have this opera into which she could lose herself with such abandon. The role of Mabel was exactly to her taste—and so, she had discovered, was acting. The good Lord knew, she'd had plenty of practice in the art. Her whole life sometimes seemed to Marjorie to have been one long, insufferable act. At least this role was fun.

Throwing her arms out in a gesture worthy of Loretta Quarles herself, Marjorie sang with gusto, "'. . . to find her daylight break with such exceeding beauty?'"

Then Mr. Kettering took her arm to lead her off the stage as, at the same time, the pirates crept onto the stage behind Mabel's sisters. Marjorie breathed a sigh of relief at having once again thrown off Jason's determined pursuit.

Her sigh was premature. The Pirate King was supposed to grab hold of Ginger Collins, who was playing the role of Edith. As Marjorie and Mr. Kettering passed Jason, however, he latched onto Marjorie's arm instead.

An undignified tug-of-war took place at the back of the stage while singing was continuing up front. The audience, believing it to have been staged that way on purpose, giggled. Marjorie finally wrenched herself away from Jason and scampered offstage as if pursued by demons—which is exactly what she felt like.

Shaking her arm, which hurt, she grumbled, "Daft gudgeon."

"I don't understand, Miss MacTavish. Did Mr. Proctor change the marks?"

Glancing at Mr. Kettering as she rubbed her arm, Marjorie felt a wholly unjustified stab of guilt prick her. None of this was her fault, confound it! "Nay, he didna. Dr. Abernathy seems to be rewriting the script as he goes along."

"How very odd."

"Aye, it's odd, all right."

"What's going on with the two of you?"

Turning, Marjorie saw Mr. Proctor eyeing the stage and looking confused. As well he might. "I'm sorry, Mr. Proctor. I don't know what's gotten into Dr. Abernathy tonight."

"Hmm." Stroking his chin, Mr. Proctor watched the stage with keen interest. "Perhaps he's doing a little improvising of his own, as you did, my dear, when you entered stage left earlier instead of stage right. That went over very well, and his improvisations seem to be pleasing the audience, too." He beamed at her. "The two of you are wonderful at this! We shall have to stage more Gilbert and Sullivan offerings for future missionary fund-raisers."

Marjorie would participate in another opera if Jason Abernathy was in the cast when hell froze over and Queen Victoria rose from the dead. She didn't say so, merely offering a noncommittal "Hmm" in response.

Her next appearance would be tricky, since she'd have to be onstage with Jason. She didn't trust him at all any longer. He seemed willing to play any underhanded trick in order to get her to talk to him. But why?

She didn't figure it out before she had to walk out onto the stage once more. The pirates had just decided to marry all of Mabel's sisters even though the girls didn't want to marry them. Holding her arm out, palm up, in a "stop" gesture, Marjorie stepped boldly into the melee. "'Hold, monsters! Ere your pirate caravanserai proceed, against our will, to wed us all, just bear in mind that we are Wards in Chancery, and Father is a Major-General!'"

And, for the rest of the act, Marjorie did her best to dodge Jason. Fortunately for her, one or the other of them was singing most of the time. As soon as the curtain fell—to thunderous applause—she dashed offstage and headed straight to the ladies' dressing room. He couldn't get at her there unless he wanted to cause a real rumpus, and Marjorie believed, for all that he was an unconventional sort of person, that he wouldn't dare cut up in a church.

She turned out to be right. *Thank God, thank God.*

"Whatever is Dr. Abernathy pursuing you for, Marjorie?" asked Kathleen O'Riley, the girl who was playing Kate.

Mopping perspiration from her brow and grabbing the frilly white peignoir and nightcap in which she would appear in the second act, Marjorie said, "I have no idea, Kathleen. I think the man's slipped a cog." And, because she didn't want to talk about it anymore, Marjorie threw the gown over her head and hoped Kathleen would be gone when her head emerged.

She wasn't. "Hmm," said Kathleen, slipping on her own peignoir. All the daughters would be thus attired throughout the Act II.

Marjorie went to the dressing table and sat down, trying to look as if she were adjusting her makeup.

That ruse didn't work, either. Kathleen had a sly look on her face that Marjorie didn't appreciate when she sat next to Marjorie on the dressing bench.

Frustrated, Marjorie demanded, "Well? Do you know more about it than I?"

Putting a hand on Marjorie's shoulder, Kathleen said contritely, "I'm sorry, Marjorie. I don't want to snoop into your business."

"Thank you. I wish more people were of your stripe." Once more, Marjorie's old friend, guilt, reared its ugly head. "Sorry I snapped at you."

"Think nothing of it."

Kathleen proceeded to powder her nose. Marjorie dabbed on more lip rouge. There was a general buzz in the room as all the Major-General's daughters and Mrs. Proctor congratulated each other on what looked like a smashing success. Marjorie had almost calmed down when Kathleen blurted out, "I think the man's in love with you!"

Marjorie goggled at her in the mirror.

"I do. And I think he's wonderful and don't know why you keep avoiding him."

Unable to think of a thing to say, being thunderstruck, Marjorie just stared into the glass at the other girl's reflection.

"Oh, I'm sorry again. I know it's none of my business, but he seems like such a fine man, and you're such a fine woman, and I just don't know why you keep trying to stay away from him."

"Um . . ." But Marjorie was still unable to think of anything to say.

Kathleen's eyes grew large and she gasped. "Unless . . . Oh, Marjorie, please don't tell me that he's a villain in disguise! Do you know something the rest of us don't? All the Major-General's daughters have been dying to have him pay us attention, but he has eyes only for you. Is there something we should know?"

"Er . . . no. He's quite a . . . a good man. Most charitable, in fact." Blast. She hadn't meant to give the impression that Jason was anything but an upstanding gentleman—even if he was in love with another woman and had seduced and abandoned Marjorie without a second thought.

Or . . . perhaps that wasn't exactly true. He'd certainly been giving her second—and third and fourth—thoughts this evening, curse him. And she didn't want to hear his excuses, either. They'd only make her feel worse. If such a thing was possible.

Kathleen's brow furrowed. She was very young. Probably ten years younger than Marjorie, whose chest twanged unpleasantly as the age difference registered. *Ye're not getting any younger, Marjorie Mac-Tavish. Perhaps you should have loosened up sooner after Leonard died.*

Second-guessing was an unprofitable occupation. Loretta was forever telling Marjorie so. Besides, it wasn't as if she could have overcome her fears sooner than she had. They were . . . confound it, they were phobias. Phobias were tough nuts to crack. Loretta had told her *that* as well. Time and time and time again.

"Then I don't understand," Kathleen said after a moment of thought. "He seems so fond of you, and if he's an upstanding gentleman . . . Well, it's none of my business." She laughed. "And I didn't mean to upset you."

A glance in the mirror told Marjorie that she'd begun to scowl. With effort, she changed the scowl into a smile. "You didna upset me, Kathleen. But truly, there's not a thing in what you say."

"No?"

"No." Marjorie's voice was, perhaps, the tiniest bit too firm. "We're merely acquaintances."

"Oh, surely you're more than that!"

"Nay," said Marjorie, deliberately stony this time. "We're not."

"Oh." Kathleen stared at Marjorie for a couple of seconds, shrugged, and walked away.

Bother! Even in the ladies' dressing room, she couldn't get quit of Jason Abernathy. Marjorie powdered her nose with excess force, then sneezed as she waved powder dust away from her face with her hand.

It was all Jason's fault.

* * *

Damn the woman! She was more elusive than a will-o'-the-wisp. But she couldn't escape him indefinitely. They were going to be onstage together again at the end of the second act, and he'd by-God get her to marry him then or know the reason why.

After touching up his makeup, Jason did his best to avoid the rest of the men in the dressing room. He didn't feel up to chatting, and they were all in a state of ecstasy that corresponded poorly with his own foul mood and frazzled nerves.

Finally, he got sick of the cursed ebullience going on around him and left the men's dressing room to wander around backstage. If he could, he aimed to tackle Marjorie before she took to the stage, because they'd be pretty much separated after the start of ACT II until the final scene. He wasn't sure his heart would hold out that long. At the moment it was thudding painfully in a combination of frustration, anger, and confusion.

"Jason!"

Mr. Proctor's voice startled Jason into a leap of alarm.

The older man chuckled. "Sorry. Didn't mean to scare you."

Feeling foolish, Jason muttered, "No, no. My fault. I was lost in thought."

"Thinking about your role?"

"Er . . . yes." Like hell.

"You're doing a splendid job, my boy. Splendid! This is the best production I've ever been involved with. Isn't Mr. Kettering doing well? And to think he only started learning his part two weeks ago."

"Yes. Right." What the devil was the man talking about? Oh yeah. Jason had forgotten all about the vile Hamilton St. Claire, whose memory would be revered in San Francisco because nobody wanted to hear about his villainy.

Straining to come up with something approaching conversational aptness, he said, "Yes, Kettering's doing a great job. He's got a fine voice." That had better be good enough, because he couldn't concentrate on anything other than Marjorie for any longer than a second or three.

"Our *Pirates* is definitely a hit. Perhaps we should extend the run for another weekend."

"What?" Jason hadn't been listening.

"Another weekend. This seems to be such a success. We could make more money for the missionaries if we extended it another weekend."

"Oh. Yeah, I guess so."

"But wait." Mr. Proctor frowned. Jason wished he'd get on with it. "We'd run into the Christmas season if we did that. The choir is planning a cantata."

"If we did what?" At the look of disapproval he received from Mr. Proctor, Jason made a huge effort and recalled the subject under discussion. "Oh. Christmas. Right. Not a good idea, I guess. Don't people usually stage *A Christmas Carol* at Christmastime?" He was proud of himself for creating and delivering that speech without the benefit of his brain's involvement.

Ah, but look! The women were gathering. Jason watched intently. All the Major General's daughters except Mabel would be onstage at the beginning of the second act. Perhaps he'd have a chance to talk to Marjorie then. He'd have to work fast, because she was scheduled to take to the stage right after the first chorus.

"*A Christmas Carol?*"

Jason, who had no idea why Mr. Proctor had

begun chattering about *A Christmas Carol*, glanced at the gentleman to find him looking at him with a questioning glance. What did this mean? "Er, *A Christmas Carol?*" Damn the fellow. Jason wished he'd go away and leave him alone. He needed to talk to Marjorie, curse it!

"You mentioned *A Christmas Carol*," said Mr. Proctor.

He had? "I did?"

"Jason, are you feeling all right? You seem a trifle . . . er . . . unfocused. Are you nervous about the play, my lad? Because you're doing a brilliant job."

"Unfocused? Er, no. I'm fine. Well . . ." Damn it, how did he get himself into these verbal tangles? "I'm just going over lines in my head." That was good. He should have thought of it sooner.

"Ah. I see." Mr. Proctor bestowed a fond and benevolent smile upon Jason, which made him feel guilty. "Well, keep up the good work, my boy. You're one of the best Pirate Kings I've ever seen."

"Thank you."

The orchestra struck up the opening chords of the second act's overture, and Mr. Proctor turned to gather his stage daughters together. "It's time to take our places, ladies."

Quiet tittering and the rustling of petticoats grated in Jason's ears and upon his nerves as the women followed Mr. Proctor onto the stage, the backdrop to which had been changed and was now a ruined chapel by moonlight. Why was it that all the women in the world gabbled so much? Except Marjorie. She never gabbled. She—

There she was! With a hasty apology to the women into whom he bumped, Jason scooted through the throng of maidens only to discover Marjorie missing when he got to where she'd been. Damnation. Well, she couldn't get around him forever.

Slinking sideways through the small space behind the back curtain, he made his way to the other side of the stage. Where she wasn't. Damn it!

That had been a close call. Marjorie had nearly suffered a spasm when she'd seen Jason chatting with Mr. Proctor after she'd finally dared leave the ladies' dressing room. Quickly, she darted off the staging area, muttering about having forgotten something. She lurked near the ladies' dressing room, intending to bolt inside if Jason sought her anywhere but backstage.

He didn't. It came as a great relief to her when she saw him slide behind the curtain and make his way to the other side of the stage. By the time he realized she wasn't there, she'd be onstage again, and they wouldn't have to share it again until almost the final scene. Good. She needed a rest. All this constant vigilance was quite nerve-wracking; it was making her tired.

Sure enough, Marjorie had just stepped out onto the stage when she glanced offstage and saw Jason glaring at her. Let him glare; Marjorie had a song to sing. As Jason glowered from the sidelines and Mr. Proctor drooped pathetically on what was supposed to be a decrepit tombstone, Marjorie belted out, "'Dear father, why leave your bed at this untimely hour?'"

And the audience lapped it up. When the policemen showed up and Mabel sent them off to glory by dying in combat gory, she could hear the roars of laughter even through her solo. Encouraged, she put all of her formerly suppressed dramatic skills into her role, mentally thanking Loretta for teaching her how to make broad, sweeping gestures that were typically antithetical to Marjorie's more reserved nature.

Not that night. That night, Marjorie was Mabel, the open, good-hearted, unrepressed daughter of Major-General Stanley, and one, moreover, who knew her place in the world and what to do about it. In other words, Mabel was about as unlike Marjorie as a female could get.

At one point, when she was singing, "'Go to death, and go to slaughter; die and every Cornish daughter with her tears your grave shall water,'" she thought about Dr. Hagendorf.

By heaven, this was practice! She was practicing how to be open and unrepressed so that, perhaps, she could become more open and unrepressed in her life. How funny.

The next scene—in which the Pirate King tells Frederic that, since he was born on February 29, he wasn't actually twenty-one years old yet, but only five-and-a-quarter—was a huge hit with the audience. Watching from the wings, Marjorie's heart twanged painfully as Jason swashbuckled all over the stage. He really *did* make a perfect Pirate King. She wondered why she'd not noticed his particular flair for the dramatic and comical until now.

"He's wonderful," a voice whispered in her ear.

Turning, Marjorie saw Kathleen, her hands clasped to her bosom, watching Jason as if enraptured. "Aye," she said. "He's vurra good."

And why the devil was this young girl mooning over Jason Abernathy, who had to be in his mid-thirties at least? By all the laws of God and nature, the chit ought to be pining for Mr. Kettering. Silly creatures, girls.

Scanning the group of stage sisters at her back, Marjorie sought out Ginger Collins. Ah, there she was, the ninny, still behaving well as if she had learned a salutary lesson. And a good thing too.

Mrs. Proctor, as Ruth, sang, "'Ha! Ha! Ha! Ha!'"

Jason sang, "'Ho! Ho! Ho! Ho!'"

The audience roared.

Kathleen sighed in Marjorie's ear. Vexed, Marjorie whispered, "And isn't Mr. Kettering doing a fine job?"

"Who?" Kathleen looked at Marjorie and then back at the stage. "Oh yes. Mr. Kettering is doing very well. And he learned the role in such a short time, too."

Not much interest there obviously. Fool girl didn't know what was good for her. She had no idea that Jason Abernathy only allowed himself to love Chinese women.

Marjorie's heart gave a hard, painful spasm. She pressed against it with her palm and told it to stop doing that.

The rest of that scene went splendidly. By dint of quick maneuvering, Marjorie managed to avoid Jason just barely as he exited the stage and she entered. She saw him standing in the wings scowling at her when she spoke to a woebegone Frederic. "'All is prepared, your gallant crew await you.'"

And so it went. And the audience went with them. As Frederic and Mabel sang about him returning in 1940 when he'd at last be able to celebrate his twenty-first birthday, the audience laughed so hard that both Marjorie and Mr. Kettering had trouble controlling their own humor.

A glance at the wings helped Marjorie; it was difficult to maintain one's glee when one was being stared at so hatefully by the man one loved.

Confound it, she did love him. It galled her to admit it, since he was so utterly unworthy an object of her love.

The police contingent entered, and Mabel and her sisters urged them on to defeat the pirates. A tricky situation was coming up, and as she sang, Marjorie attempted to think of a way to stay away from Jason while they were both offstage at the same time.

Nothing worthwhile had occurred to her as she launched into her last bit. "'He has done his duty. I will do mine. Go ye and do yours.'" And she had to leave the stage.

Blast. She didn't see Jason anywhere. That meant he was going to pounce as soon as she was free of the audience's scrutiny.

Sure enough, Marjorie felt her arm seized in a grip like iron just as the Sergeant of Police started in on *A Policeman's Lot Is Not a Happy One.*

She hissed, "Ow! Unhand me, you brute!"

The sergeant sang, "'When a felon's not engaged in his employment.'"

"Damned to that. I'm going to make you listen to reason, Marjorie MacTavish."

The policemen sang, "'His employment.'"

"Leave me be. This is my favorite song in the whole opera. I want to hear it."

"'Or maturing his felonious little plans.'"

"You can hear it tomorrow. Right now, you're going to listen to me."

"'Little plans.'"

"Am not."

"'His capacity for innocent enjoyment.'"

"Are too."

"'Cent enjoyment.'"

"Let me *go!*"

"'Is just as great as any honest man's.'"

"Damned if I will until you listen to reason."

"Jason." Mr. Proctor tapped Jason on the shoulder.

"Damn!" But he dropped Marjorie's arm.

Marjorie instantly scuttled away, listening to what Mr. Proctor was telling Jason. Could the dear man honestly be attempting to rescue her?

"You've got to start singing offstage with the rest of the pirates on the other side in a minute."

Oh. Of course. Mr. Proctor was only reminding Jason that he had to take his spot. Nobody would *ever* rescue *her*. *She* was *unworthy* of rescue.

Marjorie sensed that she was being irrational, but she was too angry to worry about it right then. Shooting her another black scowl, Jason stalked behind the curtain to the other side of the stage. She repressed an urge to stick her tongue out at him. Bluidy damned man.

She continued to think black thoughts as she went to the ladies' dressing room, adjusted her white peignoir and frilly nightcap, and picked up her candle for the last scene. She couldn't even come up with a smile for Kathleen, who was likewise employed. Marjorie thought she probably ought to be shocked to be appearing onstage in a frilly nightdress, but she was too miserable. She shuffled back to the sidelines to watch the proceedings onstage with a heart that felt as if it had gained ninety pounds.

A barrage of applause interrupted her brooding, and Marjorie heard the chorus of pirates singing from the other side of the stage. Good. She could avoid Jason forever now. Well, except for one point when he'd be offstage at the same time she was. But she could hide in a curtain then. And then there was the very end of the opera when they would be onstage together, but surely not even Jason would disrupt the opera's finale just to badger her. She hoped.

Codswallop. She would cope; that's all there was to it.

The notion of having to cope through another several performances of the opera made her heavy heart twinge unpleasantly, but Marjorie told herself to take one day at a time. It wasn't as if she could do anything else.

Unless she killed herself.

That thought so shocked her that she squared her shoulders and told herself *no* man was worth *that* much. Her heart would ache for a while, and then she'd get over it. She'd gotten over Leonard, hadn't she? Well . . .

Bother.

She watched and listened glumly, anticipating a nerve-wracking couple of weeks. But at least she could go home and hide after each performance. And be with the bairns. Her heart went all soft and gooey when she thought about Oliver and Olivia.

"I think we have a hit on our hands, Miss MacTavish."

Turning, Marjorie saw Mr. Kettering. She smiled at him. "Aye, I think so, too." He was such a nice boy.

Boy?

With a deep sigh, Marjorie agreed with herself.

He was a boy. Unlike Jason, who was a man. Ah, well . . .

Titters erupted from the audience when the police tiptoed down the stairs and into the sanctuary to crouch in the aisles as they hid from the pirates. Frederic, the pirates, and Mrs. Proctor assumed their marks behind the decrepit chapel's ruined window through which they would step a moment later.

Marjorie actually smiled at their exaggeratedly cautious skulking as they sang, "'With catlike tread, upon our prey we steal.'" Mrs. Proctor and Mr. Kettering were quite comical as they peered around, searching for enemies and making a terrible racket.

Then there was Jason. Marjorie had never seen anyone throw himself so wholeheartedly into a part. He was absolutely perfect.

She sighed again. For a little while there, she'd believed he was perfect for her, too. Which only went to prove, if more proof were necessary, that she was a bluidy baffin. But she didn't have time to dwell upon her many failings and idiocies. Jason would soon be exiting stage left, and Marjorie had to hide.

Far sooner than she would have liked, she was forced to leave her refuge inside the dusty velvet curtain and join the rest of the women for the last scene. Sticking as close to Ginger and Kathleen as she could, she managed to duck past Jason, although she did have to arrive onstage a trifle early in order to do so. Nobody seemed to mind. Well, except for Jason, who was plainly grinding his teeth and seething.

Marjorie told herself she didn't care. She wished it were so, even as she and the other women started singing. "'Now what is this, and what is that, and why does Father leave his rest at such a time of night as this, so very incompletely dressed?'"

Not much time left. At the end of this song, the Pirate King and Frederic would reappear onstage and the final scene would commence. Then there would be bows, and then sweet escape. Marjorie was *very* tired.

Aye. There he was with Mr. Kettering and the fellow who was playing Samuel, another pirate.

Tossing aside the staging directions, Jason marched over to stand beside Marjorie as he sang, "'Forward, my men, and seize that General there! His life is over.'"

As the pirates grabbed the general, Jason hissed at Marjorie, "What the devil is the matter with you? Why are you avoiding me?"

Marjorie and the girls sang, "'The pirates! The pirates! Oh, despair!'"

The pirates sprang up, singing, "'Yes, we're the pirates, so despair!'"

"Because you used me, you horrid creature," Marjorie hissed back.

"I did *what?*" Nobody watching would know that Jason was shocked, but Marjorie could tell he was by the tone of his whisper.

The Major-General sang, "'Frederic here! Oh joy! Oh rapture! Summon your men and effect their capture!'"

Marjorie cried, "'Frederic, save us!'" Under her breath, she added, "You used me. You love Jia Lee, and you . . . used me." Even though everyone else was paying attention to the play, she couldn't make herself admit in public that she'd lost her virtue to Jason Abernathy, who was in love with another woman.

With wonderfully comical zest, Mr. Kettering sang, "'Beautiful Mabel, I would if I could, but I am not able.'"

The pirates sang, "'He's telling the truth, he is not able.'"

"You're crazy! The only woman I love is you!" Then with gusto Jason once more broke into song. "'With base deceit you worked upon our feelings!'"

Marjorie gaped at him. Had she understood him correctly? Had he just declared that he loved her? *Her?* Marjorie MacTavish?

Since she was at present Mabel, she didn't stick her finger in her ear to clear it of fluff, but she felt every bit as wild as Mabel must have when she clutched her hands to her bosom and cried, "'Is he to die unshriven, unannealed?'"

The girls in the chorus sang, "'Oh, spare him!'"

At the same time, Marjorie arched her brows in a question for Jason, who had drawn his sword and was about to run General Stanley through with it. He saw her question and answered it with a vigorous nod. Marjorie felt rather lightheaded as she sang, "'Will no one in his cause a weapon wield?'"

"'Oh, spare him!'" the girls chorused.

The audience bellowed with laughter when the police contingent, who had been lolling in the aisles, suddenly jumped up and sang, "'Yes, we are here, though hitherto concealed!'"

Marjorie pointed at her bosom and mouthed, "You love *me?*"

The girls sang, "'Oh, rapture!'"

As the struggle between the police and the pirates commenced and the police sang, "'So to Constabulary, pirates yield!'" Jason maneuvered himself over to Marjorie again. "Well, of course I do! What the devil did you think?"

Right before he was wrestled away from her side by a policeman once more, Marjorie whispered, "But you held her in your arms!"

For a few seconds Jason was too busy staging the fight that the pirates eventually won to respond to this allegation. Eventually, he managed to get himself close to Marjorie again. "Damnation, you can't hold that against me," he hissed furiously. "She threw herself at me! I couldn't very well drop her, could I?"

As Jason and the pirates began singing their victory song, Marjorie mulled over his explanation, trying to recall that awful sojourn at the police station. She hadn't been in the best condition to make judgments, she guessed, having suffered horribly, both physically and mentally, before, during, and after her plunge into the ocean. The mere recollection made her shiver, which went well with the operatic conditions prevailing at the moment.

As Marjorie mulled these things over, the sergeant of police was leading up to a mighty climax. "'To gain a brief advantage you've contrived, but your proud triumph will not be long-lived.'"

By Jupiter, Jai Lee *had* been the one to precipitate that embrace!

Jason sang, "'Don't say you are orphans, for we know that game.'"

And Jason had held on to Jia Lee as she'd cried. Marjorie frowned, that remembrance not sitting very well with her. But she now recalled, he'd looked at her the whole time the Chinese girl had been sobbing in his arms.

"'We charge you yield, in Queen Victoria's name!'"

Jason sounded suitably baffled when he sang, "'You do?'"

"'We do!'"

Perhaps Marjorie had been the least little bit overzealous when she'd assumed that Jason was in love with Jia Lee. She supposed that, under the circumstances, when the poor girl had thrown herself at him, it had made sense that he hold onto her. After all, she'd been through an ordeal, too. Probably a worse one than Marjorie's, actually, if you removed Marjorie's phobia from the equation.

The pirate crew all knelt and bowed their heads in submission. "'We yield at once, with humbled mien, because, with all our faults, we love our Queen.'"

Was it her imagination, or was Jason singing that song to her? He was supposed to be gesturing at the statue of Queen Victoria that stood in a corner of the stage. Marjorie felt herself blush.

"'Yes, yes, with all their faults, they love their Queen.'" The policemen all took out big white handkerchiefs and started sobbing into them. The audience bellowed with glee.

Mrs. Proctor took to the stage then, holding her arms up in a dramatic gesture. "'One moment! Let me tell you who they are.'"

Somehow or other, Jason had again managed to get himself close to Marjorie. "How the devil did you come up with the notion that I love Jia Lee?" he whispered harshly from the side of his mouth. The other pirates tried to ignore him.

Caught somewhere between total confusion and absolute joy, Marjorie stammered, "Well . . . but you embraced her."

Jason rolled his eyes heavenward the moment before Marjorie joined in the chorus singing, "'They are all noblemen who have gone wrong.'"

Mr. Proctor warbled, "'No Englishman unmoved that statement hears—'"

"I can't believe you thought I loved that woman. I felt sorry for her, for God's sake."

—"'Because, with all our faults, we love our House of Peers.'"

As Jason knelt in mock solemnity before the statue of Queen Victoria, Marjorie wondered if she'd been mistaken when he'd declared his love for her. She'd like to ask him, but her pride held her back.

Mr. Proctor sang energetically, "'I pray you, pardon me, ex-Pirate King! Peers will be peers, and youth will have its fling.'"

With head bowed, Jason again spoke to Marjorie in a grating whisper. "For God's sake, I love *you*."

She hadn't been mistaken! Rapture filled Marjorie's bosom as the Major General sang, "'And take my daughters, all of whom are beauties!'"

Her heart full to bursting, Marjorie sang, "'Poor wand'ring ones! Though ye have surely strayed, take heart of grace, your steps retrace, poor wand'ring ones!'"

How she managed to sing her final solo, Marjorie never did know, but sing it she did, and the audience loved it. And then, as the entire cast robustly sang the final chorus of *Poor Wand'ring One*, and she was supposed to waltz across the stage with Frederic, she suddenly found herself in the arms of Jason Abernathy.

He, who was supposed to be waltzing with Ginger Collins, sang directly to her. "'If such poor love as ours can help you find true peace of mind, why, take it, it is yours!'"

And, as the orchestra struck its final chord and the audience leapt to its feet, clapping wildly, Jason Abernathy and Marjorie MacTavish kissed each other. Right in front of God, their audience, and the entire cast of *The Pirates of Penzance*.

Marjorie was sure she heard Loretta's voice above the rest shouting, "Brava! Bravo!"

EIGHTEEN

The faint fragrance of sandalwood hung, elusive and enchanting, above the bed. The first musical cries of early-rising Chinese street vendors floated up from Grant Street. The first few motorcars of the day passed beneath the window. A bump and the metallic chink of a tea kettle being placed on an electrical hot plate told Jason that Lo Sing was up and about in the clinic. Soon, Jason knew, the click of Mah-Jongg tiles would be added to the mix of harmonious notes that made this neighborhood San Francisco's—and Jason's—beloved Chinatown.

In other words, the world was waking up, and Jason, who had just made passionate love to the woman he adored, knew it was a kinder and better place than it had been only twenty-four hours earlier. Sunshine tapped at his window, asking to have the curtains drawn aside so it could enter and brighten his bedroom.

What the sunshine didn't know was that Jason's bedroom was already as bright as bright could be. Because Marjorie was in it. Marjorie. His own bright and shining star. The woman he loved. The woman who loved him.

"You do love me, don't you, Marjorie?" He already knew the answer, but he needed to hear her say it.

"Of course I love you, Jason, you bluidy man."

"It's a good thing. If you didn't, I might have to change my opinion of you after what we just did." He held her luscious—and lusciously naked—body tightly in his arms, not intending to let go of her anytime soon. "Anyway, even if you don't love me, it's too late. We're getting married whether you love me or not."

"Don't be daft," she advised him.

"Too late for that," he whispered into her wonderful, wonderful hair. "I'm totally mad. Madly, passionately in love with you."

"Och, Jason."

She turned into his arms and his masculinity stirred to attention yet again. He was pretty sure he'd never get enough of her. "I love you, Marjorie."

"I love you, Jason."

Their kiss was just getting interesting when it was interrupted by the shrill jangling ring of the candlestick telephone on his desk in the corner of the room.

"Damn."

"Ye needn't answer it." Marjorie's voice was a sweet whisper.

The damned phone rang again.

"If I don't answer it, it'll keep doing that, and it hurts my ears."

"Aye, 'tis annoying, all right." With a sigh, Marjorie rolled off his body.

Although Jason felt a shaft of disappointment, he reminded himself that they could resume this pleasurable activity any old time they wanted to.

With a sigh of his own, he climbed out of bed, his

feet coming to rest on the warm Chinese carpet, then led by his own personal shaft, which had been coaxed to rigid life by Marjorie's gloriousness, he went to his desk and picked up the phone. Detaching the receiver from its cradle, he spoke into the horn on the candlestick. "Dr. Abernathy."

His eyebrows lifted, his manhood drooped, and he turned to grin at Marjorie even as he listened. After a moment, he said, "Don't you know it's impolite for a gently bred lady to call a bachelor's establishment before"—he eyed the clock on the mantelpiece—"half-past seven in the morning?" To Marjorie, he mouthed *Loretta*.

To his delight, Marjorie swung her own heavenly legs over the side of the bed and sat there naked without even looking self-conscious. Astonishing. He listened for a second, chuckled, put his hand over the mouthpiece and told Marjorie, "She says she's no lady."

Her musical laugh made his manhood stir again. "We both know that, Loretta dear. Why—"

Loretta interrupted him, he chuckled again, and he didn't bother covering the mouthpiece this time. "She says that if she has to be awake at this ungodly hour because of the twins, we can jolly well suffer, too."

Another smile from his darling Marjorie made Jason weak in the knees. Therefore, he sat. The wooden seat of his desk chair was chilly on his naked rear end, but he endured. After listening for quite a while, he sighed. "You probably ought to talk to Marjorie about this, Loretta. I don't know anything about weddings."

Still smiling, Marjorie got up from the bed, donned Jason's Chinese silk robe, and went to him. She deposited herself on his lap and took the receiver from him. His attention to the ensuing conversation was divided as he fondled Marjorie's breasts.

"Good morning, Loretta." She slapped Jason's hand lightly. He didn't desist, deciding to wait for a firmer indication that she wanted him to stop what he was doing.

Fortunately for him, Loretta was a first-class gabber. He'd untied the silk robe, turned Marjorie on his lap, and was nuzzling her breasts by the time she had to speak again.

"Aye, that would be nice," Marjorie said as Jason gently took her right nipple between his teeth and nibbled. As he did so, he pushed the robe from her shoulders.

"You will? Thank you. That would be vurra nice of you." A pause ensued, during which Jason lifted Marjorie from his lap, pushed the robe aside, slid it from her free arm, and gestured for her to take the receiver in her other hand so he could get rid of the damned robe altogether. Bless her, she did exactly what he wanted her to do, and without even an argument first.

"Aye. I'd like Reverend Sargent to conduct the service."

Jason didn't know how she could concentrate on her conversation with Loretta. It was all he could do to keep listening under the circumstances. He repositioned her on his lap so that she straddled him.

"Your house? That would be so nice, Loretta."

Marjorie's gasp as he slid into her ended the telephone conversation as far as Jason was concerned.

Taking the receiver from Marjorie's hand, he spoke into it.

"Marjorie will have to finish this conversation with you later, Loretta. Something's come up." And he replaced the receiver on the cradle.

Laughing softly, Marjorie said, "How rude of you!"

Jason said, "Too bad."

And then they both lost themselves in the timeless rhythm of love. Right **there** on Jason's desk chair.

Four weeks later, at seven o'clock on the eve of Christmas, 1915, Marjorie MacTavish walked slowly down the grand staircase in the Quarleses' mansion on Russian Hill. Captain Malachai Quarles was at her side to give her away to Jason Abernathy. A string quartet cunningly located in an alcove off the hall played a lovely Vivaldi piece that Marjorie preferred to the more traditional wedding march. Before the marriage ceremony had commenced, Mr. and Mrs. Proctor had sung a lovely rendition of *I Love You Truly*.

Loretta Quarles, clad in crimson satin (in honor of the season) and a broad-brimmed hat, served as Marjorie's matron of honor. Isabel FitzRoy, another survivor of the *Titanic* disaster and a good friend of both Marjorie and Loretta, was a bridesmaid. So was Jia Lee, who looked quite lovely in her own crimson gown and hat. Marjorie couldn't help but notice that Lo Sing could scarcely take his eyes off her.

Eunice FitzRoy, Isabel's ten-year-old daughter, served as Marjorie's flower girl. A sober child, she still smiled as she carried her white wicker basket of fir twigs and red roses. The entire house was decorated for Christmas with swags of pine boughs and red ribbons cascading down the bannisters of the broad staircase; wreaths everywhere; and candles glowing from wall sconces and candelabra decorated with red ribbons, pine branches, and pine cones.

Jason, in black tie and tails and an intensely white shirt, his hair cut short and his eyes sparkling like blue diamonds, awaited his bride at the foot of the stairs. Lo Sing, similarly clad, stood beside him as his best man. Marjorie watched Jason as closely as he watched her while she descended the staircase.

Thanks to Loretta's munificence, Marjorie wore a cream-colored satin gown with beaded lace trim with a veil that trailed behind her down the stairs. She carried a bouquet of white orchids and red roses with accents created of pine needles.

The only slightly odd note to the occasion was the soft grinding of a motion-picture camera that was capturing the entire ceremony on film. Loretta had bought the camera several years earlier in order to assist Isabel and her then husband-to-be, Somerset FitzRoy, in preparation for a dance contest.

The huge hallway itself was filled with rows of chairs filled with people. Everyone from the cast of *Pirates* had come, even Ginger Collins, who had commenced weeping even before the music started. Mr. Kettering and Kathleen O'Riley sat next to each other, Marjorie noticed as she scanned the crowd. Pleased, she hoped they'd be the next couple to marry. She liked them both. Most of the congregation of the Columbus Avenue Presbyterian Church was also in attendance.

Dr. Hagendorf, holding the hand of his wife Irene, smiled benevolently, as if he believed he'd had a hand in the successful reaching of this conclusion. Marjorie had to agree with him.

She'd never been happier in her life. And to think that not four years earlier, she'd thought she'd never be happy again. Yet here she was, in San Francisco, California, being married to the most wonderful man in the world in the most luxurious setting she could imagine.

Marjorie didn't think life could get much better, although she aimed to make the attempt. She and Jason had discussed things, and they'd agreed that, as much as they loved Chinatown, they would only live above his clinic until they started a family. They'd already begun looking for a house to buy on the outskirts of the city.

A family. When Leonard had left her in that bluidy lifeboat on that tragic night more than three years since, Marjorie had believed her hopes for a family had been wrecked forever. But now she had Jason, and soon she would have a family.

Indeed, when she thought about it, she had a family already. With Loretta and Malachai, Isabel and Somerset and Eunice, and Jason and Lo Sing, she'd created a family. Right here. In America. The notion made her heart swell as she reached the foot of the staircase, Malachai stepped aside, and Jason took her hand. Beaming upon the two of them, Reverend Sargent began reading the vows.

Four hours later, as the clock struck eleven and the guests, full of food, champagne, good fellowship and the happiness of the season and the ceremony, began to depart, Jason and Marjorie stood beside Loretta and Malachai in front of the massive fireplace. An enormous blue spruce tree, decorated with electrical Christmas lights and hundreds of ornaments Loretta had collected over the years, took up nearly a quarter of the huge front parlor of the Quarleses' mansion.

"We've done it," Jason said, hugging Marjorie to his side.

"It's not so bad, once you get used to it," Malachai said with a wink.

Loretta smacked him on the arm. "Beast."

Marjorie, her heart brimming with joy, held her hands out to Loretta. "I can't thank you enough for all you've done for me, Loretta. If it weren't for you, I'd not have met Jason."

"For several years, you were sorry you *had* met me," he reminded her.

"Aye, that's so. Because you were such a cappit auld gagger."

"Was I?" Jason opened his eyes very wide.

This time, it was Marjorie who smacked her man. "Aye. That means you were a mean old joker, ye haggis-headed gameral."

Jason's broad grin made Marjorie giggle.

"It looks as if I'm going to be learning a new language, doesn't it?"

They all laughed. Then Loretta sighed. "It all went very well tonight, didn't it?"

Tearing herself away from her husband—her *husband*!—Marjorie hugged Loretta hard. "It was perfect, Loretta. It was an absolutely *perfect* wedding!"

Everyone agreed.

Complete Your Collection Today
Janelle Taylor

Available Wherever Books Are Sold!

Visit our website at **www.kensingtonbooks.com.**